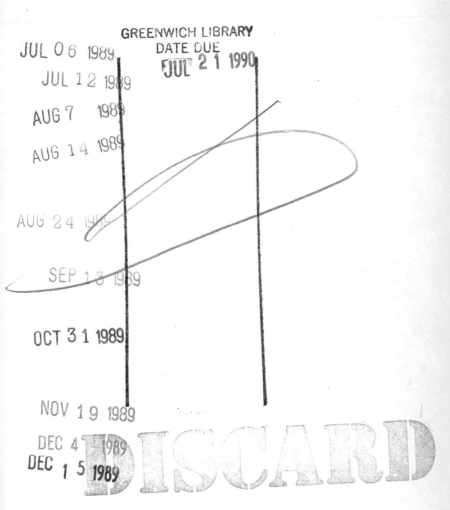

BLITZ!

BLITZ!

Molly Lefebure

St. Martin's Press
New York

BLITZ! Copyright © 1988 by Molly Lefebure. All rights reserved. Printed in the
United States of America. No part of this book may be used or reproduced in any
manner whatsoever without written permission except in the case of brief quotations
embodied in critical articles or reviews. For information, address St. Martin's Press,
175 Fifth Avenue, New York, N.Y. 10010.

Library of Congress Cataloging-in-Publication Data

Lefebure, Molly.
      Blitz! / Molly Lefebure.
            p.   cm.
      ISBN 0-312-02873-3
      1. London (England)—History—Bombardment, 1939–1945—Fiction.
   2. World War, 1939–1945—England—London—Fiction   I. Title.
PR6062.E4196B57 1989
823'.914—dc 19   89-4095
                                                                              CIP

First published in Great Britain by Victor Gollancz Ltd.

First U.S. Edition
10 9 8 7 6 5 4 3 2 1

For
Margaret de Krassel-Lane

Principal Characters

PAUL DUCHAMP *a surgeon attached to St Jerome's Hospital, London*
ANN DUCHAMP *his wife*
MRS BUSBY *Ann's mother*
ODILE DUCHAMP *elder daughter of Paul and Ann*
MORWENNA DUCHAMP (Thingy) *their second daughter*
ELIZABETH *cook and general domestic in the Duchamp household*
FERNAND LEGRAND *Odile's friend*

SYBIL SPURGEON *next-door neighbour to the Duchamps*
PAM SPURGEON (Jampot) *her daughter*
HUGO SPURGEON *Sybil's elder son*
JASPER SPURGEON *Sybil's younger son*

SIR JOSELIN SOWERSBY *of Parrocks Hall, Stellafield*
LADY SOWERSBY (Dottie) *his wife*
VICKY SOWERSBY *their daughter*
FLIGHT LT. JOSELIN SOWERSBY RAF (Jos) *their elder son*
FRANCIS SOWERSBY (Frank) *their second son*
HARRIET HOPE-WARRINGTON (Hal) *Lady Sowersby's widowed sister*
LAVINIA HOPE-WARRINGTON (Boggy) *her daughter*
NANNY BRADSHAWE *the old family nanny at Parrocks*
ELIOT *butler at Parrocks*
GILES J. SOWERSBY JNR. *a distant Sowersby cousin from the US*
HOMER MOUNTJOY *friend of Giles's, also from the US*

FLIGHT LT. PHILIP PLUMBTON RAF (Pongo)
POPPY PLUMBTON *his wife*

MARIE TOOLEY
MICK TOOLEY *her husband*
STEVE TOOLEY *Marie's eldest son*
JOSIE JAMES (née Tooley) *Marie's eldest daughter*

Violet Pollock *her second daughter*
Nelson Tooley *Marie's second son*
Rhona Tooley *her third daughter*
Pete Tooley *Marie's youngest, and last, child*
Gert Pollock *Marie's sister*

Posy Cowper *full-time District Air Raid Warden, ARP*
Flo Cowper *her widowed mother*
Henry Cowper *Flo Cowper's only son, Posy's brother*
Mrs Loftus *housekeeper to Ernie Cowper, Flo's brother-in-law*

The Reverend Clem Irving *a young curate with an East End Mission*
Sister Sunflower-Lupin *sister of Sunflower-Lupin Ward at Plashett Wold Burns Unit*
Miss Isabella Widgeon *warden of Tulip House*
Miss Honora Whitebeam *her assistant, friend and lifelong companion*
Lily *servant at Tulip House*

Part One

CRY HAVOC

I

Posy Cowper, a full-time salaried District air raid warden attached to Cuddwell Number Seven Post, stood at the junction of Unity Street and Tollemache Terrace scowling and casting impatient glances at her watch. The time was precisely ten minutes past ten. The air raid had been in progress for ten minutes. Three minutes after the warning had sounded a bomb had dropped on the Post Office in front of which Posy was now standing. The Post Office had been reduced to a pile of rubble; it had been fairly busy at the time of the incident and several people who, at the sound of the warning, had raced out of the building in an attempt to reach the basement air raid shelter at the further end of Tollemache Terrace had been caught by bomb blast and flying glass. An ambulance had arrived upon the scene with admirable promptitude and had removed six walking wounded. Four other persons, all seriously injured, remained lying upon the pavement awaiting help.

An ARP Heavy Rescue lorry now drove up and five members of personnel tumbled out. Their leader, in ordinary life known to Posy as her local newsagent, advanced and said, "Morning, Pose. Any idea how many people may be trapped under the ruins? Heard any cries for help?"

"Not a sound," responded Posy tersely.

The squad vanished to the rear of the Post Office. Posy remained in position on the street corner. The casualties lay motionless and silent where they had fallen. Otherwise Posy had the place to herself. From a distance came sounds of shouting, whistles blowing, ambulance and fire-brigade bells shrilling and clanging. Posy, who loved to be in the thick of things, shifted her feet and muttered impatiently. On her head was her steel helmet, her respirator in its canvas bag was slung at the "Ready" position on her chest. Completely prepared and on the alert, looking capable of coping single-handed with any number of Germans should they suddenly come round the corner, Posy glared hard at nothing.

"Excuse me, Miss Cowper, might I have a word with you please?"

The voice came from a small wispy girl in a belted raincoat who had suddenly appeared from nowhere and stood holding a notebook and pencil at the ready as she stared up at Posy with big, earnest, blue eyes. Posy rasped, "What d'you want, Miss Duchamp?"

"If you could tell me a few details about this incident. The *Gazette* wants a big story on this. . . ."

Posy cut the girl short. "Your editor should know better than to send his reporters to take up the time of people like me in an air raid. All I'm telling you is that you, as a civilian, when an air raid alert sounds, should take the nearest available cover and remain there till you hear the All-clear."

"But Miss Cowper, as a reporter it's my job to find out what's going on and to. . . ."

"I don't care what your job is, you're a civilian and it's your duty to get under cover and keep out of danger. We've already got enough casualties to deal with without adding you to the list. So off you go, see?" Little Morwenna Duchamp, obviously realizing that further argument was pointless, folded her notebook and scuttled away up the street. Posy, with an expression of satisfaction, watched her retreating figure. Miss Duchamp, who had only recently come to work on the *Cuddwell Gazette*, had found digs in Posy's mother's house, and, though a pleasant enough little girl, should not have attempted to take advantage of a privileged position; at least, that was how Posy saw it. Miss Duchamp wouldn't dare to ask any other member of ARP personnel for help with her newspaper story! All members of Civil Defence knew that they mustn't give the Press details of enemy attacks, or anyone else come to that. It was a simple matter of national security. There was an official Information Officer and the *Cuddwell Gazette* should have approached him. Little Morwenna Duchamp needed to learn to mind her Ps and Qs.

After which, Posy Cowper once more glared at her watch. Where on earth were those ambulances for the other casualties? She herself had been on the scene of the incident within minutes of the bomb falling and had summoned assistance without delay. Since when, apart from removal of the walking wounded (who hadn't required transport) and the arrival of Heavy Rescue (who had now disappeared) absolutely nothing had happened. What a way to fight a war!

At length, unable to stand this inactivity any longer, Posy strode rapidly up Unity Street, blowing angry blasts on her whistle as she went. These blasts should have brought fellow ARP workers hastening to her; but not a soul appeared.

She turned out of Unity Street and almost at once tripped over an enormous hose-pipe. This, like a giant anaconda, squirmed along the gutter in the direction of a throng of firemen and ambulance men jostling among a viscera of hose-pipes outside Woolworths, watched by a crowd of sightseers, including Morwenna Duchamp. Posy bore down upon this assembly. She plunged among the sightseers, "Hey you, take cover! This is an air raid, not a Punch and Judy show!"

A couple of St John's Ambulance men were in the crowd; Posy leapt upon them like a tigress. "I'm looking for some of you lot! There's four bad casualties lying outside the Post Office, dying for want of help!"

"Keep your hair on, duck. We know all about them; all under control. Ambulance on its way there now."

"Under control my foot! I summoned an ambulance twenty minutes ago!"

"Out of the way, out of the way there please!" A fireman, all brass, leather and authority, pushed Posy back into the crowd; at the same time a Salvation Army officer, carrying a bawling toddler who had lost his mother, collided heavily with her, almost knocking her off her feet. "Out of the way please!"

Posy declared, loudly, to nobody in particular, "I wash my hands of this bedlam!" She returned to the Post Office. No wonder, she thought to herself, they were calling this a Phoney War!

It was April 1940. Posy had been one of London's air raid wardens for the past two years; she was also an instructor in first aid, holding classes not only in her home borough of Cuddwell, but in a number of other eastern suburbs into the bargain. She was recognized as a first-rate instructor; wasn't ashamed of admitting it herself.

The recruits who attended her classes saw before them a strapping, strident-voiced spinster in her mid-thirties; firm-jowled, her hair cut in a no-nonsense shingle, the glance of her sharp eyes dauntingly direct, her eyebrows heavy and well marked. There was universal astonishment when it leaked out that this brawny, boot-faced Amazon rejoiced in the name of "Posy".

Posy prided herself upon being a pragmatist. As early as 1936 she had decided that it was well on the cards that the rise of Hitler's Germany would result in another war and therefore she had started attending first-aid classes and lectures on fire-fighting and anti-gas precautions; in spite of the fact that at this point in time the idea of Civil Defence had been a joke with most people, while others had condemned it as a form of active warmongering. In March 1938, after Hitler had overrun Austria, the Home Secretary, Sir Samuel Hoare, had broadcast an appeal for at least a million men and women to enrol in a Civil Defence service. Less than half that number had responded; among them had been Posy. Air raid wardens were officially described as "the backbone of the Air Raid Precautions System" and the ARP system was the "fourth arm of the nation's Services". All this had sounded great stuff to Posy, who saw herself as blessed with a particularly strong backbone. A pity that not all her fellow citizens were similarly endowed! Take this present ARP exercise, for instance. Civil Defence had been told that it was to be taken very seriously indeed; be as "near like the real thing as possible". Well, if this was being serious, snorted Posy to herself, then God help the nation when the real thing truly came along.

Her head burning with these indignant ruminations, Posy found herself back outside the Post Office. The four casualties were still where she had left them. Two lay supine. Around a third a knot of people were now gathered, apparently arguing heatedly among themselves. The fourth casualty had propped himself in a sitting posture against a shop front and was smoking his pipe and placidly watching the scene before him.

Posy joined the agitated group; two young VAD nursing recruits with a first-aid kit; one Special Constable and a Red Cross auxiliary, the last being an elderly woman with purple cheeks and frizzy grey hair. She was kneeling beside the casualty prodding him and asking repeatedly, "Do you feel any pain? Try to answer if if you can; do you feel any pain?"

"What's going on here?" demanded Posy.

"We can't get any reaction out of this one at all," replied the auxiliary.

The casualty, a stout old man in a raincoat, who was lying with his eyes closed, at last replied, without opening his eyes, "I can't talk."

"What d'you mean, you can't talk?"

"I'm unconscious, aren't I? That's what it says on my label, don't it?"

"Can't see any label," said the auxiliary.

"All the casualties are wearing labels specifying their injuries," said Posy. "If not, someone has slipped up badly."

The old man, with weary resignation, put his hand in his trouser pocket and produced a tie-on luggage label. "There you are. Says I'm unconscious, don't it?"

"But you're supposed to be wearing the label, not lying with it in your pocket!" said the auxiliary.

"It come off, duck. Go on, read it. Says I'm unconscious, don't it?"

Posy took the label and read aloud, in clarion tones, "Unconscious. Internal blast injuries. Fractured ribs. Respiratory distress."

"Golly!" said one of the VADs, "There's not much we can do for him."

"Out of the way, please," said the Special Constable in the accents of the male of the species about to take over from the weaker sex. Thrusting the Red Cross auxiliary aside he dropped on his knees beside the old man. "Help me turn him on his face, will you?" he snapped to no one in particular.

"On his face? What for?" enquired Posy.

"Respiratory distress requires artificial respiration," responded the Special triumphantly. "Come on, help me turn him over."

The old man began to wheeze. "Hold hard, mate. I'm not a sack of coals, you know."

"You lot give me the shudders," said Posy. "Who taught you to give artificial respiration to casualties with fractured ribs?"

"Blimey!" said the Special, abashed. "Forgot the fractured ribs."

"You'd be more help, constable, if you went and made sure of an ambulance for these people." Posy was icy. "I've done all I can to get one, but they're not taking any notice of a mere warden; perhaps the arm of the law will carry a bit more weight."

"Do my best," said the Special. He hurried off, glad to get away.

"What a prize looney . . . Here, help this old chap up and let him get his breath back," said Posy, glancing at the old man, whose ears had gone an alarming shade of blue. "We don't want a real casualty on our hands."

Leaving the VADs and the Red Cross auxiliary to deal with the victim of the Special Constable's zeal, Posy went to inspect the other casualties. "They're not going to leave us to die out here, are they?" enquired the next unfortunate, a borough councillor of public spirit who made a point of participating in everything, and had eagerly volunteered to be a casualty, but who was clearly now regretting her enthusiasm. "I've a feeling someone needs a good shaking up somewhere along the line," she added ominously. "Help me up, would you? You've no idea how hard this pavement is." Posy helped the councillor to her feet. She said, "I'm nipping into that café on the corner to get a cup of tea. The ambulance people can collect me there. I'm labelled a broken leg, but they'll have to make-believe a kindly passer-by carried me to food and shelter."

And so saying the councillor vanished into the café. At the same moment somebody tapped Posy on the shoulder; she looked round, to see the man with the pipe. He said, affably, "Well, now I've been left to bleed to death I'm going home to make sure that at least I have a decent funeral. Ta-ta!" He walked over to the other old man and the pair exchanged a witticism Posy couldn't overhear. The two men then went off together. The VADs and the auxiliary likewise departed from the scene. Seconds later the Heavy Rescue squad emerged from behind the Post Office and clambered into their lorry. Posy strode over to them. "Were there any casualties? Have you got 'em out?"

"All under control," said their leader. "All-clear's just sounded, too, so it's back to the depot to brew some char."

"But the All-clear isn't sounding till thirteen hours!"

"Look, this whole exercise is only pretence, innit? So we're pretending the All-clear's sounded, see?" And with a volley of guffaws Heavy Rescue rumbled away. After a second or so of glaring in the direction of the vanished lorry Posy turned brusquely to the final remaining casualty; a woman lying patiently on the kerbside, staring with wooden stoicism into the gutter a few inches from her nose. Posy stooped over her. "No sense in you lying there any more. Pretend the ambulance has taken you off to hospital. Pretend the blooming war's over, if you want!"

"Orright," said the casualty. She scrambled to her feet and brushed down her coat with her hands. "Well! That's it then, innit?"

"That's it."

The final casualty departed. Posy, left alone, opened her report book and wrote a long entry. From the distance came continuing sounds of the exercise, in full swing; but as far as Posy was concerned the show, such as it had been, was over. "A complete frost!" she exclaimed to herself, repeatedly. "As much like the real thing as possible, my foot!"

The trouble was, of course, that so far the war itself had never shown any sign of becoming the real thing. Six months, now, since Hitler had invaded Poland, and Britain and France had declared war on him, but no attempt had been made by the Allies to attack him, and Hitler, for his part, had not attacked them. "All quiet on the Western Front" with a vengeance! Resultantly, everyone had become lulled in a sense of false security: people said Hitler was scared to take on France and Britain and would sue for an armistice without going into action, or, if he did try to fight, would discover that he had left it too late; had missed the bus. As for the possibility of air raids occurring, this was believed in less and less with every day that passed. With such a lack of reality permeating everything and everybody, it was no wonder that the various branches of ARP had lost an alarming number of personnel; half those needed for today's exercise were simply not available.

Nevertheless, all that said, it made no difference to how Posy saw things. She still believed Hitler meant business; she didn't trust him an inch. Idiots, people were, to think otherwise. Yet could she jolt them into realizing what lay in store? No; it was like banging her head against a brick wall.

Deeply disgruntled, Posy returned to Number Seven Warden Post. Sammy Ross, the Post warden, an old soldier who prided himself on imperturbability and savoir-faire, and whose role in today's exercise had been to remain at the Post, in touch with HQ, was seated at his desk carefully drawing up a chart. "Here's my report to incorporate with yours," said Posy. Sammy retorted, "I don't need your report: I got one all finished and ready for despatch, thank you! What's known as efficiency."

"But how did you write it without my observations? You don't know what happened at my incident."

"What happened doesn't matter," responded Sammy serenely. "It's all make-believe. I reckon, from what I've already heard, that the entire thing's been a prize cock-up, but that's got nothing to do with my report. Want to read it?"

"D'you realize that, at my incident, all the walking wounded were picked up by ambulance within five minutes, while the really serious casualties never received any attention whatsoever and to all intents and purposes were left lying in the street to die?"

"Just what I'd expect."

"But it's not good enough! We aren't going to carry on like that when the real thing starts, are we? Good heavens, this exercise was planned to show up where we need to improve our strategy: here you are not even bothering to send in a proper, factual report. *You* need improving, for one!"

"Miss Cowper! Can't have my subordinate speakin' to me like that!" Sammy looked up from his chart with a warning frown.

"I can't help that, Mr Ross. I've never minced words in my life and I don't intend to start mincing 'em now."

Sammy had already learned to temper his valour with discretion when it came to dealing with his redoubtable second-in-command. Accordingly he changed the subject.

"I've put you down, in the next round of the sector table-tennis championships, to have me as your partner in the mixed doubles, and that woman what's her name, telephonist with the warts from the Report Centre, as your partner in the ladies' doubles. Okey doke?"

"Suppose so. But look here, getting back to this exercise, d'you really mean to tell me that you aren't going to send in a true report of what really happened?" Posy glared at Sammy indignantly. "I've half a mind to tell that young girl reporter on the *Gazette* what fine tricks you're up to, I really am."

"For gawd's sake don't go telling sensational tales to the Press: last thing we want is to destroy public confidence in Civil Defence. When Hitler gets here, *if* he gets here, we'll show 'im. Until then, keep your hair on. And now do me a favour and go and get some dinner and leave me to carry on with this ping-pong chart in peace. Savvy?"

Posy responded with one of her famous snorts. Sammy said, "No use you trying to reason why and all that caper, Miss Cowper. Yours but to do and bloody die, see?"

"Along with a lot of other people if they're all left lying out in the street waiting for help that never comes, like they were today."

Posy signed off in the duty book and departed. Officially the ARP exercise was still in progress, but who cared? Gloomily she marched home.

II

". . . want you lot to get this absolutely straight: you've got to know the exact location of your pressure points so that you can jamb your thumb down hard and pronto on any one of 'em at any time, any place, anywhere: in the dark just as well as in the light, because once Hitler starts bombing us, as bomb us he now surely will, we're as likely to be raided in the night as broad daylight."

Tuesday the fourth of June, Posy Cowper conducting her Thursday evening Civil Defence first-aid class at Stoke Hartwell. "Now I'm going to call each of you up here on this platform, in turn, and I'm going to blindfold you and then I'm going to lie down here on the floor as if I was a casualty and tell you one by one which artery I've had cut by flying glass and you're to stop the bleeding, see? I shall say, 'temporal artery' or 'femoral artery' or so on and so forth, see? And heaven help those of you what fumble about; because if you can't bother to learn your pressure points off pat then you might as well say goodbye to the idea of being in Civil Defence, for there's one thing for sure and that is when the bombing starts there's going to be arterial bleeding and if there's arterial bleeding there's no time to stop and look up pressure points in your first-aid manuals. . . ."

And Posy, producing a large handkerchief with which to blindfold her pupils, suited action to the word and began calling up her class, one by one. Odile Duchamp, seated well at the back, her moment of summons surely some ten minutes away, began reading a letter from her sister, Morwenna, which Odile had found awaiting her on her return home from work to Foxwarren Avenue, that evening.

47 Rushton Road,
Cuddwell

Mon. June 3 1940

Dearest Odo,

Just a quick line from this hard-pressed newshound to say it seems ages since I last saw you — I keep hoping I'll be able to wangle a Sunday off so that I can get home for a few hours, but, as I think I've already told you, there used to be five reporters on this rag: now, thanks to call-up, there are only three, including me, and I'm still such a cub that I'm only considered fit to be given assignments that Gilroy, our senior reporter, is above covering, or Stoppard, the other reporter, is too busy to handle. Once there would have been three juniors to do all the dog's-body stuff that I now cover single handed, so you can well understand why I work a fourteen-hour day every day and spend all day Sunday trying to catch up with writing copy! Ah well, *there's a war on!* And with that weary catchphrase I'll stop my beefing — though actually I'm not beefing really, for in spite of the gruelling hours and constant nose to the grindstone, I'm still enjoying my reporter's life enormously.

Isn't the news awful? The way Hitler is sweeping across France, everything crumbling before him! No doubt the French will successfully counter-attack at some point, but they're leaving it late! Is there any news of Papa yet? I'm terribly worried about him over there in France. And any news of our cousins in Paris? And your Fernand, have you heard anything of him? How ghastly it all is! And happened so suddenly! Only a month ago Mr Chamberlain was still Prime Minister and had barely finished telling us that Hitler had missed the bus.

How's Mummy? Racing round like a whirling dervish with the WVS no doubt. Please give her all my love, and to grandma too, and not forgetting Elizabeth, and say I'll do my utmost to see them soon. Any news of Pam and her bed-pan larks? Have you finished your first-aid course yet? Poor old you, I wouldn't want to be in one of Posy Cowper's classes! She's a dragon and no mistake! Takes a fiendish delight in hauling me over the coals whenever she gets a chance. Luckily we don't see much of her at Rushton Road at present; now the war has really begun properly at last, everyone is rushing back to join Civil Defence and Posy is busier than ever training them all like mad.

We see even less of her brother, Henry. He's a bit younger than Posy, and very different in personality: quiet, the sort who keeps himself to himself, though always polite and pleasant enough when he speaks to you. Works with the Gas Board. His mother says it's a job that carries a lot of responsibility. She's obviously very proud of him.

What a bore we can't have a good gossip over the blower any

more; we poor civilians, now this emergency is on, as good as forbidden to telephone except when absolutely necessary, and then keep it short as possible. And having no phone here at my digs doesn't help, and of course I can't make or receive private calls at the *Gazette* office. Still, we can always write to one another — so long as I can find time!

All for now, Odo. Have to write some copy. Kisses and hugs all round,

Morwenna

Odile folded the letter and replaced it in her handbag, thinking to herself that Morwenna, so far, had come out the lucky one in this war. Most unfair, seeing that she, a mere sixteen-year-old schoolgirl, had had far less to lose than Odile, who, three years Morwenna's senior, had been poised on the threshold of a whole new wonderful life at university in Paris; now all snatched from her!

Morwenna, when war broke out, had been evacuated with her boarding school from the east coast into the safer inland countryside. Within a fortnight she had run away and returned home. She had refused vehemently to be sent back, though her mother had protested, "You can't ruin your education just because there's a war." To which Morwenna had replied, "But I don't need to be educated! You know I'm going to be a novelist." "You're going back on the next train, child." "Okay. But I'll only run away again, *AND NEXT TIME I WON'T COME HOME!*"

Odile, watching this little scene between parent and child, had seen her mother quail. Perhaps, if she had had a husband at home to back her in this crisis, she might have won the day and Morwenna would have returned to school; but Papa had already left for France with the RAMC to organize field surgical units. Odile had done her best to reinforce her mother. "Don't be such an ass, Morwenna, of course you must go back to school! Mummy's perfectly right. Who d'you think you are, anyway? Emily Brontë?" But Morwenna had merely thrust out her jaw and stared back in stony silence. Their grandmother, Mrs Busby, could be heard muttering, "No discipline whatever!"

A small, slight girl, looking as if the first breath of wind would blow her away, Morwenna, since nursery days, had possessed a will of iron: a power of obstinacy so intimidating that her family, in sheer self-defence, had cultivated the art of compromise when coping with her. This pattern once more repeated itself. Terms were drawn up: Morwenna need not return to school while the war lasted, but might stay at home (Stoke Hartwell, a leafy suburb verging on Epping Forest and far removed from the centre of London was not in an expected danger-zone for air raids) and do a secretarial course ("Always useful for a girl"). Papa had assured them all, before leaving for France, that once the French army got to grips with Hitler the war would be over in a matter of weeks. Morwenna would be back at school in the New Year.

But by the New Year no fighting had yet taken place. Morwenna had finished her secretarial course and, without consulting anyone and lying boldly about her age, had got herself an advertised job on the *Cuddwell Gazette*, whose editor, driven desperate by the call-up of his staff, was prepared to employ, for the first time in his life, a female reporter. Poor old Mummy had made no attempt to conceal her horror; sixteen years old and working as a newspaper reporter in Cuddwell: only twelve miles distant, geographically speaking, but as different from Stoke Hartwell as chalk from cheese! Stoke Hartwell was "a nice place to live" (non-Stoke Hartwellians called it a "snobby place"). Whereas Cuddwell, lying nearer London, was a lower middle-class and working-class neighbourhood: highly respectable and self-respecting but far removed from Stoke Hartwellian concepts of living.

However Morwenna could not be dissuaded and to Cuddwell she went; worse still, she insisted upon taking digs there. "I can't come home every night, Mummy! I have to cover evening assignments, and work through weekends because we're so short-staffed." Odile, seeing that their wretched mother was by now on the point of nervous breakdown, had had the brilliant idea of approaching Posy Cowper, in whose first-aid class Odile was now enrolled. Miss Cowper came from Cuddwell, she was clearly the epitome of respectability, and might well know somebody, equally respectable, who could offer Morwenna lodgings. Accordingly Odile had timidly approached Posy, who had replied that her mother had just lost her lodger; a bachelor, very quiet, had been called up, and she was looking for someone else, quiet and respectable, to take his place. Morwenna seemed to fit the bill perfectly and within twenty-four hours was established at 47 Rushton Road, Cuddwell.

As for Odile, she had remained at home at Maytrees, Foxwarren Avenue, Stoke Hartwell, entirely at a loose end. Simply to have something to do she had, like Morwenna, learned shorthand and typing and, still hoping against hope that the war would be over before it had properly started, had taken a temporary job in a local estate agent's office while, as a vaguely patriotic gesture ("Doing one's bit"), for one evening a week, she had enrolled on the course in first-aid.

She genuinely wished she could be more like her mother, who, at the outbreak of war, had hurled herself without reservation into the Women's Voluntary Services and devoted her entire time, nowadays, to doing this, that and the other, wherever directed, "to help the war effort". Perhaps it was easier, mused Odile, for people of her parents' generation. Having lived through the last war, they were better able to acclimatize themselves to the wartime conditions Odile found so frustrating and wearisome. The disruption of normal patterns of life: all one's friends scattered and abruptly lost touch with, the young chaps called up, the girls racing to volunteer for this and that or, their education cut short, taking jobs; the blackout; shortages of everything from tennis balls to lipstick; no decent shows in the West End; no nice shopping jaunts and outings. All the fun suddenly gone out of life.

At present Ma was away from home; had been absent for over a week, on yet another WVS war effort thing. She was incurably vague and so, as usual, hadn't had the remotest idea where she was heading for, or why; had simply packed a small bag of essentials and gone off with Sybil Spurgeon who lived next door and was also in the WVS. "Another job for us to do! Expect us when you see us!"

Whereas Odile spent her time mooning around, yearning for her lost yesterdays, and wondering despairingly if she would now ever have any kind of a decent tomorrow.

She took another letter from her handbag. It was written in French, in a masculine hand and its envelope bore a French stamp. One of the scores of letters with which Fernand had plied her since last September when, like all Frenchmen of call-up age, he had been conscripted on the outbreak of hostilities; becoming a raw recruit in the depths of provincial France, housed in barracks named after Joan of Arc.

It's all totally soul destroying! Even the stuff they issue to polish our boots has the most repulsive smell: you wonder where they *find* such

23

boot polish! And the senior officers! Their antedeluvian chauvinism and obsession with the spirit of Verdun is beyond belief; you long to bellow at them to drop their preoccupation with the last war and turn their attention to this present mess. Old dodderers! It would be a farce, if it weren't so desperately tragic.

She knew all his letters by heart but continued to read and re-read them; she loved to see his handwriting and touch the paper he had touched.

Are they true: the tales we hear of all those patriotic Frenchmen rushing up to the Front in 1914 praying that the war wouldn't be over before they had their chance to get to grips with the Boche? Either it's a fairy story, or our generation is remarkably different from theirs! None of us lot shows the slightest desire to pour over the Maginot Line and capture German villages!

More complaints: about rifle drill; square-bashing; starvation of the intellect; wretched food; barrack-room doldrums; off-duty hours of excruciating boredom hanging around a sleepy little town where the one and only cinema was showing Tarzan films.

I wonder what I've done to deserve such a fate! I suppose it's because I've lacked dedication. I've drifted along, enjoying life as it comes; an easy-going chap. And now here I am, trapped in this god-awful spot, with heaven knows what ghastly fate ahead of me. Well, that's what comes of failing to show a dedicated spirit.

All my friends, everyone one meets in Paris, so magnificently dedicated! To communism; to socialism; to pacifism: unlimited isms to choose between. Every individual I know is totally single-minded about one specific ideology or the other. But not I! It isn't that I'm politically apathetic; I'm not. But somehow, as a reasoning man, I can never totally commit myself. Take pacifism as a case in point. I'd love to be a pacifist: nothing nicer! The idea of being forced to take up arms to preserve our rotten imperialist system revolts me; but unfortunately I'm the sort of chap who'll instinctively punch any chap on the nose if he threatens to punch mine, which counts me out as a pacifist from the word go. Wouldn't you agree?

She and Fernand had met the previous August at Bolbec in Brittany, where the Duchamps had been spending a month, as they did each year, together with their French cousins from Paris. Fernand Legrand, a first-year law student at the Sorbonne, had been staying at the same hotel with his parents and sister.

Odile had lived in a golden trance of swimming and boating with Fernand, of wandering along the cliffs with him, of tennis singles with him on the sunny courts redolent with the scent of pine trees, of sauntering hand in hand with him round the harbour at night, with the village lamps dancingly reflected on the water and the little lighthouse at the end of the quay flashing in rhythmic harmony with the myriad other lighthouses signalling into the night all along the rocky coast of Morbihan. Always with Fernand.

Odile herself had been due to enter the Sorbonne to read history in the coming October, encouraged to do so by her father. She would live in Paris with her uncle, aunt and cousins. Everything, it seemed, would work out like a dream!

Then her bliss had come to an end, abruptly; just like that. Thanks to Hitler.

In her mind's eye she was with her family having breakfast on the sunny hotel terrace overlooking the beach. Her father had suddenly announced to her Uncle Nicolas, "The sooner I can get Ann and the girls back to England the better. There'll be a regular stampede of English back across the Channel within the next few days and I want to be ahead of the rush. Pack our things today, leave tomorrow."

Morwenna, her mouth full of croissant had enquired, "But just because Hitler and Stalin have signed a non-aggression pact, why does that mean we're on the brink of war?"

Thursday, the twenty-fourth of August, and the news of the Hitler-Stalin pact had just reached the ears of a startled world.

"Because," Uncle Nicolas had replied, "it puts paid to a united front of France, Britain and Russia, to restrain Germany. And a united front with Russia was our last hope of preserving peace. Now Hitler can blackmail us with his bombers, and play merry hell where he chooses, secure in the knowledge that Stalin, for one, won't intervene to stop him, even if the French and British finally find the nerve to call his bluff."

Papa said, "Hitler isn't bluffing. I've no doubt the French army could knock him sideways, but no army, however good, can prevent bombers getting through, and that's where Hitler has us." Then he started his usual doom and gloom about mass terror attacks by

25

Hitler's bombers. "The point is, will the civilian populations of Paris and London hold out long enough under that kind of annihilation, giving the field troops time to go into action; or will civilian capitulation mean that the military are obliged to come to terms with the enemy?" And so on. Ma, who was knitting herself a beach cardigan, counted stitches under her breath, desperately trying to concentrate, shutting out the talk. Aunt Madeleine, rolling her eyes piously heavenwards, murmured as she invariably murmured when Papa got on to mass terror attacks, "One can only hope and pray that it will all blow over! It's too terrible to contemplate!"

Odile sat listening and almost choking with combined contempt and despair: contempt for these miserable elders who, having experienced one frightful war's slaughter in their youth, seemed, like sheep, to accept the impossibility of preventing the fresh doom hanging over them. All they ever did was talk, or fall back on pious hope! As for her despair, that was for her own bright dreams that war would send crashing.

"Ready to come for a walk?" Fernand's voice, as he bent over her.

"Yes!" Odile gulped down the last of her coffee and sprang to her feet.

Fernand was already running impatiently down the steps leading from the hotel terrace to the beach. Odile scurried after him.

"Where are we going?" she asked as she caught him up. "Round the headland to the next bay, like we did yesterday?"

"No. There isn't time."

"The tide won't be up for ages yet."

"The tide has nothing to do with it. My family's leaving for Paris. There's my mother calling me now!"

Sure enough, from behind them came Madame Legrand's voice, "Fernand!"

"Ignore her," said Fernand. "We must have a few last moments alone together." He took Odile by the hand and, walking with rapid strides, hurried along the beach. "My father is in a real panic about this latest crisis," he continued. "So, in the middle of breakfast, after one glance at the morning paper, he announces that we must go home to Paris without delay. He seems to be expecting the Germans to arrive at any moment."

"My father's just the same," said Odile. "He's hauling us back to England tomorrow. I was wondering how to tell you."

On the surface, everything was just the same as usual. The distant blue and white incoming tide glistened in the sun and the gulls fluttered and called above the breakers. On the beach in front of the hotels a group of people were lining up to do their morning exercises under the guidance of the *Maître Nageur*. Nearer at hand another group were briskly playing volley ball. An old woman, who spent all day every day on the beach under a vast sunshade, had already arranged herself and the sunshade to her satisfaction and was comfortably peeling herself a peach.

They reached a place where some big fallen rocks blocked them from the view of the hotel and Madame Legrand. Fernand stopped, took Odile in his arms and kissed her. "You'll come back to France if there isn't a war?" he asked.

"Of course. I'm due to start at the Sorbonne in October."

He kissed her again, then stared hard into her eyes as if searching for some oracular truth in their depths. Then, "You won't be back. You know it. You know there's going to be a war this time, just as well as I do."

Odile's eyes filled with tears; she couldn't speak.

"Fer-nand!" Madame Legrand's voice again.

"*Merde!*" said Fernand. "I shall have to go." A scallop shell lay on the sand at their feet; swiftly he stooped, picked it up and handed it to Odile, with a mock ceremonial bow. "A little souvenir of your stay at the seaside, *mademoiselle*."

"Thank you, *m'sieur*! I shall treasure it for ever."

He linked his arm through hers, pressing her close to him, and in silence they retraced their steps, back to the hotel.

The German tanks had rolled towards Warsaw; the Polish High Command had ordered a general retreat of the troops into southernmost Poland, there to regroup. It was a matter of hanging on till the French were ready. They should have been showing signs of active intervention by this time! But. . . .

Fernand's letters contained frustrated accounts of how the army was helping farmers gather record fruit crops. "*Mon dieu!* What a farce this all is! My career and prospects disrupted to become an orchard-cropping peasant! Millions of our chaps called to arms, and here they are playing among peaches and plums! We've declared war; for God's sake let's make war, and get it done with! France has gone senile, like her High Command. Impossibly chauvinistic – and impotent!"

Nonetheless, fruit picking wouldn't, couldn't, go on for ever. In his next letter Fernand struck a new note: even he wasn't above a little chauvinism. "The news from Poland certainly sounds grim! However, as yet Hitler's troops have met with no real opposition; the Poles are admittedly brave, but perfectly archaic. Whereas the French military machine is the best in the world. Just you wait till our *poilus* get their teeth into the Germans. The war will be over in no time, that's a promise! And then, we'll start to live! You and me together!"

Odile, once she had begun work at the estate agent's office, instructed Fernand to address letters to her there. It wasn't discreet to have his stream of correspondence constantly flipping through the letter box at Maytrees. Even Ma might begin to smell a rat! Odile suspected that her parents could have second thoughts about letting her go to Paris and the Sorbonne, when peace returned, if they knew that she and Fernand. . . .

He kept optimistic about their future. "I know that in this I am not being *strictly* rational, beloved Odile, but how can I possibly fail to survive this idiotic war when I know that you're there for me at the end of it all?"

His face was before her as clearly as if he were beside her; the depths of his large dark eyes under their thick, straight black eyelashes; his strongly marked eyebrows; his full mouth; the sooty little mole just below his left jawline. . . .

"Miss Duchamp, let's have you next!"

Startled from her reverie by Miss Cowper's clarion call Odile jerked from her seat and began stumbling dazedly towards the platform. Next instant she was blindfolded and Miss Cowper was bawling in her ear, "Carotid!" Odile began wondering where in hell she would find a carotid artery?

"Come on, come on! Don't forget I'm bleeding to death!" roared Miss Cowper, from where she now lay prone at Odile's feet.

Odile dropped on her knees, put out a tentative hand and took a grip on the first portion of Miss Cowper's robust frame that her fingers met. "No go!" shouted Miss Cowper. "Carotid, I said! I don't keep it down there!"

The class began to titter as, wildly fumbling, Odile tried squeezing at random whichever bits of Miss Cowper came to hand first, to be greeted by a bellow of "No!" each time. The tittering turned to unabashed laughter. Finally Miss Cowper cut Odile short

28

with, "All right, you can stop; I'm dead. And a fat lot of help you're going to be to anyone in an emergency!"

She bounced to her feet, grabbed hold of Odile and applied a hideous grip to a point deep in the base of her throat, an excruciating jab of pain that brought tears to Odile's eyes. For a moment she feared she was going to pass out. "That's your carotid, m'girl! Now, don't you forget it!" Odile thought she would rather die than be saved by Miss Cowper, who, slipping the blindfold from Odile's head, dismissed her from the platform with, "Don't know why you bothered to sign on for these classes if all you intend doing is waste my time, and yours."

The instant she sank down on her chair Odile's thoughts flew back to Fernand. How exactly his reaction to this wretched war coincided with hers! "A farce, if it weren't so desperately tragic!"

And tragic, perhaps, was to be the final word. All very well to speak breezily of French *poilus* getting their teeth into the Germans! Hitler's tanks had invaded France three weeks ago; the French front had been pierced, news bulletin after news bulletin told calamity – and not another letter had come from Fernand.

III

"We shall go on to the end. . . . We shall defend our island, whatever the cost may be. We shall fight on the beaches, we shall fight on the landing grounds, we shall fight in the fields and in the streets, we shall fight in the hills; we shall never surrender."

"Of course we're all going to fight!" said Mrs Busby, putting down her *Daily Telegraph* from which she had been reading aloud to Elizabeth. "Does he suppose that we English aren't going to make a stand?"

"Oh, of course Mr Churchill knows that, ma'am! That's what he's saying."

"I don't mean Churchill. I mean Hitler."

"I don't know, ma'am. Maybe he thinks we'll be easy to finish off, like all those foreigners."

Maytrees, Wednesday the fifth of June. Mrs Busby, an aggressively spry lady in her seventies, was breakfasting with Elizabeth, the domestic, herself a good sixty. Mrs Busby hated eating alone and in any case had come, over the years, to regard Elizabeth as more companion and friend than servant.

"In my opinion," continued Mrs Busby, as she finished reading the report of Churchill's fighting speech in the House of Commons the previous day, "I don't think that that speech is aimed at the British public. *We* all know *we're* going to fight! It's intended for Hitler, in case he thinks we're going to fold up like everyone else has, and for the Americans, who are always so frightfully slow on the uptake and have to be *boomed* at!"

"I think you're right, ma'am. *We* don't need it."

The telephone rang. "That will be my daughter, to say she's on her way home, at last," exclaimed Mrs Busby, optimistically. Elizabeth answered the phone: returned saying, "It's Dr Duchamp, back from France, ma'am. He says he's safe and well, but too busy with the wounded they've brought back from Dunkirk to be able to get home. We are to expect him when we see him."

"Paul! Thank God for that! I was terrified he might be captured by the Germans!" Mrs Busby, normally not noted for displays of affectionate interest in her son-in-law, was obviously genuinely relieved to hear that he was safe. She added, "Is he at the hospital?" "St Jerome's? No, ma'am. Dashing from one surgical unit to the next, he says. What a muddle everything has become, all of a sudden! Nobody knowing where anybody is or what they're up to."

Ann arrived home, without warning, the next morning, reappearing as abruptly as she had left in the first place. "Been to Folkstone," she explained laconically, as she entered the garden-room where her mother and Elizabeth were having their elevenses by the open french-windows. "Helping with the troops when they came ashore," continued Ann, and, in the same breath, "Any news of Paul?"

"He telephoned yesterday," replied Mrs Busby. "Safe in England, but busy with the wounded. Wonderful how we've managed to bring so many men back, isn't it?"

"Bloody miracle," responded Ann, kicking off her shoes and flopping down on the sofa. "Bloody miracle," she repeated, as she lit herself a cigarette and inhaled deeply. She rarely, if ever, used that kind of language; but, as she looked half dead with exhaustion, her mother decided to let the lapse pass unremarked.

The British public had only just had released to them real news of the Dunkirk rescue operation and even now had merely received outline information. Those who had taken any part in it maintained, on their return, the extreme caution in discussing it that they had been told they must observe; resultantly Ann now proved irritatingly uncommunicative about what had gone on at Folkestone, merely saying that apart from a few hours' sleep snatched nightly, this was the first chance of a breather she'd had in ten days.

Elizabeth brought her coffee. Ann sipped it, and lit another cigarette. Bliss, sheer bliss! She promised herself that she would spend the next two or three days lying on the swing seat in the garden: she could never remember having felt so completely, damnably worn out!

The telephone was ringing. "If that's for me I'm out — unless it's Paul!" exclaimed Ann. Elizabeth took the call and came in with a pitying glance for Ann. "It's Mrs Spurgeon, ma'am. She says it's a matter of urgency."

Ann, with a groan, rose and went to the telephone, hobbling like an old woman on her stockinged feet. Why on earth Sybil, like Ann just back from Folkestone, couldn't put her feet up with a silent vow to let other people deal with all matters of urgency for a few hours at least. . . !

"Hello, Sybil. Don't tell me you've already found something else for us to do!"

"A message from HQ, an emergency first-aid post and mortuary need scrubbing out as a matter of urgency, I'll pick you up at fourteen hours, okay?" As usual Sybil spoke in a wild gabble.

"We've only just this instant arrived home! You may feel spry as a lark but I. . . ."

"We're the only two available, everyone else is still scattered along the south coast doing their bit for the boys. See you at fourteen hours and don't forget to have an old mat to kneel on. Bye-ee!"

Ann hobbled back to the sofa, poured herself another cup of coffee and lit another cigarette. "Sybil has found us a mortuary to scrub out after lunch."

"Oh ma'am, I hope you aren't overdoing it!" exclaimed Elizabeth, with genuine concern.

"Only wish I were young enough to overdo it," said Mrs Busby vehemently. "Give Hitler a good doing over I would, if I had the chance!"

31

Ann, feeling ashamed of her momentary failure of morale, thought of all those swarms of exhausted tommies who had come pouring off the boats at Folkestone, having stood for ages on the beaches of Dunkirk and in the water, under fire, waiting to be taken on board the rescuing ships which in their turn were bombed and sunk in all directions. Some notion of what Dunkirk was like had reached her from snatches of conversation overheard among those to whom she had served piping hot cups of tea hour after hour for ten long days; tea for which they had thanked her with a gratitude which brought tears to her eyes at the thought of it. Those poor chaps really knew the meaning of exhaustion! So what in the world was *she* beefing about?

At two p.m. on the dot Sybil showed up, with an impressive array of cleaning equipment stowed in the boot of her car. Although they were detailed for a scrubbing job, WVS discipline demanded that Ann and Sybil should be immaculately turned out in WVS uniform. Designed by couturier Digby Morton to be simultaneously trim, attractive and practical, the suit of soft green tweed with an interweave of grey was worn with a dark red jumper and a plain, pull-on felt hat, suitable for either town or country. Ann, at forty still youthfully pretty, with a fresh complexion and loosely waving light brown hair without trace of grey, looked very nice in the outfit; though regretfully aware that an inch or so off her hips would improve the hang of the skirt. Sybil, on the other hand, approved of her own appearance in uniform and rightly so, for if anything could help her angular figure, uniform did: it made the angles look more natural, while the Sybilline lack of flesh meant that neither skirt nor jacket bulged inelegantly. That hat was less successful on her. With her large flashing spectacles and protruding teeth Sybil was not, as she put it, a "hatty person".

Ann's piece of old mat installed in the boot with the other things, off went the two women; Sybil, an erratic driver, whizzing along Foxwarren Avenue at a spanking pace, her few hours' rest at home seeming to have restored her completely to her usual frenetically energetic self. She was one of those wiry, taut, nervously restless people who apparently never tire; moreover her own fatigue-proof constitution made her intolerant of any hint of weakness in others. A fanatical believer in fitness, Sybil perceived positive moral virtue in health and strength, which she associated with a clean, vigorous outlook on life in general. Prior to post-Munich disillusionment,

Sybil, like many another of her kind, had nourished an enthusiasm for Hitler's National Socialism and its enticingly wholesome slogan, *Kraft durch Freude* — "Strength through Joy" — which she had zestily intoned upon her return from summer jaunts in the Black Forest. "Hitler has really injected a new spirit into the German people. We could do with a little of something of that sort over here!" A remark which had provoked instant reaction from her elder son, Hugo, who loudly let everyone know that he was a Communist and believed in a United Front against Hitler. However, Sybil's admiration for the Swastika had evaporated abruptly with Hitler's invasion of Czechoslovakia in March 1939; when war broke out between her own country and Germany, six months later, Sybil couldn't wait to get her teeth into the promoter of "Strength through Joy" and bring him to the ground.

Now, as she drove, Sybil jabbered away at top speed about the latest family crisis to have engulfed her, this time involving her daughter Pam, a junior probationer nurse at St Jerome's. "No sooner in the house than collapsing on me in floods of tears, wailing something or other about someone called Nicky — apparently some young naval officer it seems blown up at Dunkirk. First I've heard of any naval officer! Of course daughters of today never tell one a thing! From what I can gather they were secretely engaged though they couldn't have known each other for more than a few weeks; I suppose we must expect this kind of thing from our offspring in wartime but quite honestly my dear what with Hitler *and* one's own children one certainly has one's time cut out trying to cope with it all at once!"

To this, Ann made indistinct sounds of general sympathy; at the same time she was unable to prevent an unfortunately smug expression appearing on her face, as she thought how very different was the relationship she enjoyed with her own daughters, who always told her everything.

Sybil continued, "I've already enough trouble on my plate with Hugo! I daren't mention any of *that* to his father, who's having a bad enough time evacuated to Southport. Well there I go: careless talk costs lives and I *shouldn't* say where he is, top civil servants being doubtless marked men and *so* important."

Ann repeated her sounds of sympathy. She never knew whether to be amused or exasperated by Sybil. At the same time this didn't prevent Ann from feeling sincerely sorry for Sybil: basically a good egg (as Ann phrased it to herself), and blessed with two perfectly good younger children, a son, Jasper, and daughter Pamela, but really most unfortunate in Hugo (whom, of course, Sybil completely worshipped in the way of mothers with first-born sons). Hugo, an Oxford undergraduate in his final year and therefore exempt from call-up, had suddenly returned home, a fortnight or so ago, announcing that he had come down from Oxford for good, without finishing term or sitting for his finals, and was intending to register as a conscientious objector on the grounds that all war was pointless and society a fraud and he was opting out of the farce for good and all. Saying which he had packed a bag and left home to stay with pacifist friends, he hadn't said where. Sybil, not unnaturally, had been distraught and had spent an entire evening weeping on Ann's shoulder; after which they had drunk brandy and sodas together to help pull Sybil round, and Ann, for the first time in her life, had returned home reeling and had had great trouble in inserting her latch-key in the front door lock. "There's a war on!" she had heard herself saying aloud, over and over again, as she had fiddled with the key. "There's a war on!"

And now, of course, poor Sybil had Jasper to worry about too! Aged nineteen, he had gone to France with the Territorial Army, just at the point when the Phoney War ended and Hitler's tanks erupted into Blitzkrieg. Heaven alone knew where the boy was or what had happened to him! Ann had noticed poor Sybil's strained expression at Folkestone, scanning the faces of the returning troops, hoping against hope.

Ann had always wanted sons because Paul had so much set his heart on sons. Paul, born in England of French parentage, held a dual passport; bilingual, in the Great War he had served as a liaison officer with Field Ambulance, on the Western Front. His family had, down the generations, produced highly reputable doctors, scientists. It was natural that Paul should want sons to carry on this tradition. His one brother had been killed at Verdun. In Paris his only sister had four daughters. Ann had been well aware that it was up to her to produce boys.

She herself had lost her father (a Regular soldier) and two brothers at the Front. But when, in 1921, she and Paul had at last started a family, three years after their wartime marriage, they had nursed no fears that any son born to them would face the horrors they themselves had just passed through: they shared the universal conviction that, following the carnage of the recent conflict, there must never be, *could* never be, another war.

The birth of their first child, a daughter, Odile, had been an unmitigated joy; a girl was lovely to start a family with and there'd be a son next time. Ann had quickly tried to become pregnant again, but it was not until nearly three years later that she had conceived once more, while on a family holiday near Morwenstow in north Cornwall. During the ensuing nine months no attempts had been made to refer to the contents of her womb by any name more specific than "Little Thingummy"; Ann hadn't wanted to tempt Providence. As the final weeks of the pregnancy had passed she had developed a sense of certainty that the new arrival *must* be a son. A daughter it had been. They had named her Morwenna, after the Cornish saint. However little Morwenna, in the family circle, was known as "Thingummy" or "Thingy".

Ann had continued trying for a boy, but had produced no more children. Despite her disappointment she was happy in her daughters and Paul too, though he had so badly wanted a son, nonetheless adored the girls, as Ann frequently and contentedly remarked, though he tended to worry about them more than Ann did. For instance, he had feared that Odile had grown too serious about that Legrand boy at Bolbec, but Ann had reassured him, "Oh, don't worry; it's nothing more than a holiday enthusiasm. It'll be years before Odile is serious about anyone!"

Odile was now nineteen, old enough to be called up had she been a boy. Ann, these days, felt increasingly thankful that she had been blessed with daughters rather than sons.

Sybil was saying something. "It's a relief to know the powers-that-be are making sure our first-aid posts are in order."

"Is this place we're scrubbing out some vast undertaking that will occupy us for the rest of the week?"

"I don't anticipate we shall find there's an awful lot to be done," said Sybil. "The place was requisitioned last summer when we were all expecting Hitler's bombers to appear in swarms the instant war broke out and I think it was blacked out and more or less got ready then."

Ann made no response. She was thinking of those months before the war when Paul, together with colleagues from London's other leading hospitals, had been called upon by the government to prepare for enormous numbers of air raid casualties. Ann had been

35

one of the optimists who had refused to believe that war was on the way: to jolt her complacency, Paul had confided to her that the official estimate for air raid casualties was four hundred thousand within the first twenty-four hours of an all-out bombing attack. Armageddon, in short.

Ann had been obliged to accept that, in the case of war, there might well be air attacks; indeed, if she hadn't accepted that possibility she would never have troubled to join the WVS, essentially a Civil Defence organization. But she couldn't convince herself that Hitler might inflict a kind of H. G. Wells *Things to Come* holocaust upon London. She had assumed that somebody in Whitehall had decided that some lurid exaggeration was needed to inject a touch of alacrity into a decidedly apathetic country. This she still privately believed. Moreover she remained essentially optimistic about the war in general. Paul had always insisted that, if civilian morale held out after the initial wave of terror-bombing of Paris and London, Nazi Germany would be polished off in the field in no time. Well, Paul had been wrong about Armageddon, but he couldn't be wrong about the essential superiority of the French army: everyone knew it was the best in the world. True, at the moment Hitler's troops weren't exactly being polished off at high speed by the French, but a whirlwind attack such as Hitler's couldn't last. The French would counter-attack; the British would soon be back in the fight again; the war could still be over within a few months.

She voiced this line of thought to Sybil. "Hitler can't keep this up, you know. We've had to evacuate our troops from France, but. . . ."

"We'll be back there in no time. As for Hitler, he's burning himself out."

Sybil slowed the car as they approached an old drill-hall set among Victorian terraces, with a Methodist church on the corner. "The keys are at the ARP post behind the church," she said. She stopped the car by the church and Ann popped out to collect the keys, armed with which the two women let themselves into the drill-hall, built at the time of Queen Victoria's Diamond Jubilee. Sybil and Ann stepped cautiously into a place of pitch blackness; every window had been boarded over as a combined precaution against flying glass and a method of blackout. Gasping exclamations to one another, the pair groped round the walls in search of light switches. At last Ann found some and turned them on.

She and Sybil were standing in a small annexe at the front of the main drill-hall. To the left of this annexe was a room planned as a makeshift office; a desk and a filing cabinet were placed ready in it, together with an old swivel chair. A portrait of Queen Victoria in her Diamond Jubilee regalia still adorned the wall. There was also a kitchen of sorts with a cold water tap, a primitive earthenware sink and a rusty gas cooker. All the walls throughout this part of the building had been freshly distempered white, but the floors had been left filthy, the grime of years overlaid with the mess made by whoever had boarded the windows and whitened the walls.

"Going to take the rest of the day to get this clean," said Sybil.

She and Ann filled their buckets with water and put them on the cooker to heat. They then took off their smart tweed suits and donned dungarees. Ann lit a cigarette, looked round with a slight shudder and said, "What a ghastly dump! Who on earth decided to use this as a first-aid post?"

"I wonder what lies down this passage?" said Sybil.

"The main hall, I suppose. And maybe the WCs. There must be some kind of convenience. Pity the poor first-aid staff stuck here!"

So saying, Ann walked down the passage and opened a door into the main hall. It was blacked out like the rest of the building. She discovered a light switch and exposed more dreary whitewashed walls, another filthy floor. Sybil joined Ann to inspect he hall. "Take hours of scrubbing!" they groaned to one another. Ann crossed the hall and tried a door at the further end. It opened and she stepped into a rear annexe, packed with stacks of what looked like long, narrow, dark brown cardboard cartons folded flat.

"What on earth are these?"

"What?" asked Sybil, peering into the annexe.

"Hundreds and hundreds of flat cardboard folder sort of things."

"Lord only knows," said Sybil. Ann meantime took one of the cardboard objects down from a stack and began to examine it, merely out of curiosity.

It was a kind of very large, heavy cardboard box, much longer than it was wide, and folded flat like a collapsible cake box, for convenience of storage. Ann partly unfolded it, still wondering what its purpose could be.

Sybil said, "Oh God, it's a coffin!"

"A coffin?"

"Yes, don't you see? Prefabricated coffins. Stacks and stacks of 'em."

Ann stood without speaking, still holding the half-opened object, seeing that it was indeed, as Sybil said, a coffin. A kind of cold, impersonal numbness came over her. She looked at the stacks of the things around her; she noticed now that they were graded in various sizes, from large ones, like that which she held, to small ones. All ready for Armageddon.

"Put it away, and let's get out of here," said Sybil.

Ann, still too numb to be able to say a word, automatically refolded the thing and replaced it on the stack from which she had removed it.

She then followed Sybil back through the drill-hall and into the kitchen, where the water in the buckets was now hot enough for them to use. Neither of them spoke about what they had just seen. Within minutes they were both on all fours and scrubbing their way across the front hall floor.

It was not until just after nine that they arrived back at their respective homes, both totally exhausted. Elizabeth greeted Ann with her customary resumé of events which had occurred during the time that her mistress had been out: "Dr Duchamp is home, ma'am; he arrived about an hour ago. Miss Odile is at the cinema. I've kept you some supper. The doctor and your mother have had theirs. Shall I bring it into the drawing-room for you, on a tray?"

"Yes please, Elizabeth."

Ann limped into the drawing-room where the nine o'clock news broadcast was drawing to a lugubrious close with the information that German tanks were rolling the French back in all directions.

"Paul, darling, thank heaven you're home all in one piece! You must have had a ghastly time!" cried Ann, flying to him.

Paul, with a set face, switched the wireless off and rose to embrace his wife. Mrs Busby, always forthright, exclaimed, "Looks worse for the French every moment! I always said they wouldn't stand up to a real crunch and, you see, events are proving me right."

Paul swivelled upon her. "The past few weeks I've seen old women like you lying dead by the roadside, in bomb craters, dive bombed by those bastards!" He choked on the words, gulped some whisky, then continued, in a taut, cutting voice, "My good, idiotic Anglo-Saxon relic, what we're living through now is the massacre of Europe, in cold blood. The British aren't going to be spared, don't think it! And see how you'll stand up to it!"

"I think, Ann, I shall go to bed." Mrs Busby rose, trembling, and walked shakily from the room. Ann, after a moment's hesitation, hurried after her. "Mother, let me help you upstairs."

"No thank you, my dear, I can manage."

"You really invited that outburst, you know. Poor Paul; he's had a most upsetting time and is obviously worn out. . . ."

"Naturally I understand that he's tired and upset. As for being Anglo-Saxon, that doesn't worry me one jot. Thank heaven for Anglo-Saxons! And I confess that I shall be shortly having my seventy-fifth birthday, but nonetheless that doesn't mean I'm a *relic*!" She glared furiously over the bannisters at her daughter's pale, upturned face, and then limped stiffly out of view.

Ann returned to Paul. "What on earth possessed you to call mother a relic! She'll never forgive you."

"Your mother should have been throttled years ago."

"Paul, really! If only out of respect for me. . . ."

"What about a little respect for me, eh? You damn well know it's not true that the French. . . ."

"But something has gone terribly wrong, somewhere along the line, Paul."

"Yes. We've allowed ourselves, for years, to be blackmailed and intimidated by a gang of vicious thugs, and now we're reaping the whirlwind."

There was a brief silence. Then, "France can't really be going to fall!" Ann burst out, like someone who had earlier received a stunning blow and was only now, suddenly, stabbed by realization.

"I agree it's almost impossible to believe that a marvellously civilized nation, that has taken a thousand years to develop, can perish, within a month, at the hands of a crude butcher. But," Paul spoke slowly, staring, without seeing, at the garden, twisting his whisky glass round and round between his hands in a kind of anguish, "that, God help us, is what is going to happen."

IV

The *Cuddwell Gazette* editorial offices and printing press were located in a big gaunt building, part of a now defunct tannery, at the end of a cul-de-sac behind the parish church and noisy, stall-crowded market square, historically the town centre. Eight-thirty every morning, bar Sundays, saw Morwenna eagerly hurrying through the square, chaotic with stall-holders setting out their fruit and vegetables. A short-cut across the churchyard brought her to the cul-de-sac, along which she sped, to dive into a dark doorway and up a flight of dirty stairs to the first floor, where, on a dismal landing, a door on the right bore the awe-inspiring name, "Editor". Next was the sub-editor's room, beyond this the reporters' room.

Monday the seventeenth of June. Morwenna pelted up the stairs, sniffing the all-pervading odour of newsprint as if it were Chanel No. 5. From the room marked "Editor" could be heard the voice of Mr Walters, already at his desk and involved in clearly hectic telephone conversation, bawling his head off at some unfortunate at the other end of the line

In the next room Mr Macpherson, the sub-editor, a round-shouldered man in his shirtsleeves, had lit his first pipe of the day and was gloomily scanning his copy of *The Times*. During the past ten days Paris had been declared an open city and had fallen to the Germans; the French government had retreated to Bordeaux; the French army was everywhere in apparent disarray; talk of counter-attack carried less and less conviction. The newspapers and wireless bulletins chorused a mounting crescendo of disaster. All this was reflected in the expression on Mr Macpherson's face as he stared at his *Times*.

Morwenna wished him a polite "Good morning"; he grunted a reply and continued to read. At this moment Mr Walters whirled out of his office, shouting, "Couldn't wait for his bloody call-up papers! So bloody keen in his country's hour of need that away he had to rush and join up off his own goddamn bat! No thought of what that means to this bloody-gorblimey paper!"

Mr Macpherson raised his head in enquiry. "Haven't lost Gilroy, have we?"

"No, not yet, it's young Stoppard gone off to terrify the Hun. I thought we could count on him for another six months at least. Not that he was much to count on but anything's better than nothing. Christ orl-bloody-mighty! Gilroy due to be called up any moment and I'll be landed with you, Miss Doochamp, as my one and only reporter. Strewth! What a bloody nightmare!"

Mr Walters seemed on the brink of spontaneous internal combustion. He continued to bawl at Morwenna, "From now on your gotta cover everything that's down for Stoppard in the diary, plus your stuff in the diary too, and God help you!" Morwenna nodded, big eyes fixed on Mr Walters, wondering how much redder he could grow in the face before exploding. "Gor blimey! bloody Hitler!" and Mr Walters vanished back into his office. Morwenna scuttled into the reporters' room, scruffy and uncomfortable looking, but Mecca to Morwenna, with its desks, each equipped with a battered typewriter and a wooden chair. The desk by the window was Gilroy's; Morwenna, as cub reporter, had the one in a corner; the desk by the fireplace had been Stoppard's. Morwenna, with a businesslike expression, now began removing all her things from the corner desk to that by the fireplace.

She was pleased, on the whole, that Stoppard had left. It would mean a lot of extra work for her, but on the other hand it also meant that she automatically moved a step up the ladder and had more responsible jobs to cover.

Having taken over Stoppard's desk Morwenna next inspected the diary to discover what she had to take over in the way of his assignments. She found that he had Coroner's Court that morning, an interview with the sanitary inspector in the afternoon and a Parks and Open Spaces Committee meeting in the evening. Her own diary entries included a Townswomen's Guild meeting at two p.m. and a Boy Scouts' concert party in the evening.

She wondered how on earth she would fit it all in. She stood staring at the diary, frowning in fierce concentration. At this point Gilroy arrived; a thin, dark-headed youth with a long pointed nose and inquisitive brown eyes. "Morning honeybunch, contemplating suicide?" he said genially.

"Not really, though I'm going to have an awful lot of work to do now Stoppard's gone. You've heard that he's joined up, I suppose?"

"Mac's just given me the news. Nice enough bloke, Ken

Stoppard, but as a journalist not the world's greatest. You'll make a damn sight better reporter than he ever was, or had any hope of being," said Gilroy, encouragingly, as he seated himself at his typewriter and began furiously turning out copy. Morwenna wrote up a couple of weddings left over from the previous day and took this copy to Mr Macpherson, who was chatting glumly with Mr Walters about the morning's news from France. Mr Macpherson received the copy from Morwenna. "These all the weddings up to date, Miss Doochamp?"

"Heavens no, Mr Macpherson! I've a huge list of weddings, long as my arm; the problem is getting round to them all. Everyone in Cuddwell seems to be getting married."

"Just like it was in the last war; everybody getting spliced," said Mr Walters lugubriously, his tone that of someone referring to an outbreak of a particularly obnoxious contagion. He added, fixing Morwenna with an aggressive glare, "Don't ever let me hear you're leaving me in the lurch to get married, Miss Doochamp. Don't want any of that wedding-bells stuff from you."

"Heavens no, Mr Walters I shall *never* marry! I intend dedicating myself to my career!" replied Morwenna fervently.

"Good-oh, Miss Doochamp. I breathe again," said Mr Walters, turning away hurriedly and diving into his office. Mr Macpherson, knocking out his pipe, said, "And don't forget, Miss Doochamp, I want that inquest stuff written and handed in before you go off to dinner."

"Okey-doke, Mr Macpherson. See you later!" And off went Morwenna to Coroner's Court; the first time she had covered it and therefore a great professional thrill for her.

In the courtroom press bench she found Pym, her rival from the *Mercury*, a breezy seventeen-year-old. He was sympathetic about the load of work fallen upon Morwenna as a result of Stoppard's departure; the *Mercury* staff was becoming similarly depleted. "Still, if you and I get together and share the load, strictly on the QT, I'm sure we'll survive this desperate hour," he said, grinning at her. "Let's hear what you've got on your plate." Like a couple of conspirators they divided up their assignments: "I'll do the Parks Committee, you do the concert party and we'll swap the dope over the blower afterwards."

"Fine," agreed Morwenna. She added, suddenly sounding a little shy, "Are you going to Cuddwell Ratepayers' Association tomorrow night, and if so, would you cover it for me? You see, tomorrow's my sister's birthday and my grandmother's too and my family's throwing a sort of celebration and if possible I mustn't miss it. Stoppard was going to oblige me, but now. . . ."

"By all means, if you'll cover the Royal Orphanage whist drive and dance on Saturday for me, to allow me to go on the spree."

At this point the Coroner entered, and silence was called for by the usher. Morwenna opened her shorthand notebook and prepared for action.

V

Morwenna arrived late for midday dinner at her digs at 47 Rushton Road. In the bright and comfortable kitchen-cum-dining room Mrs Cowper and Posy were seated, eating. Mrs Cowper, looking up with a cheerful smile, said to Morwenna, "Hello duck. We started without you; hope you don't mind. Yours is all ready, kept hot in the oven."

"Heard the news?" asked Posy. "The French have thrown in the towel."

"When all's said and done, we're much better off without 'em,' said Mrs Cowper.

"Much better off," agreed Posy, grinning buoyantly, like one who had had a load fall from her back. "Now we can get down to fighting the war good and proper!"

Morwenna, frozen rigid with horror and staring aghast, stammered, "I don't believe it! It's not true! It's a false report; the French will never surrender!"

"Came over on the one o'clock news," said Posy. "It's true alright." She poured herself a fresh cup of tea. Mrs Cowper, bringing Morwenna's plateful of shepherd's pie and peas to the table said, "It means we know where we stand, and that can only be for the good."

Morwenna spent the rest of the day listening to people saying more or less the same thing to each other in voices more cheerful than she had heard on the streets for a long time. "Better off without them!" "Now we know where we really stand!" "Get on with the job, now we can, and no messing about!"

You would never have guessed for an instant that the British had lost their chief ally. "They're all mad!" thought Morwenna grimly. She wondered what Frank would have to say about all this.

Morwenna, despite her fervent avowal to Mr Walters that she intended dedicating herself to her career, had recently fallen in love.

She and Frank had first met six weeks ago at Pam Spurgeon's nineteenth birthday party. The war made parties at home difficult, so Mrs Spurgeon had let Pam invite a few friends to dine and dance at the Hungaria. Odile and Morwenna had, of course, been invited; since childhood they and Pam had always gone to one another's birthday parties. For Morwenna this would be her first time at the Hungaria, one of London's ritziest places to dine and dance. Every right-minded girl dreamed of a date at the Hungaria! Morwenna could scarcely wait for the evening to arrive. There was only one snag, and that was a serious one: she was far too busy on the *Gazette* to hunt around for something special to wear. She resigned herself to the Liberty blue velvet smocked frock trimmed with palest pink and turquoise that had so thrilled her when it had been bought for her to wear at a wedding ten months ago, but which now seemed hopelessly juvenile. She did her best to age herself by sweeping her hair up and fixing it with blue combs and a blue bow, which she prayed might stay put.

It was the most appalling hair in the world to have been cursed with, as Morwenna groaned to herself daily. Its colour, palest ash blond, she dismissed as wishy-washy, while in texture it was so fine and slippery that, within moments of being dressed, it would be in all directions, adding to her general wispy, fly-away appearance. The only way to keep it reasonably neat was to grow it long and fasten it in plaits; at school she had worn these hanging down her back but nowadays, at work, she wound them round her head, a style she disparaged as hopelessly old-fashioned and Gretchen-like — but what alternative was there if she didn't want to look like a wild thing out of the woods?

To heighten this woodsy impression, Morwenna was further afflicted, as she saw it, with eyes too large for her face. Worse still, her frequent smile was broad and slightly lop-sided, revealing

44

brilliantly white, rather gappy teeth (at school they had named her the Cheshire Cat) and whenever she laughed her nose and eyes wrinkled in wicked glee: no wonder her father used to tease her mother by saying that the Cornish piskies had had a hand in producing Morwenna.

All most disheartening, and also jolly unfair, because Odile had everything denied Morwenna: Odile's hair was true golden blond, she had regular features, a lovely smile, a soulful expression (especially coveted by Morwenna) and well-marked eyebrows (Morwenna's, being the same colour as her hair, scarcely showed). Well, it was no use moaning, but it *was* a pity that one sister should have been blessed with such marvellous good looks, while the other—!

Morwenna told herself firmly that, at the Hungaria, she must remember not to laugh or smile (Cornish pisky, Cheshire Cat) but to maintain an aloof, mysteriously pensive expression, sort of Garbo as Queen Christina. With this resolve, Morwenna applied a last careful coating of lipstick, and a touch of blue mascara (an old block discarded by Odile); but mascara was a mistake, because it accentuated her eyes, so that now she looked like an owl! However, too late to do anything about it; an owl she must resemble for the rest of the evening. With a last disgruntled grimace at herself in the mirror, off she hastened to catch her train.

The Hungaria was crowded; lots of uniforms, lots of glamorous, self-assured young women who made Morwenna increasingly abashed by her smocked frock and not yet seventeen summers. Pam, looking remarkably pretty and poised in a chic coral-coloured silk dress, introduced Morwenna to the rest of the party, all of whom, with the exception of Odile, were strangers to her; Morwenna had expected to find old buddies from the former Stoke Hartwell "gang", but not so. Even Odile, at first impression, seemed like a stranger; dazzling in a new red chiffon dress with sequined shoulder straps, bright red lipstick and nail varnish, and smelling ravishingly of *Je Reviens*.

Another surprise: Pam had as her escort not her brother Hugo, as Morwenna had taken for granted would be the case (Pam had always had a fearful crush on Hugo and was in heaven if she had a chance to go out with him!), but a young sub-loot in the RNVR called Nicky ("Don't breathe a word to my mother about Nicky, *please*!" hissed Pam in Morwenna's ear as the introductions were made).

"Would you like to come to the cloakroom and tidy your hair before we all go to our table?" murmured a low, considerate voice in Morwenna's ear. The speaker was a tall, dark, attractive girl, madly svelte in emerald green; Morwenna limply nodded agreement and followed this intimidatingly elegant figure to the ladies' cloakroom. It was some indication of Morwenna's state of daze that it was not for several moments that she realized her guide was already known to her: Boggy Hope-Warrington, who with Pam was a junior probationer nurse at St Jerome's hospital. Odile and Morwenna had recently spent an afternoon with Pam and Boggy in town, going to the Empire Cinema in Leicester Square, taking tea afterwards at Lyon's Corner House nearby. Boggy on that occasion, in nurse's uniform, with cape and cap, had seemed simply a jolly, dimple-cheeked, eighteen-year-old; now here she was looking totally mature and worldly-wise, obviously knowing her way around at the Hungaria, and bestowing on Morwenna the sort of kindly sympathy grown-ups give to the young. One glance in the mirror showed Morwenna that her hair did indeed need tidying; her already flushed cheeks flushed a deeper pink with chagrin that Boggy had noticed it instantly and had come to her rescue.

While Morwenna struggled grimly with her hair, Boggy lit herself a cigarette, using an elegant little lighter and a silver cigarette-holder, which so immensely impressed Morwenna with their sophistication that she began to fear that she might show herself up, this evening, as totally out of her depth. Meantime Boggy prattled brightly, "What a wonderful idea of Pam's to have her birthday party here! And lovely of her to ask my cousins, Jos and Frank; she knows how I adore them both and as they were on leave it seemed a marvellous idea their making up the party, chaps being in such short supply at present."

"Oh rather!" agreed Morwenna heartily. To be honest she hadn't even registered the cousins, having been in such a state of blurred confusion when the introductions had been made that she had merely murmured "How d'ye do" and "Hello" at random.

"Naughty of Jos to bring along the Plumbtons without asking Pam first!" gurgled Boggy. "But then Jos is most fearfully naughty, always." She rolled her eyes and dimpled, savouring Jos's naughtiness. "He can get away with murder! Still, they seem an awfully sweet young couple, don't you think? Aussies. Pongo Plumbton, by the way, is in Jos's squadron."

46

"Oh?" Morwenna hadn't registered the Plumbtons, either.

"Ready for the fray, my dear? Then shall we go?" Boggy, with a motherly smile, escorted Morwenna from the cloakroom to rejoin the others.

They were led to their table; waiters, bustle, music, couples revolving on the dance floor. No sooner had the party sat down than they at once leapt up again, in pairs, to dance. Morwenna found herself seated alone at the table. She realized, with profound mortification, that she was odd one out at the party; the youngest present, she had been invited no doubt out of kindness, indeed under the circumstances Pam could hardly have asked Odile without Morwenna. But no partner had been provided for her. Little girls of sixteen don't get proper partners. She began to wish, very much, that she hadn't come.

The music stopped, the dancers returned to the table. Morwenna found herself seated between Frank and Pongo; the latter, slightly built, with a genial open face and schoolboy's happy grin, had something engagingly touching about him and Morwenna soon found herself in conversation with him. Not so with Frank. He, in army officer cadet's uniform and looking horribly bored, struck Morwenna as unattractively morose and, as she put it to herself, stuck-up. His brother Jos, on the other hand, was all laughter and high spirits; tall, dark, unbelievably good looking; a fighter-pilot in the RAF. No wonder Boggy adored him; anyone would adore having a cousin like that!

The music struck up again. Pam and Nicky moved on to the dance floor. The next instant Jos was asking Morwenna to dance. He held her lightly, looking into her eyes with laughing grey-blue ones. He danced divinely, of course, and because he danced well she too danced well. In short, this was suddenly, miraculously, turning out to be the glamorously sophisticated occasion she had associated with the Hungaria! When Jos led her back to the table she felt like a different person; years older, poised, self-assured. She flashed a brilliantly happy smile around the company. The first course was now brought to them; everything was delicious. The wine, excitement, her delight all mounted to Morwenna's head; her cheeks grew pinker, her eyes shone.

Next Morwenna danced with Pongo, then with Nicky. By now Morwenna had completely forgotten that a mere half an hour ago she had been wishing that she hadn't come! They were all treating her like one of themselves, an equal in years and experience. It was all turning out to be the most marvellous fun; she had never been happier in her life!

Elated, she reseated herself at the table. Opposite her Poppy Plumbton was laughing noisily at a story told her by Jos. She was the type that Odile called *jolie-laide*; too much forehead and a big, irregular nose. Her large, mobile mouth was generously lipsticked an exciting shade of Shocking Pink, her eyes were the colour of periwinkles. A loose bob of tawny hair fell to her bare shoulders. She had a smashing figure and a golden tan, and wore a perfectly cut, backless dress the colour of her lipstick and a slender gold chain round her long, smooth neck. In short, she was a sizzler! And without even being pretty to start with! Morwenna stared at her in envious fascination. Somehow or the other she too must learn the art of how to transform her naturally unfortunate appearance into something irresistibly sexy and riveting.

At this moment one of Morwenna's combs fell out of her head on to the floor. Frank politely retrieved it for her. Morwenna, blushing furiously, put it back in her hair. Pam said, laughing, "Trust you, Morwenna, to shower combs all over the place!"

Boggy, shaking her crop of short, crisp curls said merrily, "Thank heaven for a natural mop! I hate things stuck in my head!"

"Nothing in your head whatever, is there, Bogs?" said Jos, teasingly. Poppy, who clearly possessed all the social nerve in the world, asked Boggy why she was called that of all things. "My two awful Sowersby cousins," replied Boggy, rolling her eyes at Jos and Frank. "I'm really Lavinia, but that made Lav for short, and lav of course meant bogs, and bogs turned into Boggy. Awful, these juvenile names one gets stuck with for life."

"I sympathize," said Pam. "At school they always called me Jampot. Why exactly, I don't know — all lost in the mists of time — but the name stuck like a label."

"You *must* remember! It was because you ate all the jam straight from the pot at a midnight feast," said Morwenna. Odile exclaimed, "Really, Thingy, that's not the sort of tale with which to embarrass your hostess."

"And why Thingy?" drawled Poppy, arching her eyebrows that were sophisticatedly drawn in with pencil; she had plucked out all her own. Morwenna, staring at the eyebrows and wondering how she would look if she did the same with hers, made no reply to

Poppy's question, but Odile answered for her, "Because she's a thingamajig, a thingummy. As you can see."

"And now someone ask me why I'm called Pongo," said Pongo. "And the answer is I haven't the faintest, but I've a suspicion it had something to do with my tennis shoes." They all laughed loudly.

"Children, children, enough of this," said Jos, affecting a paternal tone. Then he asked Poppy to dance. Nicky danced with Pam, Pongo with Odile. Boggy was suddenly recognized by an officer in the Welsh Guards who bore her off to the dance floor, Morwenna was left sitting with Frank.

He was tall like Jos, even taller, and his voice was exactly like Jos's, but there all resemblance ended. Frank had flaming red hair, thousands of freckles and irregular features and was as withdrawn in manner as his brother, by contrast, was life and soul of the party. Now, after a moment or two of constrained silence he said to Morwenna brusquely, "I deplore this custom of ruining dinner by constantly jumping up to dance, and I'm afraid I refuse to participate. So forgive me."

"That's all right," rejoined Morwenna. "I've been on my feet all day doing funerals, so I don't mind a little sit down." In point of fact she had never in her life felt more exhilarated and eager to dance than she did at this moment, but was not going to admit this to a boor like Frank!

He, meantime, was giving her a most curious glance.

"Forgive me for being inquisitive, but when you say, 'doing funerals', does that mean you're engaged in the undertaking trade?"

"No, no, no! I do funerals as part of my training to be a writer."

"I don't follow! Explain."

"Well you see, I'm going to be a novelist . . ." Morwenna paused to eat a piece of toast and pâté. Frank said, "I don't see how burial of the dead can prepare you for a life in literature."

"Oh, I don't *bury* them!" And Morwenna, forgetting all about Queen Christina, gave one of her unrestrained peals of laughter, her mouth spreading in wide glee, her nose wrinkling and her eyes screwing up. Frank, as if he found it infectious, laughed too. "I don't bury them," repeated Morwenna earnestly, when she had regained her composure. "I *cover* them."

Frank cocked an eyebrow at her. "Am I to see you as a kind of Antigone, scraping earth over the fallen? Covering, merely, rather than interring?"

49

"No, no, no! I *cover* funeral stories as a newspaper reporter. You see . . ." And Morwenna embarked upon an animated account of life on the *Gazette*. Frank listened with apparent interest. Then she asked him, "What do *you* do?"

"Nothing of any importance," replied Frank. "An eternity of drilling and marching, marching and drilling. Nothing that could possibly interest anybody." He sounded so fed up that Morwenna thought it best not to pursue the subject. However, after an interval of silence she tried again. "You didn't want to join the Air Force, like Jos?"

"Me in the Air Force? Heavens no. Zooming about in aeroplanes: last thing I want to find myself doing."

"I always think I'd enjoy flying a plane."

"I don't see why *you* need bother. Don't you fly as a natural course of things?"

Morwenna, not sure how to take this, searched for a wittily snubbing answer; she couldn't help feeling that he was rather rudely making fun of her. Then he burst out with a growl, "God, how I loathe places like this, crowded with idiots and thick with cigarette smoke! They always give me a headache. Yet most people seem to love this kind of thing. What's your idea of a really good time? Mine's anything but this torture."

Before Morwenna could reply everyone came back to the table again. More eating, more wine; then up they all jumped to dance once more. Morwenna and Frank remained at the table as before. This pattern repeated itself several times. Frank barely spoke a word to her, but looked increasingly glum, while Morwenna wondered if it would be unpardonably rude if she crept away and went home? It was now obvious to her that Jos, Nicky and Pongo had only asked her to dance at the start of the evening out of courtesy; nobody really wanted to dance with her. Frank was the rudest person in every respect that she had ever met. She had been right when, earlier, she had wished that she had never come to the Hungaria!

Once more everyone returned to the table. Now champagne was brought and a cake with candles. The band played "Happy Birthday". Pam blushed and laughed and everyone clapped and cheered. Pam then blew out the candles; the cake was cut and slices of it served to each of them. The champagne made them all, with the exception of Frank and Morwenna, delightfully merry. A series of toasts were proposed to Pam; more champagne was ordered. Morwenna sipped hers and stared at nothing in particular. Then she noticed Jos giving her a brotherly glance. He smiled and rising said, "What about a dance, Morwenna?" She knew he was prompted by kindness to ask her and she should have danced with him simply in appreciation of his kindness, but she didn't want to dance when she was only asked out of warm-hearted pity, so she replied, "No thank you."

"Don't you like it here, Morwenna?" asked Pam with a note of near maternal concern in her voice. "Aren't you enjoying yourself? Odile and I thought you'd be thrilled to come this evening!"

Morwenna, blushing at being openly spoken to like a small child, managed to reply politely, "Oh yes, it's very nice, only . . ." Before she could say more, Frank intervened. "It's not her kind of thing, really. She's used to banquets and balls at Soria Maria castle as a guest of the Troll king. That sort of thing."

"Really Frank!" exclaimed Boggy. Everyone was laughing again. Morwenna, near to tears, jumped up from the table. More combs flew out of her hair, the blue bow slipped over one eye. She pulled out the bow; her hair fell down, she felt totally abashed and ridiculous. She fled to the ladies' cloakroom. Boggy, having flung Frank a look of furious reproach, hurried after her.

Morwenna had locked herself in the loo. When she emerged it was clear that she had been crying. She approached a mirror and began powdering her nose and then fastening up her hair. Boggy, hovering solicitously near, murmured, "Can I help you tie that bow? Fastening bows in one's own hair is always so frightfully difficult, I always think." So saying she began skilfully dressing Morwenna's hair. "What fabulous hair you have, Morwenna! I'm green with envy!" Morwenna forced a polite smile; nobody on earth could truly want slippery fly-away hair like hers, Boggy was being nice. Boggy continued, in a low, sympathetic voice, "Personally, little one, if you'll take my advice, just forget everything Frank said. He's a rabid eccentric, always says and does the wrong thing. He doesn't mean to be rude or hurt your feelings or anything like that, but he's impossibly egg-headed and out of touch and he gets these weird ideas and says things without thinking, and, all in all, is quite the family madman. So don't, please, take him and his odd remarks and behaviour to heart. . . . Now, though I say it myself, I've really made you look lovely! So let's join the others, shall we?"

They returned to the table. It was deserted, save for Frank; the others were back on the dance floor. He stood up as they approached; Morwenna forced herself to look him levelly and coolly in the eye. Suddenly they smiled at each other. "I suppose you wouldn't care to dance?" he said, cocking an eyebrow at her. "Love to," said Morwenna. And that was how they had fallen in love.

They made a date to meet again the following weekend, Whitsun weekend. But on Friday, May the tenth, the day before their arranged meeting, Hitler had invaded the Low Countries and the real war had begun. All leave for the Services had been cancelled, and had remained cancelled. Frank and Morwenna, like countless other wartime couples, were obliged to resort to carrying on their romance by exchanging a steady flow of letters.

VI

June the eighteenth 1940: the midday post brought Morwenna a letter from Frank.

He was, he explained, like all troops at that moment, poised at the ready in case Hitler, now with the French channel ports at his disposal, should decide to beard, or more correctly mane, the British lion in his den.

I must say that though the threat of invasion is, in one sense, perfectly ghastly, at the same time an attempted invasion of this country by Hitler and Co would be quite fascinating. Nobody's invaded us from overseas since 1066 and it will be most interesting to discover the differences between the reception that we gave William and the reception we give Adolf. My bet is that the humour of the natives will be much the same, at least I hope it will, while the result will be rather different.

You recall, of course, what Wace of Jersey tells us of the night before the Battle of Hastings. How, when it was time to fight the battle the English were "extremely hilarious, very full of laughter and very cheerful. The whole night they ate and drank; never throughout the night did they lie in bed. You might have seen them stir about, skip, dance and sing." And they were singing, we're told on good authority,

> *Bublie crient e weissel*
> *E laticome e drinckeheil,*
> *Drinc hindrewart e drintome*
> *Drinc helf e drinc tome.*

Which in rough translation reads, "Be blithe: let him come and drink hail" (in Anglo-Saxon times a host handing his guest a cup would wish him *Was Hail*, to which the guest replied, *Drinc Hail* — which is why we still go a-wassailing at Christmas.) Continuing with song: "Drink towards me and drink to me, drink half, and drink it all up" (in the lusty North, where I come from, we still drain the glass, or preferably bottle, toom.)

I must say that I personally think that this will be a much better song to be caught singing when Hitler comes than that dreary dirge, "Land of Hope and Glory". And I expect him to find us all "extremely hilarious, very full of laughter and very cheerful" — but not with drink; with bloodyminded high spirits. For *I* think the Normans were wrong about the English; it's true they had been drinking all night, but they weren't drunk; they were simply in fighting fettle. They're funny people, the English. You watch them now: as things are turning really grim and nasty they're all growing more and more cheerful, with great grins all over their faces; and next they'll start laughing — and when the English start to laugh, take my word for it, that's when Hitler will have to watch out!

A postscript, squeezed into the margin, sideways along the edge of the paper, said, "After all this rigmarole it is unnecessary to repeat for the umpteenth time that I love you!"

Morwenna read the letter on the train as she travelled homewards to Stoke Hartwell for Odile's birthday party. She wondered if Frank were right about the English; it was true that, since the announcement of the fall of France twenty-four hours ago, everyone she had met had seemed unexpectedly cheerful about the catastrophe: but nobody was downright *laughing*.

The train arrived at Stoke Hartwell. Morwenna got out, and began walking homewards up the hill, bracing herself for the family ordeal which doubtless lay ahead. Odile's birthday celebration, this year as every year, would be part of a threefold festivity. Odile shared her birthday with her grandmother, Mrs Busby; moreover the eighteenth of June was also Waterloo Day and therefore an important date in the British calendar and of especially warm significance to Mrs Busby, whose great-grandfather had distinguished himself by playing a particularly dashing part in a charge against d'Erlon's intrepid infantry, among whom had been Paul's great-grandfather. This gave a certain piquancy to the annual Waterloo Day celebrations at Maytrees, Paul being as proud of his great-grandfather's Gallic valour at Waterloo as Mrs Busby was of her ancestor's verve. In addition, of course, there was Paul's determined opinion that the battle had been lost to the French because Napoleon was suffering from haemorrhoids. Mrs Busby's response to this was always a brisk, "Ah, he should have kept himself fit, like Wellington. No slouching, there!"

The family for obvious reasons, was always thankful when Waterloo Day was over.

As she neared her house Morwenna met Pam Spurgeon with the Spurgeon dachshund. Morwenna hadn't seen Pam since she had lost her Nicky and the change in her appearance came as a shock. Hours of weeping had made Pam's eyes seem smaller and her nose larger, her complexion was splotchy, her hair hung lifeless and dank. Morwenna felt unexpectedly shy in the face of such plainly grievous mourning.

Pam said listlessly, "Hello Thingy. Home for the birthdays?"

"Yes," mumbled Morwenna. "Coming to the party?"

"Ma and I will be there." Pam was doing her best to sound normal. "Come for a walk with me and the dog? It won't take long."

They walked, without speaking, down the road and turned off along a walled lane leading to a bridle path into the Forest. They plunged among the trees, walking over silky green grass bright with buttercups. Pam let her dog off the lead, he capered and bounded round them. A fallen tree provided a seat for the girls; they sat down and watched the dog enjoying himself sniffing out a rabbit.

At last Morwenna managed to say, "I was terribly sorry to hear about Nicky. You do know how much I'm sorry, Jampot?"

"Please, you'll make me cry. I . . .I spend an awful lot of time crying, these days; it's silly, I know, but I can't help it." And with these words Pam broke down, crumpling on to Morwenna's shoulder and weeping unrestrainedly. Morwenna, not knowing how

54

to comfort her, put her arms round her and hugged her tightly. "Poor, darling old Jampot! Oh, Jampot, poor darling."

"I shall never get over it, never!" moaned Pamela, her face burrowing deep into Morwenna's shoulder.

"You feel like that now, Jampot love, but you *will* get over it in time. You really will, just wait and see!"

"The trouble is, I was so stupid! I was so *silly*, and *stupid* . . . and I'll never have the chance now to put it right."

"Put what right?"

"Well, you see . . ." Pam, fumbling for, and finding, her handkerchief, blew her nose into it despairingly. "Nicky," she drew out the word with a kind of pain, "wanted me to spend a weekend with him last time he was on leave, and like a fool I wouldn't."

Morwenna, after a pause, said, "Well, I suppose it seemed the right decision at the time."

"I can't imagine why I was such a fool! Only, I thought of what on earth Ma would say, if . . . And then, there's everything you're always taught, to put you off the idea . . . Oh, it was stupid of me! I shall never forgive myself, never! And he wanted it so much!"

"Oh lor, Jampot! You weren't to know it was his last leave."

"I should have realized that, when there's a war on, every leave might be the last."

Morwenna breathed a long sigh. Poor, poor Jampot!

"I suppose we'd better find that dratted dog before he's run off too far," said Pamela at last, after she had choked and blown her nose some more. The girls rose and went further into the woodland, calling the dog as they went. When they had found him it was time to return to Maytrees.

The party started with the customary birthday greetings, gifts, kisses. Everyone presented Mrs Busby with bouquets and the drawing-room was scented by early carnations, roses, lilies and double stocks. The health of the birthday celebrants was proposed by Paul and pledged in cider cup. The atmosphere of the party was determinedly cheerful, but laced with unspoken thoughts, impossible to avoid, of what was happening elsewhere. Ann, this year, had made her mother promise that there would be no allusions to the 1815 victory. Mrs Busby had rejoined, "That goes without saying! One doesn't kick people when they are down."

Odile, as usual, was asked by her grandmother to play the piano and rippled off a selection of Chopin waltzes and mazurkas. Sybil

Spurgeon remarked, in a pause in the music, "We mustn't forget Mr Churchill is speaking to us after the nine o'clock news."

"We won't forget," responded Ann. "Though I'm afraid it's bound to be grim!"

Just before nine Odile closed the piano, Paul switched on the wireless; the room reverberated with the weighty strokes of Big Ben. The news itself was heavier than the clock chimes. The extent of the split between the former Allies (a split that widened and deepened every moment, like an angered crevasse in a glacier) was appallingly apparent from the fact that Pétain's cabinet had ordered the French ceasefire without notifying the British troops. "*Au fond*, Weygand has always detested the British for defeating France at Waterloo," said Paul, "while Pétain, a devout Catholic, has never forgiven them for being Protestant. The role that the past and its prejudices plays in the present is the overriding tragedy of the human race!"

The only cheering note in the news was that the British, the previous day, had repeated a Dunkirk episode with resounding success, using larger vessels, and fetching away from France a further hundred and thirty-six thousand British troops and twenty thousand Polish.

Then came an announcement that a General de Gaulle, former military adviser to Paul Reynaud, would be broadcasting from London, on the BBC, to all fellow Frenchmen at ten o'clock. "That's the tank expert man, isn't it?" said Ann. "Yes. Mentioned in despatches by Weygand, a week or two back, for his attack on the bridgehead at Abbeville," replied Paul. "At least *he's* managed to get out of France. He'll be a thorn in Pétain's flesh from now on, if I'm not mistaken."

The Churchill broadcast began. The voice, solemn, sonorous, rolled and reverberated over them. Once more he told them how desperate was their plight, yet how firm was the will of Britain to fight on.

Morwenna, glancing round the listening faces, hoping at least for smiles, noted that the universal expression, disconcertingly, was a blank amounting to something apparently close to boredom.

The voice rose slightly in pitch as it progressed, quickening in urgency, though totally confident. The listening faces remained curiously unmoved.

"What General Weygand called the Battle of France is over. I expect that the Battle of Britain is about to begin. The whole fury of the enemy must very soon be turned on us. Hitler knows that he will have to break us in this island or lose the war. If we can stand up to him, all Europe may be free and the life of the world may move forward into broad sunlit uplands. But if we fail, then the whole world, including the United States, including all that we have known and cared for, will sink into the abyss of a new Dark Age made more sinister, and perhaps more protracted, by the light of perverted science. Let us therefore brace ourselves to our duties, and so bear ourselves that, if the British Empire and the Commonwealth last for a thousand years, men will say 'This was their finest hour'."

After he had finished speaking there was a silence during which Ann reached out and switched off the wireless. Then she rose from her chair. "I think we should drink the health of our Prime Minister, don't you?" Amid polite expressions of approval she opened the drinks cabinet and fetched out a bottle of Paul's best cognac. He made a slight movement of protest, then thought better of it. Elizabeth, meantime, had whipped out glasses. Ann, carefully but swiftly, poured stiff tots and Elizabeth handed them round. Ann then raised her glass. "To Winston Churchill, and the Battle of Britain!"

Everyone rose to their feet, echoing the toast. They drank. They all sat down again. Then, to Morwenna's immense satisfaction, they turned to one another and began merrily laughing among themselves, like children who shared some happy, delicious secret.

VII

Morwenna received another letter from Frank.

What did you think, My Love, of Winston's Waterloo Day speech? Pericles to the life! Harrow's a better school than Eton gives credit for. Listen to this, and you'll instantly understand what I mean. Here's Pericles, "We must realize that, both for cities and individuals, it is from the greatest dangers that the greatest glory is to be won. When our fathers stood out against the

Persians they had no such resources as we have now; in fact, they abandoned even what they had, and then it was by judgement rather than by luck, by daring rather than by natural power, that they repulsed the foreign invasion and made our city what it is today. We must live up to the example they set: we must resist the enemy in any and every way, and endeavour to leave to those who come after us an Athens that is as great as ever." Now, substitute "Nazee Germany" for the Persians, and "Britain" for "Athens" and you're hearing the voice of Winston. Bloody marvellous stuff!

But what I'm really writing to say is, I'm going on a course next weekend and I've worked out a complex and cunning timetable that means (if all goes according to plan, which it probably won't!) that I can manage two hours in London on Friday afternoon, this coming Friday. I'm sorry it's such short notice, but I've only just heard about it myself. I'll be waiting at the top of the Duke of York's steps at two o'clock (fourteen hours). Not at the bottom, not halfway up, nor halfway down, but at the *TOP* (of the steps, *not* the column). I shall wait there till three; if you haven't shown up by then I shall loiter in St James' Park. If wet, I shall wait in the Abbey, Poets' Corner, until four, unless I find it veering dangerously near to their closing time — can't risk getting locked in! Do you understand all this, and think you'll be able to find me? Four o'clock is Cinderella hour, for me; then I *must* go. Do your utmost; with this invasion scare on I've no idea when we shall be able to meet again.

Friday, the day the *Gazette* went to bed, was not a good day for taking the afternoon off, though occasionally Mr Walters would dismiss Morwenna early simply because he got tired of trying to restrain his language during moments of crisis. This particular Friday God was good, sending the Minister of Supply to inspect a local factory making Service uniforms. Morwenna was detailed to cover the story. By skipping lunch and getting Pym to cover the story for her, Morwenna reckoned on making the meeting with Frank.

Friday was a sunny, breezy day. Morwenna arrived at the top of the Duke of York's steps on the dot of two o'clock. The steps were deserted, except for some courting pigeons.

Morwenna spent the first ten minutes of waiting enjoying the green vistas of tree-lined Mall and shrubby, sunshiny park. Soldiers, sailors, airmen, from all over the world — London had become the centre of the fight against Hitler. Morwenna felt a peculiar happiness at the thought that she was part of it. In a strange way this was a jolly good hour to be living through, she told herself, even though you might not believe it unless you were actually here, living it.

But where on earth was Frank? Surely he hadn't gone to the Abbey by mistake, having confused himself by his own complicated directions? Maybe he hadn't been able to get away? Maybe the course had been cancelled? Or maybe he'd simply forgotten!

Bored and disgruntled with waiting, she tried to divert herself by tilting her head as far back as she could to look up at the effigy of the nursery-rhyme famous "grand old Duke" himself. He was so high above ground, posturing atop his column, that it was difficult to see him well, but Morwenna was able to make out that a pigeon was perched on his head, and his shoulders were white with pigeon droppings.

She was suddenly seized hold of from behind and Frank's voice said, "No, I'm not up there, though I quite appreciate you must be wondering where I've got to."

Morwenna, taken wholly by surprise, uttered a startled yelp. "Gosh! You made me jump, creeping up on me like that. I wasn't expecting you from that direction."

"I wasn't expecting to come from that direction myself; got on the wrong bus. How confusing London buses are! And what's happened to all the taxis? Let's go and sit on a seat and look at the ducks while I recover from the experience of being whooshed towards Pimlico when I expected to be heading for Piccadilly."

He took her hand and led her across the grass. Since their meeting at the Hungaria party he had received his commission and in officer's uniform he looked younger than she remembered. Morwenna, suddenly feeling unexpectedly shy, walked without speaking. They found a seat by the lake and sat down. Various kinds of duck paddled in the water or waddled on the grass verge. People strolled past, idling in the sunshine. Sparrows hopped and cheeped.

Frank looked almost fearfully at Morwenna, she, equally nervous, eyed him. In silence he put his arm round her as if making an experiment. At last he said, "Yes; you are real. I had been beginning to wonder if I'd dreamt it all."

"Me too!"

They burst out laughing together. Suddenly everything was recovered between them. Frank said,

"What shall we do? We have just over an hour and a half, in broad daylight, in central London on a fine day with sufficient people around to put any satisfying clinches, on seat or grass, entirely out of the question. It's too late for lunch, it's too early for tea, and we haven't sufficient time to go to a cinema even if we wished to. Otherwise, the world's our oyster until four o'clock. What do you suggest?"

"I don't know." Morwenna, thinking it enough simply to be with him, pensively fondled his right hand, then found herself gazing curiously at it. Why, until you were in love, didn't you care what kind of hands a man had? Frank had freckled, finely articulated, long hands. He also had a deep gash, now healing, on his thumb, and a recent graze extending across the back of the hand to the wrist.

"What *have* you been doing?"

"Practising the arts of war, my darling." He spread out both his hands and scrutinized them himself, in rueful dismay. His left forefinger had a piece of plaster round it, his left thumbnail was black. "I'm so awfully useless at doing useful things with my hands. Some chaps can do anything: tie knots in barbed wire, dismantle concrete gun emplacements, tear bathroom fixtures out of walls — no end to the things they can do. I watch in amazement."

"Why do they tear bathroom fixtures out of walls?"

"*Joie de vivre*," replied Frank, with an airy gesture. "You don't know half of what goes on until you join the army. They say the navy is even more illuminating."

"What sort of arts of war do you practise?"

"Simple, primitive, Stone Age stuff. Nothing closely connected with the twentieth century. At the moment we're so frighteningly short of arms and equipment lots of chaps haven't even got rifles! Everything had to be left behind in France. If Hitler invades within the next few weeks things are going to be very sticky; if he holds off for two or three months I think the odds are that we shall beat him back into the sea."

"There was something I wanted to ask you, about the battle of Hastings," said Morwenna. "You said that the English were all laughing and skipping about in fine fighting fettle, and what I want to know is why, if they were in such high feather and all that, they didn't win the battle?"

60

"An interesting question. Accepted opinion has it that they didn't throw in enough men, and furthermore they were over-eager and over-confident. Harold wasn't able to choose his ground; he had to fight where he stood, or retreat, and so he chose to fight. His front was far too small; some of his troops were forced to withdraw for sheer lack of fighting room, while the rest provided a close-packed target for William's bowmen."

"I hope history isn't going to repeat itself!"

"The future alone will tell! We live with the tiger at the gates. Shall we try to find somewhere less well populated? Maybe Green Park. I should awfully like to kiss you but I simply can't summon the nerve in front of all these ducks."

They walked across St James' Park towards the barbed-wired and sandbagged Buckingham Palace with the Royal Standard flying over it. "The King's there," said Morwenna. "Of course," said Frank. "Where else should he be?"

Across the road, in Green Park, all was shade and solitude. "The emptiest park in London, thank God," said Frank. Under a tree they stopped and kissed.

Suddenly Frank looked up and muttered urgently, "Let's get away from here!"

Morwenna followed the direction in which he was looking: a couple much like themselves, except that the man was in RAF blue. Frank repeated, even more urgently, "Let's go! They'll see us!"

"But darling!" Morwenna was terribly amused. The French always told funny stories about English embarrassment at being caught kissing, or even holding hands, in public. Frank, now flushed bright pink, was certainly running true to form. Morwenna said, "They haven't even spotted us. All they've eyes for is one another."

But Frank merely tugged at her with increased urgency. "For God's sake! I don't want 'em to see us!"

Suddenly Morwenna recognized the advancing couple: Jos Sowersby and Poppy Plumbton.

Frank wheeled Morwenna round and began hauling her away rapidly. "It'd be too embarrassing for them for words to find themselves face to face with us."

Morwenna then realized that his anxiety was on behalf of his brother.

"Let's shove on into Hyde Park," continued Frank. "Easier to lose 'em there, if by chance they wander that way too."

He strode off at cracking speed, Morwenna scuttling hard to keep pace with him. "Anyway," muttered Frank, to himself rather than to Morwenna, "it's nothing to do with us what they get up to." But a few seconds later he resumed, in a troubled mutter, "Nonetheless, the wife of a brother officer who's supposed to be his best friend. . . ."

"I'm certain they didn't see us," said Morwenna reassuringly. "And that's the most important thing."

"Precisely. Incident closed."

Hyde Park, beautiful as it was with early summer, was nonetheless now part of a front line awaiting the start of battle. Barrage balloons, sandbagged ack-ack gun emplacements, slit trenches, barbed wire, uniformed figures, greeted the eye in every direction. Nannies with their prams and little charges had long since gone from the scene; so too had the former myriads of scampering and barking dogs gleefully exercising; the small children come to sail toy boats; all deckchairs, all bands and bandsmen, all riders in Rotten Row. The flower beds were now vegetable allotments; hastily erected blockhouses were strategically sited in glades and vistas.

Morwenna, gazing around, said, "In one way it's awful to see Hyde Park like this, but in another way it's jolly exciting."

"Think how we'd feel if London, like Paris, became an open city."

"Oh, London would never forgive its inhabitants if they made it an open city."

They strolled across the park and found a sequestered seat in the bend of a path winding through a shrubbery; here they hugged one another without restraint. Presently Frank pushed back Morwenna's pale blonde hair from her forehead and asked, "How old are you?"

"I'll be seventeen the end of this month. Why?"

"As you only look about fourteen it's a natural question. One would hesitate to produce a fourteen-year-old bride. Indeed, I'd be shoved in clink, and you'd be sent to a remand home, or whatever they call 'em. Damn, would you credit it; here come two bloody old women! They've got the whole damn park to sit down in and they have to choose this particular corner! You'd have thought Providence could have spared us a mere sixty minutes alone together." He leapt up as he spoke and hauled Morwenna to her feet. "Let's try Kensington Gardens. Maybe the gods will be kinder there."

They hastened from the shrubbery. The Serpentine shone before them; a stretch of wind-ruffled water with here and there a rowing boat.

"A boat! That's a good idea! Nobody's going to swim out and insist on sharing our boat," exclaimed Frank. "And if they do I'll knock 'em on the head. Come on! We've still got just under an hour."

"Let me row," begged Morwenna, as the boatman on the landing stage propelled a boat into position for them to step into. "Please let me row. You can steer." She adored boats and water.

"By all means; I'm in no way averse to taking it easy while a toiling female sweats!" And Frank accordingly seated himself on the cushion in the stern while Morwenna, looking ridiculously small in comparison with the oars, the thwart on which she perched and indeed the craft in general, proceeded to arrange herself to her satisfaction before starting to row. The boatman gave the boat a mighty shove and, clear of the shore line, Morwenna began to pull.

"This is grand!" exclaimed Frank, leaning back with a sigh of luxury. "I can admire you, and the view, and let things rip, as Agamemnon said as he lowered himself into the bath tub."

There was a strong headwind and despite Morwenna's pulling they made little progress. Frank asked, "D'you want me to take over? I will if you like, if you're finding it too hard going."

"No, no, it's bracing!" responded Morwenna stoutly. "I'm loving it."

Frank burst into a whoop of laughter. "I believe you, Thumbelina, though thousands wouldn't."

Morwenna rowed, on he sat staring at her. The boat inched, doggedly but laboriously, towards the centre of the Serpentine. Frank felt in his pocket and brought out a small notebook. He said, "We must exchange addresses. Addresses of where, unless the whole world falls apart, we have some reasonable chance of contacting one another. I've got your address in Cuddwell, but not your basic home address, nor have you mine." He scribbled in the notebook, tore out the page and handed it to her. "Unless things become totally grotesque, like Goering taking over our house as a hunting lodge, you should always find somebody there who could give you at least some idea of what might have happened to me. Now give me yours."

Morwenna told him her Maytrees address; he wrote it in his notebook and replaced this in his pocket. Morwenna folded his

63

piece of paper and put it in the zipped inner receptacle of her purse.

"More than that we cannot do," he said. "You won't forget me, will you?"

"Forget you?" Morwenna, in her astonishment, stopped rowing and stared at him wide eyed.

"That's all right; all I wanted to know," he said. "Row on, little darling."

Morwenna resumed her pulling. The wind-ruffled water made small smacking sounds against the sides of the boat. Frank, who had removed his cap for comfort, lolled staring up at the sky. "Amazing how, if you stare at blue sky hard enough and long enough . . ." he began, in a musing tone, and then broke off with an abrupt yell of "Oh, damn!" He jerked bolt upright. "I've left my bloody swagger stick on that seat!"

"Which seat?"

"That last one we were sitting on, I suppose. I don't know. Now you've got me wondering — it might have been that first seat, in St James's Park. In which case it's certainly a gonner! Oh damn and blast! That's the third bloody swagger stick I'll have lost since I got my commission. Damn tom fool useless silly idiotic things. . . . Come on, change places with me and let me row back to shore, quick. I'll have at least to see if I can find it."

At peril of capsizing they changed places and Frank, with big splashing strokes, jerked them back towards the landing stage. "I'm sorry about my language," he said, after some five minutes of hard rowing. "It's the bloody army. What my blessed mother will say if she hears me give mouth like that I shudder to think."

"You should hear Mr Walters when we go to bed."

"I'm certain that you are doing no more than use professional jargon, so I'll pass that one; but if and when you meet my mother, my love, lay off that kind of innocent prattle. She'll hideously misconstrue!"

Morwenna giggled and sighed simultaneously. "Will it be *ages* before we meet again?"

"God knows! There's no point in surmising. We can but wait and see. All leave's cancelled for the present. And that's that." He glanced at his watch once more. "Fifteen bloody minutes to four! Now, look here: the instant we touch shore I'm going to leap out and run like blazes back to that last seat. If the stick's not there, then I'll just have to say goodbye to it. I haven't time to run all the way back to St James'. You beach the boat and follow on and we'll rendezvous in the bosky. Get it?"

"I hope I'll find you."

"Don't worry; if you lose me, I've certainly no intention of losing you. I may lose swagger sticks but I've damn well no intention . . . Here goes!" The boat slid within a yard or so of the landing stage, Frank gathered himself up and took a flying leap. The boat rocked violently; Morwenna scrambled to get the oars. She swung the boat round and pulled it in. The boatman, coming to her, said, "What's up with him? Spotted Hitler?"

"He's left something on a seat."

"Left his cap behind in the boat, too."

"Oh crumminy, so he has!" The boatman handed Morwenna the cap. In the distance Frank's long legs were carrying him in great bounds towards the shrubbery. Morwenna, flourishing the cap, screamed, "Frank!" He turned about, waved his arms wildly in reply, his voice coming in a shout of, "Don't worry! I'll find you!"

But he didn't. Morwenna followed him to the shrubbery; she found the seat, but no swagger stick, and no Frank. She waited, but there was no sign or sound of him. She searched other shrubbery paths despairingly, without result. She couldn't linger; four o'clock was Cinderella time for her too. She left Hyde Park at a brisk double, clutching Frank's cap.

The following evening she returned home to Maytrees for a short weekend break. While she was sitting in the drawing-room playing bezique with her grandmother, Frank telephoned.

He said, without preamble, "You lunatic! Where in hell did you . . .?" He sounded highly vexed.

"Darling, what on earth . . .?"

"Why in hell didn't you stay put? I all but gave myself a stroke racing round and round trying to. . . ."

"You told me to follow on!"

"I did. I agree. All my fault as usual, doubtless." He subsided.

"I've got your cap. You left it in the boat. Shall I post it to you?"

"Left it in the boat, did I? Wondered what I'd done with it. No, don't post it — the chances are it will never catch up with me. Keep it and let me have it next time we meet, though Lord only knows when that will be." He continued, "I've only got a split second to talk, so if there's anything vital we should tell each other, now's the time."

"Did you find your stick?"

"No. Must've left it on that other seat, or maybe in the dratted bus. When it comes to me losing things the possibilities are endless."

Morwenna started laughing. Frank continued, "It doesn't matter a damn, losing little things like swagger-sticks and caps, but it's bloody ridiculous to lose one another. It augurs poorly for the future, if we're going to carry on the way we've started. We must make it a golden rule, henceforth, that we never. . . ."

There was a sharp click cutting him off in mid-sentence. The line went dead, then the dialling tone resumed its smooth purr. Morwenna waited to see if he would come back on the line again, but he didn't. She couldn't call him; she had no idea where he was. She returned to her grandmother and bezique.

VIII

Frank in a brief scrawled note of a few days later.

"I'm so sorry we were cut off like that. All my fault, I'm afraid. I put my elbow on the thingamajig."

IX

DO NOT GIVE ANY GERMAN ANYTHING. DO NOT TELL HIM ANYTHING. HIDE YOUR FOOD AND YOUR BICYCLES. HIDE YOUR MAPS. SEE THAT THE ENEMY GETS NO PETROL. IF YOU HAVE A CAR OR A MOTOR BICYCLE, PUT IT OUT OF ACTION WHEN NOT IN USE. IT IS NOT ENOUGH TO REMOVE THE IGNITION KEY; YOU MUST MAKE IT USELESS TO ANYONE BUT YOURSELF. . . .

The Stand Firm leaflet, *If the Invader Comes*

Sybil and Ann, for hours and hours on end, thrust copies of it through front door letter boxes as part of a nationwide house-to-house distribution.

> The civilian must obviously do nothing which would be of the slightest help to the enemy, but on the contrary hinder and frustrate him; and if his help is asked by the military, as it may well be, it is his duty to answer wholeheartedly any call, however exacting, that may be made upon him . . .

The leaflet concluded,

THINK BEFORE YOU ACT. BUT ALWAYS THINK OF YOUR COUNTRY BEFORE YOU THINK OF YOURSELF.

The purpose of the Stand Firm policy was to avoid, above all else, the catastrophic congestion of the roads by fleeing refugees such as had occurred in France and Belgium. If and when the invasion came, British civilians were to stay put, while the fighting went on around them. The message was not only thrust home, literally, through domestic letter boxes, but appeared on the front page of every newspaper and was repeated at regular intervals over the wireless.

The safest place to hide while fighting was going on would be in slit trenches in back gardens: families were urged to dig trenches and make all precautions now, well in advance. Instructions were issued on how to buttress slit trenches; other leaflets explained how to construct emergency field kitchens out of old bricks, sheets of tin and old stovepipes.

"Always supposing," sighed Ann, "that you can get hold of an old stovepipe."

The Stand Firm policy was far from meaning, however, that the civilian population was to adopt a purely passive role. As the leaflets made clear enough, "The Government has always expected that the people of these islands will offer a united opposition to the invader."

Once invasion was imminent martial law would be proclaimed in Britain; under this, any soldier might legally order any civilian to do anything.

It was now not so much a case of "if the invader comes" as "*when* the invader comes". A few people might still be found, of course, scuttling around saying that Hitler would never try it, but they were in a small minority. The directives being showered upon the civilian population were, in themselves, an indication of what officialdom grimly expected. "During Occupation do not believe, or spread, rumours." During Occupation!

Invasion would be announced by the ringing of church bells. Until that moment the ringing of church bells was banned throughout the country. The Stoke Hartwell church clock, that chimed each quarter of an hour, had already brought more than one nervous Stoke Hartwellian to the verge of heart failure during the small hours.

The clock was chiming the half-hour now, as Sybil and Ann wearily trudged homeward across Stoke Hartwell village green after twelve hours of pretty well non-stop leaflet distribution. It was seven-thirty in the evening and normally, at this time, the green would be tranquil and silent, with only one or two strollers in view. Now the scene was very different. The barrage balloon that occupied a furthermost corner had been there for the past six months; everyone had grown used to it. But a squad of the newly formed Local Defence Volunteers, drilling with broomsticks (they as yet had no real weapons) was a novel feature, as was the small concrete blockhouse that had suddenly sprung up at the crossroads, apparently designed to bar the *Wehrmacht* from entering the Rose and Crown public bar. The ancient iron railings outside the old schoolhouse had been removed to be melted down for munitions and were, with much clatter, being loaded on to a lorry.

A group of prosperous commuters, who normally would have been relaxing at home after their day's work in the City, were now half killing themselves digging slit trenches across the green. The bank manager, a keen cricketer, could be seen in the distance on a ladder set up against the Stoke Hartwell Cricket Club pavilion, painting out the Stoke Hartwell and leaving only Cricket Club; the signpost by the stone drinking fountain had similarly been removed in the interest of giving the enemy no help with knowledge of his whereabouts when he arrived. Two elderly women were briskly emptying buckets of scraps into the municipal pig bin that had been installed near the bus-stop. Ann and Sybil exchanged "good evenings" with them. The raucous shouts of the LDV sergeant drilling his recruits (all at least middle aged and many seriously out of condition) rang through the air, making conversation difficult. "Hope those rifles the Yanks have promised our boys don't take too long in arriving," said one of the bucket-emptiers. "Time's running short." "My hubby's in that lot," said the other woman, nodding at the squad. "How it will affect his rheumatism I daren't think. He could hardly get up the stairs to bed after his last session."

"Doubt if I'll make the stairs myself, tonight," said Sybil. She and Ann then resumed their homeward plod. Arrived at their respective front gates each woman hobbled indoors; ahead of them, in a few hours' time, lay an all-night ARP exercise in which they were to be in charge of a mobile canteen.

"Whew!" gasped Sybil, as she dropped at last into an easy chair and sipped the tea she had been thinking about, with longing, for the past few hours. Upstairs her son Jasper was running a bath. Among the last of the British troops to have been brought from Dunkirk he had been in a bad way on arrival in England and, after a brief spell in hospital, had been sent home to recuperate for a few days. Seven months in the army had changed him from a podgy jolly boy into a tough, muscular, young man. Sybil privately lamented her lost baby.

Jasper, now in the bath, was splashing recklessly and blithely bawling a selection of favourite army choruses. Sybil, secure in the knowledge that she had half an hour or so during which she would not be disturbed, went to the brush and broom cupboard (a place where other members of the family were not prone to rummage) and fetched out a broom handle with a carving knife lashed inexpertly to it with twine. This amateur pike was of Sybil's own making and she was not yet satisfied with it.

She poured herself another cup of tea, settled in her chair and unwound the twine and then made a fresh attempt to attach the knife so that it would make a firm extension of the broom handle. This she had already attempted to do four or five times without success. She knew that Jasper would make a far better job of the thing, but she was too horrified by what she was doing, embarrassed by it almost, to bring herself to let any other person into the secret of her dark resolve to follow Churchill's dictum, "You can always take one with you."

Perhaps it would help if she first fastened the knife to the broom handle by india-rubber bands and *then* made it fast with the twine?

She found some rubber bands, poured herself more tea to fortify herself, and started fiddling desperately with knife, broom handle and bands.

From upstairs came a cheerfully bellowed ditty, addressed to Hore-Belisha, until recently Secretary of State for War,

> We're going to join
> We're going to join
> We're going to join Belisha's army!
> Ten bob a week,
> Fuck all to eat,
> Bloody great boots
> And blisters on your feet,
> If there hadn't been a war
> We'd have buggered off before!
> Belisha, you're barmy!

Jasper was unaware that his mother had returned home. Sybil, struggling with the twine, scarcely paid attention to what was being sung.

> Hitler's only got one ball!
> The other's in the Albert Hall;
> Himmler
> Is somewhat sim'lar,
> But Goering's got no balls at all!

However tightly she bound the twine and fastened it, the knife still remained wobbly. To be of any use the weapon must be completely firm and trustworthy for one single, fatal thrust.

> Fuck 'em all!
> Fuck 'em all!
> The long and the short and the tall. . . .

"May I come in?" Ann's voice. She had arrived unnoticed via the garden and the open scullery door.

"Oh yes my dear, do!" gabbled Sybil, painfully flustered at being caught red-handed with her weapon.

They say there's a troopship just leaving Bombay
Bound for old Blighty's shore,
Heavily laden with time-expired men
Bound for the land they adore. . . .

"I came round to ask you what time you want me to collect you for tonight's doo-dah," said Ann. "Do you think quarter to nine will be early enough?"

There's many a soldier is leaving the ship
There's many a sod signing on,
You'll get no promotion
This side of the ocean
So cheer up my lads fuck 'em all!

"I am so sorry!" apologized Sybil, rolling her eyes ceilingward in the direction of the raucous baritone. "Jasper's having a bath."

Fuck all the officers and WO Ones
Fuck all the sergeants and their blinking sons,
For we're saying goodbye to 'em all,
The long and the short and the tall. . . .

"There's a war on!" replied Ann wryly. Her glance travelled over the broom handle, with the carving knife crookedly fastened to the end of it. She murmured confidentially, "I've been polishing my grandfather's cutlass. It's horribly rusty, but I've been using wire wool and knife powder and I daresay it will do."

"D'you think, quite honestly, we shall ever . . .?"

"Nerve ourselves to do it? I suppose, if the crunch really comes we shall be so completely beside ourselves . . . I mean, Sybil, suppose that a German appeared this very minute charging across your lawn?"

"As an Englishwoman and one who believes her country is the finest country in the world, and worth dying for, quite apart from the fact that who wants to survive under Hitler anyway, I hope I'd do something more than cower in a slit trench! In any case," added Sybil, "we aren't digging any trenches here! I shall probably be the only one of the family left here, and as a member of the WVS *I* shall be far too busy to hide in slit trenches. It just is," she concluded, glancing at her pike, "I want to have something ready in case I need it, or get the chance, and I want it to be firm so that when I do jab at a German the thing doesn't simply buckle up leaving me to be shot with nothing accomplished."

"I don't suppose, Sybil, that we're the only ones."

"Not by a long chalk! 'The Government has always expected that the people of these islands will offer a united opposition to the invader.'" Sybil, scarcely surprisingly, knew the leaflets by heart. "The blooming Germans are going to discover that the British government hasn't been wrong for once!"

"D'you ever, at moments, Sybil, find it hard to believe that what is happening now is really true?"

Sybil drew a long breath and, gazing at the broom handle, carving knife and twine, replied slowly, "I was thinking that very same thing just now, while I was. . . ."

Her voice trailed away. A silence fell between the two women. Their eyes met, then drifted back to the broom handle and the knife.

"'Roll out the barrel! Let's have a barrel of fun!'" Jasper's roar flicked them back to speech and action.

"Collect you at quarter to nine then, shall I?" said Ann.

"I'll be ready." Sybil replaced her still unsatisfactory weapon back in the brush and broom cupboard and took a kind of pie from out of the larder and advanced with it towards the gas cooker. "Have you tried this Ministry of Food recipe yet?"

"What is it?" Ann stared suspiciously at the dish in Sybil's hands.

"Woolton Pie. Root vegetables and seasoning in white sauce, topped with pie crust. I've no idea what it will taste like: Jasper will have to grin and bear it! It's Woolton Pie or nothing for supper tonight."

Sybil, as she spoke, turned on the gas in the oven. Ann said, "I must skedaddle." She went to the doorway, then halted and in a hesitant voice almost whispered, "I've got a large pair of carpet shears. Maybe they'd be easier to fasten on?"

Sybil, brushing some milk over the pie-crust, replied, "When you've a moment to spare fetch them round, and I'll experiment."

But as it turned out there was no moment to spare. The promised rifles, half a million of them, arrived from the US, where they, made for the previous war but never used, had lain packed in grease in army stores for the past twenty years. Now they had at last crossed the Atlantic and women at various locations throughout England waited to make them clean and ready for the troops. The indefatigable WVS turned out for the task and among them, it went without saying, Ann and Sybil, detailed to work eight-hour shifts round the clock removing the thick yellow grease.

Garbed in coarse overalls they stood with their particular contingent of fellow volunteers in a commandeered gymnasium set out with long newspaper-covered trestle tables. When the rifles were brought in all the women burst out cheering, stretching out eager hands to take a firearm somnolent with fat, to revive it with rags and cleaning materials into a gleaming lethal weapon.

"Now we'll be ready for Hitler!" exclaimed some jolly, matronly voice, and everyone else repeated the refrain, laughing, "Now we'll be ready for Hitler!"

X

The preliminary air skirmishing of the Battle of Britain had started: the daily tally of fighters shot down was blared in headlines and bellowed by newsvendors like Test scores at the close of each day's play: "Seventeen for ten! Seventeen for ten, and not out!"

For reasons of security no detailed accounts of the skirmishes reached the public; apart from the tally of triumphs and losses the news dealt only in broad generalities. Everyone knew that Hitler was hammering away with his aeroplanes as a start to his invasion and that places on the coast were getting it: occasionally someone with connections in some port or dock town that had been mauled would receive tidings that enabled them to report that "They'd had it bad" there. One such flicker of illumination reached 47 Rushton Road, Morwenna's digs, in the guise of a letter for Mrs Cowper from Mrs Loftus, housekeeper to Mrs Cowper's brother-in-law Ernie, who, against all pleas and advice, had refused to be evacuated from his retirement bungalow at Southend.

"Ernie's had a stroke!" exclaimed Flo Cowper, looking up from her letter and staring with a shocked expression across the breakfast table. "Mrs Loftus says she thinks it's the aeroplanes fighting over

73

them all the time; they're having it very bad, she says, the noise is terrible. She says it's a bad stroke."

"Not surprising," said Henry Cowper, laconically.

His mother resumed reading her letter, then, "They've took him into hospital. Paralysed down his left side and don't recognize nobody. Can't talk. I suppose someone ought to go and see him. After all, he is your dad's brother!"

"'Is your journey REALLY necessary?'" intoned Henry, quoting the slogan that had now been plastered over bus terminals and railway stations up and down the country in an attempt to dissuade civilian travel at this time of imminent invasion.

"What, not to see someone that's had a stroke?" exclaimed Flo Cowper indignantly. "I call that downright inhuman!"

"Travel's very bad at the moment, Mum," suggested Posy. "Don't want to give *yourself* a stroke trying to see Uncle Ernie. Specially as it seems he won't even recognize you when you get there."

"Leave him to recover a bit and then think about going," advised Morwenna.

"I shall go if there's a funeral," warned Flo.

"Cor, Mum, you do look on the bright side always, don't you?" said Posy.

"A stroke at his age," said her mother.

"If there's a funeral, that's different," said Posy. "But give the poor bloke a chance."

Flo Cowper continued to look lugubrious. And sure enough, twenty-four hours later a telegram arrived to say that Ernie had died and that the funeral would be at Southend the following Friday at two in the afternoon. It was now Tuesday.

"You'll be coming with us, won't you, Henry?" said Flo, none too hopefully. Henry said, "You must be joking! Me get the day off to go to a funeral in the middle of an emergency?"

"Oh, come on Henry! If Pose can get away. . . ."

"My job's different." He paused to take a mouthful of shredded wheat, his main dish for breakfast. "In any case, if I was you I'd give that funeral a miss. South-east coast's not a nice place to be these days; too much going on. Uncle Ernie will never notice you're not there."

"Miss your uncle's funeral!" Flo Cowper was flushed, almost tearful, with indignation at the very idea. "Your Uncle Ern would never have missed a family funeral, or anyone else's that he felt a

74

respect for. Neither would've my Fred. Always followed their friends and relations, them two brothers did. I'm going to follow Ernie."

"Long as we don't find ourselves following him all the way to kingdom come," said Posy drily. "Still, I don't see why Hitler should stop Uncle Ernie from having a decent funeral," she added, as a spirited afterthought.

"Nor me, either," said Morwenna, who by now felt so much part of the Cowper family that she joined in all their discussions without hesitation. "Specially as you might say it was Hitler who gave him his stroke in the first place."

"You're right there, duck," sighed Flo.

After Henry had left the room, Posy said, "You might have known he'd cry off, Mum."

"Well," rejoined Flo, as usual loath to hear any criticism of Henry, "I suppose, as he says, he's too busy. Gas is a responsibility, specially just now. You and me, Pose, will just have to go alone."

They travelled by train to Southend, arriving there shortly after eleven; the tide was out and the estuary was an horizonless expanse of glistening mud. Virtually the entire population of the town had been evacuated in anticipation of German invasion; the place felt ghostly. The sea front was a mass of barbed-wire entanglements and concrete tank-traps. In the uncanny silence the cries of the gulls rang out stridently, almost obscenely.

Usually they took a bus to the end of Ernie's street; today, there being no bus, they had to walk. "We've plenty of time, that's one good thing," said Flo. "Mrs Loftus said twelve for a bite of lunch."

The funeral was at two.

The walk was quite a long one: out of the centre of the town and well into the flat seaside suburbia that lay behind it. The clean, pale pinkish pavements glinted and dazzled in the brilliant sunshine. The sky above them was a hard bright blue and empty of everything except the sun.

Almost all the houses were unoccupied, with, in not a few instances, boarded up windows. The front gardens, usually kept spruce, were weedy and reproachful. Ernie's bungalow, a nice one specially built for him, looked almost unnatural with its trimmed hedges, neatly mowed grass and tidy flower beds. All the curtains were drawn, because of the funeral.

They walked up the front path between borders of double pinks and catmint. Posy pressed the front door bell; Ernie had chimes and these rang out clearly and too cheerfully within the silent house. Mrs Loftus opened the door without delay. She looked her usual plain, competent, box-faced self, her eyes, skin, hair, mouth and spectacle-frames all the same non-colour. Usually her clothes were that same colourless colour too: tweed skirt and lambswool twinset with, for visitors, a single-strand necklace of Ciro pearls. Today she was in dark charcoal grey and without the pearls.

She greeted them with subdued affability. She had been an excellent housekeeper to Ernie and Flo held nothing against her, though she expected that Ern had left her the bungalow. On the train Flo had said, "Expect your Uncle Ern has left Mrs Loftus the bungalow," and Posy had said, "Well, that's fair enough." It was known that Ernie must have left quite a bit of money and this was to be divided equally between Posy and Henry, after some, nobody knew quite how much, had gone to the Sunshine Homes for Blind Babies.

Mrs Loftus said, "There's a little bit of lunch ready, but I daresay you'd like to see him first. He's in the back room and looking beautifully peaceful; you'd never guess he'd had a stroke. He died without regaining consciousness after the second one, which was just after I'd posted you the letter."

She led them into the back room, in darkness and heavy with the scent of flowers. She swished back the curtains with quick, unhesitating hands; there was a hard hiss of metal runners and dazzling light rushed into the room and fell upon Ernie, a tiny man, paper thin and wispy, lying in his coffin like a wizened child nicely asleep, with wreaths and flowers embowered around him. "Oh, don't he look lovely and what a lot of flowers!" exclaimed Flo.

"I put it in the local paper as well as the *Telegraph*," said Mrs Loftus. "And as he was very highly thought of by everyone who met him, though there's nobody able to get to the funeral except ourselves, a surprising number of people have sent tributes. Almost everyone's left the town," she added, "and the ones who've stayed behind are in essential occupations and with the state of emergency we're in at present people can't take time off for funerals."

"Not a good time to be buried," sighed Flo.

"Can't pick and choose, Mum," rejoined Posy.

She and her mother had brought wreaths with them and these

76

they now placed by the coffin. Flo, suddenly in tears, said, "Well, one thing, he's far better off, way the world's going!" She bent over Ernie and kissed his forehead. "Bless you, old dear," she murmured.

"Well, now perhaps you might like a bite," suggested Mrs Loftus deferentially. She pulled the curtains back across the windows and the shadows once again engulfed Ernie. The three of them filed into the front room where the table was laid with cold meat and salad. Mrs Loftus produced a bottle of Bristol Cream sherry. "A small sherry, each? You probably would like one after that journey."

They were always given sherry when they visited Ernie, but normally it was a dryer, nuttier one. Mrs Loftus, however, knew what to serve and when. Flo said appreciatively, "Bristol Cream is a good funeral sherry. It fortifies."

"Yes," said Mrs Loftus, and poured them all a little more.

Flo had been rather worried when she had first realized that all the funeral arrangements would have to be seen to by Mrs Loftus unaided. It was a lot to ask one woman to do, and Flo was anxious that Ernie, as senior member of the Cowper clan and one time head of the family haulage business, should have as good a funeral as wartime circumstances permitted. But she need not have entertained the slightest qualm, because Mrs Loftus had done it all perfectly, as was really only to be expected if you thought about it; everything was just as Flo would have wanted it herself. She could sit back, and well not enjoy it because you never enjoyed a funeral, but sit back with an easy mind, knowing that as it had started so it would go on: smoothly and with an eye for proper detail; like the sherry, for instance.

When they started lunch Flo exclaimed, politely, "I hope we're not eating all your meat ration!"

"It's his," explained Mrs Loftus.

"Don't you have to hand in the ration book?"

"Yes, you do, but the way it fell out I'd got Mr Cowper's rations but he never ate them. And with all the worry of what was going on in the sky all the time the poor old dear hadn't much of an appetite recently, in any case."

"Nice salad!"

"The lettuce and radishes come out of the garden. Try some pickle, its home ma . . ."

Her sentence perished unfinished as the windows and doors all started to rattle to a background accompaniment of distant heavy bangs and thumps. Mrs Loftus said, "That'll be the Germans attacking a convoy. I hope that doesn't mean we're in for a noisy afternoon."

"Sounds a good way off," said Posy cheerfully.

"The convoy'll be well out from here, but the planes chase each other all over the place, come swooping and fighting right overhead. He said he'd rather die than be turned out by Hitler, and that's what he did in the end, poor dear; mind you, I'm not his age and I haven't got high blood pressure."

The windows continued to rattle and the distant guns to crump. "The ships fire at the planes, you see."

"There's been a lot sunk."

"What, ships? Oh dreadful!"

"That's why there's all the rationing."

"They say that he's building hundreds of flat-bottomed barges for the invasion. Poor Mr Cowper said, 'Let's hope he gets his tides wrong and comes over and gets stuck in the mud!' A little more salad?"

The crumping and rumbling continued, grew louder. They finished lunch and went to tidy themselves and prepare for the ceremony. The undertakers arrived with the hearse and two cars. "I asked for two cars, it looks better," said Mrs Loftus. "Oh, much better! Don't want to appear to be doing things on the cheap, even with a war on," said Flo.

The undertakers, black garbed and professionally dismal, moved quietly in and out; the women sat in the front room behind the drawn curtains and chatted in muted voices. Mrs Loftus outlined how she had found Ernie seized in the bathroom and had called the doctor and he had called the ambulance. "It was a merciful end. I don't think he ever realized any of it."

The coffin was carried out to the hearse: they could tell by the tread of the men. Then all the flowers were taken out. Mrs Loftus drew back a curtain slightly and peeped. "They're almost ready for us to go."

A sudden furious blare and racket of sound as a plane burst out of the sky and ripped roaring over the bungalow, seeming to sear the very roof top, followed by a violent series of shattering salvoes of explosion, succeeded by a high-pitched droning that gradually faded.

The undertaker put his face round the door, a face smooth and unctuous as a plum. "Passed over," he said. "We'd best go, ladies, while the going's good, or perhaps have a long wait and be late at the church."

"Oh we must go! Don't want to keep the vicar waiting."

They walked down the front garden path, Mrs Loftus locking the door behind them; in the distance the dogfighting snarled, bit and tore at the sky. The undertakers, their hats removed, stood waiting in glutinously respectful stances by the flower-laden hearse. They helped Flo and Posy into the first car and Mrs Loftus into the second. The brief funeral cortège crawled solemnly along the deserted street, unseen and unsaluted, but maintaining all the niceties of funeral etiquette.

The immediate home-locality left behind, the vehicles quickened pace and soon were moving at a pretty good speed. "Going rather fast, aren't we?" said Flo. "Can't blame 'em, don't want to hang around in the middle of an enemy action," said Posy. A lot of noise could be heard; tucked away in the cars it was impossible to determine what, precisely, was happening.

The church where the service and burial were to take place was a countrified one some distance from the bungalow; Ernie had favoured it because it was pretty. He had worshipped there fairly regularly and had been generous with donations.

Between bungalow and church the funeral party glimpsed not a living soul. They arrived to find the vicar, a small, grey-headed figure, at the gate waiting for them; every now and again he glanced apprehensively up at the blue and dazzling sky. As the mourners got out of their cars, there came another frightful explosion of sound as if the heavens were splitting apart, and a high pitched tearing screaming as a plane came swooping downwards, followed by a second with guns roaring and barking. They swept across in a frenzy of sound and whirled away upward and beyond a tall screen of elms behind the little graveyard. Flo hesitated, clutching Posy, who rasped in her mother's ear, "Keep going, Mum! Ignore 'em!"

There was a fluster of the clergyman stepping forward, the mourners closing upon him and around him, seizing his outstretched hands; hasty murmurings, they didn't know what, and then parting again to make way for the coffin as the sky filled fast with fighting planes and unbelievable noise. The vicar wheeled on his heel and began striding up the yew-lined path to the church, intoning defiantly in a voice remarkably loud for so small a man, "I am the resurrection and the life, saith the Lord. . . ." The undertakers, coffin hoisted high, followed him with exceptional briskness and behind them panted Flo on Posy's arm, Mrs Loftus huddled behind them. They passed, heads bowed in terror under the tumult as much as in grief, into the refuge of the church and took their places in a single front pew, with the coffin, Flo, Posy's and Mrs Loftus's wreaths on it, standing in the aisle, and the vicar facing them on the sanctuary steps.

His lips moved, his voice reached them in snatches through the battle din:

"Lord, thou hast been our refuge: from one generation to another. Before the mountains were brought forth, or ever the earth and the world were made: thou art God from everlasting, and world without end. Thou . . ."

The rest was lost in an enormous tearing and screaming, as if giant sheets of paper were being torn across and across and screamed at the tearing. The vicar continued to open and close his mouth, continuing the service with fine desregard for all else; he moved on to the lesson, snatches of Paul to the Corinthians reached the heart-pounding and cowering women, "The last enemy that shall be destroyed is death . . ." Another of those huge, eardrum-bursting swoops of roaring and screaming noise, engines racing and whining and the guns all hell and fury, the planes clambering raging across and up the sky and swooping again; in the distance a heavy boom, boom, boom . . . "O death, where is thy sting? O grave . . ." A long drawn-out fearful descending whine growing into a roar rushing down upon them louder and louder and the three women clutching and clinging to each other and Flo praying out loud, "Oh God oh God oh God!" The engulfing climax of falling plane slammed over them and past and then exploded with a crash that brought glass shattering down from a window at the further end of the church and a great lump of plaster from the ceiling thumping into a side aisle.

The vicar continued the service undismayed. With unflinching steps he led them from the church out into the graveyard, they walked towards a large fresh mound of clay breaking the green of the grass. Beyond a distant row of small houses great clouds of dense black smoke coiled upward from where the shot-down plane was burning out.

"Man that is born of woman hath but a short time to live . . ." Flo, from the graveside, glanced up, stiffened and then pulled Posy's sleeve. Posy lifted her gaze and followed the direction in which her mother was staring in fascinated amazement. A parachute was drifting down the sky, towards them, a man suspended from it.

"Lor, he's going to land on us!"

The parachute was drifting in the direction of the graveyard. Would it clear them, or would . . .? Posy seized Flo and jerked her back to awareness of the grave, the glistening varnished oak coffin lying deep in it. Without knowing what she was doing, Flo took a handful of earth and let it drop on to the coffin, ". . . earth to earth, ashes to ashes, dust to dust . . ." A strange faint rustling sound came from the parachute passing overhead, the mourners, eyes lowered towards the grave, not daring to look up, ". . . who shall change our vile body, that it may be like his glorious body . . ." Mrs Loftus flickered a glance upward ". . . able to subdue all things to himself . . ." The parachute with its burden hanging limp disappeared behind the elms ". . . I heard a voice from heaven, saying . . ." More roaring approaching vastly across the sky and a plane glittering tip-tilted, as the vicar and Posy together in thrusting voices forced the others to keep themselves screwed down into "Our Father, which art in heaven, Hallowed be thy Name. Thy kingdom come, Thy will be done . . ." The earth and grass smelt pungently in the heat, the flowers and wreaths lay heaped in a spangle of petal-shaped colours interspersed with little oblongs of white cards: "To dear Uncle Ernie with all our love . . ." "To our good old friend . . ." "To Ern from his former workmates", "With many memories of happy times together on the bowling green . . ." "From all at Gainsborough Gardens. . . ."

"Almighty God, with whom do live the spirits of them that depart hence in the Lord, and with whom the faithful, after they are delivered from the burden of the flesh . . ." The vicar's voice moved towards the close of the ceremony as another high-pitched whine grew out of the sky and a whirling chorus of chase and echo crossed over them blotting out prayer and mourning and sensation of every kind except fear, followed by a fast tide of incoming relief as the fighters twisted and zigzagged once more into the blue distance, "And the love of God, and the fellowship of the Holy Ghost, be with us all evermore. Amen."

Dazedly, they were saying goodbye to the clergyman and thanking him. He walked with them to the church gate, sweat on his brow but holding tight close to the normal last kindly words and sympathies for funeral parties. Then they were in the cars and driving away. Flo said, "Was it a German, d'you think?"

"No idea," retorted Posy stiffly. "Wasn't looking and no more should you have been."

"Whichever he was, German or one of ours, I hope the poor young chap landed safe," said Flo.

XI

Pam Spurgeon and Boggy Hope-Warrington left St Jerome's Hospital for Plashett Wold Manor, the burns unit, in mid July in a bus crammed with fellow nurses. Plashett Wold itself, when they reached it, turned out to be a tiny market town, pure Tudor in appearance; the only sign of contemporary life being an evening newspaper placard in the main square, "Latest score: thirteen for eight." The Manor lay a good two miles distant from the town. The girls found themselves looking at an early nineteenth-century residence in Strawberry Hill gothick, with lawns, rose gardens and tennis courts. What a lovely change after St Jerome's in the heart of grimy London!

There was just time to unpack before supper; afterwards the nurses were at leisure to enjoy the grounds briefly before going to bed. They strolled to inspect the roses and the herbaceous borders and discovered a swimming pool. "We're going to have a whale of a time if we spend the rest of the summer here!" exclaimed Nurse Wendover, happily surveying the pool. "Whale, dear Wendover, is the operative word, I feel," said Boggy, with one of her gurgles. "Just you wait and see; natural born water-baby, that's me!" retorted the oversized Wendover. The others broke into peals of laughter; Wendover, poised by the pool's verge, beaming good-naturedly, looked more like a large seal than a water-baby. "Laugh away, cads," she said. "You'll laugh on the other side of your faces when you see my butterfly-stroke." Their shrieks of mirth were those of girls released into holiday mood.

*

Burns units were a recent venture, still in a pioneer stage. Plashett Wold Manor was small, but equipped for the most advanced treatment. The larger rooms in the house were used as wards, five to eight beds in a ward; the smaller rooms had been sub-divided into cubicles for crucial cases. The wards had been named after flowers and virtues: Rose, Lily, Daisy, Sunflower, Lupin, Patience, Mercy, Felicity, Faith and Hope. These names had been chosen by the owners of the Manor, Lady Grace and her sister Lady Daphne, the pair having now moved into a cottage in the grounds and visiting the unit every day with conversation and comforts and to arrange bowls and vases of flowers.

Pam and Boggy found themselves, together with four other girls, Wendover, Mertz, Spry and Markhouse, as juniors on Sunflower, a ward of eight beds with four cubicles attached and hitherto not in commission. The steadily increasing fury of the aerial battles was bringing more and more patients.

The ward's ornate gothick windows overlooked the front lawn and a horseshoe-curved herbaceous border. Across the broad first-floor landing was Lupin Ward and the two wards were presided over by Sister Sunflower-Lupin, usually simply referred to as Sister Sunflower. There were two staff nurses on each ward. The ratio of nursing staff to patients was high: the nursing was of a demanding nature.

But on their first morning, the juniors on Sunflower saw no patients; they did nothing but prepare for a convoy of cases expected that afternoon. It was all scurry and bustle, ensuring that everything was ready and nothing overlooked. Sister Sunflower appeared to make her inspection. She was a Scot, square-jawed and grizzle-haired with little bright eyes and a dogged expression. "Don't know about Sunflower," murmured Markhouse, herself of Scots descent, "looks more like Greyfriars Bobby to me."

At eleven Pam and Boggy went off duty, did an hour's physiology class, had dinner, and rearranged and put away the things that they had hastily unpacked the night before. It was then time to return on duty. They arrived on Sunflower just as the first of the new cases were brought up. There were seven of them: all severe, two crucial.

The stretchers came in one by one, carried by medical orderlies; screens went round the beds, the scent of roses and lilies that had pervaded the ward was overborne by the sweet sickly smell of burned flesh. From some of the beds came groans. Sister was everywhere at once. Two consultants arrived. The atmosphere grew tense.

Pam was told to fetch a cradle for bed Number Five. She hurried to get it, hurried back. Behind the screen, Number Five — a male body bright yellow with flavine over those parts of a hideously burned chest, arms and hands that were not hidden by dressings, his face all but unrecognizable as a face for the vast bubble-like blisters that covered it — lay motionless, a drip-feed apparatus beside the bed. The sight was both grotesque and horrifying; Pam involuntarily took a step back. Staff instructed her to place the cradle over the body. Pam was so shaken that for a moment she quite lost her presence of mind. Markhouse appeared, looking drawn; she and Pam placed the cradle carefully and draped a sheet over the cradle; air had to be kept circulating round all burns. As the two girls emerged from behind the screens the patient in the next bed, also hidden behind screens, screamed loudly; they heard a doctor's voice say something, another cry. The hypodermic tray was taken in. Pam was sent to get some more flavine for Staff and then ordered to take a chart to Number One cubicle. She had another horrifying glimpse of a body that was a mass of blistered and hanging burned flesh. The unspeakable sweet odour filled her nostrils, bringing her to the verge of retching.

In the corridor she encountered a dazed-looking Boggy, who exclaimed, "I'm not certain I'm going to be able to take this!"

"I suppose if they can, we must," responded Pam bleakly.

Each stretcher, as it came in, had two nurses to receive it. Boggy and Pamela were dispatched to cubicle Number Two where the last of this convoy's cases was about to be taken. The medical orderlies brought in the canvas stretcher; on it lay a thing of sodden uniformed legs attached to a charred and blistered mess of what had been torso, arms and head. Half the face had been burned away, the left eye gone, the nose gone; all was featureless and formless, one mass of fiery weeping blister blebs. Boggy began to sob. Staff snapped, "Pull yourself together, nurse. Otherwise you've no business here." But she herself looked appalled.

"Shot down burning into the sea . . ." one of the medical orderlies said. The name and details were not yet known; the pilot had been rushed straight to the unit, receiving plasma and blood in the ambulance. Saving him seemed less than a forlorn hope. He was immediately put on oxygen and Boggy and Pam, together with a third year Yellow Belt nurse, Stephens, set about removing his clothing preparing him for the doctors to see. In addition to the burns he had multiple fractures; right arm, clavicle and ribs. His clothing had to be cut away; in places it was burned into the flesh.

Stephens, almost as pale as Boggy, muttered, "If he survives until the doctors arrive to look at him it will be a wonder."

"Don't you dare let me hear any nurse in this ward speak about losing a single patient!" snarled Sister Sunflower, appearing suddenly, her ornate towering cap and streamers quivering with indignation and determination. "The puir lad's been rescued and brought to us by the mercy of God and now we're to bring him safe through the rest of the way." She cocked an eye at the impacted uniform stuff deep in the oozing burned flesh. "Ye'll no touch that furrther, nurse; that's best left for the surgeons." She vanished again, to return with a consultant. Pam and Boggy were sent to their tea.

Boggy gasped, "I never imagined, did you . . .?"

"Never."

When the girls returned to duty on Sunflower they were detailed to clean up the sluices, where great bins overspilled with blood-stained and serous fluid-soaked dressings. It took a good while and much energy to restore the sluices to the state of gleaming immaculacy demanded by Staff.

Pam was then detailed to remove soiled pads and dressings from cubicle Number Two. The pilot, still deep in coma, lay under protective cradles with a sheet and light blanket draped over them. His head, from which most of the scalp and left ear had been burned, was covered with white gauze dressing, a pad covered the empty eye socket; gauze dressing concealed the rest of the featureless face, leaving two nostril holes in the bone where the nose had been.

Boggy, Pam, Stephens and Staff Nurse stationed themselves round the bed and removed the covers and cradles. The stench from the burns was nauseating. Naked, except for the gauze dressings, and bright yellow with flavine where no dressings concealed the blistered and weeping flesh, the grotesque horror that they were handling was deftly and skilfully raised by the four young women, draw-sheet and pads changed, the patient carefully lowered back to a recumbent position, the cradles and covers replaced. The nurses, moving automatically as a team, performed the ritual in near silence, exchanging only the barest and most essential of remarks:

the anonymous body as it were ownerless, dispossessed, under their silent ministration.

Staff Nurse and Stephens checked the oxygen and drip apparatus, Boggy and Pam bore away the soiled articles.

So the evening wore on, with each hour bringing increasingly grim realization of the horrifying truth of what shooting down planes really meant. Three alone of the patients on Sunflower could manage nourishment by mouth and these, because of their grossly swollen and blistered lips, could take liquids only, through straws. The rest, in their extremity, were at this stage being kept alive on intravenous drips of saline, blood and dextrose. Most were still in coma; those who flickered back to consciousness required heavy sedation to control their pain.

Pam felt herself almost unbearably humbled in the presence of such suffering in young men, some her own age, who only a few hours previously had been at a peak of physical fitness. "Latest score: thirteen for eight! Hoorah! Well played!" she herself had exulted each evening with Boggy. "Great! Marvellous! Wizard; simply wizard!"

The nurses sank deeper into strained silence as the midsummer daylight waned and the tense and strangely quiet ward was prepared for the night. This afternoon and evening of duty on Sunflower had swept the nurses at one step into a new dimension of experience; it was as if they had journeyed, in a flash, from a familiar territory to some distant Scutari.

The night staff came on. Boggy and Pam, dazed by it all and scarcely aware of what they were doing, removed their frilly cuffs, rolled down their sleeves, put on their stiff cuffs, placed their capes over their shoulders and walked, speechless, side by side along a twilit gravel path to the nurses' quarters. They ate no supper but went straight to bed, exhausted; emotionally almost more than physically.

Yet, weary as Pam was, she found sleep difficult to capture. The tragic and terrifying images of the patients, above all of the occupant of Number Two cubicle, were seared upon her mind's vision and passed constantly before her as she lay staring restlessly into the darkness. But at last she slept, and then it was morning, with early sunshine and birdsong outside the window.

The day staff breakfasted, walked back along the gravel path that they had trodden in dulled horror the night before. The flowers and lawns sparkled, the sky was clear and blue. Up to Sunflower Ward, off with the cape, hang it on the peg in the changing room; remove stiff cuffs, put them on shelf, roll up sleeves, slip on frillies. And now the moment had come to face the stringencies of another day on Sunflower.

A glance at the Ward Book before going on. Pam's eye travelled down to Cubicle Number Two. The anonymous body now had a name: Flight Lieutenant Philip Plumbton. Pongo! One of the guests at her birthday party at the Hungaria, ten weeks ago. That happy, carefree evening, when she had had her Nicky with her, and Pongo had looked like a laughing schoolboy as he danced and joked and toasted her in champagne.

XII

He lay there, virtually burned out, inching steadily towards death. Sister Sunflower, who spent much time at his bedside, intoned fiercely, "I'm nae losing him without a bonny fight, I can tell ye that!"

The occupant of Number One cubicle, a sergeant pilot, had died during the night: he had been moribund when brought in and all attempts to save him had failed. Sister had had to resign herself to the inevitability of losing that patient, but for the others, even the almost equally desperately burned Flight Lieutenant Plumbton, she intended to struggle without quarter, marking out her sticking place and snarling at anyone who voiced the merest shadow of doubt over the prospects of victory.

Her expression, as she moved about the ward, was one of lively ferocity crossed with passionate concern. Her grizzled locks struggled in wisps and odd curlicues from under the cap that she somehow managed to imbue with the spirit of a Highland bonnet; she travelled at a brisk terrier trot, her bright little eyes and sharp, pugnacious little nose missing nothing. She was remarkable for the economy and precision of all that she said and did, with a terse energy of both body and mind that gave the impression of someone who moved and thought on springs. She was celebrated for the iron discipline with which she ruled her wards and her icy cool in a crisis.

Pam had met marvellously cool Sisters before now, and considered that she had already had more than her fair share of tartars, but she soon discovered that Sister Sunflower's *sang-froid* and iron hand were partnered by a quite unique sensitivity of understanding for her patients, and if her tartar's eyes could flash fire their brightness also, at other moments, held tears.

The patients, struggling from coma into vague consciousness and falling back again found, in Sister's small, almost comically plain face a potency that drew them up from the shadows into which they had relapsed and made them cling longer to the next period of awareness. Gradually she established herself, for each of them, as a rallying point. Her expression of concern, as she bent over a bed and recognized recognition, would flick into a happy and welcoming smile; her confidence in a patient's recovery stimulated his confidence in himself and fed hers further. Invisible strands of strength and reliance extended between herself and every bed; the ward became a kind of web with herself in the centre as a miracle-working spider. The consultants, distinguished and expert as they were, deferred to her as an alchemist in a class of her own. Even the greatest of the great names of Harley Street had been heard to approach her with, "Sister, I would much appreciate a word of advice."

She maintained the traditional distance between herself and the junior nursing staff, but she was capable of making even a junior nurse feel that, in the busy mind under the quivering and oddly expressive Sunflower cap, note had been taken of each striving juvenile; more, that the Sunflower heart itself was not utterly impervious to the feelings and struggles of junior dogsbodies, however inexorable the Sunflower rule over them.

Boggy, when Pam had fallen upon her, choking out that cubicle Number Two was Pongo Plumbton, had uttered a cry of anguished dismay and all but passed out. Pam had shoved her into a bathroom and sloshed cold water into her face; Sister Sunflower had suddenly stood before them, in urgent silent enquiry. Pam, forgetting in her extreme agitation that junior pros never spoke to a Sister, had blurted out, "Nurse Hope-Warrington and I are personal friends of Number Two cubicle."

"You and Nurse Hope-Warrington must carry on with whatever it is that you are supposed to be doing," had been Sister's reply. She had then turned on her heel and vanished and Boggy and Pam had contrived, somehow or other, to pull themselves together and return to the ward.

Later that morning, when the juniors were taking their break, word came that they were to go to Sister's office. Gulping back their Horlicks they hurried to present themselves. Sister occupied what had once been a small music room with a balcony overlooking the rose garden. The room was more sitting-room than office; desk and files were placed unobtrusively and the eye fell first of all upon a cosy little sofa and comfortable chairs.

This was where some of Sister Sunflower's most important work was done. Here weary consultants were revived with cups of tea (and, rumour had it, sometimes something a little stronger) and conversation far removed from Plashett Wold Manor. "Well, next time ye're up that way you must take an afternoon off from the fishing and climb up past Loch Bealach a' Bhuirich to see Chual Alumn; it's the sight of a lifetime, and a bonny walk," Pam heard Sister saying to the Greatest Man of all, one evening, as they emerged together from her office; he the size of a bull, physique matching reputation, and she like a skipping cairn terrier beside him.

In this office-parlour, too, were received the relatives of the patients, none of whom, on the occasion of their first visit, had any idea of the extent of the damage sustained by their sons (or, as the case might be, husbands) and all of whom had to be prepared for the shock.

The junior probationers now filed into this sanctuary and stood attentively and timorously before Sister. "Y'know, nurrses," she began without preamble, "that a Ward Sister will from time to time conduct her junior nurrses round the ward and instruct them on the nurrsing aspects of the various cases, and a verra valuable function that is too. But on this ward we are all too busy, working as a team trying to save these wonderfully brave young men, for me to find time to take you on a round or for you to have the time to spare for it. Nursing is always, as I need not tell you, the vital factor in good hospital treatment, but here it is utterly paramount. It is we nurrses who have to bring the patients through to the stage where they're fit and ready for surrgery; and it's a braw fight. In this unit the lives of the patients are literrally in the hands of we nurrses. The responsibility of each of us is verra gr-r-reat — (underlining the verra greatness of it with an immense rolling of her rrr-s) " — and I

89

am, as ye have already noticed mebbe, much on the ward meself; so, shoulder to shoulder with me, ye'll learrn. For this is real nurrsing, here, real nurrsing, and a fine privilege it is too and an honour to come here to nurrse these men and ye'll none of ye forget that, I know, nor give way to your own feelings of distress, for it is distressing to see such things; nor to your tiredness when ye get tired, for it is verra tiring wurrk. Thank you, nurr-ses. And now back to the ward with ye."

The care of patients on the wards always involved incessant watching and attention, as the juniors had already amply learned at St Jerome's, and routine was the basis of all ward life, but here at Plashett Wold the exacting routine and incessant vigilant care demanded by the fight for the lives of the patients was rigorous beyond anything the young nurses had imagined possible and that the older nurses had ever previously experienced. Only one or two of the Sisters, and the Matron (a white-headed apparition who made her periodical rounds of the wards wearing an inscrutable expression and nodding her head like a mandarin) had known anything like it, on active nursing service during the previous war. Sister Sunflower, it transpired, had nursed in Mesopotamia; about that ordeal she seldom spoke.

The period of greatest hazard for patients at the burns unit was the first month to six weeks. During this period of shock and intermittent coma accompanied by acute dehydration and risk of bacterial infection, the mortality rate ran at its highest. Sister Sunflower had been right about the braw fight fought shoulder to shoulder. The entire medical and nursing staff was committed, engulfed in the stark struggle between life and death; the nurses, especially, pitched to a fierce peak of hard passion of willing the burned fighter pilots to battle for survival in a conflict even more desperate than the one in which they had been shot down.

Out of the six remaining patients on Sunflower Ward two, during this critical stage, succumbed and slipped away; one after the other, within the space of a few hours. Sister Sunflower said, "Well, we've lost three now, all told; we're losing nae mair!" She had spent the night at the bedsides of the two just lost.

In cubicle Number Two Pongo Plumbton hung on, just about; occasionally flickering into something akin to consciousness and then in such pain that he had to be given morphine.

The nurses drew encouragement from the progress of Mr Alcott and Mr Beauchamp (the patients, whatever their rank, were always addressed simply as "Mr") who, less severely burned than the others (though heaven knew that "less severely" was desperate enough), were now making something rather more than precarious progress. The rest still lay maintained on intravenous drips to replace the fluid that wept endlessly from their burns, necessitating the repeated changing of dressings.

The junior pros, forbidden during their first year to handle forceps or to apply any kind of dressing or administer any kind of medicine, were confined to tasks of more or less plain drudgery: fetching and carrying, bedpanning, changing the disposable pads on which some of the worst cases had to lie, washing unburned areas of supine bodies, making beds, lifting and turning the patients, feeding those who became sufficiently improved to be fed, and so on, not to mention the never-ending cleaning and tidying of bedsteads and lockers, bathrooms and sluices. There was no end to the labour and often, at the close of the day, the young nurses missed out supper and fell on their beds, sometimes too weary even to undress.

By far the most rewarding part of the juniors' work was the role that they were expected to play in drawing the patients out of their comatosed states back to an awareness of, and an interest in, their surroundings. The fight for life that each injured man was waging was of a fundamental, gut order; the basic instinct to survive at work under dark layers of inert stupor. From these subterranean vaults, into which, relinquishing the struggle, it was so easy to sink never to come up again, the men had to be stirred and stimulated to surface. The nurses chattered and coaxed into seemingly deaf ears, to be rewarded at last by muttered curses and displays of crass irritability that were recognized as signs of recovery and therefore crosses to be cheerfully and professionally borne.

Beds that death had emptied always received fresh cases; in the skies beyond Plashett Wold the battle mounted in crescendo. The general atmosphere of the wards was maintained on a carefully muted key. Quiet normality was the note striven for in this place of grotesquely terrifying sights, sickening smells and fearful suffering. Lady Grace, gasometer-shaped, hatless, silver-haired and gowned in Ascher-printed silk two-pieces, kept the bowls and vases replenished with roses, sweet peas, jasmine and honeysuckle as serenely as if she were in her own drawing-room. Any patient who displayed the slightest awareness of, and, as time passed, pleasure in the flowers had especially fragrant bouquets placed near him. And flowers were the subject of the conversation that Lady Grace, following the example of the nurses, showered, confetti like, upon both the heeding and unheeding. "These are my second crop of roses; the first was one of the best I've ever known! The sweet peas are remarkable this year, too, quite remarkable. Of course you're far too young to remember what sweet peas used to smell like. I do my best to cultivate for scent rather than colour, but people today are awfully bad on noses. What was it that Wordsworth called it, the 'tyranny of the eye'?" She had a booming voice and as she was deaf she tended not to mind that the conversation was completely one-sided; she was used to rambling on and never hearing any replies.

She came in the mornings. Afternoons found Lady Daphne circulating, smiling and beaming. She was half the size of Lady Grace, was always in blue and never without a hat. She read letters aloud to their recipients and talked at gentle random about her dogs, cats, bee-keeping, music, and the birds that came into the garden. Afterwards she would say, "As long as the brave young chaps know that they still belong to this world and that there's at least one old lady who enjoys coming to see them for a chat!" Enjoy was a brave word, in itself, on Sunflower Ward.

Lady Daphne was marvellous with visiting relatives. Frequently she would take them back to her cottage for tea, reviving them after their ordeal. Sister Sunflower, who could not cope with teas for visitors in addition to everything else, worked hand in glove with Lady Daphne.

One afternoon Pam, emerging from the kitchen with milk for Mr Beauchamp, saw Poppy Plumbton being received by Sister at the doorway of her office. Pamela and Boggy had been wondering when Poppy would visit. Boggy had telephoned her to express sympathy and to make cautious remarks about Pongo's chance of recovery: it had been difficult to know how much to tell Poppy: "Yes, well, he is rather badly knocked about; but the surgeons work such miracles nowadays!" Poppy had responded brusquely in an attempt to maintain her self-control.

Now, in a cyclamen-coloured linen suit and plain cream straw hat, Poppy had come to visit. Pam, busy with a thousand things to be done and forced, by hospital rule, to remain unobtrusive and dutiful, could not step forward to speak to Poppy, and Boggy had been hauled away by Staff to change mattress covers. So there was no smile or encouraging word from a friend for Poppy who, courageously self-possessed as she looked, could doubtless have done with one.

Pam took the milk to Mr Beauchamp, who, like all the patients with facial burns, had to be fed through a straw. From the bedside Pam could see part of the passageway leading to Number Two cubicle and presently she saw Sister conducting Poppy along it. Poppy was looking remarkably cool, but Pam's heart bled for her nonetheless.

Poppy followed Sister out of sight and Pam concentrated all her attention upon Mr Beauchamp. "Well, and how is Mr Beauchamp; cheering up a bit now he's making such big strides on the road to recovery?" She spoke brightly, with one of her sunny smiles that patients usually found infectious, but all she received in reply from Mr Beauchamp was a scowl. He was making good progress and therefore had entered that period of anxiety, depression bordering on despair, and extreme nervous irritability that engulfed all the patients once they emerged from coma and quiescence and began to get a firm enough grasp back on life to realize the enormity of the catastrophe that had hit them.

Pam answered Mr Beauchamp's scowl with another encouraging smile. He made an attempt at speech; it seemed to be a comment on the milk, in which sulphanilamide tablets had been crushed. Pam bent her head to catch what he was trying to say. "Fucking awful stuff," he muttered.

"Oh well, drink it all up and you'll soon be on to better things," she replied serenely.

Then Pam spotted Poppy and Sister coming away from cubicle Number Two. A brief visit, that; but Pongo was at present under heavy sedation and wouldn't have known that Poppy was there — though it was true that when little Mrs Beauchamp, a bride of eight weeks, had visited her husband while he was in coma she had sat by his bed holding his hand for hours on end.

Poppy's face, under the cream straw hat, was white and set, but she seemed otherwise to be perfectly in control of herself. She passed out of view.

It was not until they met over supper that Pam had a chance to tell Boggy about Poppy's visit.

"Oh, poor Poppy! How did she take it? Was she terribly distressed?"

"Cool as custard," said Stephens, joining the conversation. "The Sunflower looked more cut up than she did."

"Must have a hell of a lot of guts," said Pam. "Underneath she'll have been fearfully upset. They've only been married a few months."

"Ghastly to have a husband lose half his head!" shuddered Mertz. "It's difficult to know which of them to be sorriest for."

"Absolutely appalling!" said Boggy. "I must try, by hook or by crook, to have a word with the poor girl next time she comes, even if it means being hauled up before Matron."

The days passed. Pongo, clambering gropingly out of the morass of coma and sedation, began to utter sounds of attempted speech. It dawned upon Pam and Boggy that he was asking for Poppy.

But Poppy, after that first visit, hadn't appeared again. Perhaps Pam surmised, she was one of those few, remarkably few people who simply couldn't face the horrors of the situation.

"She'll have to force herself to face 'em, in that case," said Boggy. "Pongo needs her. Otherwise he wouldn't keep asking for her. Think I should drop her a line and tell her?"

"Might be better to have a little heart-to-heart chat with her, next time you have a night off and go to London. A letter's a bit impersonal, don't you think, under the circumstances?"

"However much she cringes from seeing him like that, she'll jolly well have to come to grips with it, because however much plastic surgery they do on him he's never going to look anything like his former self."

Poppy didn't sound precisely eager to meet Boggy, but finally agreed to a quick pre-luncheon drink in the Dorchester bar. She was lunching in Mayfair with friends, she said; she didn't suggest that Boggy might join them. Boggy, who had fixed a hair appointment at Harrods, arrived at the Dorchester a few minutes late, to find Poppy already seated in the bar, sipping iced lager and looking equally icy.

"Sorry I'm late! Life is just one mad rush these days." Boggy, doing her best to sound bright and casual, seated herself beside Poppy. "Join me in a cocktail?"

"No thanks, I shall stick to my Down Under preference for beer."

Boggy ordered a dry martini for herself and another lager for Poppy. Waiting for the drinks to come, Boggy told herself that it was no use beating about the bush, the subject of Pongo must be

discussed without delay. Accordingly she braced herself for action.
was so fearfully sorry to miss you when you came down to see Pongo
she said, as the waiter put the drinks before them. "I hope I'll
around on the ward next time you come. Any idea when that will be?

"Can't say," said Poppy, raising her lager to her lips. "Cheers!" sh
said. She drank, put her glass down with great deliberation o
movement, and with equal deliberation looked Boggy firmly, almos
challengingly, in the eye. "Well, I can say, actually. If you want the
truth, the answer is, I shan't be."

"What! Never?"

"Never," replied Poppy flatly.

"But, Poppy! You must see him! You can't do that to the poor boy.
He keeps asking for you!"

Poppy lowered her eyes and stared at her glass. Boggy continued
urgently, "I know it's a shattering thing to see him like that, but it will
distress you less as time goes on and you get more used to it; and, you
know, you've got to start seeing him again sometime." Poppy
remained silent. Boggy, feeling a mounting impatience, concluded,
"I mean, Poppy, he is your husband!"

"I know, I know," replied Poppy at last, her lids still lowered. "I've
thought about it a lot. I hate agonizing choices, and my god, believe
you me, though you won't, I've been through hell over this one!"
Suddenly she raised her eyes to Boggy, and said, rapidly, "But I'm
not changing my mind, now I've once decided. I'm not seeing him
again. Not because of what he looks like, but because . . .
because . . ." She faltered. Boggy said, "Because what?"

"Because I'm leaving him. I want a divorce. The marriage was a
mistake."

"But, Poppy, you can't leave him now! He needs you desperately!
It's a terrible crisis in his life! You can't possibly mean what you're
saying. You can't realize!"

"I realize it, and I mean it." Poppy's tone was hard and level. "You
see, I've fallen in love with someone else."

"Oh?"

"Yes, 'Oh'!" Poppy mimicked Boggy's English, "Oh." She
continued, "And if I go to Plashett Wold and see Pongo and allow him
to think I still care for him, it will be far crueller than making a clean
break. To visit him would be merely keeping up a game of pretence.
Surely you can see that? Or does your Pommie hypocrisy prevent you
from understanding that honesty is the best policy?"

Boggy retorted crisply, "When you're dealing with a critically sick patient who's in no state to appreciate the nice ins and outs of a situation and wants only to be visited by his lawfully wedded wife, then I think it's up to you to put him first and to hell with honesty! And to hell with you falling in love with somebody else, too! After all, you've hardly been married to Pongo that long, have you? You aren't seriously claiming you're out of love with him already?"

"It was all done in a rush, one of these typical wartime marriages," said Poppy. "You get the idea you want to be married, and, as the future's all of a sudden uncertain as hell, you go ahead and marry while the going's good. I thought I was genuinely in love with Pongo; it seemed the real McCoy all right at the time. If we'd been married ten years instead of ten months the thing would have come unstuck, just the same, once I met Jos."

"Jos!"

"Yes. Jos. Who else? Surely you must've realized, that evening at the Hungaria? It was scarcely discreet, the way he monopolized me. I'm sure Pongo would have noticed if he hadn't downed so much champagne."

"To be candid, and you enjoy being candid, I merely supposed that Jos was flirting with you like he flirts with every girl who takes his fancy."

"Oh, I know that in the past he's been wicked where girls are concerned. He's not tried to conceal it from me. But this time it's different; we both know it's totally, absolutely different from anything we've ever felt before!" Poppy's face was flushed and her eyes shone.

She's certainly got it badly, Boggy admitted to herself.

Poppy continued, "That's why we've decided to be completely honest about it, from the word go. It's simply not on to pretend that it hasn't happened. Simply not on."

"Does Jos realize the desperate condition Pongo's in and how he keeps asking for you?"

"Jos knows Pongo's in a real dicey state. About the asking for me, no. I didn't know that myself."

"And Jos think it's all right for you to walk out on Pongo at this time?"

"Jos agrees with me that I'm right not to pretend that our marriage is still on when it's come to a full stop. Finito!"

Boggy, not daring to voice her thoughts lest she exploded completely and made a scene in public, lit a cigarette, with trembling hands, and ordered another martini. At last, feeling sufficiently under control to speak again, she said, "Have you given Pongo any intimation whatsoever that your marriage is . . . finito?"

"I was waiting for a chance. But all leave, as you know, was cancelled because of this Battle of Britain thing, and so I never saw him. And I didn't want to tell him in a letter, because that seemed a yellow way out, so, no; he doesn't know about it. I reckon, now, that it's best to leave it till he's rather more out of the wood."

"Just leave him to lie there asking for you!"

Poppy said, "I can see you think that Jos and I have put up rather a bad show." Boggy slowly sipped her martini; Poppy exclaimed challengingly, "Well, go on, say it! You do think so, don't you? So why not say it?"

Boggy said, "I think your behaviour is despicable."

"You'd rather I told, and acted, a lie?"

"Under the circumstances yes, I would."

"Typically Pommie!"

Boggy, her expression now frigidly impassive, continued to sip her martini. Poppy opening her handbag with a snap, said, "How much do I owe you for the lager?"

"Nothing. My pleasure." Boggy's tone was as cold as her expression.

"Another Pommie lie!"

"My privilege, then."

"That's a lie, too." Poppy placed a ten shilling note on the table. "That should cover it."

Boggy, impassive as ever, took another sip of martini. Poppy rose and said, "So long, then." "Goodbye," Boggy replied. Poppy walked rapidly away, head held high. Boggy, when she settled her bill, gave the waiter a generous tip and departed leaving the ten bob note still lying where Poppy had placed it; doubtless the waiter would pick it up and good luck to him.

Back at Plashett Wold Boggy gave Pam a detailed account of the meeting. Pam, as she listened, became increasingly outraged and indignant, breathing "Oh!" and "Never!" and "Really!" and finally, "Oh, my god, how disgusting!"

"It's not the falling in love with Jos," said Boggy. "It's fatally easy to fall in love with Jos; girls galore have broken their hearts over him. And I'm prepared to believe that perhaps, this time, he has genuinely fallen in love himself. But to walk out on Pongo at a moment like this, when he's so desperately in need of support, and furthermore to do it in the name of high motives of honesty and strong principles. . . ."

"Despicable!"

"That's exactly what I told her. Despicable behaviour."

"Bravo, Bogs! And did she look as if she might think better of it, and at least pay him an occasional visit?"

"Oh no. Went off with her head in the air, convinced she's doing the right thing."

"Poor, poor Pongo! It's enough to make your heart bleed!"

"Between ourselves, I think she's hoping he'll peg out before he need be told. No unpleasantness, no divorce: he just fades away, and she marries Jos."

Pam, eyes flashing, blazingly rejoined, "Well, he's jolly well not going to die on *our* ward! We'll pull him through, Bogs, we'll pull him through!"

XIII

The air battles intensified. Rumours grew of fleets of invasion barges gathered at ports on the other side of the Channel: of false starts to the invasion; that the British had met the invaders halfway and the Channel was full of burned German bodies.

Frank wrote Morwenna endless letters; he had plenty of time to write letters because he had broken his ankle on an unarmed combat course and was in hospital.

Beastly uncomfortable; former mental hospital that has been taken over by the army — no, not for mental cases, though I suppose it wouldn't surprise you too greatly if you suddenly learned I'd been carted off to the bin! I am suffering from a certain

98

sense of injustice: a friend who fell out of a tree (on the same course) has been shipped off to a ducal palace that's become a military hospital; why couldn't I have gone to the ducal palace too? Says he's lying in bed in a vast gilded chamber hung round with Titians and Canalettos and Holbeins. However, last thing I should do is grumble about such trivialities when my poor brother risks his life daily, locked in combat with the bloody bandits aloft. The only good thing about this ruddy ankle is that I may be allowed home for a week or two while I get back to walking on it. Which will hearten my mother: she won't breathe a word of it, of course, but she's desperately worried about Jos; he's the apple of her eye. However, having me around, even briefly, will be better than nothing. The same goes for Pa.

Frank arrived home at Parrocks without warning. It was late afternoon, merging into early evening, when he arrived. Everything at first seemed much as usual. The Northumberland summer air was clear and cool. A second crop of yellow roses clambered in full blow around the entrance portico, exactly as he had known they would be clambering, and it seemed quite natural that it should be Eliot who answered the bell and not Armstrong, for it was Eliot who had been butler at Parrocks during Frank's infancy and boyhood and though Eliot was now in his eighty-third year he looked virtually the same as ever to Frank who, in the way of children, had always regarded Eliot as ancient even when he had still been in his relatively sprightly sixties.

Nor did it surprise Frank to hear his mother's voice coming from the little Chinese drawing-room; always her favourite room. But it was remarkable that she should be saying, "A Lewis gun costs fifty pounds; I really do think we should try for something more ambitious than that. What about a two-thousand-pound bomb?"

At this instant there came another peal on the front door bell. "That'll be Mrs Hope-Warrington," said Eliot.

As his aunt habitually called at this hour for a pre-dinner chat and a drink it was no surprise to Frank to see her, either; but he had forgotten she would be in ARP warden's uniform. She, for her part, was astounded to see Frank.

"Good lord, so it was you who rolled up in that staff car! I passed it in the drive; never dreamt it had delivered you. How's the ankle? Heard you'd been hospitalized with it."

"Mending. They've sent me home for a short leave while I practise walking on it," replied Frank, embracing his aunt with genuine warmth. "I was in luck's way with a lift. How's the ARP going?"

"Great guns! We've actually had one or two alerts! Jerry's been payin' attention to Tyneside and resultantly there've been quite a lot of planes buzzing around. Makes one feel needed after all."

"Any bombs?"

"Oh don't carry it too far! Actual incidents — we don't call them bombs, dear boy, in Civil Defence they're always referred to as incidents — actual incidents have not as yet come our way, but we have heard the siren." Aunt Hal, as she spoke, neatly placed her cap and gloves on the hall table. She had had her hair bobbed, accentuating her resemblance to her daughter, Boggy. "S'pose you've been strafed to blazes?"

"Good lord no. I'm stationed in the heart of the hinterland. Real up-country wallah. Nothing, but nothing ever happens to me: apart from tripping and breaking my ankle."

At this juncture Eliot cleared his throat loudly and with meaning. Hal said, "Precisely, Eliot! I'm shamefully late as it is, without standing around coffee-housin'!" She advanced towards the Chinese drawing-room door. "See you after the meeting's over, Frank." And she disappeared from view.

Eliot said, "It seems to me, Master Frank, we'll have to find something for you on the ground floor. You won't be wanting a lot of stairs."

"Few as possible," agreed Frank.

"Trouble is, Master Frank, we've no sooner recovered from one swarm of evacuees than they're threatening to land us with another. Not fair on the family, in my opinion; squeezed into the old part of the house while all the comfortable new floors are taken over by jumped-up Civil Servants. Still, there it is. No use complaining."

And so saying, Eliot conducted Frank from the late seventeenth-century wing of the house (the "new" part) into the medieval Great Hall, where strategically placed screens kept out at least some of the draughts. It was here that an earlier Francis Sowersby had dined, centuries ago, upon his return from the Battle of Agincourt.

"Is it possible to rustle me up a cup of tea, Eliot?" asked Frank, as he hobbled after the butler into the small wainscotted parlour adjoining the Great Hall.

"With tea rationed as it now is to two ounces per person per week, her ladyship keeps strict hours for tea drinking. I think you would be advised to have a whisky instead, sir."

"Oh very well, Eliot. Anything you say." And Frank, who was privately gasping for a cup of tea, lowered himself into a chair and resigned himself to a whisky and soda.

"Where are you thinking of putting me, Eliot?" he asked, as the old man placed the whisky tray on a small table at Frank's elbow.

"I think the best we can do is the fossil room, sir."

"Great Scott, Eliot, that's back to the Dark Ages with a vengeance!"

"There's a war on, Master Frank."

"As you will, Eliot." There was nothing for it but resignation.

Frank's great grandfather, like many of the gentry of his day, had been an ardent antiquarian, collecting relics of all kinds, but above all rejoicing in fossils. He had housed his collection in a small room alongside the medieval buttery. It was dark and cramped, and chill in even the hottest weather, and though well enough for fossils seemed singularly unsuited to human habitation. However, as Eliot said, there was a war on.

"You may find it better than you fear, Master Frank. It has been used as a spare room once or twice recently. I'll go and prepare it." Eliot departed.

Frank poured himself a whisky and soda and drank it slowly, listening to the bees in the honeysuckle round the mullioned windows overlooking the little cobbled yard. The drowsy tranquillity of it all stole over him; he mused upon the probability, or otherwise, of it being shattered by the trampling and confusion of enemy invasion. Unlikely that German jackboots would ever tread here, but who could say? They were now stamping and clattering in equally secluded and hitherto safe-seeming retreats.

As usual, when Frank returned home to Parrocks after an absence, his first hours were spent in renewed marvelling at the place and in becoming reabsorbed into what was, for him, its unique atmosphere. Parrocks, though large enough to be in part requisitioned to accommodate a group of evacuated Civil Servants (who had recently been removed as abruptly as they had been installed) was not by any manner of means a stately home; it was not even a very large house, as ancient family houses go, but, as Sir Joselin Sowersby, Frank's father, was fond of saying, it represented nearly a thousand years of history and so there was a lot more to the place than merely met the eye. The earliest part of the building was Norman, the latest had been built in early Georgian times. "And all by Sowersbys," Sir Joselin would add. "And as we're rather a rum family it's naturally rather a rum house. That said, nowhere else like it, far as I'm concerned."

Frank shared his father's passion for the place. Whether Jos felt such a deep attachment, almost a reverence, for Parrocks was uncertain to Frank: though, of course, it would be Jos who would inherit. Frank had once had the jarring experience of listening to Jos describing how a friend of his had suddenly learned that the ancient family seat he had recently inherited was sited upon a particularly rich coalfield and how he had realized an immense fortune by allowing the ancestral home to be demolished and the coalfield exploited. Jos had concluded by saying that he wished someone would discover a prize coalfield under Parrocks. True, he had spoken jokingly, but to Frank it was an idea infinitely too appalling to contemplate, even as a joke.

Now his state of homecoming reverie was interrupted by voices and laughter, accompanied by footsteps crossing the Great Hall. His mother, aunt, and, if he were not mistaken, the vicar, Andrew Foley.

"I agree with you," Mr Foley was saying. "I don't see why we shouldn't raise sufficient for a two-thousand-pounder."

"Two thousand! We'll not raise that in a month of Sundays!" exclaimed Hal.

"Two thousand pounds in weight, Hal," said Lady Sowersby. "The cost would be round about a hundred and thirty."

"One thirty-eight, to be precise," said Mr Foley.

"And a Lewis gun is how much, d'you say?" Hal's voice.

"Fifty. And a sub-machine-gun runs at thirty," said Mr Foley.

"The tennis club is collecting for a sub-machine-gun," said Lady Sowersby. "We don't want to steal their fire! Besides, we should do better than that."

They came into the parlour. Lady Sowersby, on seeing Frank, gave a cry of astonished delight and ran to hug him. "Frank, lovey, what a beautiful surprise!"

"Didn't Aunt Hal tell you I was here?"

Hal laughed, enjoying the moment. "I didn't want to spoil it."

"Nice to see you home, Frank," said Andrew Foley. "How long are they allowing you to shake a loose leg?"

"Not very long, I'm afraid. Still, anything in the way of coming home for a few days is better than nothing."

"Mr Foley's just been lavishing guidance upon us as treasurer of our Spitfire gala fête committee and he's reviving himself with a quick sherry before rushing off to chair a vestry meeting," said Lady Sowersby, advancing upon the oak court-cupboard in which the drinks were kept and peering into it with the curiosity of one who was no longer certain of what she would find. "Only dry sherry, I'm afraid. I hope that will do? I could call Eliot to find us something else, but his knees are so rickety, we try to keep him on the move as little as possible. When Armstrong was called up, Eliot insisted on returning, as his personal war effort, and one hates putting people off doing their bit, but his knees I fear are going to prove his Waterloo."

"What on earth's a Spitfire gala fête?" asked Frank, laughing. There was something about his mother that always kept him on the brink of affectionate laughter. She, pouring out sherry for Hal, Mr Foley and lastly herself, replied, gaily, "Why a gala fête to raise money for a Spitfire, of course!" She seated herself next to Hal on the chesterfield. "Frank, darling, I drink your health. Lovely to see you again!"

"And so say all of us," said Hal. Andrew Foley rumbled agreement, Frank was suddenly nearer tears than laughter. Then Hal said, "Never raise enough to buy a Spitfire, though, Dottie. Cost a fortune! Stellafield will never manage it, even if the war lasts a hundred years which God forbid."

"Oh I know we really haven't a hope of buying a Spitfire," agreed Dottie. "We only called it the Spitfire Fund because the village was so mad keen to buy one and we didn't wish to dampen ardour. Obviously we'll have to settle for a less ambitious buy. That's what this afternoon's lengthy discussion has been about." And she sighed and sipped her sherry with the air of one jaded with talk.

"For the last time let me ask, what's the cheapest war weapon we can buy, just supposing we have to make drastic adjustments to our sights?" asked Hal.

"A hand grenade at four bob a whack is about the lowest you can go," said the vicar. Since he had joined the Home Guard his manner and style of speech had become markedly less formal. "The Infants' Bible Class has rather made hand grenades their special province. They've already donated sufficient for three: two and a half, to be precise; Sir Joselin kindly made up the deficit for the third."

"I still think we should go for a big bomb," said Dottie. "I'm sure we'll raise at least a hundred and fifty. Gala fêtes always go well."

Frank mused to himself that incredible conversations of this kind were taking place all over England. Aloud he asked, "When is this gala going to be?"

"Saturday the seventh of September, here," replied Dottie. "Saturday week."

"I'm convinced it will be a huge success," said Mr Foley. "And now I must fly to my vestry meeting." He rose to his feet. "Thanks for the sherry, dear Lady Sowersby; invigorated I take my way."

"A nice man," sighed Dottie, when he had gone, "but a horror to have on a committee. Keeps changing his mind, and throwing up fresh ideas, and causing uncertainty in the minds of the rest of those present."

"Typical of today's Church of England," said Hal.

"I don't know about that, but I do know we would have settled for a bomb weeks ago if it hadn't been for him, whereas we've wasted hours and hours in unnecessary discussion, and there simply isn't time for that sort of thing nowadays. Look Hal, why not stay to supper now that we have Frank here? It'd be rather nice."

"Love to, but I've umpteen reports and paperwork that I must do this evenin' or it'll never get done. Make it another evenin'? Stretcher-party exercise tomorrow evenin', and Land Army subcommittee the next. What about Saturday, if I can find a baby sitter for Gordie?" Gordie was Hal's seven-year-old evacuee from Islington.

Hal, Dottie's only sister, widowed during the final months of the last war and left with an infant daughter and very little money, had been given the Parrocks Dower House to live in by her ever generous brother-in-law, and there she and Boggy had made their home ever since. To the Dower House Hal now hurriedly returned, while Dottie went up to the Parrocks nursery to say good night to her child evacuees; five-year-old Barney and his sisters Queenie and Thelma, respectively six and eight years old.

Frank retired to the fossil room. His mother said, as they parted, "Dinner will be a bit late, I'm afraid; your father has been at a meeting with the Regional Commissioner, over on the other side of the county. As for your sister, these days we expect her when we see her. She's our regional WVS billeting officer, as I think I've told you, and this invasion scare means she's literally working round the clock dealing with the new rush of evacuees to the country."

Punctuality at meal times had always been something of a fetish with Sir Joselin. Frank reflected to himself that once upon a time not only would his father never have been late for dinner, but that his sister Vicky would have perished rather than fail to present herself in the dining-room on the dot of the appointed hour.

The fossil room was just large enough to hold a camp-bed, a small table with a dressing mirror, and Frank's bags. Eliot appeared, saying, "I trust it will do, Master Frank. I've done my best," and adding, with Northern forthrightness, "But do or not it's all you're going to get!"

"Fair enough, Eliot. As you have already pointed out, there's a war on."

Sir Joselin was decidedly late. Lady Sowersby and Frank sat on the terrace, had another drink apiece, and chatted amiably; principally about Jos, who had just been awarded the DFC. Through the windows of what, pre-war, had been the family's comfortable sitting-room, they could glimpse the dust-cover-draped furniture standing like ghosts, white and strange.

"It's pointless to open up and settle back when at any time we're to be requisitioned all over again by some government department, or one of the Services. Personally I've given up fretting over what may or may not be going to happen next. I simply live for the hour and do my best to be of service to my country," said Dottie. "I've only one wish, and that is to have all my family come through this war safe and in one piece. . . . Ah, here's your father! Now we can eat."

After dinner they drank their coffee in the gazebo. The evening was warm and balmy, the sunset touched the hills with amber. They chatted of this and that. Sir Joselin said, "And you broke that ankle of yours doin' unarmed combat trainin', did you? Does today's army go in for that kind of thing because of shortage of weapons, or is it some newfangled fancy of the folk at the top?"

"Oh, nothing special about unarmed combat training," replied Frank casually. "We all have to do it."

"Wondered what kind of outfit you'd landed up in. Army jujitsu team or somethin'?"

"No, no. Nothing exciting about me. I'm in the conventional infantry, a so-called intelligence officer. All painfully undistinguished and plodding. And even less impressive to be labelled anything to do with Intelligence! What it all boils down to is that

I've landed a backwater job: 'fraid they've decided they'll never make a field marshal out of me."

Sir Joselin, at this point, changed the subject, to complain of the difficulty of obtaining dog meal in war time, prompted to this observation by the appearance of his black labrador bitch, Starlight, come to seek her master's company. After some discussion of the dog-feed problem, followed by comfortable comments upon the splendid condition of Starlight despite dietary difficulties and advancing years, and the general superiority of a bitch as a daily companion in comparison with a dog, Frank said, "By the way, I'd rather like to invite a girl I know to stay here for a few days, if that's all right. I want you to meet her, because I am going to marry her."

There was a pause during which his parents remained admirably deadpan. Then Sir Joselin said, "Your mother is the one to decide whether or no we can squeeze in a guest. We're a bit short of space, these days." He added, courteously, "Of course, we'd love to meet her."

"Are we allowed to ask who she is?" enquired Lady Sowersby.

"Morwenna Duchamp, the name is," replied Frank cautiously. "Her father is a consultant surgeon at St Jerome's. Boggy knows her. Which is really how I met her in the first place."

"Oh, so she nurses at St Jerome's with Boggy, does she?"

"No. She's literary: an aspiring George Eliot with a touch of the Brontës." Frank's tone was increasingly cautious.

A slight flicker of apprehension crossed Lady Dottie's face. "How old is she?"

"Seventeen." Only just, to be precise; but there was no call to be that precise.

"Oh Frank dear, what are you thinking of?"

"Marriage," drawled Frank. "Nothing ulterior, I assure you."

"Marriage at a somewhat distant date?" suggested his father. "Seventeen, though sweet (we won't go into the matter of never having been kissed), is far too young to get married in wartime. Too young at any time, come to that, but particularly so in wartime."

"I know it's a bit young, but I think it's okay in this case," responded Frank. "She's altogether unusual and though. . . ."

"Naturally you think she's unusual because you're in love with her!" intervened Lady Sowersby, crisply.

"And, as I was saying, though peculiar in several respects is, in others. . . ."

Lady Sowersby cut in again. "Peculiar! In what way peculiar?"

"Odd, then, if you don't care for either unusual or peculiar," retorted Frank. With a slow and languid movement he put down his coffee cup on the gazebo's stone balustrade. This affectation of bored, languid movement and drawling speech, so exactly his father's pattern of behaviour when up against a difficult situation, alerted his poor mother to the fact that Frank was going to make a fight for it.

"Odd?" Sir Joselin, cocking up his left eyebrow, was drawling too, now.

"Strange! Weird! Wonderful! Not belonging to this earth! You'll understand, when you meet her. A faery!" Frank gestured, one of his airy gestures. Sir Joselin said, "All there?"

"How d'you mean, sir?"

"Well, not potty, or anythin' of that sort?"

"Potty? No, certainly not! Quite the reverse: exceptionally intelligent, in fact. But slightly — no, more than slightly, distinctly — abnormal."

"Naturally!" rejoined his mother. "You're abnormal yourself, and like attracts like, but I wouldn't be too sure about not being potty!"

"Easy, Dottie, easy!" intervened Sir Joselin.

"Mad keen to marry, I suppose?" continued Lady Sowersby. "Girls of that age are always dying to become brides."

"Don't know," drawled Frank. "Haven't asked her."

"Not proposed to her?" Sir Joselin exclaimed.

"Not formally. Not yet. But it will be all right. We understand each other."

"You haven't mentioned any of this to her at all?" asked Dottie.

"Any of what?"

"Oh, Frank, don't act so daft!" exclaimed his mother. "I really lose all patience with you at times! You win all these double firsts and things and then talk like a village idiot!"

"My dear, please! Village idiocy is not infrequently a form of high sagacity," said Sir Joselin. "You mustn't confuse the situation by comparing Frank with what he is not. Give me the village idiot every time, when it comes to making sense," he added. "Now Frank, m'dear feller, try to bring yourself down to the mundane level on which your mother and myself operate, and tell us what precisely, or more or less precisely, is the nature of the understanding that you have with this . . . er . . . boggle, or hobthross, or whatever it is you've been caught by."

Frank reflected for a moment and then said, "I don't think I altogether care for the word 'caught'."

"Fairies catch you," returned his father, with an air of one who knew his ground. "Not with an eye to marriage, or improvin' their social standin' or anythin' of that sort, but simply because they get struck with a fancy for you. . . ."

"Joselin darling, don't you think . . ." Dottie tried to intervene. Sir Joselin continued, "It's decidedly dangerous to become involved with the Little People, and I hope, for your sake, my dear boy, that you're mistaken in the identity of this young person and that she's a human being after all. Damn uncomfortable spouses, fairies!"

"Shall we be serious for a moment?" suggested Lady Sowersby.

"'Pon my soul, Dottie, Frank's asked for our advice and I'm offerin' him my considered. . . ."

"I didn't ask for your advice, Father," said Frank. "I made a statement."

"Very well then, you made a statement. But you must have realized that it would give rise to comment. Your mother's comment is that —"

"My comment," said Dottie firmly, "is that if Frank hasn't already mentioned marriage to this child, he would be well advised to say nothing and wait until she is a few years older, when things may look a little different. After all, do you really suppose, Frank lovey, that her parents would agree to an engagement, let alone a marriage, at the age of seventeen? She would require their permission, you know."

"A sound comment," said Sir Joselin. "Mine would be that, unless this child genuinely *is* a fairy in which case of course, my dear chap, you're sunk, and have my heartfelt condolences, you should give yourself time, and the girl too, to grow older, and see a bit more of life, and then, if you still feel the same way about each other, why, my blessing upon you both and good luck!"

Frank made no reply to this for a moment or so. Then he said, "And may I still invite her to come and stay here for a few days, if she can manage it? For even if you're neither of you over-anxious to meet her, I'd like to have her here. I greatly enjoy her company."

His parents exchanged a glance: a question, an answer; agreement; unspoken, but as effective as any voiced exchange.

"Ask her by all means, as long as she doesn't leap to any unsound conclusions as a result," said Lady Sowersby. "I know we can rely upon you to be sensible."

"Be most interested to meet her," said Sir Joselin. "I s'pose she'll be visible? Not one of those little Tinkerbell thingummies that flit around unseen and go ting-a-ling-ling?"

XIV

Frank wrote to Morwenna, next morning before breakfast, in order to catch the first post. He wrote it on a postcard, for all the world to see, and kept it admirably concise and to the point: "I'm home here at Parrocks, on a short sick leave. Join me here *immediately* if you can possibly manage it. I'd like you to meet my parents — and they would equally like to meet you — I've told them I'm going to marry you."

Directly after breakfast Lady Sowersby drove away to a WVS committee meeting. Sir Joselin, too, was out all day engaged on unspecified business. As for Vicky, Frank had not yet set eyes on her: she had returned home late the previous night and had gone out again at some unearthly hour this morning.

Frank spent the day practising walking. In between he rested on a garden chaise-longue on the terrace and thought about Morwenna. He knew she would come to Parrocks if she could, but would she be able to get time off from that wretched newspaper? It was a frightful bore not being able to telephone her: 47 Rushton Road having no telephone, and catching her at the *Gazette* office an impossibility.

At one point his old nurse, Nanny Bradshawe, appeared with Barney, Queenie and Thelma. Like Eliot, Nanny Bradshawe had emerged from retirement to resume her old job at Parrocks as a way of "doing her bit". Considerably younger than Eliot and remarkably sound in wind and limb, she was genuinely enjoying the rather bizarre experience (for all parties concerned) of transforming three little street urchins into rosy-cheeked, scrubbed and shiny occupants of the Parrocks nursery; empty for many years but now once more resounding to childish voices, laughter, teases and tantrums.

"I don't know how you manage it," Frank said admiringly. "Och, it's nothing," rejoined Nanny Bradshawe, who hailed from the other side of the Border. "If I could manage you, Master Frank, I could manage anything!"

The children were greatly disappointed to learn that Frank had not been wounded by the Germans, but had tripped over a tree root. At first they had stood staring at him in awe, as a hero; now they rapidly became undisguisedly condescending. "What a silly thing to do," said Thelma. "Yes, silly billy!" shrilled Queenie. Barney, in glee, echoed, "Silly billy!" "Enough of that!" said Nanny Bradshawe. "Let you bear it in mind as a lesson: always watch where you put your feet." She then marched the trio away for what she called "a wee constitutional".

At four o'clock, just as Eliot was serving Frank tea on the terrace, there was a sudden sprang of roaring sound overhead and a plane shot across the sky immediately above them, flying low. They both jerked to stare upward. "It's a Hun!" Eliot shrieked, as if on a hunt and suddenly sighting the fox.

The plane was so low they could see the Nazi crosses on its undercarriage as it passed over them and, as it banked slightly, the swastika on its rudder, and the top of the pilot's head. Eliot stood hollering and shrieking: thin, drawn out view-halloos. Frank joined in. The plane vanished behind the shoulder of a hill; the noise of its engine died into the distance.

"Pity we hadn't something handy to take a shot at the bugger!" said Eliot regretfully, after he'd got his breath back.

"Awful pity," agreed Frank. "Thought he was going to drop in for tea."

No further excitement occurred after that. Sir Joselin, when he returned home after dusk, reported that it was rumoured that a Messerschmitt had been shot down some ten miles away. "That bandit Eliot and I saw," said Frank. "So low I swear I could have got him with a rifle."

The night passed quietly, the morning was brilliant with sunshine. Frank thought to himself that, with luck, Morwenna should get his postcard that day.

Once again the family was due to disperse on various missions.

"Oh, such a beautiful day!" sighed Dottie. "And I have to spend it collecting scrap! However, there's a war on. Wonder if those 'Cogs' are ready?"

"Those what?" laughed Frank, who found the idea of his mother as a scrap merchant more than a little hilarious.

"Marvellous organization, your mother's rag and bone collectin' outfit," said Sir Joselin proudly. "Twice a week she drives the lorry. . . ."

"Round the village dumps," explained Lady Sowersby. "Old iron and bottles and jam jars, and then we have drives once a fortnight for bones, and paper, and scrap rubber and so on. Wonderful what we get! And the schools, you see, have this 'Cog' system of junior salvage groups. I've organized our local branch; it's been frightfully successful! Saturday mornings in term time and two mornings a week holiday times, collecting from house to house, with donkey carts and old prams and wheelbarrows. I tell you, it's quite a turn-out! In the past six months they've helped us to double the amount of salvage collected."

"Nanny Bradshawe takes out the the nursery goat cart," said Sir Joselin. "Tremendous hit. It's about to set off now; let's go and watch. Too priceless for words!"

In the stable-yard Queenie and Barney were already sitting in the cart, Queenie holding the reins and ostensibly driving. Thelma, holding the goat by its halter, walked alongside the animal. Nanny Bradshawe walked the other side of the equipage. As they started out of the yard the children struck up with the "Cogs" song "There'll Always Be a Dustbin", to the strains of "There'll Always Be an England". Sir Joselin burst out laughing. "Capital!" he said. "Capital, what?"

He then went to dictate letters to the estate office secretary. Lady Sowersby drove off in her lorry. Frank, left to his own devices, limped slowly to the gazebo. He had equipped himself with a pair of binoculars and planned to while away the morning with a little bird watching. The view across the valley towards the Border was wide and beautiful; he seated himself on the broad stone seat in the gazebo, the stone comfortably warmed by the sun, and swept the view through the binoculars. The clouds rode, white and silver and without menace of rain, well above the hills that were green, purple or tawny as the light caught them; on the pastures of the high ground black cattle browsed, and white sheep; in the valley bottom the fields, planted with crops as a wartime measure (of latter years they had been largely turned over to grazing) were buff and yellow and ruddy gold, or green with kale and turnips.

The river curved and shone among the park trees, and down a straight smooth ride went the goat cart with Queenie and Barney perched in it and Thelma and Nanny Bradshawe walking either side of the goat, taking a short cut to the village. The road along which Lady Sowersby was driving made a wide detour down to the old ford across the river and then swung back to the village lying just outside the Parrocks park at its furthermost point. The way round by road was three times the distance, or more, than through the park.

A family of four buzzards circled high overhead, mewing kitten-like. A party of jackdaws were in the home paddock, a pair of ravens in the distant sky above Gow Crag, a jay screamed a grating cry in the woods on the right of the park and some crows joined in; they had in all likelihood sighted the old vixen who, regular as the seasons themselves, took up residence in an earth in the thorns there when summer ended and cub-hunting began and her favourite lair on the fern bank became unpleasantly popular with hounds.

Frank scanned the ground between the trees in the hope of a glimpse of the vixen, but she was not in view. So he shifted his scrutiny to the goat cart, which amused and touched him. He, when the size of Barney, had ridden in it with his brother Jos at the reins and later he, Frank, had graduated to holding the reins. Frank could remember Vicky walking holding the goat's halter. And Nanny Bradshawe, always stout and cheerfully firm, walking the other side, as she walked now.

He swept the landscape ahead of the cart and its company: he found the wooden bridge at the end of the green ride; by the bridge stood a small, sturdy boy, Gordie, Aunt Hal's evacuee, come to accompany the goat cart. Gordie cast a stick into the water from one side of the bridge, hung over the white wooden handrail to watch the stick pass under, then darted across to the opposite rail of the bridge and craned over to see the stick emerge. Then he climbed up to stand on to the lower rail, holding the top rail in both hands, and traversed sideways along the rail the full length of the bridge. Then he climbed down off the rail and crossed to the opposite rail and climbed on to that and repeated the traversing act all the way back to the end of the bridge where he had first started.

Then he glanced to see how far away the goat cart was, and it was still a good way off, so he had more time to kill. He began hopping across the bridge on one leg.

Halfway across the bridge he seemed to find hopping tedious: he stood, both feet firmly planted on the ground, staring ahead of him at a herd of deer that had been grazing under the trees on the further side of the river but, disturbed by something — perhaps the old vixen — were now running at good speed across the open ground towards a spinney on the left, running from the right where the jay and crows had been calling.

Gordie looked to see what had started them running, and Frank, watching through the binoculars, saw the child stiffen and become immensely attentive. Probably he had spotted the vixen. Frank, with the binoculars, examined the ground under the trees to the right, but he could see nothing. The boy was meantime creeping forward, close to the bridge rail, as if viewing something but anxious not to be viewed in turn. Frank still could not make out the fox, or whatever it was that Gordie had seen. The boy moved stealthily to position himself behind a tree.

After a moment or two Gordie cautiously peeped out from behind the tree. He was watching something beyond him, in the covert. Frank swept the covert again, but again without result. Gordie turned from the tree, crept back across the bridge and began running as fast as his small legs would carry him up the ride towards the goat cart, but keeping to the side of the ride, close to the trees, rather than running up the open ground in the centre of the ride.

Frank, immensely intrigued, again examined the spot at which the child had been staring while stationed behind the tree. A sudden movement caught his eye: something grey, the right height for a deer's head but not the right colour. No sooner had he seen it than it was swallowed up by bushes and didn't reappear. Frank directed his gaze back to Gordie.

The child, plainly rather out of breath by now, was still scuttling towards the goat cart, which advanced steadily down the ride. At last the gap between cart and Gordie was closed and Gordie, scarlet in the face with exertion, was giving Nanny Bradshawe a graphic account of what it was he had seen. After a minute or two, during which Nanny Bradshawe flung several hasty glances in the direction from which Gordie had come racing, the old woman turned the goat's head in the direction of the trees to the left of the ride and led the cart across to them, while Gordie, obviously the bearer of hot tidings, resumed half-running half-trotting towards Parrocks.

Frank saw that Nanny Bradshawe was guiding the goat cart back to Parrocks too, unavoidably at a much slower pace than Gordie.

What it was that Gordie had seen Frank could not fathom. The grey object had disappeared into cover; it was not the right colour for a bull and Frank could not think of anything else that might have caused Nanny Bradshawe to instruct Gordie to race off with a message while she turned tail with her little party and headed for home. Bulls were the only things Frank had ever known to alarm Nanny Bradshawe.

Gordie was now within hailing distance of the gazebo. Frank leaned over the parapet and shouted, "Hey! What's up?"

Gordie, going slowly now and panting hard, came up the steps from the park to the gazebo. Breathless, he gasped, "It's a German, guv!"

"A German! Are you sure?"

"Yes, guv!" Gordie had changed into a sturdy, rosy, freckle-nosed country child, but he had not lost his London accent. "Saw him plain as plain. German pilot!"

Frank surveyed Gordie a little dubiously. It would be unwise to raise a full hue and cry on the word of a seven-year-old.

Gordie meantime drew heavy gasps, regaining his breath. At last he managed to say, "He was a German all right! I could see his eagle and swastika . . . He was creepin' about under the trees."

"Did he see you?"

"Don't think so."

"You better nip up to the house, to the tower . . . you know where I mean, do you?"

Gordie nodded vigorously. Frank resumed, "Go up the spiral stairs and knock on the little oak door you'll see, with the rose carved over it. . . ."

"Yes, I know!"

"My father's in there. Tell him; he'll do whatever's necessary. I'll stay here and keep a watch out."

"Right y'are, guv!" And away went Gordie.

Frank took up the binoculars again. He scanned the ride, the bridge and the trees beyond. A grey-clad figure briefly flitted into view, then dived into cover again.

It seemed an age before Sir Joselin and Gordie, hand in hand, came hurrying towards the gazebo.

Frank said, "He's there, right enough. Just spotted him."

"I've telephoned the police and alerted the Home Guard," panted Sir Joselin, out of breath with excitement.

Frank handed his father the binoculars and Sir Joselin took a long look, then said, "No sign of anything in the park, except Nanny Bradshawe and her little lot. Don't like to see them there, I must say." He continued to scan the park. "Where did you spot that wretched Hun?"

"He was about a hundred and fifty yards right-handed from the spinney where that dead oak is. About three o'clock from the oak itself," said Frank.

Sir Joselin stared hard through the binoculars, as before. "Nothin' visible at the moment." He continued staring. "I say, that's a good effort!" he exclaimed suddenly. "Trod, Andrew Foley, Mowdie and Jonah, all armed and going through the trees, headin' for the wooden bridge. They certainly turned out quickly! Who says the Home Guard's a bunch of old fogies, what?" He handed the binoculars back to Frank.

Sure enough, the four men, none of them in uniform, but each armed, Trod, Jonah and the vicar with rifles, Mowdie with a shot gun, were stalking cautiously but at steady speed, down the park, through the trees, towards the wooden bridge.

Gordie began scrabbling with his feet in an attempt to clamber on to the gazebo parapet. "I want to look, guv!"

"Of course, my dear chap! You were the first to sight him; must have a chance to view the run." Sir Joselin sympathetically bunked Gordie up on to the parapet. The child sat with his legs dangling over, Sir Joselin gripping him round the waist to make sure he didn't fall.

"There's Mowdie creeping through the bushes by the bridge," said Frank. "Once that lot are over the bridge they'll be close to where he was when I last saw him."

"If he spots 'em and starts running he'll be checked by the ox-bow," said Sir Joselin. "Great handicap for him that he doesn't know the ground."

At this point Eliot turned up. "A young lady, Master Frank, has just telephoned from London to say she'll be arriving here on Saturday. Says she's expected. I explained you were unable to come to the telephone and asked her to send a wire advising us when she arrives at the Halt and she'll be collected. Have they ketched him?"

"Not yet. Got him pretty well surrounded, though. Trouble is, though we've an idea of his whereabouts they've only the sketchiest notion, and if we try shouting to them we'll alert him," said Frank.

"Best keep mum," said Sir Joselin. "If he breaks cover, then holler."

They stood straining their eyes until they could feel their eyelids stiffening. The Home Guard party, stooping low to the ground, one by one crept across the wooden bridge and vanished into the trees the other side.

Suddenly Gordie piped, "There he is!" At almost the same instant Eliot, who could no longer distinguish soup from serving-spoons but had not lost his keen fox-hunter's long-distance vision, burst into an ear-splitting shrieked view-halloo. Frank swept the glasses round, searching frenziedly, ."Where?" "By that dead tree!" squealed Gordie.

Eliot continued to holler; Mowdie stepped out from cover and stared in the direction of the house. Frank, forgetting his ankle, pulled himself on to the parapet, and pointed, left arm extended, towards the oak tree. Sir Joselin said, "Pipe down now Eliot. Object achieved." Eliot, near to expiring with excitement and the effort of hollering, leaned against the parapet, eyes glued in the direction of the dead oak. "Gone back into cover," he whispered hoarsely. "No matter. Showed himself just when needed," responded Frank. He raised the binoculars once more.

Mowdie and his companions were now creeping from tree to tree towards the dead oak.

Nanny Bradshawe, hearing the hollering, had stopped the goat cart, had looked to see Frank pointing and was now staring towards the oak tree. The children and the goat were staring likewise.

For a few moments all was still, nothing happened. Frank said, "Now, if he breaks cover again for God's sake don't shout, Eliot. Mowdie knows where he is."

Another pause. Then Eliot said, "He's yonder."

"Where?"

"Under yon ash tree, Master Frank. Now he's gone into the ferns."

"Yes. I can see his head," said Frank. "Now he's out of view again. Can see the ferns moving, though. He knows he's been sighted, that's for sure."

Another pause. Sir Joselin murmured, "Lost track of him completely now, far as I'm concerned."

"Still in the ferns," said Frank. "There he is, raising his head!"

"Mowdie's right behind him, t'other side of ferns," said Eliot. He had totally abandoned his butler's demeanour and was a hunting veteran, pure and unabashed.

"There goes Foley. Now Jonah! And there's Trod! Good chaps; they've got the ferns surrounded!" Frank was exultant. Gordie shrilled, "They'll catch 'im now!"

There was a long pause during which the four members of the Home Guard and their quarry alike crouched motionless, hidden from each other and each side waiting for the other to make a move. This waiting game continued for an interminable length of time. "Silly buggers, they're leaving it too long," groaned Frank. "He'll bolt!" He literally gnashed his teeth.

"Bolt, and with all that cover they'll lose him again!" Eliot gnashed his teeth too.

Another pause, during which they all watched on tenterhooks. Then, "He's breaking cover! It's a bolt, sure enough; it's a bolt!" And Frank burst into a shriek, echoed by Eliot.

"He's running through the trees, over there, guv!" squealed Gordie, pointing for Sir Joselin's benefit.

"Heading straight for the goat cart!" Frank sounded horrified. "Making right for it." He stared hard through the binoculars. "Don't think he's seen it, though. Not yet."

"Poor old Nanny! What will she do?" groaned Sir Joselin.

"That German's certainly moving. Ah, he's seen Nanny and the cart now. . . . Not stopping, though. Making a dash to pass it! . . . Oh, I say! Oh, bravo! Oh well done, Nanny! Oh bravo indeed!" Frank began to laugh, to whoop. "She's ketched him! By jove she's ketched him! Oh, bloody good show Nanny Bradshawe!"

"Got her teeth in him fair and square!" whooped Eliot.

The German, not seeing Nanny Bradshawe and the goat cart until the very last moment, had attempted to dash past, swerving; but he had stumbled slightly as he swerved and Nanny had stepped out, planted herself in his path and caught him firmly by the arm.

"Not turnin' nasty, is he?" asked Sir Joselin, peering anxiously.

"No, no, just looks flabbergasted. Oh, that's rich!" Frank burst out laughing again. "Thelma's pitched in now and grabbed him by the leg. And Queenie's climbing down from the cart and . . . by jove, she's pitching in too! Grabbed him by the other leg. And now Barney's trying to get down!"

"'Pon my soul, this beats all!" said Sir Joselin. "Never heard the like! Medals all round, what?"

"Here comes the Vicar. Nothing wrong with his legs, even if he's short on grey matter! He's up, and Trod and Mowdie. . . . They're all in for the kill now."

The knot of people clustered round the captured man. Frank said, "Hope Nanny gets the brush."

"No sign of the Law," said Sir Joselin. "Aha, there he is. Silly chump, full-tilt on his bike in quite the wrong direction! Miles off course! Gave him full instructions too!"

The captive, meanwhile, was being marched towards the house. Nanny Bradshawe followed with her little contingent.

"Come along Gordie, we'll go down and meet her and give her an escort of honour," said Sir Joselin. "Always did say that the British nanny was God's greatest gift to Creation." He lifted Gordie down from the parapet and the two set off together.

Eliot turned to Frank and said, with a long sigh of satisfaction, "By gum, lad, I wouldna missed that for a' the tea in China!"

XV

The prisoner, a *Leutnant* pilot of about nineteen or twenty, was escorted into the Great Hall. Sir Joselin scanned the mud-stained and clearly exhausted prisoner.

"Better let him sit down before he falls down. He's obviously all in, as well as scared of what we may be going to do to him. Frank, you know German; find out who he is and how he got here, and assure him we don't intend stringin' him up from the beams. Eliot, you'd best arrange a bite for him — do as we'd have our own lads done by, y'know. Meantime I'll ring the Chief Constable."

Frank hobbled across to the prisoner. He proved unwilling to answer questions, or indeed to hold any conversation at all. Sir Joselin, returning, said, "Found out anything about him?"

"Only that he was shot down and baled out yesterday afternoon," replied Frank. "He's perfectly within his rights not to say more to us. He's almost certainly that chap we saw flying over here yesterday tea time."

"Black Maria's on its way," said Sir Joselin. "He'll soon be with officialdom and feeling more secure; obviously thinks he's fallen into the hands of brigands, what? Rum lot, the Germans! Wish I spoke the lingo sufficiently to ask him what the hell he thinks he's doing fighting for that blackguard Hitler."

"Don't think you'd get much joy out of him," said Frank. "But I'll ask him if you like."

"No, no," said Sir Joselin. "You're right; it wouldn't serve any purpose. No doubt he's convinced he's savin' civilization from the Jews! Well," drawled Sir Joselin, reseating himself, "I don't mind bein' lined up with Joshua."

At this point Mrs Kelly, the housekeeper, came in with a tray of potted meat, rolls and coffee. She was determined to get a glimpse of the German. Her great-great grandmother, as a young girl, had seen Bonnie Prince Charlie riding south with his troops at the time of the '45, a tale that had been handed down in the family, and Mrs Kelly was going to hand down this morning's historic moment to her own posterity.

She placed the tray at the end of the long, ancient table for the captive to help himself and, having taken a good steady look at him so that she wouldn't forget, she returned to her kitchen.

The *Leutnant*, despite his obvious qualms, could not disguise his hunger and addressed himself to the rolls and coffee without ceremony. At this point Lady Sowersby turned up, flushed and excited. "I'm told you've caught a. . . ." Then she saw the captive. "Dear me, he's terribly young, isn't he!"

"Not too young to be an infernal menace," said Sir Joselin drily.

Eliot went to the front portico to keep an eye open for the Black Maria when it came up the drive. He had scarcely been gone five minutes before the company in the Great Hall heard a vehicle drive up. "That'll be the police," said Frank. The prisoner poured himself more coffee and helped himself to the final roll. "He must be allowed to finish his rations before he's carted off," said Sir Joselin.

Steps in the passageway. Eliot reappeared, carrying a silver card-tray on which lay two impeccable engraved cards. Eliot extended the tray to Lady Sowersby, who raised an eyebrow as she picked up the cards. Who on earth . . .? People weren't using cards any more, in wartime.

Eliot, noting her expression of surprise and curiosity, murmured, "Two American gentlemen, m'lady."

The name on the first card that she glanced at was quite unknown to her; Homer J. Mountjoy III, from Areopolis, Ga, USA. She wondered what on earth could be the reason for an American from Georgia, a total stranger, to be visiting Parrocks at a time like this. Enormously puzzled, she picked up the second card. In a flash all became clear:

> Giles J. Sowersby Jnr.
> Parrocks
> Aldermary, SC, USA

Dottie, without comment, passed the cards to Sir Joselin, the Sowersby card uppermost. He read it and his face lit up with mingled amazement and pleasure.

"My word! Historic day this is turnin' into, what? Show 'em in, Eliot."

"Here, or should they go in my little drawing-room?" ventured Dottie, with a glance at the *Leutnant*. Sir Joselin said, "Fetch 'em in here. Why not?"

Eliot departed. Frank asked, "Who is it, father?" He could see that the callers were something of a sensation.

"Your cousin, a kind of nephew of mine. I can't on the spur of the moment work out exactly how many great-greats down the line from Giles who left Parrocks for the brave New World in, let me see, must have been sixteen-fifty-four, or maybe five: couldn't stand England under Oliver Cromwell, and no wonder! Went to Barbados. It was his grandson who made a strike for the Carolinas, where they had rice plantations. Met this boy's father in nineteen-hundred, I believe, in London; I was eleven at the time and he was much the same age. Over here with his mother; large woman. Saw the Troopin' of the Colour. Bakin' hot day. Wore rather a silly sailor suit."

At this point Eliot showed in two RAF flying officers. The first of the pair required no introduction, he was obviously of Sowersby extraction: tall, good looking, with grey eyes and a cast of feature that marked him unmistakably as a kinsman of the handsome Jos laughing out of a silver-framed photograph placed on the oak chest between the windows, yet with rusty brown hair that indicated a touch of the rufous strain carried by Frank. To Lady Sowersby the newcomer came as a distinct shock: he bore a singular resemblance to Sir Joselin as a young man.

Giles Sowersby advanced into the Hall, introducing himself courteously but confidently as he stepped forward. Sir Joselin greeted him with unfeigned warmth; a family greeting. Lady Sowersby kissed and embraced him; Frank exchanged a vigorous handshake. Homer Mountjoy was then introduced; he was as tall as Giles but exceptionally slim, inclining to droopy, with long fair moustaches, receding fair hair, and amused, sleepy blue eyes. Both young men spoke with soft, languorous southern drawls, enchanting to the English ear.

"We've joined the RAF, as you can see," said Giles, with an engagingly boyish, almost bashful smile. "Homer and I have been buddies ever since we can remember. He's kin through my mother's sister, we've always done everything together, so we're doing this one together too."

Sir Joselin raised his hand slowly and brought it down in a hearty ceremonial clap on Giles's shoulder. "Well done!" he said. "That'll show 'em!" He then repeated the ritual with Homer, "Great stuff! Bravo!"

"Wonderful!" echoed Dottie, all smiles and shining eyes. "Good show!" said Frank.

"We'll have a drink and a pow-wow when we've seen this feller here off the premises," said Sir Joselin lowering his voice confidentially and indicating the prisoner by a jerk of his head. "Shot down yesterday afternoon about ten miles away and finished up on my back doorstep, nabbed by old Nanny. Pilot of a . . . whatsit . . .?"

"Messerschmitt Bf 109," said Frank.

The two new arrivals were clearly well brought up young men who had been taught to behave themselves with the utmost politeness in other people's houses; accepting anything, however strange, as perfectly natural, and not gaping. This courteous approach, combined with a slight general bewilderment of finding themselves precipitated into a medieval hall and accorded a reception that completely belied any idea of the English as a nation of cold fish, had prevented them from grasping the finer points of what was actually going on. They had noticed, fleetingly, beyond the Sowersby enfilade of handshakes, embraces, shoulder-clappings and general enthusiasm reserved for long lost sons, that a gloomy young fellow in uniform was seated ravenously demolishing rolls and coffee while four dishevelled characters, all armed, one apparently a clergyman, stood round him, grimly watching him eat. It looked remarkably like a hold-up of sorts, but surely could not be!

Now, all was explained. The young man eating rolls, upon closer scrutiny sure enough was in *Luftwaffe* uniform, with the eagle and swastika emblem above his right breast pocket and his pilot's badge, also of eagle and swastika equivalent to a RAF pilot's "wings", worn slightly lower on his left. The reason for the grim-faced armed guard was clear. Yet this did not make the situation any the less extraordinary, for extraordinary it was: the great medieval hall; the tableau of prisoner and armed custodians; the trim and tranquil Lady Sowersby; the hobbling Frank, an obvious embryo Sir Joselin; above all, Sir Joselin himself, a clear manifestation of the past surviving in the present, and taking the present excellently well in his stride, too, judging by his unperturbed handling of a *Luftwaffe* pilot and a couple of Americans all landed upon him unheralded and simultaneously. Lastly, but not least, there was the antique Eliot, whose knees were now almost seized up as a result of the morning's excitements, but who still tottered back and forth with the expression of one who knew the house would fall down if he ceased to function.

He reappeared once more. "The police, sir."

"Aha, here at last! Direct 'em into the courtyard, Eliot." Sir Joselin turned to the guard. "March our prisoner into the yard and line up. We might as well hand him over with a bit of style. Frank, explain to him that he's being handed over to the constabulary who will hand him in turn to whatever it is the RAF call their military police. And tell him he's a lucky young chap to be out of the war before the rest of Uncle Sam's young chaps arrive. One swallow doesn't make a summer, but two are a promisin' sign of spring."

Frank once more addressed a few sentences to the *Leutnant*, who made no rejoinder, but simply pushed back his chair, rose to his feet, faced Lady Sowersby, clicked his heels smartly together and jerked a stiff bow. He was then marched into the yard where he was handed over to the three uniformed policemen who presented themselves through the archway in the outer wall.

"Decent enough young chap at heart, I daresay," said Sir Joselin. "But anyone sportin' swastikas is makin' it plain he's struck a bargain with the devil. And now I think we'll have a spot of celebrative lunch: break a bottle of champagne. It's not every day in the week that we capture a German, and have a long lost Sowersby return to the fold, bringin' a fellow ally with him, what?"

Later in the afternoon Sir Joselin took Giles and Homer on a tour of the house and the family portraits, first drawing their attention to the photograph of Jos. "We've had Sowersbys at every notable battle from Flodden Field to Ypres; now we can add the Battle of Britain! Keep him in here with us so that at least he remains by proxy in the family circle. Pity he's not here for you to meet in person. Been awarded his DFC, y'know. Great chap. Forgive my pride. Can't help it." He then led the visitors out of the Great Hall and into the new part of the house. In the dining-room he stopped before the portrait of a youth still little more than a boy, with wavy auburn hair flowing to his shoulders, his eyes wide and intelligent, the faint smile on his lips apparently about to burst into open laughter.

"There he is, Giles; your great-great-great-great-great-great grandfather and namesake. Think I've got the number of greats right. Nice lookin' young chap, what?"

"Sure looks fun to know."

"No doubt he was. Pity we can't meet him in the flesh. Five brothers there were, all told, and all fought for their King against Cromwell. We've four of them in here, but the fifth, Raiseley, the Colonel, hangs up in the tower in the room that was his during his lifetime. For one thing, I've no doubt he prefers it up there, and the other reason is that it's not a suitable portrait to hang in a state room; facially it's a good enough resemblance, but the poor chap looks mouldy. Now, we all know he's a troublesome sort, but I wouldn't exactly accuse him of being mouldy; wouldn't want to judge him harshly in any way at all. A gift of seeing into the future, which is what he's famous for, must be decidedly uncomfortable for the poor feller to live with, don't y'know?"

Homer and Giles exchanged broad, happy smiles behind their host's back. Parrocks was proving to be every bit as good as they had hoped.

"Now this — " and Sir Joselin stopped before a small and ancient portrait of an exceptionally ugly woman whose unfortunate appearance obviously could not be entirely blamed upon the ineptitude of the artist. "This is the lady to whom we Sowersbys all owe a vast debt. Imagine having to hop into bed with her! But that was what Ewen Sowersby did in the year fifteen hundred · and five, or thereabouts. Family all as poor as church-mice, you see, after having been on the wrong side in the Lambert Simnel uprising. This poor creature here was the daughter of a rich merchant in Kendal; the wealth of wool, y'know. Nobody would marry her. Her father tried to bribe suitors with an immense dowry, but one look at that face, and that put paid to it. Until at last Ewen Sowersby came along, drew a deep breath, closed his eyes, and married her, and the fortunes of the family changed overnight! Started re-building; started branching out! All due to her."

Slowly the enthralled visitors paced with Sir Joselin down the Long Gallery while he, so to speak, introduced Sowersbys to them without pause. "No portrait of the Sir Francis who fought at Agincourt, alas, but there's a stone effigy of him on his tomb in the village church. The Sir Francis who fought at Waterloo, over here between the central windows, had two horses killed under him and lost his right arm. My father, here on my right, God bless him, fought in the Boer War, returned home safely and was killed near the main gates here when his horse was scared by a back-firing motor-bike. His heir, my brother Francis, here next to father, was killed on the Somme a year previous to that in which yours truly got knocked abaht a bit at Ypres. Yes, that's me. Young man when that was painted. Never look like that again!" He paused, shook his head and smiled. "Those were the days: young and full of fire. What? And now m'dear chaps, we'll saunter across this landing, passing my own dear mother on the way; how's that for a lovely face? My sister there; she died when quite a gal. Not a beauty like my mother. Rum thing that, y'know. Sowersbys more often than not marry pretty women, and produce handsome men, but by Jove, they seem to defy nature and produce string after string of plain-faced daughters. Rum!"

They had now reached the main staircase and descended it slowly, down to the entrance hall. More family portraits, together with the trophy heads of big game, gazed down upon them. "That's my great uncle in militia uniform, and that next to him is a kudu bull," said Sir Joselin. "Easy to confuse 'em. That's my grandfather; True-Blue old country squire. And that's my uncle: he bagged most of those poor animals. Mad keen big-game hunter.

Plenty of money for big game huntin' and stuffin' things in those days."

"Do you think a house like Parrocks will have any place in the post-war world, sir?" asked Giles. Sir Joselin, who had been swinging his right foot slowly forward, preparatory to stepping down from the final stair, with great deliberation swung it back and re-assumed a firm stance. "No idea, m'dear boy. But if we can last almost a thousand years in the face of fearful odds I don't see why we should have to throw in the towel during the final half of the twentieth century. Wait and see, shall we? Wait and see!"

XVI

"Glory be, how am I supposed to persuade Mr Walters to give me a few days off?" Morwenna had exclaimed to herself when she read Frank's postcard.

But no persuading had been required. No sooner had Morwenna arrived in the *Gazette* office than Mr Walters had told her that he wanted her to take a week's holiday, starting the coming Saturday. "Sorry it's such short notice, Miss Doochamp but as Gilroy expects to be off to serve King and bloody country in a fortnight's time, it's best for you to take a break now. Once Gilroy's gone, holidays on this newspaper will have about as much chance as a snowball in hell."

"Thank you, Mr Walters. It'll suit me fine." To herself she had exclaimed, Lordy lor! Destiny with a vengeance!

Vicky Sowersby offered to meet Morwenna off the six o'clock train at Stellafield Halt. "It's absolutely no trouble to me, Frank: I have to meet the train, in any case, because I've a fourteen-year-old schoolgirl travelling alone on it and she must be collected. So if you'll give me a brief idea of what Morwenna looks like, so that I'm able to recognize her. . . ."

"Blonde," said Frank, vaguely.

Despite Vicky's pressing, he seemed quite unable to provide her with further details, and Vicky was left to comment to herself that Man was the craziest of the Almighty's creations and Frank the craziest of men. She also reminded herself, reassuringly, that as no more than one or two passengers ever alighted from a train at the Halt it shouldn't prove too difficult to identify a seventeen-year-old blonde.

Vicky, at twenty-six, was the oldest of the three young Sowersbys: from the first moment of Jos's arrival to join her in the nursery, when she was two, she had been overshadowed, and a second brother, Frank, who had arrived three years later, had clinched her one-down position as a mere girl contending with two males. Moreover Vicky, if not as downright ugly as her unfortunate ancestress from Kendal, was extremely plain, her only redeeming features were her large, gentle eyes and a touchingly open smile — though she was usually far too shy to smile at strangers. She was loving kindness personified and Frank adored her; he was almost sorry that the war and the WVS had "brought her out", as her mother put it, ridding her of some of her shyness and giving her a veneer of confidence that already made her noticeably different from the Vicky of the old days. Old-style Vicky would never have driven off with a cheerful wave to meet strangers from a train!

The train, as usual, was late. Vicky stood on the little deserted platform, chatting with the old man who was now the sole member of railway staff at the Halt. He had been listening to the wireless: heavy fighting in the air all day; vast numbers of enemy planes shot down though the final figures weren't in yet; the past forty-eight hours had seen the heaviest fighting of the whole Battle of Britain to date. "Working up for something, Jerry is," said the old man. "Mark my words, he's working up for something!"

The train was signalled, appeared puffing round the bend, drew up to the platform, stopped. The first passenger off was the fourteen-year-old schoolgirl, a scruffy little thing with long pale hair tied with a bow all askew, smothered with smuts and with a rucksack wearily slung over one shoulder. She came slowly towards Vicky, who stepped forward to meet her saying kindly, "Hello! I'm afraid you must have had rather a tiring journey, dear."

"Pretty dreadful," said the little girl. She was well spoken, even though she looked so scruffy. "Fearfully crowded. I had to stand in the corridor, and we kept stopping, nobody knew why."

Vicky was about to explain that she was the WVS billeting officer and would be taking the child to her billet, but at this moment she spied from the corner of her eye the only other passenger to have left the train: a tall girl with freshly permed fair hair, pink lipstick, blue slacks, high-heeled shoes, and a bright pink jumper to match the lipstick. What *was* Frank thinking of?

"How d'you do? I'm Vicky Sowersby, Frank's sister." Had to be polite.

"Oh?" The girl gave an embarrassed leer. She was chewing some kind of sweet. Vicky decided there and then that Frank would have to be told that this horror simply would not do!

At Oxford Frank had held strong radical ideals. Without doubt he had felt it incumbent upon himself to choose a girlfriend evidently not of his own class. Vicky was no snob, but she did not approve of his choice. Frank was no longer at Oxford and would have to grow up.

However at the moment there was no alternative but to take the Horror back to Parrocks.

Vicky led the two girls to her car. "I think you had better get in the back," she said to the Horror. "This little girl will be getting out before you, so she had better travel in the front with me."

The Horror had an old, heavy suitcase. This Vicky put in the boot and the little girl hoisted her rucksack in beside it. The Horror got into the back seat, the little girl next to Vicky, and off they went.

The Horror put another sweet in her mouth and chewed it noisily.

Vicky said to the small girl, "You're going to be on a farm with some awfully nice people; I'm sure you'll like it. Have you ever stayed on a farm before?"

The child fixed her with enormous, contemplative blue eyes but said nothing.

"There'll be horses and cows and sheep and pigs and chickens," rattled on Vicky. "Maybe you'll learn to milk a cow. That'll be fun, won't it?"

The child continued to survey her with wide, serious eyes.

"I know you'll have a lovely time, Mary, and I'm sure you're going to enjoy it once you've settled in," continued Vicky. The poor saucer-eyed, tongue-tied little thing was probably feeling horribly frightened and homesick.

"I think there must have been some kind of error," said the small girl at last. "My name's not Mary."

"What is your name, then, dear?"

"I'm Morwenna Duchamp."

"Good heavens!" Vicky was so startled, the car nearly went into the ditch.

The Horror said, squelchily through her sweet, "I'm Mary."

Morwenna burst into a peal of laughter. Vicky felt a tide of relief sweep over her that Frank hadn't invited the Horror to Parrocks; at the same time, Frank's choice was still most peculiar. A little girl like this? Dear me, dear me!

"I'm frightfully sorry to have made such a mistake," said Vicky aloud. "I'm afraid Frank was more than vague in his description."

"Oh don't bother to apologize," said Morwenna, still obviously much tickled. "I gather I'm not going to learn to milk a cow now?" she added, with a flash of naughtiness that reminded Vicky even more strongly of a small child teasing a stupid adult.

Mary in the back said, "Have I gotta milk a cow, miss?"

"You're going to have the time of your life, Mary," said Vicky firmly.

They arrived at the farm. Vicky escorted Mary into the farmhouse. Morwenna wound down the window, breathed deep gulps of the clear, cool northern air and listened to the farm sounds. Vicky rejoined her, saying, "Well, I hope she'll fit in, but I doubt it." She added, "Let me repeat once more, I'm awfully sorry to have made such a silly mistake."

Morwenna started laughing again. "It doesn't matter, honestly it doesn't." She added, "Good thing you sorted it out in time."

"It is indeed!"

They arrived at Parrocks. Frank was sitting on the portico steps, waiting for them. He greeted Morwenna with a warm hug, and the unromantic remark, "Covered with smuts like Tom Kitten in the roly-poly pudding!" Lady Sowersby appeared. Frank introduced Morwenna to her; poor Dottie shook hands somewhat weakly. Vicky then showed Morwenna up to her room. "I'm afraid we're in the old attics, for the duration. I do hope you don't mind."

"Not in the least. I adore attics."

In the Great Hall Dottie commented to Sir Joselin, "Straight from the schoolroom with a vengeance. She looks about twelve."

*

Hal joined them for dinner that evening and, over sherry on the terrace, was soon engaging Morwenna in a brisk interrogation about air raids.

"Have you had any alerts in Stoke Hartwell?" was the first question. Morwenna replied, "My mother says they've had several alerts, but I'm not living there now but in Cuddwell, which is an east London inner suburb; I work there, on a newspaper. We're having alerts nearly all the time at present, because of the dogfights going on overhead, but we haven't had any bombing yet."

"You say you work on a newspaper?" said Giles. "Which newspaper is that?"

"Oh, one you'll never have heard of! The Cuddwell *Gazette*. But everyone has to start somewhere. I'm a full blown police court reporter now, which is most unusual for a female!" she added proudly.

"Indeed yes!" said Sir Joselin. "A real innovation. How does the Bench take it?"

"They can't object, poor old things," replied Morwenna blithely. "All our men reporters have joined up, bar one, and he's going any moment now, so there's only me left to cover police court. To cover everything."

"Poor old things!" repeated Sir Joselin, with a gleam in his eye. "Nonetheless, I can't say I altogether pity them. The appearance of a little sprite in the press bench of our court room in these parts would cause a bit of a stir, no doubt, but can't say I'd object. Brighten things up, what?"

"Are you a beak? Oh dear, I suppose you are!" Morwenna looked somewhat dismayed at the thought of what she had said, but then added, "Oh, but ours are a really stuffy old lot. They don't look a bit like you. They've all got at least one foot in the grave."

"Like to see the ones with both feet in the grave," said Sir Joselin. "How do they get to court?"

Morwenna burst out laughing. As usual, when she laughed everyone else found they wanted to laugh too. Lady Sowersby, however, remained dubious. "You're rather young for a career of that kind," she ventured.

"I suppose I am, really," admitted Morwenna. "But you see it's a result of the war. And," she went on, "it suits me down to the ground, because as I'm in training to become a novelist I have to make a close study of human nature."

"Well, I think we had better go in to dinner." Dottie rose as she spoke. She was aware that Frank's eyes were dancing with amusement not unmingled with a certain degree of triumph. Nevertheless, Dottie thought to herself as she led the way across the garden, the fact that the child had experienced alerts under skies full of fighting planes and worked in police court still didn't alter the fact that she was only seventeen. And seventeen was seventeen. The war might be making seventeen-year-olds highly precocious in certain respects, but fundamentally they were still merely just out of the schoolroom. Still had to grow up!

Dinner was a most pleasant occasion. The laughter and chatter of the young people present reminded Dottie of what she and her husband missed so much, now that Jos, Frank and Boggy were all absent from home. It was true that they still had Vicky, but somehow one never thought of Vicky as young. Dottie, in fact, now always thought of Vicky as a contemporary, rather than as a daughter. A sensible, sound, reliable stalwart of the WVS: Never let you down.

Just as the summer pudding, a most delicious looking thing, was on the point of being served Eliot announced, "A telephone call from Miss Lavinia, m'lady. She's at Stellafield Halt and wonders if she might be collected."

"Boggy!" There was general astonishment.

"She's received a week's holiday from hospital at short notice," responded Eliot. He prided himself upon always knowing more about family comings and goings than the respective members knew themselves. He added, "What shall I tell Miss Lavinia about being met? She is still on the telephone."

Vicky, jumping up from table, said, "I'll fetch Boggy, I have the car and I'm well off for petrol." And off she went, without further ado.

"What an angel she is!" exclaimed Hal. "For it's true her petrol allowance is far larger than my meagre ration. How squalidly calculating we have all become," she added. "Like peasants!"

They took coffee on the terrace. Giles, seated between his aunts Dottie and Hal, exclaimed, "My, this is turning out to be quite some visit! All my life I've wanted to see your Parrocks, and it's sure living up to my highest expectations."

"I'm so delighted we've had the opportunity to welcome you here," replied Lady Sowersby. "And I hope the day is not too distant when we may visit your Parrocks."

"You'll be more than welcome, ma'am! Though as far as the house goes, we've nothing to show you like this house here. The grounds are good, Sherman never touched the grounds, but the house went up in smoke. It was built to look like this house, of course."

"Like this house looked before Cromwell sent it up in smoke," said Sir Joselin. "Your six Gs grandfather handed down a reconstruction of what this house had been like in his boyhood, before the Troubles began."

"And what is your present house like, Giles?" enquired Hal.

"Small, in relation to what went before. My great grandparents were left pretty poor; all the South was left pretty poor. So they built what they could afford. In the States it's considered an old house, but you'd simply call it mid-Victorian if it were over here. Mid-Victorian Southern style! I brought a picture of it to show. And of my parents too. Forgot clean about it till this minute, you've kept Homer and me that entertained. Like to see them?"

"Oh, please!"

Giles produced a small wallet containing snapshots of his Parrocks and his parents, the gardens, gorgeous with a wealth of magnolias and azaleas and wisteria. Over these Dottie and Hal gasped, "How absolutely beautiful!"

"Spring is the time to come. When you come you must make it spring!" said Giles eagerly.

Lady Sowersby responded, "You almost make me believe that we shall do it."

"Of course you'll do it! We'll sit together on that seat, under the magnolia, right there, and we'll talk about how we sat on this seat, right here." Giles indicated the seat and the magnolia in the snapshot as he spoke, then patted the seat that he and his aunts now occupied. Dottie watched him, smiling at his infectious enthusiasm. "I'm so glad you've come over here to us, Giles," she said. "So awf'ly glad! It's such a truly Sowersby thing to have done. The two Parrocks are going to be proud of you!"

Vicky arrived back with Boggy. Cries of greeting, much embracing. Upon seeing Morwenna, Boggy uttered a kind of glad whoop of amazement and they exchanged kisses, both giggling like mad. Boggy said, "Sister Sunflower decided that, as we're run off our feet with fresh cases daily and it promises, alas, to get worse, half the nurses shortly due for a holiday were to take it now before things are utterly too demented, and the other half, which includes poor dear old Pam, are to postpone theirs until things have quietened down again — which is like saying, 'Wait till Doooomsday.'"

Everyone then began asking about the nursing, how she was enjoying the burns unit, and so forth. Boggy rather brushed the burns unit aside. "Oh, it keeps us pretty busy," was all she would say.

Presently the young folk drifted away to the gazebo to watch the sunset. With the light almost gone and Hal calling from the terrace that Boggy must come because they were going home, Boggy murmured to Frank, "Any news of Jos?"

"Not for a couple of days or so. But no news must be taken as good news, under the present circumstances."

Boggy wondered for the thousandth time if she should mention the Poppy business to Frank. What good would it do? Frank could do nothing about it, could he? But, having decided that it was pointless to discuss the matter with him, she nonetheless found herself saying,

"One of the boys we're nursing is Pongo, Poppy Plumbton's husband. Remember him?"

"I do indeed."

"He's terribly, terribly burned, still hovering between life and death. She refuses to visit him, in spite of the fact that she knows he keeps asking for her."

"Oh?" Frank's tone was guarded. "Why should that be? I mean, what reason does she give?"

"Well, I hardly like to mention it, only I can't help wondering if you . . ." Boggy paused; she knew how loyally Frank was attached to Jos and she was afraid that, if she sounded too critical of him, Frank might flare up in his brother's defence.

"Know Jos and Poppy are having an affair," answered Frank.

"How do you know that? Did he tell you?" exclaimed Boggy, amazed.

"No. I discovered it purely accidentally," said Frank. "And I'm keeping it under my hat. As I would advise you to keep it, Bogs. We can none of us do anything about it."

"You don't think that if you spoke to him . . .?" ventured Boggy.

"I do take an exceedingly dim view of it when Poppy tells me, cool as custard, that she jolly well doesn't intend ever seeing Pongo again, *and* intends getting a divorce, and Jos is entirely in agreement with her, and they're desperately and hopelessly in love and all that, while Pongo is lying there in agony with half his face burned away. . . ." Boggy's voice was rising in indignation.

Frank said, warningly, "Yes, yes Bogs, it's sickening; but don't let the whole world know. It'd shatter Ma and Pa, and under the circumstances one doesn't want them . . . I mean they're worried enough about Jos as it is. And as for speaking to him, at this present moment in time he's completely taken up with the battle and I don't see him to speak to any more than you do, and, what is more, even if I were to run into him this evening, I'm afraid I wouldn't raise the subject; it might turn out to be my last ever conversation with my brother, and I'd hate it to consist of a beastly wrangle over something that's purely his private affair anyway."

"But I'm nursing Pongo, and I've discussed the matter with Poppy, and I can't pretend I know nothing about it."

"Okay, Bogs; professionally yes, you know about it," said Frank. "But when you get home here, you don't. There's nothing we can do at this point in time; repeat, nothing. Perhaps later on. . . ."

"Later on will be too late," said Boggy grimly.

"That may well be," replied Frank, with a sigh. "But nonetheless, nothing can be done at the moment."

Boggy said, closing the conversation, "I hope you're not annoyed I raised the matter, Frank. It just is that, if you saw Pongo. . . ."

"Oh I know, I know; it's particularly hard on you, Bogs, for you're witnessing the receiving end. It's tough. Truly tough."

Hal advanced towards them. "Must be off home now, Boggy. I should think you must be feeling pretty tired."

"Worn out," responded Boggy. And suddenly she sounded it.

XVII

Next morning, before they all set off to church, Sir Joselin took Morwenna on a tour round the house, the courtesy which he extended to every guest who came to stay. She responded to the various highlights of the tour with an enthusiasm which delighted her host. In the second-floor chamber of the Norman pele-tower she paused, with an expression of particular interest, before a blotchy and damp-damaged portrait of a carrotty-headed man. "He's awfully like Frank. Who is he?"

"Colonel Raiseley Sowersby, died fighting for Charles the First," said Sir Joselin. "Come up on the roof, remarkable view!"

The view thrilled Morwenna. "You don't find it too bleak?" he asked her. She turned her full, serious gaze upon him, "Oh no! The desolation of this place is most soothing after the rigours of advanced civilization."

"She is distinctly a little odd, as poor Frank warned us," commented Lady Sowersby, when Sir Joselin repeated the conversation to her afterwards, "but personally I think she is more a character out of Jane Austen than a fairy. I can see, and hear her, in the Pump Room at Bath! 'Did you enjoy your stay at Parrocks, Miss Duchamp?' 'Indeed, sir, yes; the desolation of the place was most soothing after the . . .' what were the exact words?"

"'Rigours of advanced civilisation.'"

"'The rigours of advanced civilization,'" repeated Dottie. She added, after a moment's pause, "I do see that in some ways she would suit Frank admirably."

It was proposed that in the afternoon Giles and Homer should be taken to Kirock Tower, a long-deserted pele out on the moor, reputedly haunted by the victims of the robber band that had at one time held the tower as their fastness. So, luncheon over, they set out: Vicky, Giles and Homer, Boggy, Morwenna and Frank, the latter pointing out that if, on account of his ankle, he couldn't keep up, or decided to turn back, the others were not to worry about him.

They took an old green road rising from the valley bottom to climb slantwise up a fellside rusty purple with now fast fading heather. Frank, holding Morwenna's hand lightly in his, limped at the rear of the party, discoursing upon their route. "This is an exceedingly ancient and bloody road we're following, my love. The reivers, Sowersbys leading them more often than not, rode out this way in forays against the Scots, and they returned this way with their plunder. And it was along this road, in their turn, came the Scots, out for revenge on the English. Very lively it was, in those days, or, if you prefer it, very deathly. Which, more often than not, amounts to the same thing."

The others marched ahead, laughing and joking. "I wanted to draw Giles's attention to this road," continued Frank, "for it's an historic one for us Sowersbys, but I fear he's more interested in chatting up Boggy."

Morwenna laughed. "Never mind, darling; *I'm* interested in your road!"

Frank drew a long breath that was almost a sigh. "It's not going to be an easy one." He held her hand more tightly. "About this business of our getting married. . . ."

Morwenna had been wondering when that subject would be introduced.

"What did your parents say when you told them?" she ventured.

"They were far from encouraging. Just the reverse, in fact. Pointed out your tender years, the hazards attached to early marriage, particularly in wartime; advised caution, and waiting, and so on and so forth."

"I must confess I'm not altogether surprised," said Morwenna, with a sigh that matched Frank's. "I suppose I *am* rather young, in actual years. And I look it, what's worse. Your poor sister, thinking I was her evacuee child and telling me I was going to milk a cow!"

Frank burst out laughing and put his arm round her, drawing her close to him. "My poor evacuee child!"

They had now dropped well behind the rest of the party. The road gained the brow of the hill and struck out across the open moor. A narrow track appeared forking away to the right towards a small ravine opening between heather banks. Frank said, "This way!" They gained the shelter of the ravine. "With luck we're shot of that lot," said Frank. "The gathering of the clans is a lovely thing, but enough is as good as a feast and I am now decidedly satiated. And to think I was reckoning on a few days of bliss alone with you! I haven't even kissed you properly yet." So saying, he took her in his arms and started making good the omission with an enthusiasm that almost squeezed the breath out of Morwenna.

At last he said, "We'd better shove a bit further down this gill. I wouldn't put it past that lot, with their passion for family reunion, to come after us and round us up back into the herd."

The track was too narrow for them to walk side by side: Frank led, with Morwenna following, further and further into the lonely folds of hills. The track widened, they were able to walk abreast again. Once more Frank took Morwenna's hand. "How, d'you think, would your parents react to the notion of your getting married in, say, six months' time?"

"I'm certain they'd be against it. For I'd still be under eighteen. I shan't be twenty-one and free to do what I choose for another four years."

"Four years! We may both be dead by then; me, anyhow. We can't possibly wait four years!"

"Not possibly!" agreed Morwenna.

"So we'll have to work out a plan of campaign." Frank spoke with obvious relish; how he enjoyed plans of campaign! "I presume," he continued, as he helped Morwenna down a particularly rocky step in the path, "I presume that if, in six months' time when I come of age, we elope, your parents will then agree to our marriage, if only to make an honest woman of you."

"Oh, bound to!"

"It seems to me, then, that an elopement in six months' time and resultant marriage must be our ultimate course of action. But, as six months is a hell of a long time to postpone anything during a war, I think that, as a temporary ceremony and precaution against losing one another — and you know how good we are at that! — we should bind ourselves in traditional style with a handfasting."

"What is that?"

"A handfasting means that you join hands and live together as man and wife until a book-a-bosom, in other words an itinerant priest, arrives on the scene to sanctify the union. You see, in the old days priests were few and far between in these parts and travelled from parish to parish, and life was too uncertain for much waiting around for a priest to turn up, once two people had decided upon one another. Like it is today."

Morwenna gave him a long and thoughtful look.

"Obviously, with me in the army and things as they are, we can't set up in domesticity together," he continued. "But we have reached a point, I'm convinced, and I take it you are too, where we are ready to become man and wife. The fact that we can't go ahead with this next, logical, step is entirely due to our parents. I'd marry you like a shot, tomorrow, if I could! If you'd have me."

Morwenna gave a half-laugh, half-sigh; raised his hand to her lips and kissed it caressingly.

"Handfasting is traditional and perfectly reputable. For people like us in times like these it's a legitimate step in the right direction," went on Frank. "In any case the handfasting rules give you a chance to change your mind; a trial period of one year and a day (unless the parson appears before that), after which, if both parties desire it, the union becomes permanent. If one or the other at any time during the course of the union wishes to say, Enough! well then, you can part, just so long as the one who decides to get out accepts full responsibility for the children, if any; which, by the by, under terms of handfast are considered legitimate, though I wouldn't exactly care to put that to the test nowadays."

"I can't say I would, either."

"I don't see why that problem need arise, however. We're intelligent responsible people and with care there's absolutely no reason why we should have trouble. . . . But I don't want to rush you into anything. On the other hand, though we may each have a lifetime ahead of us, equally the church bells may ring out at any time, I don't mean wedding bells, I mean invasion bells."

"Yes," said Morwenna, thinking of Pam and her Nicky. "Yes," Morwenna repeated.

"Yes? You'll be handfasted?"

"Yes."

"Come on." He began hurrying her along the track.

"Where do we do it?"

"There's a special place. It's not a thing you do just any old where!"

The ravine down which they were hurrying, Frank now apparently miraculously cured of his limp, suddenly opened out to give them a view of a deep and almost perfectly circular glen lying below them, a green hollow scooped out of the hills. The burn racing beside them down the ravine spilled into this hollow to join another little burn already glittering there; the two narrow threads of water merging into a larger burn with pools and small cascades.

"This," said Frank, stopping so that they might survey the place properly, "is what in these parts is called a beef tub; in other words, a hollow in the hills where the reivers hid stolen cattle. Cammerburn Pot they named this one. They posted sentinels on these tops round the tub; if the alarm were raised they could get the cattle away pretty quickly." He added, "I know this part of the world better than the back of my hand. I'm so obviously intended for rapine and robbery, murder and violence in these hills!"

"What a pity you didn't come on the scene a bit earlier in time."

"Yes, three hundred years ago would have suited me fine, as long as you were around too." He pointed into the glen at their feet. "You see where the burn in the Pot bottom, Cammerburn, is joined by this little burn running past us now? Well, that spot where they meet is marked as you see by a rock, and that's the Grayne Stone, and that's where the handfastings took place. It's an old magic place; if we get handfasted there we shan't come unstuck in a hurry, I promise you!"

And, with these words, he started hurrying her downhill again.

"Why is it called the Grayne Stone?" panted Morwenna.

"Because, as I've just said, it marks the spot where the two burns join, and in this part of the world a join is a grayne."

The hillside became steeper and steeper, willy-nilly they went faster and faster, till in the end they were running down, virtually unable to stop themselves; Morwenna clinging to Frank and uttering cries that were half-gasps, half-laughter. Then the gradient eased out and they slackened pace and walked hand in hand across smooth green turf to the Grayne Stone.

Here they stopped. Everything was still and perfectly silent, except for a pair of mewing buzzards circling high overhead, and the burn bubbling and babbling at their feet. They seemed to be the only two human beings left in the world.

"In the old days," explained Frank, "several couples would come here for a kind of mass handfasting, though the numbers involved could never have made up what we would call a mass! The first of May was a favoured occasion; the ancient Celtic festival of Beltane, when great fires were lighted, and magic rites performed; 'Beltane' itself means a 'great fire'. The ancient handfastings took place round the ceremonial fire, and afterwards the couples concerned went off into the night. Midsummer was another great time for fires, and handfasting; and so was Lammas-tide. We've missed all three, we've no fire, no fellow handfasters, it's broad daylight, and we don't know the ritual, so. . . ."

"So . . .?"

"We shall have to invent a ceremony, adapted to our own time and circumstances. As long as we're in the right place, which we are, and perfectly serious about what we're doing, which we are, we shall be all right. But first of all we have to make a very careful note of the day: which is Sunday the first of September, Anno Domini nineteen hundred and forty, fifteenth Sunday after Trinity, and tomorrow we have a new moon. You have until September the second, next year, by present calendar reckoning, in which to change your mind, my child, unless a parson comes along between now and then and splices us in church, after which, of course, you will *not* be able to change your mind because you will have plighted your troth to remain married till death do us part and a vow is a vow, in my book at all events. Agreed?"

"Agreed." Morwenna nodded her head in emphasis.

"Good. Now we stand facing each other here by this stone, and we hold one another's right hand, and we repeat an ancient oath that our local witchdoctor once taught me, that should be just as good for handfasting as for guarding a secret — which was why he taught me, to guard a secret."

Frank and Morwenna then faced one another and joined hands, and Frank intoned, "May my right hand be cut off. . . ."

"May my right hand be cut off . . ." repeated Morwenna.

"And the water by my feet turn to stone. . . ."

"And the water by my feet turn to stone. . . ."

"And this stone to water. . . ."

"And this stone to water. . . ."

"And the grass wither and die. . . ."

"And the grass wither and die. . . ."

"And night fall at noonday. . . ."

"And night fall at noonday. . . ."

"If I forget what I have vowed to remember."

"If I forget what I have vowed to remember."

There was a moment's silence, broken only by the burn's voice, while they continued to stand motionless, holding hands. Then Frank, with a great shout, picked Morwenna up and spun round with her, holding her aloft, whooping his head off. The sky, fellsides, and green turf spun wildly before Morwenna's eyes, and then, just as abruptly as she had been swung into the air, she found herself slamming down into the heather with Frank on top of her bringing a gasp from her.

Frank stared into her eyes, a long stare, then put his mouth hard on hers in a kiss that went on for ever, the buzzards mewing high in the sky above them and the burn running; heard but not heard;

until, penetrating even their mutual insensibility to all else but themselves and each other, the buzzards' mewing became lost in a distant female voice calling,

"Coo-eee! Coo-eee!"

"Flaming hell!" Frank struggled up to peer out of the heather. The intruder's cheerful "Coo-ees" were now alarmingly close. "Bloody Vicky! And the rest of 'em in full cry behind!"

Morwenna smoothed down her skirt and pushed back her hair; she had lost her hair ribbon and knelt, peering for it in the heather, as Frank, trying to stand up, lurched forward and only stopped himself falling by propping himself against the Grayne Stone. Vicky, approaching them with a wide, friendly smile, changed her expression for one of anxiety. "Frank, are you all right? I saw you go down in the heather, but I didn't realize you'd fallen and hurt yourself."

"Tripped, my bad ankle," replied Frank shortly. Morwenna, glancing up at him, noticed that he had gone rather white. "Oh darling, are you really hurt?"

"I thought you were playing some kind of game," said the puzzled Vicky. "I heard whooping and shrieking as though someone had caught a fox, and couldn't make it out, and then I saw you with Morwenna, doing a sort of apache dance. . . ."

"Exactly what we were doing," retorted Frank, coldly. "One comes out here, from time to time, and apache dances." He began limping, almost staggering, away from the place, towards the others who were now hurrying forward, all noisy amusement. Morwenna, her ribbon retrieved, jumped up and hurried after him.

"What a crazy pair!" gurgled Boggy. "Capering around: we thought you'd gone mad!" She added, "We decided to come back this way to show Giles and Homer the Pot. Tell them about it, Frank. You can tell about it all so much better than we can."

"I've been telling Morwenna: done my stint of tourist guiding for the day. Tell 'em yourself. I'm shoving off home. Take me twice as long to get there as you lot."

Boggy, pulling a slight face at his brusqueness, began explaining about the beef tub. Frank, looking morose, headed towards home; he was limping really badly again. Morwenna walking beside him, said, "I didn't realize you'd fallen. I thought. . . ."

"You didn't imagine I intended hurling you to the ground like a vanquished barbarian and myself on top of you with such insensate violence? You must think I'm a lout."

"Everything happened so suddenly! And you did say rapine, murder and mayhem!"

Frank started to laugh, in spite of himself. "Suiting action to his word!"

"With a vengeance! Nearly brained me!"

He took her hand again. "You'll have to complain to the WVS billeting officer. Tell her the nasty farmer is knocking you about, throwing you around, trying to crack your skull by hurling you on to stony ground." He put his arms round her, stopped and kissed her, all atonement and remorse. "To hell with it, I might have hurt you badly. Rendered you a crippled and gibbering imbecile for life."

"And you wouldn't have been able to get rid of me, either. We're handfasted now, don't forget!"

"After a year and a day. . . ."

"Not at all. I'd be the equivalent of a helpless result of the union."

"All the same," he said thoughtfully, as they resumed walking, "bloody nuisance intruders that they all are, my damn sister especially — apache dancing, I ask you — perhaps it was fortuitous. We don't really need any little handfasted legitimate bastards to complicate what is already an unpopular betrothal, as it were. And if we hadn't been interrupted . . . what do you think?"

"I think perhaps it *was* lucky Vicky came along. And I think we'd be advised to stick to your plan of campaign: intelligent, responsible people, darling, who take care."

"Do you think you can steal downstairs to the fossil room tonight? And we'll be magnificently responsible and arm ourselves with all due precautions. It's no use me trying to stagger up to the attics; all the floorboards up there. . . ."

"Everything creaks. I can hear Vicky whenever she turns over in bed."

"Precisely. So, amended plan of campaign: the fossil room, precaution and silence." Arms round one another they walked on in blissful accord. Then Frank said, half jokingly, half grimly, "When we get home we'll find there's been a telephone call ordering me back to my unit immediately. Just you wait and see."

"Oh, darling, please not! What a frightful notion!"

Frank made no reply. Morwenna, glancing at his face, saw that he wore a strangely bleak expression. When they reached the house Eliot met them. Frank, without waiting for the old man to speak, said, "A telephone message for me?"

"Yes, Master Frank. Ordered back to your unit. The call came about half an hour since."

At the time, or thereabouts, when Frank had said there'd be a telephone call.

Morwenna looked at him now with enormous eyes. He shrugged and said, attempting lightness, "The second sight! We all have it in these parts, don't we Eliot?" Eliot replied, guardedly, "Some do, sir." He was now wearing a troubled expression akin to that of Frank.

"In point of fact," Frank resumed, when Eliot had departed and Morwenna and he were alone, "there's nothing really spooky about it, so there's no need to stare at me saucer-eyed. I've been more than half expecting to be called back at a moment's notice, with the whole country in a state of alert, as it is, over this invasion lark: like everyone else in the Forces, including the halt and the lame, I should be with my unit; it was sheer luck I broke my ankle and got a few days' convalescence and was able to come home, and even greater luck you were able to be here too. True, we've only had twenty-four hours together, but twenty-four hours are a damn sight better than nothing."

"At least we were given time to be handfasted."

"We were, my darling. It would have been dangerously pushing our luck to find ourselves in the fossil room this time round. Never push your luck! And now, if you'll excuse me, I think I'd better pack." He kissed her on the top of the head with a sigh, and left the room.

Giles and Homer were leaving after tea; Frank arranged a lift with them for part of his way. Everyone tried hard to make tea a carelessly cheerful, lighthearted occasion. Frank and Morwenna scarcely spoke to one another; conversation between them had dried up. At last it was time for goodbyes to be said; everyone rose and headed for the front of the house, where Homer had parked ready the car that he and Giles had borrowed for this leave. Frank contrived to get Morwenna to himself for a brief moment. Suddenly very near to tears, she clung to him tightly. He said, "Don't worry. I'll be back. God knows what may be going to hit us in the next few weeks and months, but whatever happens don't think for one moment I shan't turn up in the end for our rendezvous in the fossil room. Handfasted to you and Parrocks, I am, for ever and a day." He kissed her eyes, as if to kiss the tears away. Morwenna, murmuring an almost incoherent, "Yes, I know," relinquished her hold on him and let him go.

Everyone in the hall was embracing, hand clasping, exchanging thanks and goodbyes and good lucks. Morwenna stood still and unspeaking in this whirlpool of departure; she heard Sir Joselin saying to Giles, "This old house has sent out many a young man of our line to battle, and welcomed them home when they've done what they had to do; so don't forget this is where you head for when you've finished the job, what?"

"I'll be back, sir! Don't you worry!"

"They all say that," thought Morwenna. "Be back. Don't worry."

"And you too, m'dear feller, splendid meeting you, consider yourself one of the family. We shall be most hurt if you don't head for Parrocks whenever you can, with or without Giles. . . ." Sir Joselin pumped Homer's hand up and down with a ceremonious rhythmic action. Homer bowed an old-fashioned, solemn bow. "Sir!"

"We really do mean it when we say consider yourself one of the family, Homer!" exclaimed Lady Sowersby, turning from giving Giles a warm embrace. Homer bowed again. "Ma'am!"

Frank, whose uniform accentuated both his height and the colour of his hair, crossed the hall to his mother. "Goodbye, Ma!" He bent down and kissed her, then kissed Vicky and Boggy; exchanged hugs with Nanny Bradshawe who had come downstairs to see him off; shook hands with his father; went down the steps, shook hands with Eliot who was standing by the car, holding Frank's bag. "Goodbye Eliot, wear the door for me and keep all safe till I get back!" "Yes, Master Frank sir, I will that!" replied Eliot, handing Frank the bag and looking very serious.

Homer got into the back seat of the car; Frank sat next to Giles who was driving. The three young men raised their hands in gestures of farewell. "See you soon!" "So long, and thanks a million once again!" "We'll be back!" The car crunched slowly across the gravel, gathering momentum, and vanished down the drive.

XVIII

Yes, it *is* Tuesday, the third of September. Almost impossible to believe,

 my darling love,

that we said good-bye as recently as Sunday: a mere forty-eight hours ago — seems more like forty-eight years; and as for the handfasting, that seems more like four thousand years distant in time! Perhaps it was. What *is* time, in any case? Nobody knows. And there isn't enough of it at my disposal, this afternoon, for me to ramble on, speculating on the subject. Well, at least we were given the time to become handfasted; but I have a distinct feeling we have done it all before. Do you feel like that too?

This is really a "night before the battle" letter; for one thing is certain: if Hitler doesn't have a try at invading us within the next fortnight, then autumn conditions in the Channel will oblige him to postpone the attempt till next spring. Personally I believe everything points to his giving the thing a try within the next few days. I'd like it to be while you're still at Parrocks; in the event of invasion no place can be guaranteed safe, but you'd be a lot better off at Parrocks than in London, which is bound to be a prime target for attack. It would put my mind, well, not at ease, because under no circumstances can one have one's mind at ease at a time like this, but I would worry about you less if you were at Parrocks.

But whatever happens, I don't want you to worry about *me*. I have a strong presentiment, mounting close to conviction, that I shall survive what's coming. I may be wrong, of course; possibly it's a common delusion before action begins. But there's little point in my survival if you fail to survive too — which is why I do beg you to take care and not expose yourself to any greater danger than you need. Damnation! here comes the corporal wearing an expression so portentous it can only mean that we have run out of soap, or Private Crumb (his real name!) has come over queer again (I'm not making it up — every now and again he does this coming over queer, but what to do about it I'm not quite sure; maybe it's his natural condition; on the other hand it may be an early symptom of something which may make him the most frightful liability just when the Germans roll up; I suppose we can always shoot him accidentally, if need be). One thing you can be quite sure of; the corporal (who is about to enter) with a look of doom like that on his face isn't going to say anything serious like, "Hitler has reached Colchester, sir, and we're ordered out to prevent him getting any further!" The chap, for anything really serious, puts on a loopy smirk. I'm gradually getting to know the ropes. Here he is! Ah! "This 'as got nothing to do with the war, sir!" I must stop; continue this breathless tale in my next, if there is a next! What a stupid way to end a letter! Bless you for ever, little darling. F.

4 September 1940

Dear Boggy,

Just a quickie to say we've already had a change of address: as from tomorrow our squadron is no longer stationed in Northumberland, but moves south to reinforce a squadron that has been having a tough time of it, lost quite a lot of its pilots. Can't tell you more than this, at present, but both Homer and I see it as good news: means we really shall be right there in the Battle of Britain, and that's what we came over for! This said, it was swell to be posted to Northumberland. Though only a brief posting it gave me time to visit Parrocks, and get to know you all — a weekend I shall never forget! Another advantage of being in the south is, I'm nearer you — I shall take you up on that promise of yours to show me the sights of London first chance we get. Homer joins me in sending best wishes and saying it was worth crossing the Atlantic just to meet you! Here's to seeing you again soon!

Roars,

Giles

Darling Thingy,

Thanks for the pc of Hadrian's Wall; is that where you've been?
Ma, as usual vague as hell, says you told her you were off on a
week's Youth Hostelling on the Border: wish you had told me you
were going; I'd have joined you. My God, do I need a break!

I've had the most frightful row with Papa. I made up my mind
to join de Gaulle's *Forces Françaises Libres*; went to their head-
quarters at Carlton Gardens; told me to come along again, for an
interview. Unfortunately needed my birth-certificate, being
under twenty-one and a British citizen; had to ask Ma for it and
she informed Papa of what I was intending to do. He blew a
gasket. Uniformed services, either French or British (unless
nursing services), are not for decent young women: licentious
soldiery and all that and Free French likely to be especially free!
Went on to say that as I seem content enough with my present job
(who says so?) best to stay in that until we know whether Hitler is
going to invade us or not. At present moment in time wisest course
is to be home here in Stoke Hartwell; STAY PUT. And so on.

To make matters worse, on my way back from Carlton Gardens
to Piccadilly, I ran into that boy, Jean-Paul Monier, who was a
friend of Fernand's and used to stay at Bolbec and play tennis
with us, d'you remember? Now over here, and in the FFL. We
recognized one another at once, hailed each other in French and
had a long talk. I asked him if he had any news of Fernand (I've
heard nothing from him since France was first invaded — four
months ago!) and Jean-Paul thought Fernand must have been in
some very bad fighting, but knew nothing more than that.

Jean-Paul most enthusiastic I should join FFL and fight to
liberate France, kept repeating to me de Gaulle's slogan, *La France
a perdu une bataille, mais la France n'a pas perdu la guerre.* After which
inspiration, all I get is stay bloody PUT at home! Oh god! if only I
were twenty-one and could do what I wanted! Oh this beastly
war! it has ruined everything I ever set my heart on, and now,
final straw, being underage devastates my last chance of doing
something that I want! I feel that not only my life is in shreds, but
that my heart is too! My life is over before it even began! At
nineteen! Get in touch with me the *instant* you return and relieve

the desolation into which your dementedly frustrated and unhappy sister has fallen!

Odo

Parrocks
Saturday September 7th
(9 a.m.)

Dearest Frank,

Morwenna and Boggy left here together half an hour ago; Vicky has driven them to Newcastle to catch the London express. I fully understand why you wished Morwenna to stay on here and no, darling, of course didn't mind a bit your telephoning yesterday evening to ask me to put it to her! Your anxiety over her being in London at this time is perfectly natural, but she was absolutely determined to return to her newspaper; we simply could not persuade her to stay on. I must say your father and I rather admired her for it! We loved meeting her, she is a charming little thing, tho' needs time to grow up. However your father and I have said our say on that.

As for poor Boggy, she had no choice but to return to her hospital though fortunately as it is buried in the depths of the country she should be reasonably safe. My heart will be with all you young people over the weeks ahead; I fear we have some dark days to face, you will all be in my thoughts and prayers. So far as your dear brother Jos is concerned, your father assures me that the longer a fighter pilot goes on, and the greater expertise and experience he consequently acquires, the more likely is he to survive. I cling to that hope! Whereas I am painfully anxious for Giles and Homer, who are being flung, green, into the height of the battle. They'll each be flying their first combat sortie any time now; let's trust that some guardian angel will be around!

Must now say goodbye. We have our Spitfire Gala Fête today and as you may guess the next eight hours or so will be frantic! Let us know how you continue to fare, Frankie dear!

Your ever loving
Mother

147

Dower House
Parrocks
Sunday September 8th 1940

Dearest Lavinia

Am anxious to hear that you arrived at Plashett Wold safely
and look to you for a line when you have time to write.
Meanwhile I'm scrawling this hasty note to reassure you that we
are all perfectly safe in this part of the world, in case rumour
reaches you of our great invasion scare of last night; Eliot (who
as usual knows *everything*) having informed us that only parts of
the country were alerted, so that possibly you may know nothing
of it!

Gordie and I had stayed on for supper at Parrocks after the
Spitfire Gala Fête. Such a pity that you two girls had to miss it
— the most tremendous fun and a huge success! Raised well over
three hundred pounds and have donated it to the county Spitfire
fund; Stellafield should be proud of itself! However, to get on
with my tale! At eight-thirty in the evening, just as Gordie and I
were on the point of returning home, the church bells rang out.
Invasion! You could hear them ringing from all the steeples for
miles around! I left Gordie at Parrocks and went off to my
Warden's Post; sat there all night, next to the blower, waiting for
something to happen, but nothing whatever did. However good
deal of commotion in the village with the Home Guard marching
about and at Parrocks they thought they were on the point of
capturing another Hun but turned out to be Sandy Routledge,
the local road mender, one of the Home Guard, who had lost
himself in the dark. This morning the place is thick with
rumours.

Your uncle Joselin has it, from the Regional Commissioner,
that an invasion attempt was made across the Straits of Dover
and at points up the east coast as far as Harwich. The code word
"Cromwell", meaning "invasion Imminent", was sent out at
eight p.m. to the Southern and Eastern Commands and soon
after to other parts of the country. Meantime an invasion fleet of
barges crammed with German troops was annihilated by the
Royal Navy and a small German bridgehead established briefly
near Folkestone was wiped out after murderous fighting. Also,
heavy air attacks on London have taken place.

Eliot has it that the Home Guard has been extensively involved in action against German parachutists throughout the east and north-east all night and that the Germans have all had their throats cut!

Our vicar has just popped in, on his way to church, to say that, according to the Rural Dean, an invasion attempt has definitely been made, and as definitely repulsed, and Mr Churchill has decided that, in the interests of security, the episode shall be described as a "false alarm" with no mention whatever made of it on the wireless or in the papers, as though it had never taken place! Certainly there has never, at any time since the church bells rang, been any reference on the wireless to an invasion alert in any part of the country — not even that the bells were rung — and there's no hint of any kind of invasion attempt in any of this morning's papers. All very rum! However, as I said when I started this letter, I'm telling you what happened here (and precious little it was, thank heaven!) so that you will know we're all safe if the rumours reach you, and repeat we'd appreciate a line from you some time to set our hearts at rest that you haven't been in the thick of things at Plashett Wold.

Must now dash off to church myself, it being a National Day of Prayer to mark the anniversary of this wretched war, and myself having to represent the ARP I daren't miss it, though having had no sleep all night I feel more like bed than church!

Take care of yourself my dearest child. Love from us all,
Mummy

Part Two

FRONT LINE

XIX

Marie Tooley and her family party of daughter Josie, Josie's year-old twins Gerry and Gary, ten-year-old Rhona, and little Pete, arrived back in London shortly after two o'clock that Saturday afternoon, the seventh of September, sunburned and weary after a week's hop-picking in Kent. Their journey had been a wearing one. Pete, a particularly troublesome twenty-two-month-old, had a battered wooden folding pushchair into which he, like an infant Houdini, was tied with a complicatedly knotted clothes-line, from which bondage he staged a non-stop series of unbelievable escapes. Rhona was in charge of Pete and the pushchair; a thankless responsibility, for when at last she got the wriggling liberty-loving Pete tied down he never stopped yelling and bawling until he had freed himself once more, whereat the exasperated Marie dashed at Rhona with angry reprimands and thumps for having allowed Peter to escape.

Usually, when Marie returned home from hopping with her brood, her eldest son, Steve, met her at London Bridge Station to help her carry her things, but he had now joined the Home Guard and was somewhere in the country, as a training instructor; Marie was vague as to details. All she knew was that what it boiled down to was Steve couldn't meet them and it was merry hell having to manage without him!

Josie, married to a seaman in the Merchant Navy, lived in Stepney with her Aunt Gert. Because Josie couldn't travel across London with her twins single-handed, Marie, Rhona and Pete were going out of their way to accompany her to Aunt Gert's; they would then, after a cup of tea with Gert, walk down Bromley Street to the Commercial Road and there board a bus for Silvertown. "And shall I thank my stars to be home!" thought Marie to herself. "Back in Lucknow Passage; sit down in my own kitchen, see my Violet again; can't wait for it!"

Violet, Marie's second daughter, a sparkling brunette of

eighteen, had not gone hopping but had stayed at home to take care of her stevedore father, Mick Tooley. Marie was now seeing in her mind's eye the jug of stout, the saveloys and pease-pudding that Vi would have ready as a celebrative homecoming supper; over this repast Marie would tell Vi and Mick all about the hopping and they'd have some good laughs.

With the haven of Lucknow Passage as a beacon to keep her going, Marie footslogged across London Bridge to the Monument, the panting and perspiring Josie beside her, Rhona pointing out to the goggle-eyed Pete the ships and barges on the river. "That's the docks, away down there, Pete, and our house. That's where we're going when we get on the Tube."

"Good old river, good old Thames!" said Marie, kindling to the London scene as she always did when she came back to it after the annual hopping. "You can't beat London! Look Pete, there's Tower Bridge, see?"

At the Monument they plunged underground; Marie with an air of desperation. She hated underground travel; "You always get lost in the Tube!" But Josie, younger and more confident, guided them safely on to the District Line, and then it was straight through to Stepney Green station. And there was the good old Mile End Road, broad and busy; cross that, and there, pretty soon, was Stepney Green itself, with an actual strip of grass surviving to support its name. They walked to the end of the Green, turned into the maze of narrow streets beyond and, after a final back-breaking couple of hundred yards or so, reached Gert's little shop on the corner. "Thank gawd!"

The shop door, half-glazed, but the pane partly obscured by an open/closed notice and advertisements for Woodbine cigarettes and Wills Gold Flake tobacco, opened with a sharp ping! of its bell. And there, in the tiny dark little shop that smelt of dust and soot and cat and newsprint, sat Aunt Gert in her wheelchair: hugely stout, triple-chinned, smiling, wearing her customary garb of brown woolly cap and (except in the hottest weather) an old coat over a clean cotton-print apron. Today, because the weather was warm, she had exchanged the coat for a cardigan.

The tea-tray was all ready and waiting on the oilcloth-covered table in the room behind the shop; Josie had the kettle boiling on the gas-stove in no time. The twins had their nappies changed and were put upstairs in their cot to sleep; Rhona was given a sherbet dab, out of shop stock, to keep her happy; cups of tea were handed round, Aunt Gert taking hers as she sat in her chair behind the counter; she changed the chair's position so that she faced the others in the back room. Her shoulders, over the years, had become big humped-up hillocks from turning the wheels of her chair.

"Well," she kept saying, "you've all caught the sun orright! Look fit as fleas!"

Her own face was of a waxy pallor, the complexion of a prisoner. For over thirty years she had spent all day every day, bar Sunday afternoons, sitting in her shop.

Pete, who made too much mess with sherbet dabs and so had merely been given a piece of bread and butter, now began to create, shouting and kicking his legs up and down. "He wants his flag! Give him his flag!" cried Aunt Gert. "Yes, give him his flag!" chorused everyone else, anxious to quieten Pete.

The flag, a small Union Jack on a stick, was a leftover from the Coronation when Aunt Gert had sold flags as well as having liberally decorated her own shop front with them. She had done a roaring trade in flags. Everyone in Stepney had bought them.

Pete had taken a fervent fancy to the flag the very first time Aunt Gert had shown it to him to divert his attention when he had gone off into one of his paddywhacks. Ever since, on each visit to her, Pete demanded the flag, the stick of which now had his toothmarks all over it for when he wasn't waving it he chewed it.

Josie now fetched out the flag from a chest of drawers and Pete took it and flourished it and then started biting the stick. "He'll get splinters in his mouth," said Marie. "Got real savage teeth on him now, he has."

"Yes, and if we take it off him goodbye peace," said Josie.

This dilemma, however, was immediately forgotten because at this moment the air raid warning sounded.

"Cor, the sireen! What a time of the day to choose! Just as you're settlin' down to your tea!" from Marie.

"Won't come to nothing with a bit of luck," murmured Josie.

As they had walked to Stepney Green they had heard the distant whines and cannon fire of aerial dogfighting, but they had become used to these sounds over the past few weeks and therefore ignored them. But now the skirmishing in the sky grew louder and Rhona, still sucking her sherbet dab, ran into the street to watch. It was a full-scale dogfight all right: white vapour trails twisted their cotton wool patterns across the clear blue overhead; the fighting planes glittered, their guns crackling, and the sound of cheering rose from the Stepney streets where the Saturday afternoon male populace was zestily following the fortunes of the battle exactly as though it were a football match.

Rhona, excited, came running indoors. "Seen a balloon!" she told her elders. "Little white balloon!"

"Must've been a parachute," said Josie.

"No it ain't! It's a balloon! Over there!" She waved with her sherbet dab eastwards, towards the docks. She ran out, ran in again. "Can't see it any more."

"You sit down and have a drop of tea," suggested Aunt Gert. "All finished now." The battle had retreated down river. "No more fireworks today," said Gert. "Have the all-clear next."

But then they began to hear the roaring in the sky. At first, like everyone else who heard it, they thought it must be thunder. However thunder didn't go on coming louder and growing nearer like that, and it dawned on them that it must be aeroplanes. Still, as they'd never before heard, or even imagined, a mass of aircraft on that scale it puzzled rather than alarmed them, and then Rhona went into the yard to look, though her mother told her not to, and then the child darted back screaming, "There's hundreds of 'em coming, mum!" and then the noise was shaking the very house and had become so appallingly ominous that there was no longer any doubt of what was about to happen.

XX

Aunt Gert's back yard was just about big enough to take an Anderson shelter, but Gert had not troubled with an Anderson because neither upon her crutches nor in her chair would she have been able to get down into it. So during the recent random raids, she had propelled her chair beneath the stairs and sat there, while Josie had crouched with the twins under the shop counter that, made of solid mahogany and with a thick layer of newspapers and periodicals on top, seemed as safe a place as any.

Now, as the roaring of the bombers reached crescendo point, Gert desperately wheeled herself to the stairs, Josie dashed to fetch down the twins and Marie thrust Pete under the counter. He didn't want to go and kicked and struggled. Then the bombs began to drop. Rhona dived under the stairs with Aunt Gert, Josie came panting with a twin under each arm and stowed herself with them alongside Pete. Only Marie was left without refuge and she crawled under the kitchen table as everything began to shake and shudder from the non-stop explosives raining down on the docks a mere mile or so away, a target so close that it seemed to the Stepney Green household that everything was being aimed at them. They huddled in terror, appalled into silence; even Pete lying pop-eyed and petrified without struggling or crying. Only once or twice Rhona gave a whimper and Marie ejaculated, "Oh gawd!"

At last it was over. They emerged, white-faced, shaking and dazed from their hiding places. For several minutes they could none of them find speech. Then Marie said, "Well, me and Rhona and Pete best get along home."

Despite the terrifying noise of the raid, surprisingly little damage had been done to this part of Stepney. It wasn't until Marie reached Sidney Way and the thoroughfare broadened that she saw the smoke: enormous black coils of it mounting up into the eastern sky over the docks, there to form a slowly spreading and thickening pall, an ominous red glow tingeing its undersides. In the direction of the Commercial Road the clanging of fire engines sounded nonstop. Marie had made up her mind to get home to Lucknow Passage at all costs, but even she was forced to admit that things were going up in smoke in no mean manner in the direction of Bow Creek and that perhaps it was not wise to march a small girl and a baby straight towards the trouble spot. She turned the pushchair round, saying, "Come on, you're going back to Aunt Gert's."

At Gert's Marie explained. "There's bad fires over the docks so I'll leave my kiddies and our bags with you, Gert, while I go and see."

Aunt Gert rolled big, anxious eyes at her sister. "Ooh, Marie! Mind how you go!"

"Don't s'pose it's much," said Marie breezily. "Roan, you be a good girl and help take care of Pete till I come back to fetch you." And with this Marie once more left the house, telling herself repeatedly that just because there was a fire in the docks it didn't mean *her* place was burning down.

In the Commercial Road Marie was suddenly assailed by intimations of the true extent of the disaster. Along the pavements of the broad highway came a steady westward flow of people: Marie's own East Enders, but not as she had ever seen them before or had ever thought she would see them: spectre-faced, speechless, nobody knowing where they were going, only that they had to get out. Some were grotesquely white from head to foot with fallen plaster; some were singed black, some bloodstained or roughly bandaged. Some carried babies, bird cages, pillowcases hastily stuffed with clothes. Some pushed prams into which howling infants, old suitcases, bags and bundles were all flung pell-mell. Some, aged and shuffling, could barely totter. Mothers dragged tails of crying children. At intervals, labouring along the gutter, out of the path of the speeding fire engines and ambulances, a desperate head of a household pushed a handcart loaded with rescued family goods and perhaps two or three little children and a grandmother. Marie's heart went cold as she saw this never-ending tide of calamity, but nonetheless she herself kept on walking towards the fires from which everyone else was fleeing. Must get home; home to her chap and Vi.

Suddenly a smoke-blackened woman, weighed down with heavy bags and a cardboard box with a tabby cat in it, hailed Marie. "Oi, mate! Got a pram to sell?" It was a neighbour, and Marie turned to her avidly. "What's happened?" "Give you ten bob for a pram, mate." "Ain't go no pram. What's happening up Silver . . .?" "Look, give you a quid. All I got." "I've got no bleeding pram to sell you! What's happened up Silvertown?" "Flattened, Silvertown is. And what's not been flattened is gone up in smoke."

Marie waited to hear no more but hurried off, desperate anxiety reviving her tired feet. It was not yet seven o'clock, but a heavy, orange-tinged twilight had already descended; the sky was one thick shroud of black smoke blotting out all light except that of the great arc of crimson and scarlet climbing in the east, while westward the sinking sun was lost in a despairing rusty murk.

The fires were now close and appalling; dockyards, wharves, warehouses, gasworks, all engulfed in fire, an incandescent furnace. Marie discovered that the streets, or what had been the streets, of Silvertown had been cordoned off. Everything beyond was utter confusion and conflagration: firemen running and shouting, great arcs of silver water shooting into towering infernos of flames and smoke, sparks and fiery fragments flying and whirling, everywhere enormous hose-pipes snaking over the ground, fire-reflecting water lying in pools and puddles, glass smashing and falling, masonry crashing; the air stifling with searing heat and the reek of burning. In the turmoil it was simple for Marie to slip through the cordon; but where to go next she had no idea, for she could no longer identify with certainty the features of what had become an entirely new and nightmare landscape.

As she stood staring, two rescue workers hurried past carrying a stretcher with something like a plaster-covered old bundle on it; then another stretcher went by, then two more, each burdened with a similar, shapeless, dusty bundle. Then an ARP warden came hurrying with an inert, blackened child in his arms.

Marie, shuddering, turned away and advanced hesitatingly another twenty yards or so over glass-crunching, debris-strewn ground. She should now be, she felt pretty sure, in the neighbourhood of their local pub, but all that met her eye was a great mass of rubble with a vast crater yawning in the middle of it. Some seventy-five yards further on was the dockyard wall over which poured flame-stabbed thick smoke, and, rearing up gleaming through the smoke, the row of derricks that looked over the wall, down upon Lucknow Passage; metallic monsters that were now fiery molten red.

Her sense of horrified foreboding mounting every second, her breath coming in jagged sobs, Marie continued to stumble and scramble over the piles of rubble. Shouting and desperate firemen directed great jets of water over and beyond the searing bright derricks into the blaze that raged and roared like a hurricane. Marie, thoroughly bewildered as to where she was and scarcely able to draw breath in the searing atmosphere, certain she must have reached Lucknow Passage by now but able to spot no trace of it, subsided on the rubble and gazed round despairingly. A few yards distant a half-demolished wall confronted her, with a flap of torn-away yellow patterned wall paper dangling, and a little iron fireplace, still in position in the wall, with a piece of green cotton flouncing pinned to drape the mantelshelf, and a spotty old photograph nailed over it; and though Marie couldn't see the photograph distinctly from where she crouched she knew it was of herself and Mick Tooley on their wedding day.

Marie, numb, motionless, stared at the fireplace, the dangling flap of wallpaper, the photo. Then a voice shouted behind her and a hand seized her. "Down you get from there, Marie. This is no place for you!" It was the local ARP warden, a mate of Mick Tooley. "Mick! My Vi!" gasped Marie, as she was half dragged, half carried off. "Not under this lot," he shouted in her ear. "Come on, out of it quick!" and he hauled her away just as the molten cranes began to tilt forward, to crash, bringing the dockyard wall with them, on top of what had been Lucknow Passage.

The shouts of the firemen, the roaring of the fire that came leaping now where the wall had been, were submerged by a new sound: the sirens wailing their warning again.

Marie, oblivious of everything, shrieked hysterically in the warden's face, "How d'you know they're not under that lot, how d'you know?"

"See 'em running away, up the street, just before the bombing started!" he shouted back. "C'me on, you gotta get under cover, we're in for another packet."

"Where'd they go?"

"Making for the shelter if they had any sense. And that's where you got to cut along quick yourself, Marie mate, before this next bleeding lot comes down on us."

The shelter, some two or three hundred yards distant, was one of the recently erected brick and concrete surface shelters. Steve had been very rude about it, saying it was useless and Marie was not to bother with it but must use a cellar. But Marie, as she staggered towards it, was thinking only of how she'd find her Mick and Vi there. Of this she was now certain.

Overhead the roar of the bombers drummed the sky once more, but Marie, almost collapsing as she stumbled into the shelter, was scarcely aware of it. Her Mick, her Vi!

The shelter, dim with a single hooded blue lamp, was empty apart from two St John's Ambulance men who were stooping over a groaning fireman. Marie, forgetting everything else but her quest, indeed in her exhaustion quite beyond rational behaviour, backed out of the shelter. They weren't there. It must be some other shelter Mick and Vi had gone to. She'd have to go on searching.

A violent screaming whistle, a sensation that her eardrums were being blown out and that, at the same time, she was being shut between two slamming doors. The next thing she knew she was being hoisted to her feet by a copper.

Marie, convinced that she was being arrested, started to protest, "I ain't done nothing!"

He began propelling her across open, rubble-strewn ground, hurrying her along. Marie attempted to dig in her heels.

"I ain't done nothing, straight I ain't!"

He picked her up in his arms and ran, carrying her. Marie shouted in protest. Another bomb-shriek and a crash, as her custodian ducked down with her behind a sandbagged wall. Confusion. More policemen. "I ain't done nothing! Let me go! All I done is look for my chap! You can't cop me for that you wicked lot!"

"Come on, mother, we're getting you out of here." Marie, still yelling, was put in some vehicle, quite what she didn't know, and driven off. The world, all fire and the crashing of bombs, turned into blurred nightmare out of which she bawled at intervals, "You can't cop me for looking for my chap!"

Then she was being led into a building, down some stairs, into a dimly lit room with mattresses on the floor and blanketed figures lying on the mattress. Marie, who once or twice in her life had been arrested for being drunk and disorderly, had never been in a nick quite like this before, but such funny things were happening now that there was no saying where you might end up. A woman in green brought her a cup of tea and showed her a mattress to lie on. Marie drank the tea, removed her boots, lay down on the mattress. The person lying next to her, a gaunt matron of her own age, rasped, "You copped it too, mate?"

"Yes! I ain't done nothing."

The woman said, "None of us ain't done nothing. That Goring just wants to show what he can do."

The words were no sooner out of her mouth than a violent series of crashes shook the building and the speaker abruptly pulled her blanket over her head as if to ward off the bombs. Screams, curses, shouts of terror came from other occupants of mattresses. Marie, in her state of dazed exhaustion, was scarcely aware that another terrifying raid was in progress. She lay motionless, blanket up to her chin, thinking about her chap and Vi and how, next day, if she didn't find herself in clink, she'd have to go on looking for them.

Suddenly a hand twitched the blanket and a voice from the other side of her said, "Here, look! That's all I got left." Marie, opening her eyes, found a dirty old insurance book thrust under her nose. The woman who held it, half sitting up from her blanket, bleary-eyed and with grey hair wildly disarrayed, repeated, "Lost my house, lost my old man, lost everything; all except my insurance book."

"I've not even got that, mate." Marie, when she had gone hopping, had left her insurance book with Vi for safekeeping.

The woman put her book under her pillow, repeating, "All I got left in the bleeding world."

Another woman was led in, stumbling and blank-eyed, dirty and distraught. Marie, listening to her disjointed remarks that she'd been bombed out "twice since tea time" and had her "little dog blown to smithereens by them fucking Huns", suddenly realized that this was no cop shop, but an emergency refuge for the homeless.

"What harm did a pore little animal ever do them bleeders? What harm has she done 'Itler, I ask you?" The woman sank onto her mattress and the tears trickled down her grimy face, leaving tracks where they ran. "Blow to bits a little dog! Wicked! Wicked!"

She huddled down, racked by sobs, then started up again with a screech as the whole place vibrated and shook with a crash so deafening that it seemed the building itself had been hit.

But apparently it had not: voices shouted and ambulance bells shrilled in the street outside. A near miss, thought Marie; and now she was too exhausted to care whether she got bombed or not. Her eyes closed; she was fast slipping to the point of blessed oblivion. But then the insurance book was thrust under her nose again and the husky voice from the next mattress repeated, "All I got left, look! Lost my house, lost my old man. . . ."

"Yes mate, you told me."

"My insurance book, all I got left!" And once more it went under the pillow, once more its owner lay down.

Marie drifted off towards sleep again. Then, "Here, look here mate! All I got left! My insurance book!"

Marie, with a growl, rolled over on to her other side, her back to the woman, burying herself in the blanket, but minutes later came a hard poke between her shoulder blades and the voice, "Lost my house, lost my old man, lost the lot! All I got left . . ." It went on all night, it seemed to Marie, who, dropping fitfully in and out of exhausted sleep laced with the heavy throbbing of the circling bombers overhead and punctuated by sickening crunches and thuds, was herself tormented by a vision of her bedroom fireplace left stranded in a bit of surviving wall while her wedding photo surveyed the red-hot derricks crashing down, crashing down.

XXI

The bombers kept up their attack for over eight hours. The All-clear sounded at half past four next morning and shortly afterwards a lot more people were brought in to the refuge, there, as they recovered their wits and breath, to recount tales of unbelievable horror: all the dockside riverfront, nine miles of it, ablaze, and no way of keeping the fires from spreading; the warehouses, full of inflammable things, exploding of themselves with the heat; brandy and rum kegs that burst, showering blazing spirit; timber yards where the great draught from the flames sent huge burning timbers tossing up into the air, like straws, to come down streets away and start fresh fires; paint and rubber stocks going up in flames higher than St Paul's; gasworks blazing; power stations blazing; whole streets a sea of flame from end to end; great rats the size of dogs swarming from the wharves; the river itself on fire at one point, covered with a sheet of molten liquid sugar; the whole of dockland being devoured by flames; all the fire-pumps of London in use and didn't make no difference; sky red all over like it was on fire itself; hundreds and hundreds of people dead; their houses blown down by bombs and then the poor bleeders roasted to death trapped under the wreckage, or else killed trying to get out.

Visions of the Stepney Green family meeting this terrible end, her Pete and Rhona, Josie and the twins and Gert, brought Marie up from her mattress and groping for her boots. The electricity had failed during the night; hurricane lamps now lit the refuge, adding to the general atmosphere of forlorn confusion. Marie joined a queue of women using the emergency chemical closet before getting out to confront the horrors of the new day. In the queue Marie found an acquaintance who had lived just round the corner from Lucknow Passage and who had spent all yesterday afternoon in the shelter where Marie had hastened in the evening hoping to find her Mick and Vi. According to this neighbour, Mick Tooley and Violet had never at any time appeared in the shelter, from which all the occupants had been evacuated by the police when the afternoon raid had ended and Silvertown had been cordoned off. "Must've gorn to some other shelter, mate," concluded the neighbour.

Information gleaned from the closet queue revealed that this refuge was called a Rest Centre and that there were places of the same sort in various parts of the East End, and some further out, and some, rumour had it, even out in the country and if you hadn't nowhere to go of your own accord you got moved on to these distant Rest Centres to make room for other people; you might end up in Kingdom Come before you knew where you were, as one member of the queue put it.

"Don't mind where I go, as long as I don't have to spend another night like the one I just been through! Hell couldn't be worse!" said someone else.

Everyone agreed that this was the thing to do: get up the Mile End Road to the People's Palace. For it was to this centre of former entertainment and relaxation that the mayor of Stepney and his local government officials had now removed themselves, after having been bombed out of their own premises.

Marie, desperate with anxiety for her family, refused the tea and biscuits she was offered and hurried away from the Rest Centre. This, though she hadn't realized it last night when she had been taken there, was less than a mile distant from Gert's place; a short walk that Marie this morning found awful. The hour was still very early; the scarlet and furiously angry eastern sky was inflamed with fire glow, not sunrise. In the eerie red-tinged half-light Marie groped through a landscape of wreckage; shops down, houses down, gaping craters surrounded by great heaps of rubble where yesterday had stood solid buildings that had looked as if they would last for centuries. The air reeked of smouldering fire that waited to burst into life again; the ordinary East End daybreak sounds of people trudging off to work, milk carts going their rounds and voices hailing each other with "good mornings" were replaced by the now inescapable ambulance bells, the agitated shouts of rescue workers and the exclamations and lamentations of families who, creeping out from the cellars and basements where they had cowered all night, now saw, dimly revealed, the extent of the havoc.

Marie, on feet sore and blistered after last night's walking, limped down one battered street and up the next, dreading what she might find when she reached Gert's, yet with no alternative but to hobble on and face whatever she found. Suddenly, into her mind still dazed by last night's experience, the realization flashed that her Mick and Vi had known that, before returning to Lucknow Passage from the hop-picking, Marie had planned first to see Josie and the twins back to Gert's. Stood to reason, when Mick and Vi found themselves bombed out they'd have gone to Stepney Green, gone there to join her and the kiddies! But, because she'd raced hurrying off to Bow Creek, she'd missed 'em! Must've passed each other, somewhere along the way. Yes, that was it! Mick and Vi had been with Gert all the time!

An enormous tide of relief swept over her. Forgetting the rasping blisters on her feet, she broke into a ragged, agonized trot that soon brought her within view of Gert's street corner. Marie, heart in her throat, almost dared not look.

Half the street was down, but Gert's shop on the corner had survived the night, though the shop door itself was now paneless. Marie, weak with relief, lurched and staggered towards it. Mick and Vi and all of 'em, safe. "Thank gawd!" she said aloud, meaning it from her heart, as she pushed at the shop door only to find that, though the glass was gone, the door itself was locked. "Oi!" she shouted into the shop. "Oi. It's me!"

Shrill cries from the back room, then Josie came to let Marie in. "Oh gawd Mum! We was wondering if we'd ever see you again!" gasped Josie, in tears. "Got Dad and Vi here?" Marie asked. "Dad and Vi?" Josie sounded startled at the question. "Ain't they been with you at Lucknow?"

"Ain't no Lucknow left. Ain't no Silvertown left. Ain't nothing left up our way."

The interior of the shop was in near darkness; in the back room a single candle showed the grey, tear-streaked, hollow-eyed faces of Gert and Rhona.

"What's happened, Marie?"

"Lucknow's gone," repeated Marie. "Found it all gone when I got there. But Mick and Vi was seen starting off to a shelter before it happened, see, so I know they're safe. Thought I'd find 'em here."

"No. Not been here, they ain't," responded Gert.

Marie sank into a chair, her expression clouded with despondency once more. "They must've been took to one of them Rest Centres like I've been at. Gawd knows where they'll end up! Once you get in one of them places, Government can cart you off anywhere they fancy. Take 'em weeks to get back to Stepney, I shouldn't wonder. Weeks!"

"Where d'you say you been, Mum?" shrilled Rhona. Marie replied, "What they call a Rest Centre, though how you're s'posed to rest I dunno; bleeding hard mattress with people moaning up your ear 'ole all night! Got took there by the police, like being carted off to the cooler."

"Whatever you been up to?" gasped Gert.

"Nothing. Just looking for Mick and Vi. Got nabbed hold of by a copper; thought I was getting my collar felt. Then they took me to this here Rest Centre. Say there's several of 'em, see? So that's where Mick and Vi's been took, though what one I don't know; and they don't let you stay there; they move you on, gawd knows where. Maybe miles away by now, miles away! And how am I to find 'em?" Marie was nearing tears of desperation.

"They'll turn up, Mum," said Josie. "If that's all that's happened to 'em, they'll show up before long. But I warn you, I'm not spending another night like we've just had, not here in Stepney I'm not!" Her voice, risen high, cracked. Gert said, "Come on, char's made; pour a cuppa, gal. Feel better after a cuppa tea! Thank gawd there was some water left in the kettle; there's none in the tap. They must've bombed the mains."

Josie, hands shaking, poured cups of tea.

Gert continued, "Thought we was all gonners last night, I must say." And again she repeated, as if she couldn't get over the fact that they were still alive, "Thought we was all gonners, and that's the truth! Cor, what a night!"

"Just what I'm saying," said Josie. "You'll not find me spending another night like that. I'm getting out."

"Won't be another night like that. Old 'Itler's run out of bombs," said Gert. "Dropped all he's got at one fell swoop. Never be able to keep that up."

"Not going to chance it," said Josie. "I'm getting out."

"Where you going?" asked her mother, staring, puffy-eyed with exhaustion, over the rim of her tea cup.

"To the Town Hall for a start. They evacuate you from the town Hall, don't they? You best come along too."

"I'll stay here and risk my luck with 'Itler," said Gert unhesitatingly. "This is my house and he's not going to get me out of my own house! I've been living here forty years now, and I reckon that if the Lord wants me he knows where to find me. But it ain't right for little nippers and their mothers to be in bombing like that, so off you go while there's time."

So, after the twins and Pete had been brought downstairs from the bedroom where they'd been put to sleep following the All-clear, and, after they had been fed, Josie placed the twins in their basinette, Pete was tied in his pushchair with Rhona in charge as usual and, leaving Gert declaring that they weren't to worry about her, she'd be all right, the party set out, Marie laden with their hopping bags of spare clothes and basic necessities, "Lucky we never unpacked!"

Out in the street they found themselves part of a straggling procession of people, all with the same object in view: to get themselves and their families away from Stepney as quickly as possible. Marie, after a hundred yards or so, hesitated, then stopped and stood surveying her fleeing neighbours. At last she said, in her most delphic style, "There's more to life than being safe, y'know!"

"What you mean, Mum?" Josie sounded anxious; she half suspected what would come next.

"What I say, gal. More to life than being safe."

"Want to stay alive though, doantcha?"

"Gert's right," continued Marie. "Not going to be turned out of her own house by 'Itler. Well, he's bombed me out of Bow Creek, but he ain't going to bomb me out of Stepney: not 'alf he bleeding well ain't! Born and brought up in Stepney, I was; never left Stepney till I married and got took up Bow Creek. But now I been bombed back to where I belong, as you might say, and no blooming 'Itler's gonna turf me out from where I belong. Here I am and here I'll stay until that bleeder puts paid to me altogether, or else gets put paid to himself, *which*," wound up Marie with relish, "is a fucking dead cert he'll be, and sooner that what he expects. Sauce of some people, thinking they can knock down everybody else's houses flat as pancakes, and bleeding get away with it!"

"But Mum . . ." wailed Josie, appalled by these uncompromising sentiments.

167

Her mother said, "You go into the country if you want; nothing to stop you. But I'm going back to Gert, with Pete and Roan." And so saying Marie swung Pete's pushchair round to face the direction of Stepney Green.

A decision of Marie's nine times out of ten became a decision of the whole family. And so, when Marie, Pete and Roan reappeared in Stepney Green, Josie, with the twins in their basinette, was close on her mother's heels.

Gert stared at them in surprise as they all trooped in. "Didn't expect you home so quick! What's the matter? Forget something?"

Marie started unstrapping Pete from his pushchair. "We've come back to be with you, Gert. You're right; no use letting old 'Itler turn you out from where you belong."

"Well, I won't make no bones about being glad to see you walk back through that door, Marie! But whether these little nippers should be here. . . ."

"My kiddies stay with me!" replied Marie shortly. "If we cops it, then we all cops it together."

Gert said nothing. From the very start she had been keen that the children should leave London, but Marie, like many other mothers, had taken a dim view of the government scheme to evacuate all the children into the country upon the outbreak of war. "I'd rather keep my kiddies home with me. Families shouldn't be split up, specially when there's danger."

Finally Marie had reluctantly agreed to Rhona being evacuated with her school. Marie, too, could have gone into the country with baby Pete, her youngest, but she had stood firm in her refusal to leave her chap, Mick, and their twenty-two-year-old Steve, Violet, and young Nelson aged fifteen. Josie, following her mother's example, had announced her intention of remaining in Stepney with her infant twins. Steve, who had fought with the International Brigade in Spain and knew what bombing civilians meant, had urged his mother to change her mind, but she wouldn't listen. Presently months of phoney war had made Marie, together with thousands of other parents, impatient over the long separation from offspring in the country. "When's the Gover'ment going to let me have my kiddie home? Took her away because of the bombing. We ain't had no blooming bombing and not going to get none if you ask me! Old 'Itler would've done it by now. I want my kiddie back!"

And Marie had decided that Rhona, after the summer holidays, should not return to the country village where she had languished over the past twelve months, but should instead stay home in London, and to hell with Authority! "Whose kiddie is she, anyway?"

Parents all over the metropolis had made the same decision. Now events had proved them drastically wrong.

Marie, having uncompromisingly made clear that there would be no desertion from Stepney until the outcome of the war had been settled one way or the other, turned her attention back to her chief worry; what had happened to her husband and daughter? "Tell you what, Gert. My Mick and Vi, I don't think they've been took away. If you ask me, they're up Brick Lane with Mick's mum and my Nelson."

Old Mrs Tooley Senior lived in Brick Lane, conveniently near St Jerome's Hospital where she worked as a night scrubber, going out every morning at half-past-five to scrub her appointed area of hospital floor. Since the first alerts had started, Nelson had moved in with his grandmother to keep her company, he being a competent, confident youth who could be relied upon to steer her safely through any emergency.

Gert shook her head. "No, ain't up Brick Lane. Young Nelson came round here this morning, just after you'd gone, asking after you. Hadn't got his dad, nor Violet with him. Thought they must be with you, Marie."

Josie said, "Bet you was right first time, Mum. Bet they've been took to some Rest Centre."

"Give 'em a day or two; they'll turn up orright," said Gert reassuringly. "Likely they was among that lot they say was brought away from Silvertown by boat, down the river. Don't know where they've ended up, do we?" She continued, determined to make the best of things, "Time we all had something to eat, anyhow. Have to be cold, got no gas, got no water, got no lights, got no nothing: but there's a yesterday's loaf and some cheese and a bit of cold bread pudding. That'll have to do."

The comfortless meal eaten, Josie said, jumping up, "Well I'm not sitting under these stairs tonight, I can tell you; so now I'm off to find a shelter for me and the twins, I am, even if you lot are staying here."

"Nelson says there's a lot of people been down that Barrico Hold last night," said Gert. "Big cellar under a warehouse; people used it last war, when the zepps came over. Nelson's taking Mrs T. down there tonight. I think you should go too, Marie."

"You come with me, Mum?" said Josie.

"Might as well go down there as any other hole," responded Marie lugubriously. "What about you though, Gert? Means leaving you on your jack if we all go."

"You go," said Gert. "Take the kiddies and go. I'll be orright." She forced a small, brave smile, repeating, "I'll be orright, Marie. Better hurry off. You want to be safe below ground before the sirens start up again, if they do!"

XXII

Odile alighted wearily from the bus which had brought her back to Stoke Hartwell village green after a day of doing nothing in particular at the estate agent's office further down in the town. Stoke Hartwell was far enough away from London to have escaped any bombs during the past two appalling nights but most people had been kept awake by the sound of the constant stream of bombers heading for the docks and by the echoing reverberation, like thunder on the horizon, of high explosives and many Stoke Hartwell families had slept in the solid underground bunker shelters that they had had installed in their gardens. Odile, Elizabeth and Mrs Busby had slept in theirs. Odile's mother, early on Saturday evening, together with Mrs Spurgeon, had been summoned from home and their mobile canteen called into active service. When darkness fell and the huge fire glow appeared in the sky over eastern London, Odile, staring at it in horror from an upstairs window at Maytrees, had groaned to herself, "Hope the old mater hasn't been sent anywhere in that direction!"

Now, as Odile walked despondently along Foxwarren Avenue, she heard herself being hailed by a voice she didn't recognize. She swung round; a tall figure, in blue dungarees filthy with soot and plaster dust, caught up with her. Hugo Spurgeon! His begrimed face crumpled with exhaustion, his eyes inflamed and swollen with grit, smoke and lack of sleep, he was almost unrecognizable as the Hugo she had formerly known; an elegant, good-looking, blond youth, affecting the heavy tortoiseshell spectacles, tweedy suits and languid style of an intellectual. Odile, remembering that Pam had told her that Hugo had gone to live in some quarter of darkest London, exclaimed, "Oh, Hugo, have you been in that awful bombing?"

"All alive and kicking, in spite of the lavish attentions of the *Reichsmarschall!*" croaked Hugo, his voice all but destroyed by the dust and smoke he had inhaled and swallowed. He added, wryly, "Sorry I look a trifle uncouth by Stoke Hartwell standards, I've been up to the eyes and ears in rubble clawing out buried people nonstop for the past forty-eight hours. I've snatched a couple of hours or so off to dash home and grab a few extra bits of clothing and have a decent crap and maybe a bath. You've still got running water here, I suppose? You've no notion what it's like in the East End: no water, no gas, no electricity; power stations out of action, gas and water mains smashed by bombs. Sheer chaos!"

Odile murmured, "Makes me feel pretty useless, staying put here, I must confess." She added, in self-defence, "I've tried to join the Free French, but my father won't let me."

"Join the bloody Free French? How fatuous!" exclaimed Hugo crisply. "What good can buggering about with the Free French do?" They walked a short distance in silence, Odile in considerable chagrin. Then Hugo said, "Tell you what; come back to the East End with me. You see, the people there, having had next to no shelters provided for them by officialdom, are flocking down into any cellars they can find and most of these are pretty indescribable. I've discovered one, a vast place, chock-full of people, appalling conditions and nobody in charge. You won't believe it till you see it." He paused to clear his dust-clogged throat. "Come and give a hand there, Odile. A damn sight more useful than the bloody Free French, I can tell you."

"I couldn't possibly cope with anything like that! I'm not trained for that sort of thing, you know."

Hugo, surveying Odile with an expression of near impatience, drew a long sigh. "No one's trained for what's happening now. The vast majority of the firemen fighting these terrific fires are aux-iliaries, never had to face anything remotely like this in their lives before! Even the regular Fire Brigade chaps haven't experienced

171

ordeals to compare with the past forty-eight hours! You've done First Aid training, you've obvious presence of mind. You can't duck out of giving a hand, Odile. It's your duty. It's up to us all to help, one way or another, at a time like this."

Odile reminded herself that Sybil Spurgeon never tired of telling people that her grandfather had been a bishop. Hugo, suddenly and most unexpectedly, seemed convincing as a bishop's great-grandson.

"Anyway," concluded Hugo, "I'm disappearing indoors for an hour or so and then I'll take you there. You better wear slacks. The older your clothes the more suitable, for it's a filthy hole, and bring a tooth-brush and your identity card and ration book. It may be several days before you get back. Pack yourself a Thermos flask of tea, some sandwiches, a torch, and smelling salts if you have them. I share a two-roomed flat in Wapping with an AFS bloke and, if you want, there'll be some sort of a bed there for you to doss in, if you get time to doss. See you later." And with that he left her.

Odile watched him turn up the drive to the Spurgeon residence and she told herself that he must be exaggerating: thousands of people all packed together in a cellar, without anyone whatever in charge, and only Hugo aware of the situation? No; that couldn't be so! And even if it were, what on earth could she do to help? She wouldn't know where to begin.

And then she thought of her recent talk with Jean-Paul. "Have you heard, by any chance, news of your friend, Fernand?" She had felt herself tremble as she had asked Jean-Paul the question, her French hesitant with fear.

"Nothing since the New Year, when we ran into one another in Paris, on leave. He'd been posted with the Third Army Group: Besson's lot, somewhere on the Rhine, I think. I myself was miles away in the First Army, under Blanchard. We got knocked to smithereens." Jean-Paul had paused, then continued, "War's such a fearful mix up and muddle, when it all starts to happen. You can't hope to know anything beyond your own little patch of chaos."

"Of course not." She had forced a smile. "Just thought I'd ask."

"To judge by the little one heard, Fernand's lot must have been up to their chins in it, and it's no use pretending, Odile, that fighting the Germans isn't a desperate business, because it is!"

Now, in her own way, it was her turn to become involved in this desperate business. She went indoors and up to her bedroom, put on an old pair of slacks and an old jacket, packed a small overnight bag, had a cup of tea and a bun, explained to her grandmother that she had been asked to help with rescue work and would be away for a night or two. "I wish I were young enough to give a decent hand," rejoined Mrs Busby. Then Hugo was ringing the doorbell.

"Ready?" he said. "Good. Let's go."

XXIII

"I can't see why nobody official knows about it!" Odile repeated as Hugo guided her through a complexity of back alleyways. He replied grimly, "Incredible, criminal as it may seem, nobody's given any real thought to providing adequate shelters for Londoners, and above all the East End, though it must have been perfectly obvious to any moronic civil servant planning for likely hostilities that the Nazis would, at some point, try to bomb our civilian population into demanding surrender. And now that the bombing had begun in earnest, it's natural that people, not having had decent shelters provided for them, are discovering places for themselves and crowding into them without bothering to consult officialdom."

"Do you think people will be forced into surrender?"

"God knows what'll happen if this kind of bombing continues! As far as I'm concerned, after what I've seen over the past forty-eight hours I'd rather die than surrender to the bloody Nazis. Still, I only speak for myself."

They reached a narrow street up which a steady stream of people, mostly women and the elderly, with babies, children, dogs, cats, pushchairs, heavy bags stuffed with food and personal oddments, blankets and old sacks, were pouring towards a yard at the further end. "This is it," said Hugo. He and Odile inched their way up the street: huge eight and ten-storey-high warehouses enclosing them like sheer, soot-blackened brick cliff faces; buildings of almost unbelievable solidity, erected in the first half of the previous century or thereabouts when Britannia herself had been equally rock-solid.

The yard into which the people were now pouring was tradition-ally known as Barrico Hold. Until very recently it had been used by the horse-drawn drays that had conveyed warehouse goods to and from the docks. It was obvious enough, from the odour of horse that hung around the place, that the animals had not long since been evacuated to other quarters, safe from the bombing. Odile thought to herself how typically English it was that the safety of horses should be considered of greater priority than that of mere humans!

But there was little time for thinking. More and more people were joining the jostling and struggling throng and Odile clutched hold of Hugo to keep herself from being separated from him by the sheer pressure of the crowd. "What an awful place to try to get away from if a bomb fell on it!" she exclaimed in horror. "What an awful place full stop," returned Hugo.

The cellar that was their goal belonged to the biggest warehouse of the lot and was reached by two ramps, used by the drays when they drove down into the cellar to load or unload. The entrance itself had now been partly sandbagged as a precaution against blast. Down the ramps shuffled the ever-swelling crowd. Odile, clinging even more tightly to Hugo, muttered, "And do you still mean to tell me there's nobody officially in charge down here, with all these people?"

"So far as I'm aware, nobody. When I came here last night with two stretcher-party blokes to pick up someone injured in this yard there was no sign of anyone in authority whatever."

Odile was beginning to feel badly scared by the realization of what she had let herself in for.

They were now in the cellar itself; not so much a cellar as, more properly, the undercroft of the warehouse, an area so vast in extent that it reminded Odile of the crypt of a cathedral. It certainly had the merit of seeming a good strong place in which to shelter, the vaulted roof being reinforced with great iron girders supported by massive piers, these forming a series of large double-storeyed storage bays, the upper storey gained by ramps.

The pallidly filtering daylight seeping from the entrance revealed huddled white-faced people seated, or lying, in the bays, as far as the eye could penetrate into the shadowy furthermost recesses of the place — though much space was also taken up by gigantic crates of margarine, barrels and tubs, tea chests, and rolls of newsprint. A drone of sound, distorted by the cellar's echo qualities, was punctuated by the sharp yelps of children and the wailing of infants and random outbursts of shouted altercation between people disputing over where they should sit.

Odile, still refusing to believe that there was no one in charge of this incredible catacomb, stared about her searching for somebody, anybody, of at least remotely official appearance.

"If I were you," Hugo was saying, "I'd make a tour of inspection of the place while there's still some light coming in to see by. I can spot a light bulb or two among those girders, but without juice they're not much use. And though you have a torch. . . ."

Odile, seized by wild panic, clutched at Hugo as if she were drowning. "Hugo, you're not leaving me!"

"Have to. I'm due back on duty. But you'll be all right. Here, have this. Make you look a bit more like a proper shelter marshal." As he spoke he removed his helmet and plopped it on Odile's head, almost extinguishing her. "Bit on the large side, but better than no badge of office at all."

"But you'll need it yourself, Hugo."

"Find myself another one. Or," he gave her a critical look, accompanied by a rather drab grin, "maybe I'll find a smaller one for you and have that one back. And now, having settled you in, I must fly. See you later."

"But Hugo!" She held on to him with fierce desperation, gazing at him imploringly. "Hugo, there must be thousands down here already, and it's not even late yet! I can't cope with. . . ."

"Keep your nerve, and you'll do fine," said Hugo. And with this he disengaged himself from her imploring hands and began shoving his way back through the throng.

Odile's heart hammered, her palms sweated, her head spun. But, somehow, she managed to nudge herself into acceptance of the simple fact that she must either sink to the floor with the vapours, like a Victorian heroine, or follow Hugo's advice and summon her nerve. But how to summon one's nerve? And then Fernand suddenly came into her mind: Fernand facing a flailing hurricane of Nazi tank fire. Good god, Fernand had had to confront that kind of horror; had maybe died in it, and here was she panicking at the mere notion of having to pass the night in what was obviously a most secure shelter, albeit an unsalubrious one. *Courage! Vive la France!* For an instant Fernand's dark eyes, full of quizzical half-mocking smile, confronted her; then the moment lost itself in resolution and she began to look around at the great huddle of people, trying to decide what her first step in shelter-marshalling should be.

But the sight of this tightly packed throng brought a fresh wave of dread sweeping over her. All very well to speak about keeping her nerve, but supposing . . . and she imagined the place in pitch darkness, as it apparently must be once daylight had gone, and a bomb dropping and all these people starting up in one wild panicking stampede. . . . It would be frightful; too frightful for words! And what use would she be?

She decided that her first step must be to make a tour of inspection, as Hugo had advised.

Her torch was a small one and its battery would most certainly not last all night. What she really needed, she thought, was a hurricane lamp. And she decided to dodge out to a row of little shops she and Hugo had passed on their way to the warehouse. Hurricane lamps were by now in short supply, but maybe she'd be lucky. And, thinking this, she fought her way from the cellar and up the street, in the face of the oncoming tide of people.

She found an ironmongery shop; fortunately, like many East End shops, it kept late hours. In the shop were two hurricane lamps. The shopkeeper also had paraffin. However, she doubted the wisdom of having a supply of paraffin with her in the cellar. In fact it was probably a criminal offence to take a can of paraffin into an air-raid shelter. She explained her predicament to the shopkeeper who, on hearing that she was a shelter marshal, proved most helpful, letting her buy two gallons of paraffin and a can to hold it and agreeing that she should leave it in his shop, calling in each evening to refill her lamps (for she had decided to buy the two) on her way to the warehouse.

With her lamps filled, two boxes of matches, one in each pocket, a spare battery for her torch and a heavy heart, Odile returned to the warehouse cellar, to find that the number of people down there had now doubled.

In preparation for her tour of inspection Odile concealed one lamp behind some tea chests (she didn't want anyone walking off with it) and lit the other. She wished to draw attention to herself: people must know who she was. The combination of tin helmet and hurricane lamp should attract attention.

But the ingrained British habit of refusing to notice people defeated Odile. The shelterers were either trying to snatch some sleep before the raiding began, or eating sandwiches or whatever they had brought with them, or chatting or arguing with their neighbours, or simply sitting in abject and exhausted apathy or dread of what the night was to bring. Odile swung her lamp; peered here, peered there. She gained the impression that even if she had been the Man in the Moon on the prowl nobody would have shown the slightest interest! Then, abruptly, as she inspected a particularly dark corner the beam of her lamp fell on a slumbering woman's face and the sleeper woke with a jerk, shrieking, "Who the hell's shining that searchlight on me?" "Sorry!" exclaimed the shaken Odile; the indignant woman looked ready to fly at her. "I didn't mean to wake you up."

"Cor blimey, who's this toff blown in?" jeered the roused slumberer, in a penetrating voice that had heads turning towards Odile from all directions. A stout elderly woman seated near the angry protester said, "Give it a rest, Marie! You'll wake the nippers!"

Odile said, "I'm the shelter marshal." Best get that established.

Everyone was looking at her now, or at least everyone in that quarter of the cellar: they were, however, far from friendly looks; hostility put a scowl on every face turned towards her. The East Enders had an ingrained suspicion of everything official at the best of times, and in this particular moment of crisis suspicion was mingled with active dislike. Correctly, everyone blamed officialdom for the lack of preparedness in the face of the Blitz and above all for the desperate shortage of prepared and organized deep shelters.

Odile sensed that, whatever she was, she mustn't be an official official! "I've just come along to help," she ventured. "Just a volunteer."

Antagonistic voices rasped at her from out of the shadows: "You're Civil Defence from the Town Hall, aintcha!"

"No I'm not !"

"Then what you wearing a Civil Defence tin hat for?"

"I borrowed it," retorted Odile, increasingly desperate. To her amazement this reply was greeted by guffaws of not ill-natured laughter.

"Borrow the lantern too, duck?" shouted a voice.

"No; I had to buy that."

"Hard luck!"

Odile suddenly realized why the ice had broken so abruptly and the temperature had risen so dramatically in her favour. It dawned upon her that "borrowing" was a gentle euphemism for nicking, or pinching; just as nicking and pinching were euphemisms for stealing. The notion of a toff young lady volunteer shelter marshal "borrowing" a Civil Defence helmet appealed.

Odile, heartened by this step towards acceptance, continued her inspection. Unfortunately, as she progressed from one part of the cellar to the next, she had to repeat the process of running the gauntlet. But ripples of toleration spread. An old man asked her, "Are you a nurse?" Without waiting for a reply he went on, "We can do with one down here! Last night they was passing out like flies, people was; coulda done with a nurse."

The more Odile saw of the cellar, the more horrified she became. There were, she calculated, a good fifty bays and each bay held something like an average of two hundred persons. The place had never been envisaged as a refuge for people and so, naturally enough, there was no provision for them, not even of the most rudimentary kind. Apart from the entrance there was no ventilation, nor was there any water supply, the dray horses having been watered at a drinking trough at the further end of the yard. There was, of course, no sanitation of any kind; somebody had procured five or six old buckets and these had been placed in one of the bays. They had not been cleaned out properly since the night before and the floor around was soaked with urine. Human faeces stank in dark corners and the sight and smell of this part of the cellar, as Odile swung her hurricane lamp around it, made her want to retch and she turned away both utterly nauseated and appalled.

Most of the people were lying or sitting on sacks or dirty blankets or old coats or newspapers spread on the floor itself; a few had brought folding stools or deck chairs, but these last aroused resentment because they took up too much room. Some had perched themselves upon crates or tea chests. Odile, as she continued to patrol up and down, did her best to see that gangways were kept open; she also stopped at frequent intervals to introduce herself and exchange a few words. She learned that many of the mothers with young children, and the older folk, had been in the cellar ever since Saturday afternoon and were existing on the tail ends of the sandwiches they had brought with them and bits and pieces of food and cold tea, or milk, fetched by relatives and neighbours who ventured outside. Others remained down there because they were bombed out and homeless and had nowhere else to go.

And all the time more and more people were thronging in; workers who had been at their jobs all day and who were now hurrying to be in the shelter before the raiding began once more. By seven-thirty there were, by Odile's conservative estimation, some ten to twelve thousand people down there, literally squeezed together like close-packed sprats; in darkness, except for individual electric torches, bicycle lamps and lanterns: random points of light that accentuated, rather than relieved, the surrounding dark.

Odile, her lantern throwing a circle of light, continued to patrol, eternally trying to persuade people to clear gangway spaces and keep them clear. Suddenly she saw two persons picking their way towards her, each carrying a powerful electric torch. Real shelter marshals coming to take over! She was flooded with relief. She'd stay on of course, to assist in any menial role they proposed to her; but thank god, she wouldn't have to be in charge!

The two now proved to be middle-aged women in nursing uniform. "Excuse me," said one of them, "you've been pointed out to us as the shelter marshal."

"Have you come to take over?" asked Odile, expectantly.

"Oh no! We're Red Cross. We were informed there was a large cellar hereabouts, full of people, so we thought we'd come to investigate and, if needed, give a hand."

"You're more than needed, you're essential!" Odile could have hugged them.

At this instant distant sirens began to wail and, in response, the people in the cellar raised a chorus of groans, moans and curses.

The sirens died away; a heavy silence fell over the cellar. Everyone was waiting for the sound of the bombers. Odile and the nurses conversed disjointedly in hasty undertones.

"How many people do you suppose are down here?"

Odile gave them her estimate. "Some of them have been here since Saturday. A lot of them are homeless."

"Is it an officially designated shelter?"

"I can't believe so. There seems to be no ARP personnel here. Nothing whatever's been done to prepare the place. There's not even any sanitation."

"It's a scandal!"

"It jolly well is!"

The three decided to set up a kind of HQ or First Aid base in a bay near the entrance. Nurse McTaggart, as she introduced herself, was installed here with a packing case as a table-cum-chair combined and Odile's second hurricane lamp. Her comrade, Nurse Wilmington, and Odile continued to tour round and round, each taking one half of the cellar. After every half-hour they returned to base to seize a brief rest and compare notes. The company of the two nurses was an enormous relief to Odile, though they were obviously just as badly scared by the place as she was.

The bombers were now droning and thudding in the sky: bombs screamed earthwards, crashes and crumps reverberated, some in the distance, some near at hand, one or two terrifyingly close. As the night drew on the cellar grew increasingly unspeakable. The great mass of people soon produced conditions of airless fug and raised temperature that had everyone gasping and sweating as though in the tropics. The stench of dirty bodies, old clothes, urine and human filth and, overall, the near-putrefying reek of a terrorized mass of people jammed together in a confined space running short of oxygen, produced an atmosphere that could be felt against the face and in the throat like a coating of fur. Nor was there any way of improving things. The cellar could not be further ventilated and the raid was so fierce that it would have been suicide to venture outside for fresh air.

Before long people were beginning to faint in large numbers. They were clumsily manhandled towards the First Aid base and placed near the entrance to revive them. Odile, at great personal risk, dashed across the yard to the water trough to fill a couple of flasks with water, with which the nurses wetted handkerchiefs to apply to the temples of the collapsed persons. Smelling salts were held under their noses, precious drops of water and sal volatile were forced between their lips. Directly the sufferers could stand, the next batch of limp and paper-white people were lugged and carried to the nurses.

Odile made two more dashes for water, aghast, herself, at her foolhardiness, but at least it gave her an opportunity to splash cold water in her own face and breathe fresh air for by this time she too was feeling dizzy, partly from lack of oxygen, partly from sheer exhaustion.

Between helping with fainted people she continued with her patrolling round the cellar, trying to keep the narrow gangways open; trying to comfort and cheer weeping mothers hopelessly nursing howling infants; doing her best to calm elderly people verging on becoming hysterical with nervous stress; rallying those approaching collapse. Most of those to whom she spoke attempted to respond with wan smiles and jokes: but there were thousands more she couldn't get anywhere near and, in any case, it seemed to Odile that these trivial efforts of hers were as insignificant a contribution as a spatter of odd drops of rain falling in a desert. The strength and endurance of these people could only come from themselves and, close as these thousands now were to breaking point, they did not break, but huddled, muffled in a basic stoicism, waiting for the all-clear and dawn.

The hours dragged past. The cellar became a place of purgatory, endurable only because the alternative, the furious raid outside, was unmitigated hell. At one point the exhausted Odile dropped down on a bale of newsprint and lurched into a spasm of uneasy sleep, jerking awake with a choking sensation and hammering head. She shook herself, got to her feet, took up her lamp and plodded off on a fresh session of patrolling. Then she sank down in another corner. Near her an old woman, her face grey and slimy with suffering and sweat, tried to croak out a lullaby to a tiny, wailing baby, its gaping pink mouth a symbol of pitiful, hopeless protest, a helpless seagull-like mewing coming from it.

And Odile was back at Bolbec again, exclaiming petulantly to Fernand, "What a sickening business it is, having to cut our holidays short because of Hitler!"

A year ago. Only a year ago! Odile looked back on that sunny Bolbec morning and it seemed a million years distant in time.

XXIV

The All-clear at last sounded. How Odile, exhausted to her very marrow, managed to lug herself from Barrico Hold to Pennyroyal Lane, the address of Hugo's flatlet in Wapping, she never knew; she had no memory of it. Fully clothed she fell on a divan bed and plunged into stunned insensibility.

When she surfaced again it was noon. She opened all the windows to let some air into the small, stuffy rooms. She still had a severe headache from last night's lack of oxygen in Barrico Hold. The windows overlooked an old, narrow street; one of the maze of little, ancient streets on the so-called Wapping Island between Shadwell and Wapping basins. The Pool of London lay less than a couple of hundred yards distant from the house. Sitting by a window, breathing so-called fresh air acrid with smoke from the still smouldering dockland fires, Odile ate the sandwiches she had packed before leaving home and which she had had neither time nor inclination to eat before now.

The sandwiches finished, Odile hurried out to seek the local Wardens' Post. She had not gone far before she found herself caught in a crowd of people staring at a long line of hearses drawn up outside a building that she realized must be the emergency mortuary used for bomb victims. A succession of Union Jack draped coffins were being carried out to the hearses. It was impossible to tell which of the people were the bereaved and which mere onlookers: the circumstances of wreckage and homelessness had made the wearing of mourning clothes impossible; people were thankful to have salvaged any clothes at all: many still wore the begrimed, plaster-whitened garments that they had been wearing at the time of being bombed. Nor did the watching faces reveal varying degrees of grief: all wore expressions of profound sorrow together with an immense, dignified solemnity, in marked and moving contrast to the begrimed and scarecrow clothes.

The coffins continued to be carried out, some large, some small, some very small indeed. Odile, like everyone else present, was now openly in tears.

At last all the hearses were laden, the relatives got into the funeral cars standing ready further up the street, the lengthy procession began to move away at a slow march pace. The onlookers maintained their silence, broken here and there by muffled sobs and weeping. There were no outbursts of any kind: the policemen present on duty stood, like everyone else, motionless, gazing at the procession; there was just the deep, heavy silence and the occasional sobbing and the slow and steady forward movement of the vehicles, the red, white and blue of the Union Jacks on the black hearses, the white faces of the mourners.

The last car in the procession finally passed from view. For a few moments more the crowd remained fixed; then, the silence unbroken, it began to dissolve.

At the Wardens' Post a grey-faced, bloodshot-eyed warden thrust a packet of cigarettes at Odile, followed up by a cup of tea into which he spooned an alarming quantity of sticky-sweet condensed milk. Having thus fortified her with what he clearly saw as fixed necessities, he listened to her account of the cellar.

"Well," he said when she at last paused to take a gulp of tea, "I've heard a bit about the place already, but seeing there's been no trouble there and I've had enough other things on my plate to keep me run off my plates, as you might say, I haven't been to take a dekko yet. However, after this I suppose I better."

"I hope you don't think I'm making a fuss about nothing," said Odile anxiously. "It really is pretty dreadful."

"Everything's pretty dreadful, gal." He pushed the cigarettes at her again. "Still, you got two nurses down there, you say?"

"Yes. Two Red Cross nurses."

"You're spoilt, you are!" He allowed himself a weary grin. He didn't ask her how she came to be shelter marshal. Odile had feared she might run into trouble for sporting a Civil Defence helmet when she didn't belong to Civil Defence, but as she talked to this exhausted man she realized that neither he nor anyone else would be wasting valuable time and breath querying the authenticity of persons who providentially arrived on the scene to give a helping hand.

Odile had decided to see the warden because Barrico Hold was in his area and she hoped that he would be of some assistance. However, apart from giving her a cup of tea and cigarettes and promising to look in at the cellar and telling her to keep her pecker up and remember there were plenty other shelters every bit as bad as hers it seemed there was little he could do at that juncture.

Odile trudged back to Barrico. It was already filling with people. She went to inspect the unspeakable buckets; they had not been emptied and she realized with a sense of strong self-reproach that, as shelter marshal, she was responsible for this horrible chore.

She padded round the corner to the ironmonger's shop and bought some rubber gloves and disinfectant, a strong broom and a shovel. She was too tired and too short of time to attempt to get these necessary supplies from an officialdom that, as likely as not, would in any case be unable to provide them.

She returned to the cellar, donned the rubber gloves and, steeling herself, began carrying out the buckets and emptying them into a drain in the yard. Whether or not the drain worked she had no idea:

that would be a problem for later! To her surprise and immense relief Hugo now arrived, come to see how she fared. He had also brought her a helmet that fitted her better. Without ado he helped her to empty the rest of the buckets down the drain and rinse them out with disinfectant and water from the horse trough. Then he helped shovel away the muck and filth plastering the bucket bay; all this, too, went down the drain. "Tomorrow I'll get the damn sanitary people to do something about this crap hole, even if it means going to the mayor in person!" The mayor, Frank Lewey, was already proving to be a kind of human tornado, a Herculean pillar of strength; the whole borough was flocking to him. Odile had visions of the mayor himself appearing to muck out the cellar. Meantime Hugo shovelled and Odile splashed disinfectant around and swept vigorously with the broom. They were finishing this horrible chore when the nurses arrived, hardly able to contain their joyful news: the Red Cross was sending down four chemical closets! Great was the jubilation.

Hugo returned to duty. The nurses had brought a primus stove and billy cans. Nurse McTaggart now fetched water from the trough and boiled it on the primus while Odile and Nurse Wilmington again resorted to the ironmonger to ask him if he had any old cans in which they might store water. After some moments' thought he went next door to a delicatessen store and the final outcome was that Odile and her companion returned to the cellar with six two-gallon cans formerly used for pickled gherkins and rollmops. The rest of the afternoon was spent fetching and boiling water and filling these cans, ready for the night. No chemical closets arrived; it was too much to hope that they would turn up so promptly.

Steadily the people flocked into the cellar. This evening, however, their hostile suspicion of Odile was replaced by greetings. She and her two nursing companions were seen as genuine in their desire to help and did not represent official officialdom: they were acceptable. The bustling, chatty and competent nurses were turned to with particular confidence. Once more Odile thanked her lucky stars that they had joined her.

The sirens wailed their warning at the usual hour; by that time the cellar was again unspeakably overcrowded. But tonight, when the bombers came thudding across the sky, they were greeted by tremendous salvoes of ack-ack fire, a deafening barking and crashing of guns that at first stunned the cellar into silence and then roused a wild cheer of approval. This approval, however, was not entirely universal; a few of the shelterers preferred the previous three nights of no ack-ack, as Odile discovered when she bent over one grey-headed woman and bawled enthusiastically, "A bit more like it, isn't it mother, to hear us answering back?" To this the matron, rolling up disgruntled eyes, replied, "No, I wish they'd hold their peace, them guns! All this noise, you can't hear the bombs coming!" However this was a minority view.

The raid, as usual, lasted until dawn. Last night's pattern of unbearable heat, stench, lack of oxygen and consequent stream of fainting persons repeated itself, though this time there was at least a slender supply of water for people to sip as they struggled to remain conscious. There was also a stirring of a community spirit. A girl named Connie offered to patrol with the second hurricane lamp, and a group of men responded to Odile's suggestion that they should, as a team, carry fainting persons to the First Aid post. The system worked well: Odile and Connie spotting those in need of air and attention and the men then coming to take the sufferers to the nurses.

At two in the morning, or thereabouts, a man in one of the bays on the left-hand side of the cellar had an epileptic fit. This caused a good deal of excitement and upheaval among the people around him. Odile with her lamp and Nurse Wilmington with her torch hurried to where he lay writhing and making hideous sounds as if he were in the clutches of a demon. As the nurse stooped over him and Odile tried simultaneously to hold her hurricane lamp up better to light the scene and to clear a breathing space for the epileptic, there came a most appalling explosion together with the reverberating shuddering of heavy masonry falling. This was followed by a moment's silence, and then people began to cry out and scream. Odile, her heart freezing, realized that the thing she most dreaded had happened; the cellar had received a direct hit.

A boy with a good electric torch was standing beside her; seizing his arm she told him to run as fast as he could to the Warden's Post and ask for help. As she spoke she removed her helmet and handed it to him; he jammed it on his head and disappeared. Odile then began struggling her way through the people, shouting at them to stay where they were and not to panic. Other voices took up the cry:

everyone miraculously did what they were told; there was no stampede.

Part of the roof at the back of the cellar had collapsed. A cloud of dust made it hard to see just how extensive the damage was but certainly people were trapped under the bent and twisted girders and fallen masonry and rubble: their cries could be heard and a pair of protruding legs, those of a woman, thrashed and kicked. Two men darted forward to pull her free, bloodstained and choking with dust. A child wailed for its vanished mother. Odile was afraid that inexpert attempts at rescue might bring more roof down. The nurses now came hastening: there was some rapid discussion. Nurse McTaggart then remained at the site of the disaster to give immediate treatment to those pulled from the rubble, Nurse Wilmington returned to the First Aid post to attend to less badly injured people while Connie and Odile moved everyone away from the area of the cellar surrounding the fallen roof, in case any more of the building should collapse.

The chief terror of everyone present was fire. Two Boy Scouts, disregarding the hazards of shrapnel, raced outside to see if the warehouse or neighbouring buildings were burning and returned with the assurance that they were not. This meant that the cellar need not be evacuated.

And now ARP wardens and rescue workers arrived and a team of surgeons and nurses from nearby St Jerome's. From the mass of wreckage, battered survivors and dead bodies were dug out, living and corpses alike smothered grey with plaster and resembling bundles of refuse rather than humans. Odile, instructed to stand by directing the light from her lamp in one hand and an electric torch in the other, watched with strange lack of feeling as surgeons performed emergency operations within feet of her. One man trapped under a girder had to have his leg amputated before he could be freed; a nurse held on to the leg, steadying it, and was then left holding it after it had been severed. She wrapped it in a cloth and walked briskly off with it under her arm, to dispose of it in due course in the hospital incinerator, Odile supposed. The matter of factness of everyone's behaviour astounded her; her own callousness startled her; above all the cool passivity of the shelterers themselves amazed Odile: they took without flinching the sights and sounds of violence and disaster.

Perhaps, mused Odile, humanity can only absorb and respond to so much shock, fear and distress, after which the senses dull and apathy sets in? Whatever the explanation, there was no panic or display of strong emotion at Barrico Hold that night. Even the relatives of the injured and dead remained almost woodenly restrained in their behaviour.

The thing which seemed to agitate the shelterers most was that there had been a man passing and repassing round amongst them, whispering first to this person, then to another, that none of this bombing need happen if only people would listen to Hitler's appeals to reason: Hitler had no wish to fight the English working people; he'd come to honourable terms with them whenever they wanted.

"Who was this man?" asked Odile.

"No idea! Couldn't see him properly. He took good care to keep in the shadows. But he was there orright," said Connie. "Oh yes," said another woman in great indignation. "Whispered the same thing to me! Blooming cheek; make terms with old 'Itler when he'd just blown a hole in the roof and killed a lot of people!"

When the All-clear at last sounded the throng of shelterers plodded up the ramps and into the night that was exchanging black darkness for the first dimly smudged grey of dawn: the sky to the east bright red, not from a premature sun, but from old and new fires in the docks.

Odile had decided that, however exhausted she felt, she would see that the damnable buckets were emptied and disinfected before she went off duty. The nurses agreed, and the three of them each dealt with two buckets apiece before bidding each other temporary farewell. Then Odile was stumbling and fumbling through streets changed afresh overnight from yesterday's distortions: new craters, new piles of rubble, houses and landmarks gone that had been standing a mere eight hours previously. A great gash had been torn out of a block of flats near Pennyroyal Lane: rescue teams, among them Hugo, were digging in the mass of rubble. On the pavement lay a row of stretchers ready for the injured and the dead. Two ambulance men came along the pavement carrying a sagging bloodstained blanket between them. Some victims could not even be brought out all in one piece, thought Odile, with a lurch at her stomach.

The Pennyroyal Lane house, thank God, stood. Sleep; then woken up by sirens wailing; early afternoon and a daylight raid starting. Odile hastily flung on slacks, sweater, shoes and helmet and raced downstairs, but the raid was a brief one and before she could start out for Barrico Hold the All-clear sounded. Odile had something to eat, then she tidied herself in preparation for her night's work, though why anyone should tidy up prior to going to a Barrico Hold she couldn't think; sheer force of habit! There was still no running water so she couldn't wash, but defiantly she pencilled her eyebrows and lipsticked her mouth. She was then ready to march back to her battle station.

As she closed the flat door behind her Hugo came groping up the stairs, lurching and swaying like a drunk, which in a sense he was: the drunkenness of complete exhaustion. "Poor Hugo, I hope you get a good long kip," sighed Odile.

"Give me the chance and I'd sleep for bloody ever," rejoined Hugo, disappearing into the flat.

At Barrico Hold the promised chemical closets hadn't yet arrived; the buckets still had to do duty. The damaged area of cellar had been cordoned off; while Odile was boiling the first billy can of water and wondering if the horse trough would be dry before the water supply was back to normal (supposing that such a thing should ever be!) the warden turned up to see how things were going. He reported that, incredibly, only ten people had lost their lives in last night's incident; at the time it had been feared it might be more. There had been over sixty people injured. The roof would be repaired as soon as possible; meanwhile the hole would provide a nice bit of extra ventilation! He added that he had arranged for a small First Aid and stretcher party to be on regular duty at the shelter henceforth: it was an ill-wind that blew nobody any good, and last night's bomb had brought the abysmal Barrico Hold to officialdom's notice. So, from now on, things should improve down there.

All this came as an immense relief to Odile. She recounted it with glee to the nurses when they arrived; they themselves were beaming with pride because they were staggering under the burden of twelve dozen rolls of lavatory paper, "A gift from the Red Cross." "Oh goody, goody! that's an improvement on newspaper and old paper bags!" cried Odile. "Luxury unheard of for most of 'em down here, even at the best of times, I daresay," said Nurse Wilmington. "Oh there's nothing better for morale than a touch of unexpected luxury!" responded Odile gaily.

She speculated as to whether the usual vast crowd would turn up following last night's bomb; the cellar had shown itself not immune to disaster. But, to her amazement, even more people seemed to be swarming in tonight and general conversation soon revealed that the fact that a direct hit had resulted in only *part* of the cellar roof collapsing, and not *all* of it, was seen as proof of the remarkable safety of the place.

In due course a stretcher party of six with one First Aid auxiliary as an extra presented themselves. The shelterers all began to cheer and shout, "Ready for another direct hit, are you?" "Blimey, a lot of optimists turned up tonight!" Connie came to Odile and declared herself ready to patrol again; other youngsters also offered to patrol and were disappointed by the shortage of hurricane lamps. Two or three of them went out and presently returned with lamps. Asked where they'd got them from they replied, "Borrowed 'em, same as our marshal borrowed her helmet."

Just before the sirens sounded, a couple of costermongers set up a little stall in one of the bays, selling pasties, pease pudding, cold bread pudding, and jam or pickle sandwiches. This enterprise met with instant acclaim and success.

The sirens wailed; died away. At once the first bombers were heard and, almost simultaneously, the ack-ack barrage blazed out. More bombers, more barrage; explosions, crashes; shrapnel showering like metallic hailstones. Then fire engine and ambulance bells clanging and shrilling in the distance; more heavy thumps, the cellar floor itself seeming to groan and vibrate; more and more fire bells clanging in the direction of Cable Street. After an hour of this, a wild looking messenger tumbled into Barrico Hold: the stretcher party to go over to Wapping Highway; everything ablaze. Shadwell Basin, St Katherine Dock; London Docks; people being roasted alive; never saw anything like it! And away he rushed to alert others.

The stretcher party, First Aid auxiliary and Nurse McTaggart decamped without delay. Nurse Wilmington thought it best to remain, in case Odile needed her in the shelter. Odile was thinking of Hugo, perhaps still sleeping the sleep of total exhaustion in Pennyroyal Lane. Given the chance she would have rushed over there herself, to rouse and save him. But this was out of the question; her duty held her at Barrico.

Sick with fear for Hugo, Odile continued with her patrolling of the aisles and bays, chatting to people who couldn't sleep because of the terrifying sounds of the raid; trying, herself, to maintain an untroubled, cheerful exterior, in spite of being privately racked with anxiety. At one point, as she turned away from a bay and moved further along the shadowy aisle, a deeper shadow suddenly seemed to materialize at her side and someone half whispered, half muttered into her ear, close enough for her to feel a warm breath on her cheek, "You don't have to go through all this, you know. Jews are the only ones who'll benefit from this. Hitler doesn't want to fight *you*." Odile turned sharply; she sensed, rather than saw, a man, his face totally shaded by a hat brim; then he was gone, vanishing into the labyrinth of shadows and bays.

Shortly before four o'clock a woman started to call out in one of the bays; Connie went to inspect and returned at once to say that it was "Bad Betty having her baby."

Why Betty was Bad was not clear; what was apparent was that this was far from being her first child and Odile and Nurse Wilmington had scarcely reached her before the baby literally shot out, like a cork fired from a pop-gun. Odile raced for hot water, Connie drew up a corral of experienced matrons around the interesting scene to preserve a semblance of privacy, and Betty, soon comfortable and suckling the new arrival, a boy, announced in shrill and happy tones that he would be called Barry, for Barrico Hold.

The All-clear sounded. Odile, leaving the buckets to be emptied later and Nurse Wilmington to call an ambulance to remove Betty and her baby to a safer part of the world, raced out into the thin early morning darkness. Over Wapping the enormous clouds of inky smoke, burnished and stabbed with fire, told their own tale. Odile, exhausted as she was by her night in the cellar, ran, gasping and near sobbing, through the streets towards Wapping Island.

The Island had been cordoned off, not only by the police, but by fire itself: fire raging, crackling, shooting and leaping, with vast swirling smoke curtains and an endless glittering spray of sparks. The luridly lit scene was a chaos of tormented chiaroscuro: firehoses, pumps; firemen, perched atop ladders, silhouetted black against the fire glow, directing glittering jets of water that vanished into the flames; ambulances, rescue workers, police; nuns with little baskets running round popping morsels of food into the mouths of men who couldn't stop to eat; two priests kneeling over a dying fireman lying on the pavement, a rosary clutched in hands black and charred; a glimpse of a red hot cable lashing through the air like a striking snake, whizzing overhead, out of nowhere and falling, writhing, into the smoke from which it had suddenly darted, a danger over before Odile, standing beneath it, had had time to realize that she was in peril; and then the fire draught, that had tossed the cable aloft, suddenly parting the smoke clouds to give a view of St Katherine Dock incandescent, the Thames blood red, Tower Bridge luridly illuminated by the glare: the Pool, the very omphalos, transfixed by fire.

And then a loud wail in her ear, and Odile turned her head to find, distant from her own face by a few inches, the face of a woman who had been in Barrico Hold that night; Odile had had twice to ask her to clear a gangway and for that reason remembered her bony features and dirty scalp clamped with metal clip curlers; a work-worn face, contorted now into a mask of anguish and rage; a face of tragedy that Odile recognized from a totally different context, a theatre in Paris two Easters back when Paxinou had led a Greek company, rending her audience from head to foot as she had turned upon them shrieking woe and fury; as the cockney face turned now and the cockney voice, cracked and demented, wailed broken imprecation and lament.

XXV

A police sergeant told Odile that if she had nothing better to do than stand and stare she should shove back to whatever her job was in Civil Defence. She gazed blankly up into his face, which was scarlet and running with sweat from the heat of the fire. "I've been on duty all night. And my friend's there in a flat in Pennyroyal Lane," she said at last, finding, in her dazed condition, that it was difficult to put words together.

"Can't get in, can't get out for the fires. Took every living soul away in barges. The place is an inferno, as you can see for yourself," he replied, his manner softening.

"Where have they taken them?"

"That I can't say. You better get up the Mile End Road to the People's Palace and enquire there."

Penniless, hungry, exhausted and desperately anxious for Hugo, Odile, like an automaton, began walking in the direction of the Mile End Road. When she reached there the early light revealed the fresh tide of homeless, heading up the broad highway, all with fixed, desperate expressions: bewildered wanderers, utterly dispossessed. The majority, like Odile, had the People's Palace for their immediate objective. Built to provide culture (music, theatre, highbrow cinema, lectures) for the East End workers, whose patronage of these intellectual treats had been somewhat sparse, the place in its new guise as Stepney Town Hall was now besieged day and night by crowds in quest of anything and everything from a quiet place where a bombed-out mother might feed her baby and change its nappy, to a lift in a commandeered corporation dustcart to a mainline railway station, *en route* for an evacuee billet in the country.

The approach to the People's Palace had become a pram park: all the hoodless, paint-peeling, glandered, staggered, spavined, broken-down basinettes in the East End, from the looks of it, thought Odile, dumped and left by the great tide of mothers with babies who had flocked there, over the past four days, asking to be evacuated into the country and who, unable to take prams with them, had simply abandoned them. Upon this collection of knackered vehicles the newly bombed-out, trekking away from the East End, fell without compunction and, piling their bags, pillowcases and, in many instances, pets into the basinette of their choice marched off with it. Odile watched one woman wheel away a heavy old pram that must have transported tribes of babies in its day and now accommodated a canary in a cage one end, a mongrel dog sitting bolt upright and looking very pleased with himself at the other, and a bundle of clothes and oddments wrapped up in an old tablecloth stuffed between them. Where they were bound for heaven only knew and Odile, watching them jog away, found herself laughing and crying simultaneously.

She then joined the huge queue of people, numbers of them still in their night clothes, shuffling up the steps to the main entrance. Many of them came from Wapping and, listening to their disjointed exchanges of conversation, Odile gleaned some idea of their ordeal by fire. Showers of incendiary bombs had been dropped at the start of the raid, starting up furious blazes that rapidly had got out of control: "Yes, and he knew which warehouses to drop 'em on, didn't he? All the ones wot would go up like a lighted bonfire with paraffin on it. Jerry knew! There's been spies at work in the docks orright."

"Yes, Jerry knew that Wapping was full of pepper and spice; explodes of itself, all that stuff does, when it gets hot enough."

Much of Wapping Isle's fascination had lain in its historical associations with the spice trade: the very names of its ancient streets and lanes spoke of the Orient and of aromatic voyagings: Cinnamon Street, Ship Place, Penang Street, Malay Street, Pearl Street.

"All ablaze before they had time to get the pumps on it. Took us all off in barges and boats; hundreds of families. Just said, get out for yer lives! They say hundreds more've died, trying to escape. My sister and her kiddies, I ain't seen them anywhere yet. I'm afraid to ask, I tell you that, mate. Afraid to ask!"

"Say ever so many firemen have died in it too. Firemen and rescue men. Terrible!"

Odile's heart stood still. She could scarcely breathe for wild anxiety.

"Jerry knows what he's up to orright! He puts out special markers. That first mass murder raid, Sat'dy arternoon, started by him dropping a marker over Bow Creek. Lots of people saw it. Saw it myself. Wondered what it was. Little round shiny white thing, like a balloon."

"Well whatever it was, those bastards put the sign of death over Bow Creek and Silvertown. Same as they did over us in Wapping last night."

"All I hope is we give it 'em back! Fucking mass murder for them, mate, same as they're dishing out to us."

Inside the building all was a confusion of people wanting safe places to go to, travelling money, tickets, clothes, food. Some were searching for missing relatives; some, bombed-out, had found themselves an empty room or flat but needed furniture; some, unable to write, wanted letters or postcards written for them; some needed help with application forms. Tales of tragedy were being told, as plain matter of fact, on every side.

The queue of people searching for news of missing relatives was a long one; Odile stood in it for an hour, at last to be told that it was too early for detailed information about people rescued from Wapping Island the previous night. Wearily she turned away and went down to the basement where breakfasts of tea and bread and jam were being served, free of charge.

Odile took her breakfast at one of the long, clothless trestle tables where everyone sat squeezed together, many devouring their food as if they hadn't eaten for days, which, not infrequently, was probably the case. Among them was a family Odile recognized from Barrico; they greeted her with jammy grins. "What you doing 'ere, mate?"

"Burned out."

"Cor, your house copped it too?" And a new bond of friendship existed.

As she ate she listened to talk going on around her about recent German propaganda broadcasts to the British.

"You hear what that Lord Haw-Haw's been saying? How the German bombers will smash Stepney? Smash Stepney and make the dirty Jews and cockneys run like rabbits!"

"That's that Joyce, Lord Haw-Haw is. I remember him coming down here in Mosley's loud-speaker van, year before the war; up the Burdett Road I heard him over the loudspeaker saying how we was all being exploited by the Jews. Blackshirt candidate for Stepney borough council, he was."

"Yes! Come bottom of the bleeding poll!"

"Finish up bottom of the bleeding poll this time too, mate!"

And there were great guffaws of laughter.

Her breakfast eaten, Odile once again joined the queue of people enquiring after the missing; perhaps now some news would have come through. The queue was longer than ever and it seemed an eternity of shuffling forward, inch by inch, before she at last reached the clerk at the desk, only to be directed to another queue dealing with Wapping casualties. Another hour of wearisome shuffling forward, waiting and shuffling again. Then came an air-raid and the queuing people were advised to go down to the basement.

The All-clear sounded. News percolated that free midday dinners were now being served to the homeless. Odile joined the dinner queue and in due course sat down to her first hot meal since Monday midday: shepherd's pie and tinned peas, followed by suet pudding and treacle, Though greatly reminiscent of school dinners, it was more than welcome to Odile.

Then, still determined to learn what had happened to Hugo, she went back upstairs to join the enquiry queue once again. This time, to her total horror, she was advised to make enquiries at the local emergency mortuary.

Blindly she stumbled away, making for the exit into the street. Somebody caught her elbow and swung her round. "Odo!"

It was Hugo.

Odile burst into tears and fell into his arms. "Oh Hugo, I've just been told to look for you in the mortuary!" Hugo, hugging her to him, said wryly, "Not there yet!" He added, as Odile wiped her eyes and sniffed, "Mercifully, I'd reported back on duty. Now I'm trying to find out where they've taken Geoff."

Geoff was the AFS chap who shared the flat and whom Odile had not yet met.

Sensing, from Hugo's tone, that he was in a state of desperate anxiety akin to the one she had just passed through on his behalf, she said, "He'll suddenly grab you by the elbow, just like you just grabbed mine." And she attempted an encouraging smile through her barely dried tears, a smile which sadly faded when she saw the expression in Hugo's eyes.

"I don't think so," he said. "I know for a fact Geoff's gravely injured and taken to hospital; trouble is, I don't know which one."

Odile, at a loss what to say further, stood silent. Hugo, glancing at his wristwatch, muttered, "Anyhow, it's back on duty for me now. Maybe I'll run into someone who'll be able to tell me something."

"I better get back on duty too," murmured Odile.

They walked out into the Mile End Road and the multitude of prams. The homeless were still plodding westward, towards the People's Palace. Side by side, in silence, Odile and Hugo trudged eastward to their respective sticking places.

XXVI

Each morning, as Marie and her brood returned from Barrico Hold to Stepney Green, a ritual conversation was conducted. Rhona, with morbid relish, would exclaim, "Cor, hope Auntie Gert's not been blown up while we've been down the 'ole!" To which Josie retorted,

"Hope not, too! If she has, we *are* going to be in a nice way, with nowhere to go."

But Aunt Gert's shop would be found still standing, the shattered glass of its shop door replaced by stout boarding and on the boarding written, in red, white and blue chalk, OPEN AS USUAL. Inside, Gert was in her lifelong place, in her chair behind the counter, but round her now had been constructed a kind of wooden igloo of sturdy beams and slabs, known by all and sundry as her "rabbit hutch". It had been built for her by the local ARP warden, Jack Trotter. "Said sitting under the stairs was no good. Says if the house gets blown down with me sitting inside this, I can go on sitting till he comes and winkles me out."

Marie had a ritual question for Gert each morning: "My Vi and my chap not turned up, I s'pose?" And Gert's answer was always, "No, not yet, Marie."

Rhona, after one such early morning exchange between her mother and aunt, sighed, "Got the electric light back, got the water back, got the gas back, but still ain't got dad and Vi back."

"Been took a long way off, that's what." Marie shook her head despondently, her dark eyes heavy with brooding. "Know it in my bones, I do; a bleeding great long way off. Gawd knows when they'll be home. That's war for yer!"

Gradually her bewildered resignation gave way to anger. "Think the Gover'ment would've sent 'em back by now, wouldn't you? And no thought of how *I'm* to manage. Carting off the family bread-winner. . . ."

"You'll have to go up the People's Palace and ask, Marie. Tell 'em you been bombed out and your chap's missing and you've run out money and. . . ."

"Not missing! Not come back," corrected Marie.

"They're helping everyone that's been bombed out. Money, clothes. Give you vouchers to spend in the shops," continued Gert.

"We needn't never starve, Aunt Gert," piped Rhona, eagerly surveying the sweets on display. "Got all these choc'lits an' things to eat!"

"Oh you won't starve, duck! But your mum'll have to find something to tide her over till your dad comes home," explained Gert reassuringly.

At the People's Palace, Marie had a baffling interview with an

unfortunate woman clerk who, after some five minutes of preliminary question and answer during which each side thoroughly
confused the other, said, "Let's start again, shall we Mrs . . . er . . .
Tooley?" She glanced, as she spoke, at the name and address which
she had written on the appropriate filing form. "You say your
husband and daughter are missing, is that it?"

"No, not missing. Not been fetched back."

"Fetched back from where?"

"Where the Government took 'em, see?"

"Were they evacuated?"

"Well, you might call it that I s'pose. Anyway they was took into
the country to one of them Rest Centres and they ain't come back."

"Can you give me a few more particulars? What makes you think
they went to a Rest Centre?"

"Must've done, mustn't they? Where else? They was seen
running from our house to a shelter, but they never went in the
shelter, see? 'Cos I went looking for 'em later, see? And then I got
carted off to a Rest Centre myself and I was bloody lucky not to get
carted right off into the country too, same as they was, mate!"

"Where was this shelter where they were last seen?"

"They wasn't seen in no bleeding shelter. I keep telling you that!
They was seen going up the street to the shelter but they didn't go in
it; they must've gone in some other one, see? And then got took to a
Rest Centre, same as I was, only a different one, and then they got
took into the country and the bleeding Government ain't fetched
'em back and here I am with two little kiddies and no chap and
no money, ain't I?"

"And they were last seen going up the street to a shelter?"

"Yes. But they didn't go in it. 'Cos my neighbour was in it all
afternoon and she never seen 'em so they never could've gone in that
one, see? Must've gone somewhere else, see?"

"Where exactly did all this happen, Mrs Tooley?"

"Up Silvertown, Saturday afternoon."

"Silvertown? But you've given your address as Stepney Green."

"That's where I'm living now I been bombed out. My home's in
— my home *was* in — " Marie corrected herself — "Lucknow
Passage, Silvertown."

"And that's where they were last seen?"

"That's what I keep telling you!"

"Then I'm afraid I can't help you, Mrs Tooley. It's not in the borough of Stepney. We can help you, here, with advice on how to get financial help from the Assistance Board and how to claim for war damage; we can help you if you want to get your children into the country, we can help you with anything like that because you are living in Stepney, but your husband and daughter went missing in another borough and I can't help you there. I suggest you go to the police station nearest your old home to enquire."

"They ain't missing: they've gone off and they ain't come back!" intoned Marie at full pitch. "Cor luv-a-duck I never knew such a wicked state of affairs," she added, addressing the world at large. "Government carts your husband and daughter away to Gawd knows where, and then you can't get nobody to help you get 'em back!" And Marie, all indignation, marched out from the People's Palace and away down Burdett Road, exclaiming aloud to nobody, "Gawd save me from Town Halls! Useless lot of people!"

The police station near her old home was a good three miles distant. Marie, penniless and unable to spend any money on bus fares, plodded along with the weary but unrelenting determination of the East End poor. The wrecked and blackened landscape appalled her; aflame, by night, as she had last seen it, all had been terrifying; now, by daylight, it was utter desolation. A nauseating reek of dead fire impregnated the very air; the charred corpse of dockland stinking.

She reached her destination. The sergeant on duty in the office knew her by sight, as she knew him, for a few years back her Steve had been sent down, as Marie put it, for assaulting him. However Marie knew the police knew that Steve wasn't really a villain, just rather too handy at duffing up coppers: and anyway he'd got it out of his system now, with all that fighting in Spain! So when the sergeant said, "Hello mother, what can I do for you?" his manner was far from unfriendly and Marie, unfolding her tale, did so with a feeling of confidence that here was somebody who would at least show a bit of sense.

The police, however, knew nothing of Mick Tooley and Violet. "I don't like suggesting this, mother, but there are still a number of unidentified bodies in the mortuary. I think you should take a look at them," said the sergeant.

Marie shot him an appalled look. "But my Vi's not dead! Neither of 'em's dead! They've gone off somewhere and not come back, that's all."

"That may very well be, mother, but all the same, unpleasant as it is, you better go along to take a look. If you don't find them there it'll be helping us, and other people like yourself, you see. Helps us to know who we haven't got in the mortuary just as much as who we have got, if you get my meaning." As he spoke he glanced at his steadily lengthening list of persons reported missing since the mass raiding started.

The mortuary, a few streets distant, was a sooty brick building with an old-fashioned bell that you pulled, setting up a lugubrious tolling. A man in a red rubber apron opened the door. Marie stammered who she was and why she had come. The rubber-aproned man repeated, thoughtfully, "A middle-aged man and a girl of nineteen?"

"Yes, about my height she is, beautiful black hair, natural ringlets, dark eyes, lovely filbert nails. An' my chap: big bloke, dark hair, big nose."

"Wait here. Call you in a minute. Sit down while you wait."

He showed her into a small office. She sank onto a hard chair, her head spinning. After a bit the man returned and led her into a large white-tiled room smelling of powerful disinfectant, with four metal trolleys standing in the centre, each with a sheet-draped figure lying on it. "These are the only ones we got that could answer to the people you're looking for, mother." He carefully twitched back the sheet from the first trolley, to reveal the face only: a man, gashed, battered, one eye gone, the face greenish, but, even in this disfigured state, definitely not to be identified as Mick. "No." The next was a long-faced man, like a waxwork, mouth and tight-closed eyes sunk deep. "No!" Then a girl, button-nosed with congealed blood oozed from her nostrils. "No!" The next face was disfigured almost beyond recognition, but the ears were pierced with small gold rings and that definitely was not Vi. "No. None of 'em's mine, thank Gawd! Some poor soul's, but not mine." He led her back to the office; she stumbled down a step and he took her arm, supporting her. "I knew they wasn't here," said Marie. "They're not dead; just been took off, and not come back yet. They'll turn up."

"Hope so, missus. Keep your fingers crossed and your pecker up." He let her out and she went back to the police station. "No, not there," she informed the sergeant. "I didn't expect 'em to be." The sergeant took full descriptions of both Mick and Vi. "We'll circulate all this." He also took Marie's present address. "How's that son of yours, wounded in Spain? Fighting fit again?" "Yes. He's some-where in the country now, training monkeys; least, that's what he's told our Nelson. Not chimps. Gorillas. What for, search me!"

The sergeant, passing no comment upon this remarkable in-formation, went in the next room and returned with ten bob.

"There you are, mother, something from the station charity box: don't say thank you; I know you'll be short for a week or two till you get things sorted out. Let us know if your husband and daughter turn up, won't you? Good luck!"

Marie, quite bowled over by this generosity, went off in tears. The afternoon had been a severe strain, one way and another. But at least she now had money. She allowed herself a bus ride back to Stepney Green.

At Gert's everything was in a state of panic. Rhona had taken the twins and Pete out in the basinette for an airing and had not returned. Josie had searched the neighbouring streets for them but without result. It was now past five o'clock, only two hours to go to siren time. Josie, her eyes brimming with tears, couldn't think what to do next and Marie, worn out by her afternoon's experien-ces, was in no state to take cool decisions. She began to rant at Josie for having allowed the children out. Gert, all a-tremble like an anxious jelly, sat in her wooden box saying nothing; occasion-ally opening her mouth to speak, then thinking better of it and closing it again.

In the middle of this commotion Rhona and the basinette returned. Rhona brought the pram into the yard, her face was scarlet with exertion and excitement. Marie immediately darted at her and began to shake and pound her. "You naughty gal! Where you been?" Marie's cuffs and blows were particularly hearty because of her strength of feelings of joy and relief at having the children back.

At this point there was a loud metallic clang! followed by a howl: Pete had extricated himself from his straps and had fallen headfirst out of the pram, clutching a large tin of corned beef. "Cor, luv-a-duck! What's he got there?"

"He found it, didncha Pete?" shrieked Rhona. Pete, howling and bloody-nosed from the fall but still clutching the tin, aware that it was somehow a matter for prestige and pride, was picked up by Marie. "Here, stop crying, you're not hurt! Just hit yer nose, that's all. Come on, where d'you get that tin?"

"He found it, found lots of tins. Look!" Rhona began taking tins from out of the well of the pram: golden syrup, peaches, pineapple, peas, stewed steak, sardines. She unstrapped the twins and lifted them out and from under them brought packets of biscuits, bottles of pop, a jar of jam, a packet of sugar. Meantime Pete, who had forgotten his nose in his excitement, thrust the tin of corned beef in Marie's face, shouting triumphant jabberwocky that was his infant variety of speech.

"Strewth!" said Marie. "Where d'you get all that from, Roan?"

"Pete found it! He did, straight! He ran off, while we was in the Rec, and then I heard him calling and there he was in the bushes with all these here things!"

"Don't believe you! You nicked 'em from a bombed-out shop!"

"I never!" declared Rhona.

"Don't believe you," repeated Marie. "You nicked this lot from some place that's been bombed."

"But we never, did we Pete?"

"What's the good of asking him? He's too little to be able to say. Cor, makes me go hot and cold to think what'd happen if a copper'd nabbed you with that lot. Be sent straight to prison, you would."

"Copper wasn't to know what was in the pram," replied Rhona. "I sat old Pete and the twins on top of the stuff. Sat tight and said nothing, all the way home, didncha Pete, like I told you."

"Well," said the aghast Gert, recovering speech at last, "no use thinking of returning the stuff to its rightful owner, whoever that might be, because it'd be letting the cat out of the bag and get me a shocking bad name among the neighbours. But don't you let me ever catch you on the nick like this again, young Rhona, or I'll hand you over to the police myself. That's looting, that is! Get sent to prison for life, for looting."

"Well, best get moving down Barrico Hold," said Josie. "No time to waste if we're to be there safe before them sirens go off."

Last minute preparations were hastily made. Marie cut corned beef sandwiches and packed them in a bag with the bottles of pop for Rhona and Pete ("Might as well use 'em now we got 'em, but don't think I'm pleased at what you done, Roan, because I'm not. You're a wicked gal, you are!"), Josie packed blankets, nappies, milk bottles. At last the caravanserai was ready to depart and off they went, reaching Barrico Hold just in time to beat the sirens.

They now had their "own places" at Barrico, in a bay in the

corner near the First Aid Post. Here among tea chests lay Mrs Tooley Senior, in what was now recognized as her customary and rightful niche; she was wrapped in an old plaid shawl and reclined on an improvised couch of newspaper and sacks. Nelson sat next to her. His pal, Lenny Schreiber, was perched on the tea chests reading an evening newspaper.

"All turn into sardines if we come down here often enough," said Marie, squeezing herself beside Mrs Tooley. Rhona somehow inserted herself next to Marie. Josie wriggled and wedged herself into another slot and the twins and Pete, wrapped up in bits of ragged coverlet, were accommodated on available lap space.

"Heard anything of Mick and Vi?" asked old Mrs Tooley, her invariable greeting to Marie each evening. As she spoke she stared despondently into Marie's face, reading the answer there.

At that moment the sirens began to wail. "There goes Moaning Minnie!" said a woman who was, literally, sitting on Marie's feet. "Don't get no rest, do we?" "Don't never get no rest in this hard world, mate," returned Marie. "Still, it's better down here tonight, with the lights on," said the woman. "Better than being all in the dark." At this point the ack-ack guns crashed into action.

Mrs Tooley took a couple of earplugs from her pocket. "Got these at the 'orspittal!" she shouted at Marie. "Don't want to risk what little hearing I got left! Deaf enough already!" She inserted the plugs in her ears. The woman sitting on Marie's feet bawled, "Don't stopper me up with them things, mate! With your ears unstoppered you can hear if it's quiet, and you know it *is* quiet, and you can rest in peace. With them things in, you'd never know if you was copping it or if you wasn't!" Marie agreed.

The night's raiding had got off to a frenzied start; bombs screeched, guns slammed. The shelterers huddled speechless, grimly weathering the storm. Fortunately Pete and the twins, worn out by the excitements of their day, were now deep in slumber.

The raid remained intense until between ten and eleven when it eased off for a while and the vast bulk of people in the shelter dropped into restless, snatchy sleep. At midnight the guns crashed into chorus again and another noisy and frightening hour ensued; then once more the raid eased off.

By this time the heat and stench had become considerable, though the hole in the roof undoubtedly assisted ventilation and the chemical closets were a vast improvement on the buckets. Pete and the twins woke up thirsty and sticky; the twins were given their milk bottles and Pete and Rhona some of the infamous pop. Marie produced the corned beef sandwiches and Nelson said appreciatively, "Cor, where d'you get that, Mum?"

"Aunt Gert had some left from before rationing," said Marie. "Found the tin in her cupboard." At the same time Marie gave Rhona a look that said that though the lie was necessary, it didn't mean that lying was right at any old time, because it wasn't; furthermore, added the look, though the corned beef was now being eaten by everyone and enjoyed, that didn't mean that it had been all right to steal it in the first place. Far from it: Rhona had been downright wicked! *And* had come dangerously near to being sent to prison.

Rhona received this message and, with her mouth full of sandwich, did her best to assume a chastened expression. However she recognized that her mother, though still maintaining a pious front, was no longer really angry; Marie never remained angry with her children for long. Furthermore the corned beef had undeniably saved the family from what must otherwise have been a hungry night. So, after a few moments of concentrated sandwich munching, Rhona murmured to her mother, under cover of general conversation, "I only done it to keep us from starving, Mum, till Dad gets back."

For the second time within the past twelve hours Marie's eyes filled with a gush of tears at the sheer decency of the human heart. The sergeant who had given her ten bob, no mean sum, from the police station poor-box, realizing her problems without her Mick; and now this little girl running the risk of being nabbed by the coppers in order that the family shouldn't go hungry! It was wonderful, really, thought Marie, how basically good people were, even in a world like this one!

Mrs Tooley at this point removed her ear plugs in order to join conversation and asked, "Where d'you get the corned beef, Marie? Them bombed-out vouchers?"

"Bombed-out who?"

"Vouchers. Coupons. They give 'em you, up the People's Palace and you get free food with 'em from the grocer, if you been bombed out."

"You should've found out about that, Mum; you've been bombed out," said Josie.

"Didn't tell me a thing up the People's Palace," growled Marie. "Useless!"

"Did you try the Assistance?" queried Mrs Tooley. "They're helping the bombed-out."

"No, didn't go to them. I was looking for my Mick and my Vi. No time to bother with Assistance."

"Wasn't anyone able to tell you where they might've got to, Mum?" asked Josie. She was deeply attached to her sister Violet.

"No." Marie shook her head vehemently. "People's Palace don't know. Silvertown police don't know. But one thing's for certain: they aren't in the mortuary." Marie paused, the memory of the mortuary still haunting her. She added, "Whoever they was, poor, poor creatures that I looked at, they wasn't my Mick and Vi."

"You didn't go to the mortuary Mum!" exclaimed Josie.

"Yes."

"By yourself, Marie? Oh Marie! Should've asked someone to go with you. Asked me. I wouldn't have liked it, but I'd've gone." Mrs Tooley was deeply upset at the thought of what Marie had been through. "Go to the mortuary all by yourself!"

"I'd've gone with you, Mum," said Nelson. "Only had to ask." He, too, stared at Marie with deep concern.

"Didn't know I was going, till the last minute," rejoined Marie. "And like I said, they weren't there. Knew they wouldn't be."

"If they're in the country, why doesn't Vi send us a postcard?" asked Rhona plaintively. "We always send her a postcard when we go hopping."

"How can she send us a postcard?" retorted Marie. "One of the troubles is, see, Vi doesn't know where to write. Doesn't even know Lucknow's gone, I daresay."

This idea had only that moment come to Marie; it shot into her mind like a searchlight suddenly switched on, illuminating the darkness, and it struck her immediately that this *must* be the explanation of Mick and Vi's disappearance. Her face shining with relief at having found the answer at last, she continued, triumphantly embroidering her theme, "Sent a postcard to me at Lucknow, I bet she has! Then the Post Office has to find me, don't it? When you come to think of it, we're silly to expect to have heard from 'em yet."

"But what makes you so sure they're in the country, Marie?" asked Mrs Tooley.

"Where else can they be? Gone off somewhere, haven't they? Else they'd be here, wouldn't they? Only possible thing is they been took out to the country by the Government and ain't back yet. You wait; they'll just walk in some time, just walk in!" Marie's face shone with conviction.

"Seems ridiculous to me," said Mrs Tooley. "Take people off like that!"

"In the middle of these awful air-raids, I suppose you can understand it," suggested Josie. "Get as many people away as possible."

"What, and leave me and my kiddies bombed out with no money and no chap, no wage packet coming in nor nothing? Bleeding sinful!" snorted Marie.

"If you want a scrubbing job at St Jerome's I daresay you can have one, Marie. Help tide you over till Mick comes back," said Mrs Tooley. "Quid a week. We're short of a scrubber or two at the moment, what with a few going off to a safe place with their little 'uns, and others getting blown up, and goodness knows what all."

The guns started up again and Mrs Tooley put the plugs back in her ears. For the next three and a half hours there was a great deal of noise, making it very difficult to sleep. The heat and stuffiness in the shelter grew overpowering and Marie began to gasp for air. She was thankful when, just after five, the All-clear sounded. Some twenty minutes or so later Mrs Tooley began to heave and sigh in preparation for setting off for St Jerome's, where she started her scrubbing at six o'clock sharp.

Marie decided to join her: two hours scrubbing a morning, from six to eight every day of the week, Sundays included, at a pound a week, wasn't bad going in Marie's world, and it was a regular job, and Mrs Tooley said you got a ten-minute break and a cup of tea at seven o'clock. Mrs Tooley went on to other cleaning jobs after she'd finished at the hospital; Marie thought that she, too, might see if she could find a bit of extra work during the day, now that Gert and Josie were available to keep an eye on Pete.

Nelson Tooley and Lenny Schreiber left Barrico Hold with Mrs Tooley and Marie; they were messengers with Civil Defence and both on early duty roster.

It was still dark outside. A stick of bombs had fallen in a neighbouring alley a few hours earlier; a hostel had been hit and there was the now all too familiar welter of ambulances, stretchers and stretcher-bearers, wardens, rescue parties, a medical team doing emergency surgery on the pavement by the light of dimmed torches. The three Tooleys and Lenny picked their way through the confusion and debris. As they moved away from the scene, the two boys walking ahead of the women, a man flitted out of the shadows, muttering to Mrs Tooley and Marie as he brushed across their path, "Know how to stop it, don't you Mother? Revolt against the government; it's all run by the Jews. Why should you die for the Jews? Surrender, and all this will stop. Hitler's not against you, only the Jews." Then the speaker was gone again, as swiftly and silently as he had appeared.

"What did he say?" asked Mrs Tooley, who hadn't caught it all.

"Something about revolting and surrendering," said Marie. "Must be drunk!"

"That's him was in the shelter, other night, in the dark, telling the same thing to the people down there," said Mrs Tooley. "Trouble is, he slips away before you can even tell who he is."

They caught up the two boys and told them about it. Lenny said, "There's one or two of 'em around. If one of 'em ever tries whispering that sort of poison in my ear. . . ."

"Revolt!" said Mrs Tooley. "Where's the sense in it? Out of the frying pan into the bleeding fire, mate. That's all revolting would do for me."

"Same here," agreed Marie. "Not that I don't feel like it at times, but who's going to cook the bleeding dinner if I revolt?"

"Who takes over if we revolt? 'Itler?"

"'Itler and old Goring," said Nelson. "Have to give the salute when they come goose-stepping up Whitechapel Road!"

"Won't catch me doing that," said Mrs Tooley.

"Nor me!" said Marie.

"They've ways of making you," said Lenny.

"Let 'em bleeding try," said Marie belligerently.

"That's what they're doing now. All this bombing," said Nelson. "Supposed to make us East-Enders give in. March to Downing Street and tell Churchill if he don't give in we'll chuck him out. See?"

"Well, 'Itler's certainly going the right way about making us lot turn awkward," said Mrs Tooley, "but we ain't going to be pointing in the direction he hopes."

"I can be really awkward when I want," said Marie warningly.

"And don't we know it!" said Nelson, laughing.

"Look, he's knocked my house down!" said Marie. "I saw my house with all that red hot stuff crashing down on it. It had copped it before that, but that last lot finished it right off. Put pay to my home, it did. My wedding picture and all! You trying to tell me that 'Itler thinks I'm going to salute him after that? Bloke must be round the bleeding bend if he can't see that's not the right way to go about making me salute him!"

They all burst into a roar of laughter. A copper, standing on point duty in the roadway at Gardner's Corner, watched them plugging along the pavement towards him guffawing their heads off: not drunk or disorderly, but getting up cockney steam for a fight. The name "'Itler" reached him, followed by more yells of ribald laughter, and the copper, with a grin of his own under the chin strap of his helmet, obligingly held the early morning market traffic up for them and beckoned the four madly hilarious belligerents to cross the road.

XXVII

Maytrees
Foxwarren Avenue
Stoke Hartwell
Tuesday September 17 1940

My dear Morwenna,

Your mother, not having time to write herself, asks me to pen you a line. She and Sybil Spurgeon are out all night every night and much of the day with their mobile canteen and what little time they have at home is spent in trying to catch up with their sleep. I gather they have been sent to some hot spots "up at the Front" and have had several close shaves, tho' make light of it all in order not to worry me unduly. Your poor father, too, is being kept in the dark about their adventures; he thinks they spend their time sorting clothes for refugees: your mother says he must be

207

spared anxiety about his family, he's under enough stress as it is. He hasn't been home since the Blitz began; he spends his time performing emergency operations "round the clock"; when he telephones he sounds worn out. He assures me there is WORSE TO COME! I always think that the main trouble with the French is they *must* look on the dark side of things. And see where it's landed them! Expect defeat and you'll be defeated! Half the battle is keeping that silver lining in view!

Of course nothing is ever dropped near Stoke Hartwell; all the same Elizabeth and I sleep in the shelter as your father advised us. He says you never can tell if the Boche might offload a spare bomb on the way home and I think that this *is* sound advice: "Never trust a German" is my motto. We each have a bottom bunk and make ourselves quite cosy. We can hear all the racket going on over London, like distant thunder, and see the sky red with fire. I never dreamed I'd live to see London burning! Terrible to witness, even if a long way off. Occasionally our local ack-ack opens up on a stray raider and we feel we're in it a bit ourselves! But mostly ours is a Home Front War.

The gardener has gone in munitions *and* joined the Home Guard, so Elizabeth and I have had to take over the garden. She is ambitious and thinks we should keep *hens*. She even speaks of a goat! We've had a bumper fruit crop — all this marvellous weather and still continuing. Elizabeth has made over six hundred pounds of jam! All the fruit from local gardens and the sugar supplied by the Townswomen's Guild; our own ration wouldn't stretch to make a decent apple-tart. The good soul jams all day long every day; the place is like a jam factory. Of course every ounce of the jam is handed in for national use. Elizabeth sees it as her major war effort.

Three afternoons a week I make camouflage netting at the Parish Hall. I've taken this over from your mother. Rather a beastly job because of all the loose hemp; air thick with it, worse than filling feather mattresses. However it's a job that must be done by somebody. And two evenings a week I do house-to-house collecting for National Savings, and, of course, any spare moment I have is spent knitting comforts for the troops. So you see, though getting on in years, Elizabeth and I aren't slacking!

Odile is shelter-marshalling in Wapping. I admire her pluck, and yours too for sticking to your job in Cuddwell which, though not really near the docks, isn't all that far from the "fun and games"; much closer to the firing line than is comfortable and I know your dear mother worries about you both as I do, but there you are there's a war on! Your father has *not* been told about Odile. A pc arrived from her this morning saying so far she is safe and well but cannot telephone because all the lines are out of action. She will drop you a pc when she finds a moment to spare.

Well dear, let us hear a word or two from you when you have the time. What a world we live in! Everybody anxious about everyone else and nobody with the time or opportunity to keep in touch. And all due to that wretched little man Hitler! Still he will grow tired of causing all this trouble when at last he realizes that we British aren't going to give in, however great a nuisance he makes of himself. Until then, we must all hang on.

With much love, dear, from all of us at Maytrees,
Grandma

PS   What did you think of last Sunday's magnificent score, RAF v Luftwaffe, one hundred and eighty-three for forty! Howzzatt!! And Goering thought he'd walk all over us!

18 September

Still in this same god-forsaken spot,
    my little love,
Where nothing of any interest has happened since the reign of King Canute. The handful of half-wit natives who inhabit these parts at first looked upon us as a diversion, but are now bored by our presence. They had (one senses) hoped for the arrival of Germans by now and a spot of fire and slaughter to liven things up. But no; life here goes on in the same old way, just as it has since the year dot. Unless I had seen this place for myself I would never have believed that anything so utterly out of this world could have survived into the twentieth century; not in England, anyway. Hitherto I've always looked on Parrocks as out of this world, but Parrocks is metropolitan sophistication compared with this! Enough said of this tedious subject.

I'm afraid that by changing the subject I can only produce melancholy news. I've just learned, in a letter from my father, that poor Homer was shot down on his first combat sortie and never baled out. It's wretched. However, he showed marvellous spirit in joining us in the hour of need (I really mean that; not merely voicing a dreary old cliché, though it sounds like one). Nevertheless, that said, poor chap! But what's the use of lamenting? We may all be dead this time next week. Giles, as you may well imagine, is frightfully cut up, but in no wise dampened by it so far as fighting nerve goes: has shot down his first German, thereby avenging Homer (he says) and intends considerably increasing his score before he's through! Meanwhile Jos continues in the heroic vein, bagging 'em left, right and centre. Sowersbys seem to take to air battle! No desire whatever to try it myself though, as I think I've remarked before and now repeat in a loud voice. You have to be awfully careful what you say these days. A friend of mine remarked casually that he knew a little Polish and has now been whisked off to do liaison work with a crowd of Poles, none of whom speaks a word of English, while his Polish in reality consists of little more than being able to say, "Am I on the right train for Warsaw?" Which is a fat lot of help for anyone!

Enough for now; this isn't the season for expansive letter-writing. *Au fond* I'm ravaged with worrying about *you*: it was admirable of you to insist upon returning to London, but God! how I wish you had remained at Parrocks! I know I've said this before and you must be bored by it; and I've had your earnest assurances that Cuddwell is sleepy and peaceful and your concerns are entirely those of the parish pump. As war is notoriously composed of nine-tenths boredom and one-tenth frenzy I will do my best to believe that the Blitz raging a few miles from Cuddwell leaves you perfectly unscathed. May it remain that way!

Write to me whenever you can find a moment. Your letters, my darling little sprite, are the only things that keep me sane. Oh, for the fossil room! F.

> 47 Rushton Road
> Cuddwell, London E
> Thurs. Sept. 19th

Dear Pam,

Long time since we've exchanged news — though I heard all about you from Boggy when she and I were at Parrocks. What a wizard girl she is! By the way, I'm keeping the Sowersby side of my life rather private from the folk at Stoke Hartwell. However as all hell has broken loose from the skies since then I haven't seen anything of my family and everyone's far too busy to bother about where, or how, I spent my week's holiday.

Frank Sowersby writes repeatedly asking me if I'm safe. Seeing that he's stationed somewhere on the sea coast (from what I gather) awaiting the arrival of the enemy any moment, I don't want to worry him, so I write back that nothing disturbs the peace and quiet of Cuddwell: miles from dockland; all sitting back and basking in the incredible Indian summer etc. But to tell you the truth, Jampot love, we're having one hell of a battering! The Blitz, when it started, concentrated on the docks and East End; they're still receiving heavy attention, but now the whole of east and south-east London has come under bombardment. We're having the most ghastly time here in Cuddwell with things called land mines. These are truly terrible inventions: made specifically for high-powered destruction of military objectives, but now being used by the Germans on the homes of civilians! The damage done is unspeakable. I spent the greater part of today visiting scenes of disaster: entire streets gone; everywhere people digging out bodies, stretchers and big paper bags ready on the pavement. Teams of extra rescue workers have been brought in to help from other parts of London. An emergency Town Council meeting was held this evening; we had prayers for the injured and homeless, and two minutes' silence for those who had lost their lives. The mayor, in a short speech, nearly broke down; he has lost his brother. Everyone in an unconcealed state of sorrow at the distress all around us.

The past fortnight, since I returned from Parrocks, has been the most unbelievable in my whole life; in fact it doesn't seem to belong to real life at all — like being suddenly switched on to a totally different, surrealistic plane of existence. You lie down at night never knowing if you'll live to see next morning; each time the air-raid warning sounds you wonder if you'll still be around to hear the All-clear; nothing any longer retains the slightest element of certainty. Landscapes change within hours, people you've seen and spoken to regular as clockwork are suddenly gone for ever. It's beyond description.

I must admit I'm a bit ashamed of my whopping fibs to Frank that all is peace and quiet here, though it's done purely to set his heart at rest; he's obviously appalled at the thought of anything awful happening to me. But at the same time, to be honest Jampot, I *do* resent being treated like some child who should be evacuated into the country to be out of danger! I wouldn't stand for that when the war broke out; why should I stand for it now? He even went to the extent, behind my back, of asking his mother to try to persuade me to remain at Parrocks until things had quietened down. Of course, as far as I was concerned it just wasn't on! What was I supposed to do with myself at Parrocks, I wonder? Play dolls in the nursery, maybe! I'm afraid all this has rankled with me rather, but I keep this reaction to myself and forgive him because it's simply the result of his being so much in love.

I'm sure the reason why Odo has gone to Wapping to shelter-marshal (have you heard about that? If not, well, that's what she's done!) is mainly because Papa refused to let her join the Free French — not the sort of thing he wanted his nice young daughter mixed up in! Ridiculous, and insulting to Odo — she's old enough to be able to take care of herself and make her own decisions! I suppose it hasn't crossed poor father's mind that if she had been born a boy she'd have been called up by now and in one of the Services having to fight.

Mrs Cowper, my landlady, and I (and her daughter Posy when she's not on duty at her Warden's post) spend our nights in the Anderson shelter in the back garden, which is where I'm now writing this, by the light of a very feeble electric torch. So forgive, if I'm indecipherable! The sirens have just been wailing their heads off; we're in for another night of it. Mrs Cowper worries all the time about her son; she's not set eyes on him since the Blitz began; when he went off he warned her not to expect him back till she saw him: said it was going to be no picnic. It seems he's spending his days and nights repairing gas mains; miles and miles of London's gas pipes have been seriously damaged and great risks taken in mending them — gasmen just as heroic as firemen and ARP. All sorts of wonderful acts of courage are going on that we never hear about; unless you're in journalism yourself you can have no idea of the heavy censorship imposed on news, whether for papers or broadcasting. I spend a lot of my time collecting news items that never appear in print: mustn't let the enemy know a thing about what's been hit, or the damage done—with the result that we're all kept as much in the dark as the other side.

If you ever come home on a spot of off-duty let me know and we'll try to meet, though as I'm now the only reporter left on this rag any time-off for me is pretty well non-existent. Gosh, as I wrote that, you never heard such a fearful crashing and rumbling in your life! Another land mine by the sound of it, and *much* too close for comfort. This Anderson is well sunk in the ground and covered with earth and sandbags, but I assure you everything *quaked*!

I suppose you're nice and quiet down in the country, though Boggy says it's pretty gruelling work one way and another. Well, cheerio for now; have two police-court cases to write up yet. Drop me a line when you're able.

Lots of love, Morwenna

XXVIII

"Come along, Mr Plumbton, bath time!"

Pam Spurgeon, assuming her most cheerful voice and manner, breezed into cubicle Number Two where Pongo Plumbton lay on his bed, under cradles and sheet; his noseless, lipless non-face of, at last beginning to granulate, flesh bright scarlet against the white pillow, his left empty eye socket covered by a dressing, his right, lidless eye, gazing vacantly at nothing.

Dreading the ordeal that lay ahead, but resolutely concealing her qualms, Pam bent over him, repeating encouragingly, "Come along, Mr Plumbton, it's bath time, and after our bath the specialists are coming round to see how we're shaping up for surgery; so we'll have to get moving to be ready in time for them, shan't we!"

He made an indistinct sound of disgruntlement, almost of protest, his eye waking up to give her an antagonistic glare. She knew that at this moment he hated her as he hated her every morning when she came brightly to his bedside announcing that the daily torture of the saline bath had once more to be endured.

Wendover now came lolloping in behind Pam, her big fat breasts quivering beneath her apron bib, her fob watch's animated dangling emphasizing the pulsations of her too-abundant flesh. Her elephantine advance brought increased apprehension into Flight Lieutenant Plumbton's eye and he even attempted to move his head slightly. "Ready for our bath are we, Mr Plumbton?" boomed Wendover.

"Where are the orderlies?" Pam enquired of Wendover. "On their way?"

"Coming along the passage. Lovely chrysanths, Mr Plumbton; Lady Grace does you proud! Quite her blue-eyed boy, aren't you?" And Wendover wagged her head roguishly to indicate the bowl of pink and bronze chrysanthemums and autumn gold leaves that stood on the bedside locker.

The nurses stationed themselves one each side of the bed and began removing the sheet and cradles as two male orderlies entered to help lift and convey the patient to the saline bath that had been prepared, deeply filled with tepid water into which Wendover, a practised hand now, had cheerfully chucked several fistfuls of salt, declaring "That's about right I should say!" her days of cautious measuring long since behind her.

The reason why the saline bath was an ordeal for patients and nurses alike was because, apart from the initial overall pain of the raw body's immersion, the dressings that covered the remaining ungranulated areas were invariably stuck to the flesh and these had to be removed; a long and excruciating process that took place whilst the patient lay in the water, the orderlies supporting him and the nurses removing the dressings. For the patient it was physical torture, for the nurses it was nervous torment. As Boggy put it, "No one enjoys hurting anybody and we're obliged to hurt the poor blokes."

As Pam and Wendover between them performed this agonizing ritual, steeling themselves to ignore the sounds of animal protest and pain that were wrenched from their patient whenever they pulled away a particularly obstinate piece of dressing, Pam thought of the letter she had received from Morwenna that morning, "I suppose you're nice and quiet down in the country, though Boggy says it's pretty gruelling work one way and another." Boggy certainly specialized in the art of understatement, commented Pam to herself. No part of the treatment of a patient in the burns unit could be done with speed; everything took an age to do, everything caused the patient agony and distressed the nurse involved. For Pam, nursing Pongo was proving, above all other cases, a searing experience.

Pongo, in the face of fearful odds and buttressed by ceaseless dedicated nursing and, above all, the devoted vigilance of Sister Sunflower, had miraculously survived the perilous first six weeks of his fight back from the brink of death. He no longer made noises of asking for Poppy nor did his surviving eye indicate that he was watching or waiting for her; its expression, when not racked by pain or fierce with the irritability that chronic severe suffering generates, was one of patient resignation under infinite sorrow, like the gaze of a hospitalized baby deprived of its mother; no longer crying for her, having reached a point where hope itself is extinguished. This look of utter hopelessness went to Pam's heart and she found herself lavishing a care and tenderness upon Pongo that she reserved for him and him alone. She had made up her mind that, as long as *she* was on the ward, Pongo Plumbton was jolly well not going to give up the ghost, and told him so in no uncertain terms.

Now, as he writhed and twitched and moaned in the bath Pam did her best to help him with encouraging words and sounds of sympathy. Wendover joined in with exclamations of "Hold hard!" and "Whoa there!"; no need for her to be forever telling people about the gymkhana cups she had carried off in the happy days before the war; though it must have been hard on the pony that had her on his back, as Nurse Spry had unkindly commented after having heard for the umpteenth time how Wendover and steed had won the sandbag race.

At last the bath was over for another twenty-four hours and the wet, raw body was moved back to the cubicle, there to be patted dry by Pam and Wendover using a succession of pieces of sterile gauze: another long and painful process. Next came the reapplication of dressings, which junior probationers were not allowed to do. Wendover cleaned the emptied bath with carbolic and prepared it for the next patient; Pam fetched milk for Pongo and fed it to him through a straw while the second-year nurse who "specialled" him (the nurses' term for individual case assignments, another privilege denied junior probationers) set to work with the dressings, her every movement followed by Pam's attentive and envious eyes: first, with a pair of forceps, a piece of *tulle gras* (thick, grease-impregnated gauze) was picked out of the dressing box, then another pair of forceps was taken in the other hand and, using both forceps, the *tulle gras* was spread over the area being dressed. Over this was sprinkled sulphanilamide powder, then a piece of saline-soaked gauze was placed on top of this. That dressing was then complete and the next area had to be dealt with. All this, again, took a long time and Pam had finished giving Pongo his milk well before the other nurse was through. She left the cubicle wondering to herself, for the hundredth time, whether any of these young men would have wished to survive being shot down in flames had they known what prolonged purgatory lay ahead of them and also marvelling to herself, again for the hundredth time, at the basic stoicism with which they bore it all.

"How's Pongo?" Boggy asked Pam, over their midday meal. Boggy, over the past week or so, had been kept busy with patients other than Pongo and had had little opportunity to see him. "Giles and I had a good chin wag about this Jos and Poppy thing the other evening, I told you what an absolutely wizard time . . .?"

"Yes yes, told me all about that," said Pam with a grin. Boggy had managed a date in Town with Giles a day or two back and had never stopped talking about it since, always concluding her recitation with, "The poor boy so badly needs cheering up, after losing his oldest friend." Now Boggy continued, between mouthfuls of cottage pie, "Giles is awfully worldly wise; he thinks it best to let things take their course between Jos and Poppy, and if there's a divorce, well then there's a divorce, though I feel that Parrocks wouldn't take kindly to that; though as for Pongo, in some ways a fresh start mightn't be . . ." At this point Wendover joined them, and Pam gave Boggy a hard kick under the table to warn her to shut up. Wendover, however, was keen to talk about Pongo herself, saying anxiously, "On the subject of Pongo Plumbton . . ."

"Oh yes? I was just asking Pam how he's getting along," said Boggy lightly. Wendover continued, "Not getting along as well as he should be, if you ask me. I know he's granulating nicely, and all that, but basically I don't think his morale is up to par."

"Heavens Wendover, considering the hell he's been through he's absolutely marvellous!" exclaimed Pam, leaping to Pongo's defence. Wendover, who, like the rest of the staff, knew nothing of the Poppy-Jos affair and supposed that Mrs Plumbton never visited because she was one of those wives who couldn't stomach her husband's mutilations, said, "Yes yes, he's been wonderfully brave, but I'm sure that never having a wife to comfort him. . . ." She helped herself to a reckless quantity of boiled potatoes. "Let's hope to heaven they never ration these!" she added inconsequentially; then, returning to her original subject, "All I can say is that I saw the consultants confabbing with Sister Sunflower in the corridor after they'd seen Pongo and *I* thought they were all looking a trifle bleak. And if you ask me," she took an enormous forkful of food, "it's Pongo's morale that's his Achilles heel; and so I'm just wondering if . . ." Another immense forkful.

"Wondering what?" asked Boggy.

"Yes, out with it Wendover; what's the bright idea? We've a tutorial in ten minutes and you'll never down all those spuds let alone tell us what you're wondering if you don't get a move on," said Pam.

"What I'm trying to say," retorted Wendover, once she could speak again, "is that don't you think it might be a nice morale-boosting gesture for him if we clubbed together and presented Pongo with a get-well mascot? All us juniors club together and get him something to sort of jolly him up?"

"Such as what?"

"Well, have to put our heads together, shan't we?" responded Wendover.

The other juniors, when told of Wendover's idea, thought it a splendid one. Accordingly they all clubbed together and bought a toy koala bear, painted its black nose bright red, bandaged a pad of cotton wool over its left eye and hung a card round its neck saying, "Get moving! Sunflower's after you!" This they presented to Pongo, seating the bear on his locker. Pongo's eye brightened; if he could have smiled he would have been smiling. "Now mind you're jolly well soon up and about!" chorused the juniors, gathered in a knot round his bed. They then blew Pongo kisses as they left the cubicle.

"Hope the Sunflower doesn't take it amiss," murmured Pam.

"Oh don't be silly, anyone can see it's only a well intended joke!" retorted Wendover.

It therefore came as a nasty jolt when, almost immediately afterwards, they were told that Sister Sunflower wished to see them in her office.

Trembling in their shoes they filed into Sister's presence. She was seated behind her desk, writing her report on the day that had just ended in the ward; when the juniors had all squeezed into the office and had closed the door Sister Sunflower laid down her pen and rose to her feet.

"Now nurses, we're all short of time as usual; you have your suppers to hurry away to and I have my report to complete, but I'm away the morrow morn for a wee break and I don't wish to leave without a few words of thanks for the excellent hard work ye've all put in on this ward over the past weeks and the dedication you've shown to the patients. As junior probationers ye've none of ye had to do anything verra splendid, but I need not tell ye that, in nurrsing, the humblest task is as important as any other and that therefore the success we've had so far in bringing these patients of ours along their hard road of recovery has been as much due to the efforts of you junior nurrses as to any other members of staff. Thank you nurses; and now good night to ye!"

"Good night Sister; thank *you*!" came the chorus in reply. Sister Sunflower, with one of her dazzling smiles (rarely bestowed upon juniors) moved to the door, opened it and, with a gracious inclination of the Sunflower cap, showed them out.

"Say what you like, that woman really is a winner!" declared Boggy as they hurried towards the dining-hall.

"Certainly is! Absolute sport!"

Pam, as she consumed her bread-and-dripping and cocoa, began composing in her mind the letter she would write to Morwenna before going to bed. "Yes, you're right; it *is* gruelling work here; but it's worth it!"

XXIX

Morwenna, walking to work over pavements crunching with glass, as she now walked every morning, thought (as she so often thought) of her bromide letters to Frank. "Don't worry darling, nothing ever happens in Cuddwell!" She hurried up the High Street between roofless and windowless buildings; her usual route across the market square had been cordoned off, an exploded gas main had ripped the ground open during the night; a particularly frightful one for Cuddwell with bombs and land mines in every direction. The town centre lay gutted; Morwenna, taking a tortuous route to the *Gazette*, found St John's church in ruins, together with a row of shops. She more or less anticipated finding that the *Gazette* premises had been blown down too, but though the building had lost most of its windows it stood otherwise unscathed.

Mr Walters was at his desk as usual, though looking haggard. The rest of the staff, too, had survived what Mr Macpherson was calling "Jerry's special bonanza for Cuddwell"; several of them had had their homes damaged. Morwenna handed in her weekend's copy, checked the diary for the day's assignments and then hurried out to interview the Reverend Stephen Pottall, who was searching in the rubble of what had yesterday been the nave of his church. His usual benign geniality was replaced by thunderous denunciation. "This is the work of heathen! Barbarians! It's incredibly difficult to preach the Christian virtue of turning the other cheek under these circumstances. Incredibly difficult!"

"How will you carry on with your church services, Mr Pottall? I mean, people will still need to be married and have baptisms and funerals."

"I shall beg the use of a neighbouring church; my fellow clergy will be generous, I have no doubt. And as soon as is humanly possible we shall rebuild, of course. I refuse to be subdued by Satan."

"May I quote you as saying that, Mr Pottall, please?"

"By all means! The historic parish church of Cuddwell refuses to be subdued by Satan! We have stood here since the time of Ethelred the Unready. Who is Hitler, to think he'll destroy us?"

Morwenna jotted frenetically in her notebook and then raced away to cover a morning of police-court. At midday she tore home to Rushton Road for her dinner, then sped off to interview the organizing secretary of Cuddwell War Weapons Week. Following this came a long afternoon of routine local calls. It was not until well after six that she arrived back at the *Gazette* premises. Walters and Macpherson were still at their desks; they worked long hours now that the editorial staff was so drastically reduced. Morwenna sat herself down to write copy in the reporters' room (as sole surviving reporter she now used Gilroy's desk by the window and his typewriter); she handed in the finished stuff to Mr Macpherson. Mr Walters called her into his office to ask her about the War Weapons Week interview and to discuss a plan of campaign for the *Gazette* in support of WWW, as he liked to call it. By now it was past seven o'clock; he took a sheaf of papers from a drawer and said, "There's also going to be another National Savings drive and the Town Clerk's cooked up some borough shindigs for it and would like a splash story to get people initially excited. He's written some notes for Press attention, so you can take that little lot home with you,

Miss Doochamp, and read it over at your leisure, if you can still remember what leisure means, and write me a splash letting me have it by Wednesday afternoon; and don't try writing it during Wednesday dinner hour and fetching me in half a column with gravy all over it like young Stoppard used to." So saying Mr Walters handed Morwenna the Town Clerk's notes and as he did so the sirens started their wailing. "Strewth," said Mr Walters. "Jerry's early tonight! You better pack up and go home, Miss Doochamp. Hope we don't have a repeat performance of last night."

Morwenna returned to the reporters' room and began tidying odds and ends of things away; she hated a littered desk. Then she put on her coat, took up her notebook, handbag, and the Town Clerk's papers and, calling "good night" to Messrs Walters and Macpherson, she ran downstairs and was just reaching the bottom of the final flight to the ground floor when everything abruptly heeled over and she fell into a pit of rumbling, deafening oblivion.

Then it was pitch black, she couldn't breathe, something hard stuck into her back, other hard objects pinned her legs and right shoulder down. She tried to move her head, it throbbed and ached violently. She thought she must be in bed, having some shocking nightmare, and she tried to will herself to sit up and struggle out of it; but she couldn't move and after a few more desperate attempts it dawned on her that this terrible thing was real: she had been bombed and was now trapped and entombed under the rubble.

A sensation of total terror seized her. She started to scream but she was so choked with dust that her screams turned to coughing. She choked and gasped for breath. "Oh God am I going to die? Oh let me die quickly God if I'm going to!" A jumble of fragmentary dream sequences, rather than thoughts, engulfed her: she saw her mother waving to her as though waving goodbye to a school train and Morwenna on the train, peering out from a window crowded with other schoolgirls, so that she herself had only a chink to peep through and was being suffocated by all the girls piling on top of her. Then of Frank, snatching her up and whirling her round; then a crash into darkness; then struggling afresh to escape from under the smothering press of schoolgirls who were now back on top of her and suffocating the breath out of her worse than ever. She tried to shout "Get off me!" and triggered another violent fit of coughing, fighting in panic for breath between the coughs. Then blackness again.

Odile was there, in the bed next to her, as in early years when they had shared the same bedroom. She leaned over Morwenna and began striking her on the chest with hard little fists, to wake her up Morwenna supposed. Then came a scraping sound; it must be their mother pulling back the window curtains. The darkness was sharply pierced by a thin finger of light. It was morning. Time for school. From somewhere above her came a voice: not that of her mother, nor of her sister, but a man's voice calling, "Morwenna! Are you there, Morwenna?" It must be her father, though it didn't in the least sound like him.

Morwenna tried to reply but was immediately seized with another coughing fit. The man's voice said, "I think we've found her." The scraping sound began again. Morwenna realized now that she was not in bed with Odile pummelling her and her mother drawing the curtains, but that someone was trying to rescue her from where she lay buried.

More scrapings. The chink of light expanded: more sounds of careful movement, as if someone was cautiously removing the rubble stone by stone. The chink turned into a small hole, blocked suddenly as a face peered in. Then, "We've reached her! She's here!" His voice held a note of triumph. Then he called down to her, "Bear up, Morwenna; soon have you out of here now!"

Her rescuer withdrew his head from the hole; the cautious sounds of removing rubble began again. Morwenna, in spite of help being so near at hand, began drifting down a long slide of pain and shadow. She could feel the shadows closing in on her; great cold depths of them below her. A long way off she heard Posy Cowper's voice shout, "Careful! careful!" Morwenna made a desperate effort to stop herself sliding any further: she must pull herself back up to the light! She struggled to inch her way upwards, to open her eyes and stare at the patch of light above her, survive by it. As she fought in desperation she became aware of her rescuer's voice muttering and grumbling; it accompanied her tormented upward struggle. The light was nearer now; the grumbling became recognizably ferocious swearing at something that wouldn't budge. A fight was going on to save her: a fight his end, a fight at hers. He was trying to fight his way down to her, she her way up to him. This tug of struggle seemed to go on for ever. Then she heard Posy's warning cry again, "Careful!" Something went; the small jagged-edged patch of light above Morwenna burst open; light and air flooded in. An ARP rescue worker, in heavy blue dungarees and helmet, his dust-smothered face grotesquely streaked with sweat, giving him a clownish appearance wholly out of keeping with the grim realities of his job, crouched beside the opening; he peered intently down on Morwenna, who stared back at him; then she began coughing once more. Her rescuer's clown-face lit up with a radiant smile of relief. "She's still alive!" he shouted over his shoulder.

"Alive!" The word rang in Morwenna's head like a bell pealing a victory chime. Alive! Her terrible upward struggle was over! The bells chimed and pealed, so that her head whirled and spun: she was dimly aware that her rescuer, with infinite caution, had lowered himself through the opening and was gradually working his way down to where she lay. At last, after what seemed an eternity, he reached her and half squeezed, half crouched beside her, saying, soothingly (for she was now sobbing and moaning in sheer relief), "It's all right Morwenna, it's all right: be brave a little longer and we'll have you out in no time." He cradled Morwenna's head in his lap, protecting her from falling debris dislodged by other rescue workers who were now removing further lumps of rubble and bricks; working with the same infinite care as that of her original rescuer. Every now and again they called down to him, "You orright Clem? Doing orright down there?" and he replied, "Yes. Keep going. The sooner we're out now, the better."

He had a beautiful voice, thought Morwenna; inasmuch as she was capable of thinking. Quite different from the kind, but perfectly ordinary, voices calling down to him. He continued to cradle and soothe her, stroking her cheek. A lock of grey hair straggled across his forehead from under his helmet. Morwenna wondered vaguely who he was. Some elderly actor maybe who had gallantly joined Civil Defence? All kinds of people were doing such exceptionally brave things! "How are you feeling, Morwenna?" he asked her solicitously. "Fine," she whispered, trying to smile. "That's my girl!" he said cheerfully and smiled back at her; that radiant smile that had accompanied his cry of, "She's alive!" Morwenna closed her eyes: she was too exhausted to keep them open. She heard him say to the men above, "Hurry up, if you can."

"Doing our best. Can't afford to fetch this lot down on top of you," came the reply.

At last the rubble pinning her was removed; she was lifted up and passed from one pair of strong arms to the next and then Posy, dust and plaster smothered like all the rest, was hugging her and saying,

"My stars, Morwenna, you're a lucky one you are! Landed up in the one place in the basement where you couldn't have the whole blooming lot on top of you!"

"Mr Walters?" Morwenna was just able to force the words from her congested throat.

"Don't worry, duck; all be orright. We're taking you to the hospital now; be right as rain. Not a thing to worry about now!"

It was broad daylight; what time of day Morwenna did not know. She couldn't recall a thing about how she had become buried; her last memory was of going into Mr Walters' office.

She was placed in an ambulance; then she was at the hospital and being examined by doctors and X-rayed and cleaned and put to bed and given an injection of some kind, and she went to sleep.

When she woke up she found, to her astonishment, a young clergyman, a perfect stranger, sitting beside her bed. The thought seized her, "I must be badly injured if they send a clergyman to see me!" Her alarm must have shown in her face, for her visitor smiled reassuringly and said, "Don't worry! Everything's all right now, Morwenna. You're safe and sound and miraculously not even seriously hurt." He took her hand gently and squeezed it, repeating, "Don't worry."

The smile, the voice. Suddenly she realized who he was. "You're the rescue worker who dug down to me!" She added, "I didn't know clergymen rescued people."

"Oh dear," he said. "That's what I rather understood they were for."

Morwenna wondered where he came from. Reporting births, marriages and deaths all over Cuddwell she met a lot of ministers from many churches; not being what she called a "church person" herself, they rarely registered deeply with her. But she couldn't recall ever having seen this one before. Given as she was to the habit of forthright scrutiny, she stared hard at him, puzzled by his youth and dark hair. Not as she remembered her rescuer's appearance at all! At last she said, "When you were in that hole, I thought you were an old actor."

"How romantic! No, I'm afraid not."

"You had grey hair."

"I did, yes, but it washed out. Plaster dust."

Morwenna felt at a loss for further conversation; furthermore it hurt her throat and chest to talk. Meantime her visitor, turning

223

rather pink in the face, reached down to pick up something placed beside him on the floor. It was a bouquet of sweet peas and roses. "I thought you might like these." He handed the flowers to her, the pink flush on his face turned to a noticeable blush. Morwenna took the flowers. She couldn't think what to say; her eyes filled with tears and to hide them she buried her face in the flowers and sniffed hard. Then she looked up at him, "Oh, they smell *heavenly!*"

He smiled and blushed simultaneously. "Thank you," continued Morwenna, taking a further deep breath of sweet-pea scent. "Thank you for *everything*," she said with heartfelt meaning.

"What else can I do?" he said simply. "In any case, it was a team thing, digging you out; a team thing like it always is. Everyone was magnificent, including you, if I may say so. That's why I thought you deserved the flowers."

"I don't know where you managed to find such beautiful flowers in this part of London, in the middle of a war. Almost everything's been turned into vegetable allotments."

"Amazingly enough these grow near where I live, in the rectory back garden."

"Where do you live?"

"Not where you'd expect to find sweet peas. Where Poplar, Bow and Stepney embrace, near the beauteous Limehouse Cut; more commonly called the Lime'arse Scutt. Do you by any chance know the Lime'arse Scutt?"

"No. Are you the curate there?"

"I work with an Anglican Mission; what is described as a 'settlement'. And yes, I'm a curate. Though, with a war like this in progress, you can't really give labels to anyone. I'm in Civil Defence as well; it's one of the best ways of being useful."

Morwenna gave another long appreciative sniff at her bouquet. "And you live at the rectory?"

"No, no; I'm with the Mission. The rector of the parish church, however, is a neighbour and very good friend and when I mentioned I needed some flowers he most generously suggested I might help myself. Aha, here's Posy!"

Posy Cowper was approaching the bed. She too carried a bunch of flowers: dahlias from the garden at 47 Rushton Road. "Hello Clem. You here?" she exclaimed, with one of her rare, toothy grins. Clem rose to his feet and the two shook hands warmly.

"I popped in to see how Morwenna was getting along," explained

Clem, going slightly pink again. "Coming along nicely, by all accounts," said Posy. To Morwenna's amazement she bent over the bed and gave Morwenna a big kiss. "How you feeling, duck? Mum sends her love and will be along to see you soon as you're stronger." She handed Morwenna the flowers, and a box of chocolates. "Oh Posy, you shouldn't! I don't deserve all this attention!" "Forget it," said Posy. "A mercy to think you're still here to give 'em to."

"Hear, hear!" Clem stooped to give Morwenna a quick goodbye pat on the arm. "I'm off now; see you again sometime, if I may."

He walked away up the ward, stopping occasionally to speak to people in the beds. Posy watched him with affectionate approval. "He's a good'un," she said.

"I didn't recognize him at first. I had no idea who he was. What's his name, Posy?"

"Reverend Clem Irving. Came up with a rescue team from Bromley-by-Bow. Things were so bad in Cuddwell our Civil Defence had to send for reinforcements. You were lucky to have him around. Made quite a reputation for himself, he has, digging people out. Seems to have an instinct for it. Very dangerous work."

"I don't know how to thank him! Thank all of you!"

"Don't have to," said Posy gruffly. "That's what we joined Civil Defence for in the first place, isn't it?" She changed the subject. "I've contacted your mother and she's hoping to be here some time later today."

"Oh Posy, you're so good!"

"Don't talk soppy. Have a chocolate; brought 'em for you to eat."

Morwenna remained in Cuddwell Hospital over the next few days. She was suffering from shock, the effects of blast, and the dust that she had inhaled. She had a steady stream of visitors: her mother, Posy, daily, when she came off duty, Odile, Clem, Mr Pottall, Pym. Posy, on her second visit, broke the news to Morwenna that both Mr Walters and Mr Macpherson had been killed.

Posy explained how lucky Morwenna had been; the *Gazette* building had received a direct hit and Morwenna had plunged into the basement; a heavy girder supporting the flight of stairs above her had held, preventing her from being crushed by masses of masonry. Clem and the rescue team had worked all night to get her out of the wreckage and Posy, in spite of already having been on duty almost twenty-four hours nonstop, had insisted on giving a hand: "Couldn't leave you there, duck, could I, without trying to do something about it. But it was a mercy you kept coughing like that. If you hadn't coughed, and Clem hadn't heard you, he wouldn't have known where to dig. One time you stopped coughing and we all thought you'd had it."

Pym, who brought Morwenna some caramels, most of which he then proceeded to eat himself while he chatted, was breezily pragmatic. "Must be rather a quirky thought for you: if that bomb had dropped a few minutes sooner when you were still on that first floor with Wally and Mac you'd have copped it same as they did. By the way, as a matter of interest, did you hear the bomb coming? They say you never hear the one that actually gets you."

"Can't remember a thing."

"What a pity. I was hoping you'd be able to verify that one for me. What you thinking of doing now you've lost your job? Trying for something in Fleet Street? Good chance for a girl to break in at the moment, with all the young chaps gone."

"I haven't really thought about it."

"Have a bash at it if I was you. You've every right by now to describe yourself as a seasoned reporter, and you'd be wise to get dug in, in a decent job, while you have the chance. Come to that, I suppose you could take over my job on the *Mercury* when I join up."

"I don't know, Pym; don't know what I'll do." Morwenna still felt the effects of her bomb experience: she really couldn't get herself to care much about her possible future career, at this point.

Uppermost in Morwenna's mind, all this time she was in hospital, was the realization of how lucky she was to be alive. Her recollection of lying in darkness, buried and suffocating in rubble, was simultaneously hazy and horribly vivid: she woke in the night thinking she was still lying there, and the panic she had known at the time seized her again until she was sufficiently wide awake to know that she was not on the point of death, not about to be deprived of life before she had even reached her eighteenth birthday, cut off before her "noontide" as the old saying went. How nearly that had happened to her!

She lay in her hospital bed, surrounded by people who had shared her experience of brushing close to death. Many of them were seriously injured, one girl not much older than Morwenna had lost both her legs. Morwenna felt that she owed it to someone, something, somewhere, that she should do her best to help people who, like herself, had gone through the experience of being bombed, but hadn't had her wonderful good luck in escaping virtually undamaged. She owed a debt, she felt. A kind of debt of honour. But quite how to go about repaying it she wasn't sure.

In her bedside locker was a letter from Frank. She had sent him a brief note saying what had happened to her, though making light of it. His reply was vehement.

You see, you see, you should have done as I suggested and remained at Parrocks! I had a ghastly presentiment something like this would happen. All I can do now is implore you to go home to Stoke Hartwell to recuperate and STAY THERE until things have grown quieter: there's no way I can escape my fate of being at risk serving king and country (not without disgracing the family name, anyhow), but you're *not* obliged to place yourself in danger and for my sake you *must* keep away from the hot spots. It doesn't help anyone to have you blown up! Just means someone has to go to all the risk and trouble of rescuing you. Sorry to be so brutally frank, my darling, but the outcome of this war doesn't depend on your newspaper reporting. My future happiness (if I survive) *does* depend on you, entirely. You've had your share of heroics now, and can put it in a book: now trot back home, there's a sweet little love, and keep yourself safe for me.

Morwenna, much as she worshipped Frank, felt a wave of hot indignation when she read this. True, the outcome of the war didn't depend on her newspaper reporting, but if all the women trotted back home and stayed there, where would the country be? Take Posy; she needn't have stuck *her* neck out joining Civil Defence. Take Odile, risking her life in Wapping. Take their own mother, driving into the Blitz every night with that mobile canteen. There were thousands of women, hundreds and thousands of them, who could stay home and be safe if they chose; but they didn't choose. Poor Frank! he was always saying he rightfully belonged to another day and age: and he did, too. Given his way, he'd have Morwenna locked up in the tower at Parrocks awaiting his return from the battle of Agincourt!

Her sense of owing a debt to life (as she put it to herself) was now further intensified by dire news from 47 Rushton Road. Flo Cowper, though she lived less than a quarter of a mile distant from the hospital, had never once visited Morwenna as yet and Morwenna was privately a little hurt by this neglect, as well as puzzled. Each time Posy visited, Morwenna asked after Flo, to receive the same reply: "Oh Mum's orright. Sends her love." But something in Posy's manner signalled to Morwenna that things were really far from well at Rushton Road. At last Posy, who by her very nature was poor at concealment, blurted out, "The truth is, Morwenna, Mum hasn't been to see you because she's not up to it: poor Henry's copped it, and as you can imagine Mum's in a terrible way."

"Copped it! How?" exclaimed Morwenna, aghast at the thought of what this must mean to Flo.

Posy replied with a sigh, "Seems he was in the thick of things that first big night of the Blitz, superintending a very bad gas mains incident, and then there came an emergency call for help at another incident, and between one incident and the next, not to mention the dreadful confusion everywhere, it was quite a few days before it was recognized for certain that Henry was missing and so they started enquiries and the long and short of it is that Henry must've been blown to bits that first night; or the next; anyway it must've happened early on, though exactly how or where nobody knows."

"Oh Posy, how awful!"

"Happening all the time," said Posy, bleakly. "Still, that said, you never think it will happen to your own."

"Your poor, poor mother!"

"She feels it; she certainly feels it. Henry was the apple of her eye. Her only son, after all, and naturally she worshipped the ground he trod on. I'm afraid she's taking it hard, very hard. One comfort for her, he fell in the service of his country in the front line of battle, same as his own father in the last war: a hero's death in its own way, Morwenna. Because Henry knew he was going into something bad: didn't go into it with his eyes shut."

Posy, of course, was perfectly right. Henry had given his life for his fellow men as surely as any conventional battlefield casualty. Morwenna, thinking about this, felt even more strongly that she had some kind of example to live up to, some obligation to discharge.

Clem continued to visit her, bringing her bunches of sweet peas. "That nice generous rector will regret having told you to help yourself to his flowers," said Morwenna, rather naughtily. "However, they're absolutely lovely. . . . Best medicine I receive!"

"They'll soon be over now, I fear. A miracle second crop, brought on by this incredible weather. When are they letting you go home? I was almost expecting I'd find you gone."

"Tomorrow, I think."

They sat for a moment in silence, then Morwenna said, "I don't think I should stay home and do nothing, do you?"

"Surely you know the answer to that one yourself! Though whether you want to continue with newspaper work at this juncture in the war. . . . You were under a certain obligation to carry on at the *Gazette*, I can appreciate that, but with the *Gazette* gone. . . ." He paused; a slightly caustic grin flickered across his face. "I certainly didn't rescue you so that you might retire home and do nothing!"

Morwenna shook her head with a rather dismal little smile.

"It was a hell of a sweat digging you out, Morwenna. You have to make it worth my while. If you can't think of anything to do once you're on your feet again, I'll find something for you."

Morwenna looked thoughtfully at him. "Was that you swearing all the time you were digging me out?"

"Probably. I must confess I do swear when under intense . . . I know it's very wrong of me . . . I never supposed you could hear me." He looked genuinely abashed and ashamed. Morwenna said, taking his hand, "It's all right, Clem, really it is. In fact, it sort of made part of a lifeline for me. . . . Helped me pull myself up."

"I'm not sure quite what you mean by that, but if swearing helped, then thank God I swore!"

"You're rather funny for a clergyman, aren't you?" rejoined Morwenna, in her most earnest manner.

"Funny haha, or funny peculiar? Ah, I see from your expression which you mean." He stood up rather abruptly. "Only a whirlwind visit this time, I'm afraid. I have to attend a meeting." She felt that she had upset him with her remarks and said, "Clem, you make me feel awful. You come all these miles to see me and then I'm rude to you! I owe my very life to you."

"Don't be ridiculous. If I hadn't dug you out, one of the others would have done it."

"I didn't mean to be rude just now. Only you see I've never really known a clergyman properly before, not to talk to, I mean. We had one come to school to confirm us, but you could hardly call that conversation."

"Quite so."

"So you see, I don't know what to expect! I've only Mr Pottall to go by."

Clem burst out laughing; a real uninhibited peal of laughter. People in neighbouring beds turned their heads in his direction. He stooped over Morwenna, kissed her on her forehead and said, "Get better quickly. Then we'll find you a job at Tulip House."

· "Tulip House? Where's that?"

"A hostel run by our Mission. Crowded, day and night, by bombed-out people seeking help. You can't do better than come there to give a hand: believe me, you'll find yourself needed — and loved for what you do."

"In the East End?"

"Absolutely. I've already told you, on the banks of the lovely Limehouse Cut."

"Lime'arse Scutt."

"You've got it. Pronunciation perfect."

"I'll think about it and let you know."

"I'll be in touch."

He walked away up the ward, greeting people he had come to know. Morwenna took out Frank's letter, read it yet again, gave it a little kiss and, with a sigh, put it back in the locker. "You needn't fear, I've been blown up once and lightning never strikes twice, darling: but Clem is right, I wasn't saved in order to retreat back home and do nothing!"

XXX

"Tell me, Frank, have you met this girl, Poppy, that Jos is allegedly having an affair with, and is it true that her husband is in Jos's squadron, and has been horribly injured and burned, and she's ditching him for Jos?" And Vicky gave Frank a challenging look, as if saying, "And now I'm asking the member of the family I most trust to be honest with me!"

Frank's response was one of mingled amazement and annoyance. "Who's been talking to you about all this?"

"Boggy. She writes to me from time to time and her letters have been full of it; when she's not enthusing over Giles, that is."

"Damn Boggy! She has absolutely no right to discuss Jos's private life with you, or anybody."

Poor Vicky had been praying that she might be assured by Frank that there wasn't a word of truth in what Boggy had been writing about Jos, that it was all Boggy's imagination. However, Frank's indignant anger seemed to indicate that there *was* something to it, rather than otherwise. Vicky surveyed him anxiously, trying to read his face.

Frank felt her watching him and realized that he must control himself better, or he would give Jos's wretched game away. He fiddled with a piece of roll, trying to recapture a cool exterior, though inwardly he was seething. He and Vicky were dining together at Prunier's; Frank was in London for an interview and was putting up for a couple of nights at Brown's Hotel, where Vicky, in London for a meeting of WVS billeting officers, was also staying. Next day they were lunching with Jos, who was on a fortnight's leave (spending it, Frank guessed, with Poppy).

Summoning a light tone Frank at last managed to say, in an attempt to change the subject, "What's this about Giles and Boggy? Not working up a romance, are they?"

"I gather he's dated Boggy once or twice and has made quite an impression on her," replied Vicky. "As he has on everyone, come to that. The parents can't wait to have him at Parrocks again. They're almost as proud of him now as they are of Jos."

Frank, in spite of himself, ignited once more. "If Boggy prattles to Giles and he breathes a word to father and mother about Jos and that wretched girl . . . I warned Boggy that if a breath of it reached Parrocks the effect would be shattering." Frank took an angry gulp of wine. "True?" he said, to Vicky's original question. "Yes, it's true. And it's not an affair that reflects well on Jos, I hate having to say: Pa and Ma see him, especially Mother, as such a knight in shining armour that if they discover he's cuckolded a brother officer who's supposed to be one of his closest friends and who, moreover, is in dire need of all the support he can get, instead of being kicked in the teeth. . . ."

Vicky gave a heavy sigh. "Oh dear. I didn't think Boggy could be making it all up. She's horribly indignant about it and I confess I rather share her feelings now you've confirmed that Jos really is. . . ."

Frank interrupted urgently, "Look Vicky, for god's sake don't mention a word of any of this when we meet Jos tomorrow! I'd hate him to think the family is buzzing with beastly gossip behind his back."

"Frank, as if I would!"

"No no, of course you wouldn't; but it's so damn easy to let slip an unfortunate . . . I say, will you forgive me if I have another try at contacting Morwenna? If I fail this time I'll leave any further trying until tomorrow morning."

Despite the *Huîtres Prunier* and chablis which they had ordered (how on earth did the restaurant still manage to get oysters? Vicky wondered), their meal was not turning out to be the relaxed and pleasant occasion which it should have been. Quite apart from the unfortunate conversation about Jos, Frank kept excusing himself to try to reach Morwenna over the telephone, returning to the table each time in a worse state of frustration than before. He had come to London at such short notice that he had had no opportunity to contact her in advance. Why should she, and everyone else at Maytrees for that matter, choose to be out this evening of all evenings, when it was so desperately important for him to get in touch with her?

Frank had two letters from Morwenna in his pocket. The first was a scrappy little note written by her in hospital in an uneven hand that suggested to him that when her newspaper office had been bombed she herself had had a narrower squeak than she was prepared to admit. The second letter was much longer, written from Maytrees, where she was recuperating. In this she said that she was anxious to do something to help Blitz victims, rather than find another job, immediately, on a newspaper. "Everything is so appalling and unbearable in this war: why should humanity suffer like this? Nothing but disaster everywhere one looks! What has the poor world done, to deserve an Adolf Hitler?"

Tomorrow night, thought Frank, he'd make Morwenna forget bombs and disasters and Hitler! That was to say, if he could manage to get hold of her.

But this last try, too, was unsuccessful. Frank returned to the dinner table and did his best to resign himself to listening to Vicky describing her experiences as a billeting officer. In fact she was surprisingly entertaining on the subject, revealing an unexpected gift for humorously recounting her day-to-day adventures. Frank listened, laughed, and interpolated his own comments. At the close of the evening, when he was settling the bill and Vicky had gone to the cloakroom, he reflected wryly to himself that it had taken a war to make him discover that he had a truly delightful sister.

Next morning Vicky had started her breakfast when Frank joined her. He looked extremely put out. "No luck?" ventured Vicky sympathetically.

"Worse than no luck; my bird has flown, and where to nobody has more than the haziest idea."

"That sounds terrible! Hasn't her family the slightest notion of her whereabouts?"

"Only that she's gone to the East End to help a clergyman with a refuge for bombed-out people. What blankety-blank clergyman, might I ask? Didn't even know she was in cahoots with any damn clergyman!"

Vicky repressed a smile at Frank's agitation. She said, soothingly, "A clergyman scarcely sounds a dangerous rival, Frankie love."

"Apparently I've only missed her by a whisker! Got her bloody old grandmother on the phone. It seems she's so deaf she doesn't hear the telephone ringing half the time, and ditto the cook. 'Elizabeth and I were both in after nine yesterday evening, but never heard the phone ring once! *Anno domini*, I fear!'" And Frank gave what was in fact an admirable imitation of Mrs Busby. Vicky had never heard Mrs Busby's voice, but nonetheless she burst out laughing. "To cut a long and tedious telephone conversation short," resumed Frank, "the little creature went hot-footing down to dockland yesterday morning to help out this bloody clergyman. When I enquire the name and address of this pestilential sky-pilot all I get is, 'Oh, I'm afraid I can't tell you his name, I'm afraid it has quite slipped my memory; it's an actor's name, one of the old school, but that's all the help I can give you, and it's an address somewhere in the East End.'" Another imitation of Mrs Busby. Vicky, seeing Frank's fundamental distress, repressed her laughter this time and murmured, as she poured him tea, "But there must be *someone* who knows where Morwenna has gone, surely?"

"Apparently her mother knows, but she's out with a mobile canteen and is liable not to be back until god knows when. She's been home, had a kip, and gone out again. Some women don't know when to stop!" Frank added glumly, "We've been losing one another, Morwenna and I, ever since we first met. I thought we'd grown out of it, but it seems not!"

233

"Poor Frank!"

Vicky departed for her meeting; Frank finished his breakfast, tried to phone Maytrees again, once more no reply. Half an hour later he tried again; he got Mrs Busby who said that her daughter wasn't expected back now until late afternoon. "Do you think she could ring me when she returns?" asked Frank. "My number is . . ." But Mrs Busby at this point trilled "Bye-eeee!" and rang off.

Frank's interview was not until three; he had the entire morning to himself and couldn't think what to do with it. He mooched miserably along Piccadilly, through Leicester Square into Trafalgar Square; fountainless, almost pigeonless, for they, with no loiterers to feed them (feeding birds being prohibited as a waste of valuable food) had lost interest and had taken to foraging for themselves in the allotments in the parks. London, with little traffic, and those vehicles that were there mostly painted khaki or green and khaki for camouflage purposes, the shop windows all blind-eyed with protection against blast, everyone in uniform, had become a remarkably single minded city; there was an atmosphere that said most distinctly that this was a battle area. But there was no sign of despondency: it was a battle area where people were determined to keep up their spirits.

Frank alone was despondent; utterly dejected. He wandered on, down Villiers Street and along the Victoria Embankment. He, Jos and Vicky were meeting at the Savoy Grill; Frank was far too early. He leaned against the Embankment wall, staring eastward down the river, thinking that somewhere in that direction was Morwenna.

He loitered, lounged, leaned on the Embankment wall again, and at last judged himself not too ridiculously early to go into the Savoy and have a drink in the bar.

Along the Embankment, towards him, came an RAF officer; tall, thin, with a taut, restless appearance. Frank recognized something familiar about him, wondered if he knew him, and then realized that it was Jos.

"Great Scott!" said Jos, noticing Frank at that same moment. "You, like me, far too early for this lunch date?"

"Yes. At a complete loose end this morning, so I've been mooning my way across London. Naturally I'm here miles too soon."

"Not got Vicky with you?"

"No. She'll be joining us. Shall we cross over the road to the Savoy and head for the bar?"

"Precisely my intention."

Jos strained to speak with his old, easy flamboyance but he seemed to have lost his natural flair for it. His looks were drastically changed: his face was peaked with exhaustion; his mouth, that formerly had been always on the point of spontaneous laughter, was compressed; he had dark rings round his eyes and they themselves held a ruthlessness that Frank had never noticed before. He hadn't seen his brother since Pam Spurgeon's birthday celebration at the Hungaria and now that he saw him Frank was shaken. But he was even further shattered when Jos, removing his cap on entering the hotel, revealed grey threads streaking his dark hair.

They found themselves a corner in the noisy, crowded bar. The onset of autumn gales made the chance of invasion less likely, more leave was being granted and it seemed that every commissioned officer on leave in London had decided to come to the Savoy that lunch time.

"What'll you drink?" Jos asked his brother. "A beer?"

"Thanks."

Jos ordered beers. Frank was suddenly finding it difficult to know what to talk about. Jos broke the silence by asking, "And what is this interview you've landed yourself with this afternoon?"

"No idea what they want to see me about; probably they haven't either. The Army keeps things under its hat to the point where the good old left hand hasn't a clue where the right hand has vanished to in the murk, let alone what it's doing. *Obscurum per obscurius*."

"You sound fed up."

"I am fed up."

"Hits all of us these days. Fortunately there mostly isn't much time to think about it. Well, here's to the interview. May it result in rapid promotion!"

Jos smoked, Frank didn't. Jos said, "I hear you introduced the Thingy child to Parrocks."

"The who? Oh! Yes. I did. I suppose mother mentioned it to you."

"And long lost cousin Giles turned up?"

"Yes. And Boggy also was on leave. So one way and another it was quite a party."

"Bogs," said Jos acridly, "is a bloody little prattling pest and someone should quietly wring her neck!"

Frank hesitated, then said, "I can assure you, if it sets your heart at rest, that she hasn't done any prattling to the parents."

"It wouldn't make all that difference if she had. They'll have to know about it some day. If I last that long."

"You'll tell them about Poppy?" Frank exclaimed.

"Of course; have to, if we marry. Can't smuggle her in, can I?"

"You intend marrying her?"

"Don't look so aghast. There's nothing wrong with Poppy. Far from it. The people who need a few lessons in how to behave themselves are nosy little nurses who think they're entitled to run around delivering lectures on moral delinquency!" And Jos's eyes snapped dangerously.

"Remember that Bogs is at the receiving end of this thing, Jos."

"How d'you mean?"

"Well she's nursing Pongo."

There was a pause. Then Jos, raising his eyes to Frank's said, "You mustn't suppose that all this has been easy for me, Frank."

"Just the reverse, I'd imagine."

"Dead right. And for Poppy too."

Frank drew a long breath. "I don't suppose it's been all that easy for Pongo either."

"I don't suppose poor old Pongo's taken a hell of a lot of it in. He didn't have much in the way of grey matter to start with and I understand he's lost half of what he did have, so if he really grasps the situation I shall be most surprised." Jos spoke flippantly, glossing over the trauma.

Frank was determined not to quarrel with Jos. Another silence fell between them; Frank, who had gone bright pink, bit his lower lip and held back what he felt strongly inclined to say, while Jos lit another cigarette. Then Jos said, "I've never truly loved anyone before, you know, neither has Poppy; and let me assure you, it's complete and absolute agonizing hell."

"Have another drink?"

"Thanks. I suppose Vicky will spot us in this corner?"

"I should imagine so. We've still time in hand; she won't be here for at least another ten minutes."

"Has she changed much?"

"Yes. Decidedly for the better. Become a real charmer, at least in my opinion."

"Takes a war to bring out the potential in so many of us," rejoined Jos sardonically. He paused, then said, reverting to their previous topic, "Poppy was fearfully upset by that meeting she had with

Boggy, you know. You might tell Boggy that when next you see her."

"Rather you told her yourself. It's nothing to do with me. I'm not discussing any of it with anybody."

"Poppy can put on a very tough act when it's called for, but underneath she's as vulnerable as the next."

"No doubt." Frank wished Vicky would join them. "What do you think you'll find yourself doing when this Battle of Britain show is over?" he said, "Or is it now reckoned to be over?"

"Difficult to define where a battle of that kind ends. We're still having plenty of trouble with BF double-oh-nines during the day; their high flying capacities make things pretty dicey for us. Bit of a strain at times." Jos lit another cigarette; he was chain smoking and his fingers were stained with nicotine. "Everyone's a bit battle-fatigued. Shows itself in various ways. I've fallen into the pretty habit of spewing like a sea-sick novice Channel-crosser every time the damn tannoy gives the order to scramble. It's nervous reaction; I'd be the last person not to admit that I'm bloody scared each time I go into combat: sheer icy, belly-consuming fear. Fortunately it leaves me at the first glimpse of the enemy: I become a killer then. There's no room for fear when you're killing." Jos's tone of voice was completely unemotional, matter of fact. Then he glanced up and said, relievedly, "Here's Vicky."

Vicky advanced towards them, laughing a greeting. Jos stood up, laughing too. He embraced her, told her how nice she looked. "Frank said you'd improved."

"Improved! I like that for sheer cheek!" exclaimed Vicky.

"Oh, you know Frank."

"We all know Frank," rejoined Vicky, giving Frank himself a loving smile as she spoke. Poor boy, she thought, he *was* looking miserable!

Jos ordered her a sherry. She said solicitously, "You look a wee bit tired, Jos."

"Have had a wee bit of a tiring time, recently."

"Must be an awful strain, one combat sortie after the next."

"Feel it most in the arms and wrists, holding the damn plane in the turbulence set up by the fights going on all round you. Yes; tough on the poor old arms and wrists."

"Things have quietened down now?"

"Grew rather lively again last week. But nothing like it was. No sleeping in the cockpit in between scrambles. Time to climb out of the old kite and find a chair."

"You're going up to Parrocks for part of your leave?" asked Vicky.

"No. If I get there the parents will never stop lavishing the fatted calf upon me. I'd love to see them, but at this point in time I don't think I could stand it. Next leave. Besides, I'm being kept pretty busy down here." And, defiantly, he flung Vicky a dazzling smile of bravado, then burst out laughing. He continued to laugh and joke throughout lunch, as if a switch had been flicked on.

It was not until early evening that Frank arrived back at the hotel. He rushed to phone Maytrees; no reply. He found Vicky and marched her to the bar.

"How did the interview go?" she asked as he handed her a martini.

"Oh pretty well."

"Anything exciting emerge from it?"

"Where do you pick up these ridiculous notions about the British army?"

"How d'you think Jos looked?"

"I've seen him look better."

"At least he was cheerful enough. Never stopped laughing."

"Well, as he confesses himself, he's a killer."

"Lady killer, you mean?"

"Every kind of a killer, I suppose."

"What's that got to do with laughing?"

"Haven't you noticed what a jolly place London has become?"

"Yes. It's amazing."

Frank took a long gulp of martini. He looked thoughtful. "I wonder if I could become a killer?"

Vicky burst out laughing. "Oh Frank!" She checked herself, anxious not to hurt his feelings, and said, "I'm sure all the girls love you."

"I wasn't thinking of girls. No girls for me in London, this time round."

"Do you dance, Frank?" she asked, after a momentary pause.

"Not unless I have to, and then only basic steps. Don't tell me you do it."

"In point of fact I do. Part of my war effort. Fund-raising hops in every direction. Let's dine and dance; I'll teach you to tango. Essential for lady-killing."

"I repeat, I wasn't surmising about my capacity to kill ladies. And I have no intention of dancing."

"When you were a little boy I taught you, much against your will, how to tie your shoelaces. Now I'm jolly well going to teach you to tango." She picked up the telephone directory. "Shall we try the Meurice?"

The sirens sounded at the usual hour; by the time Frank and Vicky were due to set out to the Meurice the night had become decidedly noisy. "Shall we press on? Or d'you want to call it off and take shelter instead?" asked Frank.

"Oh, press on, unless you think otherwise."

"Okay, press on! If we die between here and Bury Street too bloody bad."

They spent the evening dining and dancing, Frank's least favourite form of entertainment at any time, but Vicky was clearly enjoying herself and it would have been churlish to have refused to partner her. Frank, doing his best to conceal his gloom, trampled and bumped his way round the dance floor, seeing in his mind's eye Morwenna in her smocked blue Liberty dress, seated with him at a table at the Hungaria. "I deplore this custom of ruining dinner by constantly jumping up to dance," he had said to her then and she had replied, he could still hear her bell-like tones and see those enormous blue eyes, "That's all right, I've been on my feet all day doing funerals." And where in hell are you now, my little love, where are you now?

"Game to try the tango again? Practise makes perfect you know," said Vicky.

"If you wish."

The raid overhead was now so noisy that it could be heard in the lulls between the music and every now and again the building shook.

XXXI

Tulip House, Sparrowgrass Row, Morwenna's new address, like so many other spots in East London had been named in a distant time when this part of the world had been a pleasant place of orchards and gardens, walks and groves and bowling-greens. There had undoubtedly been tulip borders and asparagus beds here once. Now the view was of muddy canal banks, gasometers and unending bricks and mortar.

Clem, who met Morwenna at Bow Road station and carried her suitcase for her to Tulip House, greeted her with the words, "Thank heaven, and I mean it, that you've come! I told you your help would be invaluable, but it's doubly so now because poor dear Miss Whitebeam has gone down with acute sciatica. It couldn't have happened at a worse time!"

"Oh well, I'm here now Clem and here I'll stay until I'm not needed any more."

"A dangerous promise to make, Morwenna."

They walked through the bomb-torn little streets where house after house was nothing more, now, than a gaping crater, or a pile of rubble. At last they reached Sparrowgrass Row, a terrace of early Georgian houses with a large one at the end, on the corner. "Here we are," said Clem. "Tulip House, once the Mission guesthouse for overseas visitors. Highly popular it was too, and even more popular our one and only Miss Widgeon, housekeeper here for forty years."

"And Miss Whitebeam?"

"Miss Widgeon's lifelong friend and companion. Two most remarkable ladies! I fear they don't come like that any more. I hope you'll be happy living and working with them, Morwenna. I've told them all about you and they're certainly looking forward to having you here."

"I hope you haven't painted too rosy a portrait of me," murmured Morwenna, rather anxiously.

"That would be impossible!"

"Oh, come off it, Clem!"

He started to laugh, put the suitcase down on the pavement at the foot of the flight of stone steps and bounded up them to rap the ornate and brilliantly polished brass knocker of the fan-lighted front door. After a moment or two this was opened by a tweed-clad, grey-headed lady, plain featured, with protruding teeth and warty moustached face that lit up with a broad smile when she saw Clem.

"You've arrived!" she said, in a voice like a bassoon.

"Yes, here we are! This is Morwenna, and Morwenna, this is

our one and only Miss Widgeon." Clem propelled Morwenna across the threshold, Miss Widgeon extended a firm hand of welcome, "How d'ye do."

Morwenna shook hands with the slightest duck of the head, as a well brought up French child should on being introduced to an elder and better. Her father had insisted that the training of his daughters in their infancy should be influenced by a certain gallic *finesse*. Miss Widgeon smiled benignly. Clem, still laughing, brought in the suitcase, saying, "Well, now she's settled in I must fly! I've a Civil Defence meeting I must on no account miss. See you later!" And he ran back down the steps, waving goodbye.

"The dear boy!" said Miss Widgeon. She closed the front door, with a final fond glance at Clem striding away up the street. "He never spares himself. And now, dear, I'll show you your room and then introduce you to Miss Whitebeam who, needless to say, is greatly looking forward to meeting you. Clem has talked so much about you."

Morwenna, with a heart that simultaneously warmed to this friendly greeting and sank a little at the idea of having been so much talked about by Clem, picked up her case and followed Miss Widgeon upstairs. The house echoed with cockney voices and the cries of children. "I'm afraid I've had to put you in a poky little room. It's all we can spare at the moment, as you will well understand when I tell you that we're trying to accommodate eighty people, whereas the most we were ever asked to house in pre-war days was twenty at a time, and even that I used to think a great squash."

She showed Morwenna into a narrow slip of a room on the first floor. It had a little brass bed, a small white-painted chest of drawers, a closet cupboard, and a mirror on the wall. Everything was painted white. The quilt on the bed was blue, pink and white and there was a small pink bedside rug. On the chest of drawers was a vase with pink roses in it. "Oh, it's an utterly sweet little room!" exclaimed Morwenna. "And what lovely roses!"

"Clem produced them," said Miss Widgeon. "To welcome you, he said. And now come and meet Miss Whitebeam."

Miss Whitebeam was considerably larger and a few years older than Miss Widgeon. At present she was confined to her chair and when she did attempt movement she supported herself on two sticks and was obviously in pain. But in every other respect she was Miss Widgeon's duplicate: both ladies came from good professional families; both were highly educated, suffragette, devoutly Christian spinsters; both had dedicated their lives to the service of the church and the East End poor. Both had grey shingled hair; both wore baggy tweed suits with box-pleated skirts, plain shirt-blouses, ties, thick lisle stockings and well polished brogues. Both spoke in Cambridge accents in the same resonant throaty voices and both were hearty, guileless, no-nonsense and kind; though neither of them would, as Morwenna well knew, countenance any falling off in discipline or breaching of code by a member of their own sex and social class. There had been several survivors of this redoubtable Old Guard on the staff at Morwenna's school; she had no doubt of the standards that would be expected of her at Tulip House.

The all-female ménage was completed by Lily, a wispy, withered little soul of advanced years, who had come to the mission as a twelve-year-old orphan and had stayed there ever since, working as kitchen-cum-housemaid. She shook Morwenna's hand with a bird-like claw, damp from washing up; her genial grimace of welcome was all broken teeth and little creases and crinkles. Morwenna was reminded of some small creature that had crept out of a crevice and would quickly scuttle back, and sure enough Lily, having come up from the basement to be introduced, almost at once popped down again, with a high-pitched manic yelp as she remembered something on the stove.

Morwenna, for one panic-stricken moment, wondered if she had done the right thing in coming here. Any doubts that she had entertained when contemplating the step had been swept aside, whenever they occurred to her, by her fervent desire to be of help to her fellow sufferers in the Blitz. There had also been the thought that if Odile had the guts to live and work in dockland then she, Morwenna, should have the courage to live and work there too: at Tulip House she would only be two or three miles distant from Barrico. But now, actually installed in Tulip House, in this all-female, all-virgin, high-principled ménage, Morwenna's thoughts turned to the lost life of masculine bonhomie on the *Gazette*: jokes and pubs and suppers with her rival Pym; the stampedes of work; the bad language and noise and laughter; the rotary machines roaring below; Mr Walters bellowing across the landing; the incessant ringing of the telephone; Mr Macpherson's demented yells of "For Jeesus Chrissake spike it!" All, all of it gone! And instead Miss Widgeon and Miss Whitebeam telling her how wonderful it was that, in spite of the Blitz, the Mission church had never once missed early morning Holy Communion.

Morwenna, forcing herself to come clean at the start, blurted, "I do hope Clem has told you I'm not really awfully religious."

"Nobody will force you to be what you are not," boomed Miss Whitebeam in response. "And the Lord brings each of us to Him in His own way!" she added with a smile.

Morwenna bit back the reply that she jolly well wasn't going to go to the Lord if she didn't want to. She accompanied Miss Widgeon down to the kitchen for eleven o'clock coffee and was introduced to some twenty persons, old folk, mothers and small children. The other people in the refuge were absent at work during the day.

Over coffee and general chat Morwenna was regaled with Blitz stories, everyone present having been bombed out; with the exception, of course, of the Tulip House staff. Morwenna felt increasingly reassured that she had come to the right place. But this sense of having done the right thing steadily evaporated as her day wore on and she was initiated into the routine of Tulip House and what helping there really meant.

After coffee she assisted Lily to prepare dinner for those who couldn't get to the emergency feeding centre a few streets distant. When dinner was ready she helped dish up; then fed a tiny boy who was too peaky to have a proper appetite and had to be coaxed to swallow each mouthful. Then, after dinner, she washed up; then she took a group of toddlers for an airing in the recreation ground while their mothers had a rest from them and enjoyed a sewing-bee with Miss Whitebeam. Then came tea; bread and marge and jam. Then Morwenna washed up the tea things. Then upstairs to help Miss Whitebeam have a bath. Then helping the mothers to put the tinies to bed so that they might get some sleep before the raiding became so bad that they had to be brought down to the cellar. Then downstairs to help prepare a high-tea-cum-supper for the people back from work. "Nursemaid-cum-scullery-maid-cum-general-drudge," sighed Morwenna to herself; and once again thought longingly of life on the *Gazette*.

The sirens wailed: "There goes Moaning Minnie!" The raid became a noisy one and they all trooped into the cellar and people from outside started hurrying in too. Clem appeared and conducted a short service, with community hymn singing, in the cellar. This was done with such simplicity and sincerity that Morwenna could find nothing to object to in it. She noticed the most unlikely looking characters joining in with the prayers and singing with genuine zeal;

there was something about Clem's way of conducting a service that was infectious. Afterwards two small girls asked if they might sing a special hymn and, being given permission, they stationed themselves stiffly side by side, hands folded in front of them over the region of their private parts and, rolling their eyes ceilingwards with pious expressions, opened their mouths wide and bawled at full pitch of their infant lung-power, "Jesus bids us shine," after which Clem, apparently delighted by the performance, warmly thanked them.

The raid had quietened by this time. Morwenna went upstairs to the kitchen and began tidying up and putting things away in the dresser. Clem joined her. He said, "Well, how goes it?" She replied, rather gloomily, "I hope nobody here will mind that I'm not awfully much of a Christian, you know Clem."

"Oh I shouldn't worry, just carry on as you are," rejoined Clem, taking a biscuit from a tin on the dresser and munching it.

Morwenna, staring moodily at him, thought to herself in a passing sort of way that if he weren't in a dog-collar you'd describe him as rather a dishy young chap. But the thought left her as soon as it came; she had other matters on her mind and felt the need to speak them.

She said, with mounting indignation, "I can understand a service like that helping people, because obviously they enjoy singing the hymns and that, but those two dreadful little girls! You don't really approve of that awful pious mouthing and face-pulling and caterwauling, do you? If that's Christianity among little children you can keep it."

Clem burst out laughing. "Really, you don't know me very well, do you, if you think I liked that! I abominate all small performing children, whether they're singing 'Little Sir Echo' or 'Jesus bids us shine'! But what you are forgetting is that their mothers taught them to put on that little display and that the said mothers are two of our choicest local specimens of heathen, and they got their offspring to learn and sing that hymn because it was their way of trying to please us and say thank you for what we've done for them here. If I had failed to go into raptures over it I would have appeared unbearably churlish and the whole thing would have been a fiasco. Now they're all very pleased and happy with themselves and surely you would admit that's something, in these dark days?"

"Yes, you have a point there."

"Thank you. And how's it going otherwise?"

"Oh, all right, I think. Everyone's very kind to me, and you're certainly doing wonderful work here."

A bomber thumped ominously overhead. Clem said, "I'm on Civil Defence duty: best get moving." He put on his helmet; Morwenna said, "And oh, Clem, thank you for the roses. They're lovely."

"Glad you liked them," he replied, his face flushing slightly in the way Morwenna was now getting to know and found rather endearing. "Last of the crop for this year, I'm afraid," he added. "Nothing left to help myself to in the rectory garden, except michaelmas daisies, and they never look happy indoors. See you tomorrow." He hurried out by the back door and Morwenna continued putting away the cutlery.

The night became increasingly savage; during the course of it a steady stream of bombed-out people arrived at Tulip House, where they were installed in the kitchen, comforted, and given mugs of hot sweet tea. Ambulances came to remove the walking wounded to hospital; others were taken to Rest Centres; some remained at the refuge. Then Miss Widgeon called Morwenna to come to her in the hall. Morwenna hurried there to find Miss Widgeon holding the arm of a dazed looking young fellow carrying a baby wrapped in a shawl. He stood mumbling, over and over again, "She's all I've got left now and I want the best for her."

"Of course," responded Miss Widgeon. "Of course. We'll do all we can." She turned to Morwenna. "Cup of tea please, m'dear. And some warm milk for baby. I'm taking him in my office, where it's quiet." Morwenna hurried away. She returned with the tea and the milk, Miss Widgeon said to the young man, "Now, let me hold baby for you while you have this tea; it will do you good." But he, with a wild look, merely clung all the tighter to the baby, his desperate clutching making the poor infant wail, while he repeated as before, "She's all I've got left now and I want the best for her."

"Of course of course," soothed Miss Widgeon, and then, in an aside to Morwenna, "Poor young chap! He's lost his wife and two other children and his mother. I fear it has temporarily deranged him."

Between them they persuaded the young man to seat himself on Miss Widgeon's sofa and sip some tea, while Morwenna gave the baby a bottle of milk. The poor father, totally worn out, sank into a sort of stupor; Miss Widgeon made him as comfortable as possible on the sofa, covering him with a rug. The baby, warmly wrapped, was placed at his side in a large cardboard box for its cradle. Morwenna, gazing at the pair with tears in her eyes, burst out, "Oh Miss Widgeon, how sad and ghastly it all is! Can you understand why things like this are allowed to happen?" Miss Widgeon replied, "It's the will of God, m'dear."

"The will of God that terrible things like this should be?" exploded Morwenna. "I refuse to believe it!"

"God's will," repeated Miss Widgeon, sadly but firmly. "God's will."

At that moment the sirens took up their sustained dawn chorus of the All-clear. Morwenna, feeling that she couldn't bear another moment of Miss Widgeon, Tulip House, and the awfulness of everything in general, shot out into the street to gulp the chilly earliest morning air. The blackout darkness was streaked with pale bars of grey over the rooftops to the east; the wind smelled of distant river. As Morwenna emerged from the rear entrance of Tulip House and turned the corner of Sparrowgrass Row, she collided with a man hurrying along the pavement, his head bent as he walked, his coat collar turned up and his hat pulled down over his face, so that he struck Morwenna as a being cocooned against the world. "Gosh, I'm sorry!" exclaimed Morwenna, in apology for having stepped into his path, thereby causing the collision. He, however, gave no indication that he had as much as noticed that they had collided; he simply hurried on and, at the next street corner, vanished; though not before there had flashed into Morwenna's mind the recognition, or what she momentarily felt to be the recognition, of Henry Cowper. So convinced was she, for an instant, that it was Henry that she called out his name. Then she rebuked herself; Don't be insane! Henry is dead! At this juncture the front door of Tulip House opened and Miss Widgeon's voice exclaimed, "There you are, Morwenna! I was wondering where you had disappeared to! You had better get a little sleep now, m'dear. You must be quite worn out."

Morwenna was thankful to get into bed. As she pulled off her clothes she realized she had been nineteen hours on the go. She slept like the proverbial log until eleven, when Lily roused her with a cup of tea. Then downstairs to the kitchen, to prepare the midday meal. She was at the sink, peeling potatoes, when Clem entered. He had been talking to the young man with the baby and had arranged that they were to go to a rest home in the country; it transpired that this was the house to which Clem's parents had retired just before the war and he had cajoled them into filling it now with bombed and homeless East Enders. "The poor young chap will be all right there for a while and it will at least give him a breather in which to sort himself out," said Clem. "Then we'll see if there's any further help we can give him."

He and Morwenna were alone in the scullery. Disregarding her wet hands Morwenna darted at Clem and seized him by the wrist, hissing in desperation, "Clem, I can't stick this!"

"Oh Morwenna! You've lived through incidents every bit as bad as this at Cuddwell! And I'm sure that if all these poor people here can stick it with such high courage then you can!"

"I don't mean the bombs, I mean Miss Widgeon."

"Miss Widgeon? But what has poor Miss Widgeon done to make life insupportable for you?" Clem looked at Morwenna in genuine astonishment. She, grabbing the potato knife and peeling great hunks of skin from an inoffensive vegetable, gabbled, "It's her ghastly brand of Christianity, that's what! Telling me all this is the will of God! Well, all I can say is that if God wills terrible things like this then he's a monster!"

"You know, Morwenna, you should give those potatoes a rest for a moment; at the rate you're going you'll hack your own fingers off."

"But Clem, you don't believe this is the will of God, do you?"

"If, by that, you mean do I believe in a God who sits in heaven and creates a Hitler to drop bombs on innocent people, no I do not."

Morwenna flung the knife down into the sink. "But that's what Miss Widgeon believes, and I can't stomach it, I tell you!"

"I don't suppose for one instant it's really what Miss Widgeon means. And it's certainly not what I mean by the will of God. But now isn't the time or place for theological disquisition; we'll return to the subject some other day, if you wish. Only for heaven's sake don't cut and run now, Morwenna; for my reputation's at stake, if nothing else. I've told everyone down here what a stalwart you are; I'd never be able to look any of 'em in the face again if you fled from poor Miss Widgeon. Besides, remember your promise!"

"Oh, I know. And all right, I'll stay. But I do find her blooming pious platitudes the most awful provocation!"

XXXII

A letter arrived from Frank. It was over a fortnight since Morwenna had written to him giving her new address and she was becoming a little anxious; usually he wrote at least once in every ten days. This letter had, she noticed, been written and posted from Parrocks.

Perhaps you may have heard, my little darling, through Boggy, of the death of my poor brother, just over a week ago. He had only recently returned to his station, following a fortnight's leave; he was shot down by a Messerschmitt during a brisk air battle off the Kent coast; a battle that our chaps decisively won, but during the course of it Jos, having shot down one German was himself shot down by another and though he baled out successfully he came down in the drink and drowned before any help could reach him.

As you may imagine this has devastated the family. My brother's body has not been recovered; fortunately we are not a family that attaches great significance to a mere discarded cadaver, so to speak: too many Sowersbys, over the centuries, have left their bones on too many battlefields across the world from Palestine to the Peninsula, Seringapatam to the Sudan; you name it, there one of us rendered up the ghost. Now full fathom five my brother's body lies in the Channel; it does not trouble me, nor do I think it troubles my parents, it is an honourable resting place for the remains of a Battle of Britain pilot. *But the loss of the man himself is grievous.* Fortunately I saw him during his leave and, even more fortunately it was an amiably fraternal meeting.

You realize, of course, that by darting down to dockland like that you missed two nights with me? I had to come to London for an interview and of course immediately tried to contact you through Maytrees — no luck! So far as they were concerned you might just as well have left for Timbuctoo.

It's a perfectly ridiculous state of affairs when I actually succeed in getting to London and can't see you because I don't know where you are. It must be understood that, however much *I* may have to roam in the course of this weary war, *you* must stay put at an address where I can always find you, come hell and high water; or, if you do need to move around, you must not go too far and you *must* leave details of where you have gone, so that I can locate you at top speed. Now this, my little sprite, I must *insist upon*. Promise me that you'll abide by this!

But I digress — as usual — from the main point of my letter. Having missed two nights together we can't afford to miss any more of the few now available. You will see from this letter that I am at Parrocks, on what is a fortnight's embarkation leave. The decision to send us overseas is abrupt and our destination, for security reasons, wrapped in mystery. I can't get down to London; my parents, reeling under the blow of losing Jos, naturally wish to have me here with them; grief has made my mother ill, and as my presence seems to be at least some comfort to her I, naturally, shall pass my leave entirely up here. I have explained that I wish to see you before I depart and this they consider reasonable; so, you're to come up to Parrocks the instant you receive this letter! You should get it by tomorrow midday, I reckon; therefore I'll telephone you in the evening at Tulip House (can imagine you, like Thumbelina, living in a tulip) and by that time you will know the details of your train and can tell me when it arrives at the Halt, and I'll collect you there, *day after tomorrow*.

Final remark: I am wondering what, precisely, we should do about Poppy. Presumably she knows what has happened? Apparently he was deeply serious about her; he assured me that he intended *marrying* her, if spared. I don't think I'm the one to write to her. Boggy certainly won't agree to write; that leaves you. Are you disposed to send a few kindly words of condolence? She doesn't deserve them, but at the same time the poor wretched girl *was* in love with him, and he with her.

And now, for the time being, I must sign off, leaving you as always with our watchword, "Parrocks and the fossil room" — Night after night after next! F.

But I can't! How can I? I just can't walk out like that! Morwenna exclaimed to herself. And instantly she became awhirl with conflicting emotions: dismay that Frank was going overseas and she couldn't see him before he went; anger with herself for having got into a situation where she was so tied to her post by moral obligation that she didn't see how she could possibly worm her way out; further self-reproach for having missed him when he came to London, and, at the same time, a certain resentment that Frank should take it so completely for granted that she would drop everything, be able to drop everything, at an instant's notice and race up to Parrocks. He, obviously, had no notion of what the East End Blitz was truly like, or what her work at Tulip House entailed! He wasn't thinking of anything or anybody but himself; or, more precisely of himself and her together. She could understand; there was nothing she herself wanted more than to drop everything and rush out of Tulip House to him this instant. But how could she?

She couldn't even linger any longer upstairs, rereading his letter. She had to accompany an old couple round to the mortuary to enquire after their missing daughter-in-law. And Morwenna tucked Frank's letter in a drawer, put on her coat and hurried downstairs.

After the visit to the mortuary came another long day of domestic chores. Morwenna barely found time to send a brief note of condolence to Poppy; a difficult one to write: Morwenna only did it to please Frank. She had just returned from posting it when Miss Widgeon told her that she was wanted on the telephone. Heavy hearted, Morwenna went to the phone knowing that what she had to say to Frank would devastate him, though she was certain he would understand her reason for not being able to go to Parrocks.

"Hello Frank."

His voice came back ringing with confidence, "Hullo darling! What time d'you reach the Halt?"

"I don't. I can't come."

"Can't come!" As she had expected, he sounded staggered.

"I can't get away."

"Oh don't talk nonsense. Of course you can. You must!"

"I can't. I'm terribly badly needed here. This house is chock-a-block with bombed-out people, there are only three of us to. . . ."

"Oh don't talk such rubbish! You're not indispensable, nobody is! Your old clergyman will easily find someone to take your place. He only has to stretch out his doddery hand and some parishioner will come running. Besides, he doesn't need you in the way I need you! Tell the silly old blighter that my need is a damn sight more urgent than his! As a Christian he should respond to such a cry from the heart."

"Frank, you don't understand!"

"Morwenna, *you* don't understand! Haven't you grasped that this is the last chance we may ever have of making the fossil room?"

Morwenna drew a deep breath. "Yes Frank, I have grasped that, and I'm terribly sorry; surely I don't have to tell you this in words? What *you* haven't grasped is that I can no more walk out on Tulip House and what's happening down here than you can turn round and say to your brass hats who are ordering you overseas that you're jolly well not going because you want to stay with me!"

"Oh don't be so bloody ridiculous darling!" drawled Frank. "The two situations aren't remotely comparable!"

"I'm afraid I see differently. I think they are."

It was now Frank's turn to draw a deep breath. "Are you telling me that you refuse to come?"

"I'm telling you I can't come."

"One and the same thing."

"Frank, that's a beastly thing to say! I'd come if I could, you know I would! You know I want to come more than anything in the world! But I've promised Clem I'll stay here till I'm not needed any more, and I assure you that at the moment. . . ."

"Who the hell is Clem?"

"The clergyman. And I've given him my word, and I can't walk out and leave. . . ."

"And you've given me your hand, don't forget!" roared Frank, furiously exploding.

"Frank darling, do be reasonable! There's a bloody war raging down here and I'm in the thick of it."

As if to reinforce her words the sirens began to wail. "There's the siren now. Can you hear it?" And Morwenna held the phone up in the hope that it would catch the sound and bring him some revelation of the stringency of her predicament, but Frank cut across with a bellowed, "No I bloody can't hear it and I don't bloody want to! Are you coming up to me at Parrocks or are you not?"

"Frank, I can't!" Morwenna's wail was sister to the desolate sirens that were now picking up the evening chorus from every point of the London horizon.

"Damn you! Damn you!" yelled Frank and crashed down the receiver, leaving Morwenna listening, appalled, to the heartless burr of the dialling tone instead of his voice.

Miss Widgeon began calling to Morwenna to help with taking the small children down to the cellar. As she lifted tinies from their cots, wrapped them up and carried them downstairs, Morwenna repeatedly said to herself that she was astounded that Frank hadn't understood. When he'd calmed down he'd understand, she told herself. He'd soon be on the line again to apologize for swearing at her and to say that of course he understood!

Morwenna spent the next two days in a suspense of expecting Frank to telephone. Each time the phone bell rang she thought, "That'll be Frank!" but it wasn't. Finally she decided that if he didn't contact her within the next twenty-four hours she would telephone him. Then a letter arrived from him: a single sheet, to judge by the slender-looking envelope. Morwenna slit open the envelope, took out the letter.

My dear Morwenna,

After much protracted consideration of the matter I have decided it is only fair to us both if I write to terminate our handfasting pact. As I explained to you at the time, a year and a day is the period allowed for one or other of the two parties concerned to have a change of mind and it being still well within that period I am writing to say, not that I have changed *my* mind, but that I fear you are too young to have rightly known *yours*: I rushed you into it, I see that now, and it would be exceedingly wrong of me to hold you to an engagement, or what is tantamount to an engagement, when you were not really given a chance to sit back and appraise what you were being hurried into doing. I am very sorry that I was so headstrong about it all; my nature, I'm afraid. At seventeen it's best to be given time to look around, and grow up a trifle more, and discover how you really think and feel about things for yourself. Farewell, sprite; Thumbelina! I'm off tomorrow. Luck attend you, as the Little People always say — as if you didn't know. F.

Morwenna, who had as usual carried the letter to her bedroom to read, let it drop to the floor from her suddenly limp hand; she fell

252

face down on her bed and lay there, inert, quite unable to move or think, almost unable to breathe.

Then her mind stirred once more; the idea flashed: Is it too late for me to telephone him, to say he's terribly wrong and of course I know my own mind? She snatched up the discarded envelope; the postmark showed that it had been posted the evening of the previous day. He had made certain that she would receive the letter too late for her to catch him on the phone. It was no use. She had lost him.

"M'dear child, what is wrong? You're white as a sheet!" exclaimed the alarmed Miss Widgeon when Morwenna presented herself in the kitchen to prepare the midday dinner.

"Bad news about a friend," replied Morwenna. She began grubbing potatoes from a sack under the sink. "Sorry to hear that, m'dear, very sorry indeed," said Miss Widgeon. She patted Morwenna on the shoulder and then turned to attend to someone who was needing help with an application form for National Assistance.

XXXIII

Fifty-six consecutive nights of Blitz had been inflicted on London to date and fifty-four of these had been spent by Odile in Barrico. At last the need to go home to Stoke Hartwell to collect some warm clothes for the approaching cold weather prompted her to organize a couple of nights off for herself. It would be nice, too, to see something of her family! Early in the war Odile had looked upon Maytrees as a prison to be escaped from: having escaped, she was able to think of her home with affection. Yes, it would be very pleasant to spend a couple of nights back there, chatting with her mother, playing bezique with her grandmother, enjoying Elizabeth's cooking. Perhaps it would even be possible to get hold of Morwenna and see her too!

It was early evening when Odile arrived in Stoke Hartwell. She hadn't warned anyone that she was coming: she thought she would give them all a lovely surprise. As she approached Maytrees she saw

Sybil Spurgeon's car turn out from the driveway; Odile waved energetically, the car stopped with a jerk, her mother, in the passenger seat, stuck her head out of the window, "Odo!"

"Hello Ma! Thought I'd come home for a couple of nights. Give you a lovely surprise."

"Lovely, darling, lovely! Have you a key to let yourself into the house? 'fraid everyone's out at the moment: help yourself to anything you can find in the larder. Sybil and I must dash; have to replenish our stock of char and wads before going into action. See you tomorrow morning! Bye darling! Bye-ee!" The two mothers were off at speed and Odile let herself into the empty house. She should have realized that her mother would be on duty somewhere or the other, but what on earth could her grandmother and Elizabeth be up to? Old women of their age!

Odile decided her first priority must be to contact Morwenna at Tulip House. The sisters had not met since Odile had visited Morwenna in hospital. Odile, like everyone at Barrico, knew of Tulip House by reputation; it was one of the several East End Missions which, even while it was all happening, were already becoming legendary for the heroic part they were playing in the Blitz. Odile was not altogether sure how Morwenna had managed to get herself involved with a Mission: it was decidedly a far cry from newspaper reporting! However without doubt it was a worthwhile way of spending one's war.

Morwenna, when she came to the phone, sounded pressed for time, "I'm serving suppers . . ." She thought she could meet Odile in Town next day. "I'm going to Debenham's to find Miss Whitebeam thick Chilprufe coms; if such things are still discoverable. Shall we meet for tea at Fortnum's?"

Odo devoted the rest of her evening to the luxury of a prolonged soak in a hot bath. Elizabeth returned just after nine; she explained that she had been to an allotment class, learning to grow winter vegetables. Half an hour later Mrs Busby limped in, exhausted by a session of collecting National Savings, house to house. "Miles, I've been tonight, my dear! Miles! I *must* try to obtain a pedometer so that I know exactly how far I've walked; not to brag, but for my own satisfaction!"

They were all in bed by ten. Odile's pleasant expectations of an evening spent chatting and playing bezique and savouring Elizabeth's cooking had borne little resemblance to reality. Odile had supped off tea, and a cheese sandwich of her own making, consumed while she was soaking in the bath. Marvellous bath though! she thought to herself with a smile, as she turned out her bedside lamp and fell instantly asleep.

Her mother arrived home for breakfast next morning. They chatted over something that Elizabeth called cauliflower kedgeree. Odile then went up to Town to have her hair permed and to do a little shopping, before meeting Morwenna.

The sisters, their first giggling and embracing over, found themselves a pretty little tea table, across which they eyed one another in affectionate scrutiny. Morwenna, thought Odile, still looked rather pale and peaky; it was taking her quite a while to recover from that bomb, and probably being in the thick of things at Tulip House didn't help. Nevertheless she had dressed up her hair with combs and put on her best coat, with a silk scarf and matching lipstick. "You're looking very jaunty, Thingy! I thought maybe you'd be in brogues and a Henry Heath hat, good-works style!"

"Not yet, though a few more months of Miss Widgeon and I can't vouch for what will happen. You don't exactly look as if you've come out of a cellar yourself," retorted Morwenna, eyeing Odile's elegant bottle-green barathea suit with touches of tartan and a matching tartan blouse.

"Don't say you don't recognize this outfit! I bought it in Paris Easter before last; only presentable clothes I have left. Dressed myself special for this occasion! Most of the time I *do* look exactly as if I've come out of a cellar. Which, of course, I have."

"You've had your hair cut off."

"Had to; had lice in it. Nits."

"You never do things by halves, do you Odo?"

"Everyone in the cellar has nits. Nits are a way of life. I was literally shorn a month ago, but now it's grown a bit and today I've had it permed, as you see. Helps to soften the convict look."

Morwenna stared critically at the crop of little ringlets all over Odile's head. "In fact, it's awfully chic. Suits you. La Dirt-Track in *Destry Rides Again*."

Odile laughed. "Dirt is the operative word in my case, I fear. You won't believe it, but the bath I had at Maytrees last night was the first I'd had in eight weeks. Sheer bliss, that bath!"

"Heavens! You don't stay in your Black Hole twenty-four hours round the clock, do you?"

255

"No. I share a flat near Victoria Park with two other Civil Defence workers. I'm afraid it doesn't boast a bathroom. Still, we were lucky to be offered the place after we'd been blitzed out of Wapping."

She judged it unwise to go into further details. The Victoria Park flat was rented from an evacuated school teacher and Odile and Hugo had it to themselves, for Geoff, seriously injured in the Wapping Island fire, was a patient in a unit for spinal injuries. Hugo and Odile box'd and cox'd it: their relationship amiably affectionate on the occasions when they happened to coincide, but wholly platonic; Hugo's emotional involvemenmt was with Geoff, while Odile was too much taken up with Barrico to have room in her life for any other interest. But such a ménage might easily be misconstrued, and Odile's habit of thinking of Morwenna as an inexperienced child resulted in further mention of the flat being avoided. Odile changed the subject. "And how are things with you? Let's hear about life at Tulip House."

"Not all that much to say about it, really. Just bloody hard drudgery, day after day, all day long, and most of the nights too."

"You're not enjoying it?"

"Enjoying it! Why should I enjoy it? I didn't go there to enjoy myself. I went there because . . ." Morwenna, as if unable to find words to explain why she had gone to Tulip House, helped herself, with a disgruntled frown, to a small cress and fishpaste sandwich. "D'you enjoy Barrico Hold?" she asked, rolling her eyes at Odile, and taking a bite of the sandwich.

"No, I wouldn't exactly say I enjoy Barrico. No, I don't enjoy it, but I can't see myself really exchanging shelter-marshalling at Barrico for any other kind of war job."

"Are you in charge down there?"

"Officially I suppose I am. But it's the sort of set-up everyone's beginning to pitch in now and help run things. There's a queer kind of real community life slowly coming into being down there. I don't feel helplessly alone any more, like I did at the start."

"You're better off than I am, from the sound of it, as far as being free from supervision's concerned! Not that I want to run Tulip House, I don't, but that damn Miss Widgeon!"

"Tell me about Miss Widgeon."

"No; too frustrating for words. I chose to go there, in any case. And in some ways I'm glad I did. It's just that I'm such a blooming skivvy all the time!"

"Poor Thingy! Still, no doubt you'll look back on it one day with a smile. Heard anything of Pam? I haven't been in touch with her for ages. And her friends: Boggy and those Sowersby brothers. What ages ago it all seems! Before the war it seemed possible to keep up with all the news about everything and everybody; now we never seem to know the half of what goes on, even amongst ourselves."

"I haven't heard from Pam myself for quite some time. I imagine that she and Boggy are kept hard at it in that burns unit; no time for letter-writing. I understand that Jos Sowersby's been shot down and killed, and Frank has been posted overseas." Morwenna tried to sound as casual as possible, but her voice trembled in spite of herself.

"That handsome Jos killed! Oh no! His poor family, they'll be devastated!" Odile exclaimed in horror. Then noticing that her sister was close to tears, she determinedly changed the subject. "Let's try to find something more cheerful to talk about! Heard that grandma wants a pedometer to measure how many miles she walks, collecting savings? If you ever see a pedometer lying around, pick it up and post it to her! And oh yes, the mater has asked me to say that, if and when there's a lull in this bombing and she can get time off from her canteen, she wants to take us both out to a concert, or a show, just to remind herself that she has daughters, she says."

"Poor mummy! I suppose she must feel rather like that at times! That she hasn't any family, I mean, except for Grandma and Elizabeth. I wonder when we shall see Papa again! I suppose all families, everywhere, have been broken up like this by the war. More tea?" With an effort Morwenna struggled to bring her own voice and manner under control.

"Ma says that Sybil Spurgeon said the other day that she'd grown so used to not having a husband she sometimes wondered how she would take to finding herself a married woman again."

"Two sides to that problem, I fancy! How's Pa Spurgeon going to feel, faced with having to return to *la belle* Sybil?"

And the sisters somehow managed to gurgle and chatter, and recapture a shadow of their old, pre-war, intimacy.

At last Morwenna said she must be starting back to Tulip House. They settled their bill, left the store and walked to Piccadilly Circus where they kissed one another goodbye with promises to meet again as soon as possible. "Tulip House is really no distance at all from Barrico. It's ridiculous we can't see more of one another!" "*C'est la guerre*, Thingy, *c'est la guerre!*" "Oh, the bloody old *guerre!*" And with these parting words, half groan, half wry laughter, Morwenna ran down the steps to the Tube. Odile remained standing pensively at the corner of Piccadilly and Lower Regent Street. After so much of the East End she felt she would like to savour the West End for just a little longer, before catching her train back to Stoke Hartwell.

The last of the homeward-bound commuters eddied round her, making for the Tube, or queues for buses. October had slipped over November's brink; the blackout came earlier now and the raids started earlier too, so the rush-hour was likewise earlier. Soon the hastening tide of people had dwindled to a trickle. The lights had already gone from London; a purple dusk had fallen, one that would never have been discernible in pre-war days of brilliant city illumination but which now embraced the buildings, the uncrowded streets, the Duke of York's column in the distance of Waterloo Place and the trees of the Mall; St James's Park forming a mysterious darkness beyond. She decided to stroll down to the Mall; by loitering she risked being caught out in a raid, but she had her Civil Defence helmet with her, these days she never went anywhere without it, and she was now too accustomed to air-raids to be over-nervous. In fact, she subscribed to the East End philosophy: "If it's got your number on it then it's got your number on it; if it hasn't, it hasn't."

So down Lower Regent Street she sauntered, through Waterloo Place to the Duke of York's steps where she stood for a moment or two staring at the shadowy scene ahead of her; the Mall, the park, the Admiralty, Horse Guards Parade; deserted, crepuscular, poised in that terrible and pregnant moment in which London balanced, every evening, between the safely accomplished day and the moment when the siren's wail would usher in another night of droning bombers, the crash of guns, the glow of fire, and the certainty that some citizens would never live to see the dawn.

She descended the flight of wide, shallow steps and began walking slowly up the Mall, under the now naked branches of the plane trees; the Mall with its broad carriageway and double avenues of trees converging to a point lost in the rapidly thickening twilight. She seemed to have the place entirely to herself; it was both ghostly and beautiful. On her left lay the park, with a glint of lake between the shadows; on her right were the pale façades of Carlton House Terrace and Marlborough House.

Odile walked slowly, lingeringly, taking an almost sensual delight in the silence, the grey and silver solitude of avenues and trees and shadows and twilight. After two months of Barrico Hold this face of another London seemed almost too lovely to be true.

Footsteps sounded, coming up behind her: a man marching, rather than walking, at a brisk, steady pace. She was overtaken by a Free French officer, a sturdy burly figure who passed her swiftly without a glance. Instantly, though she had barely caught his profile, Odile knew that it was Fernand Legrand.

For a second or so she was stunned by the realization. Then she told herself that she must be mistaken. Yet the figure moving ahead was so very much the Fernand she remembered: of middle height, broad and muscular, rapid and light in movement, determined in outline. However there was no way of being certain, unless she glimpsed his face. He was moving ahead so fast she was obliged to break into a rapid scuttle in her attempt to catch him up. If it were not Fernand; it would be ridiculous to be caught pursuing a total stranger; so she moved to the grass and ran along that, hoping her quarry would not hear her hurrying feet.

The faster she scuttled the more he, too, seemed to quicken his pace. She began to despair of overtaking him. But at Marlborough Gate he was halted by a car coming out of the side street into the Mall. Odile took a bound forward and got a good view of the Frenchman before he stepped off the kerb and shot across the road. It was Fernand.

She shot after him. "Fernand!"

He didn't heed her, but went striding ahead; forcing her to start scuttling, practically running, again.

"Fernand! Fernand!"

But still he ignored her cries, pressing onward so fast that she could almost have believed that he knew she was pursuing him and had made up his mind not to be caught.

At the top of the Mall he crossed the carriage way, swung left and began heading for Buckingham Gate. It was now nearly dark; Odile was afraid she would lose him in the shadows. She was breathless with hurrying and calling his name; her panting gasps verged on sobs. If she lost him now!

But once again he was halted by traffic and this time she literally flung herself at him and caught his arm. "Fernand! It is you, surely!"

He stared at her coldly and said, speaking in French, "It would be far better for us both if you hadn't done this."

She realized then that he had been trying to outpace and lose her.

She faltered, also in French, straining to see his face properly in the darkness, "You mean you'd rather we didn't . . . meet?"

"Yes." Or rather, *Oui*. A *Oui* so emphatic that Odile, who was still clutching his arm, relinquished her hold; her heart plunging from where it properly lodged to somewhere in the bowels of the earth. "Don't worry," she murmured, "we have never met." And, stunned by the shock of rejection, she turned down Buckingham Gate, in the shadow of Wellington Barracks, and began walking rapidly away.

Well, that was that! But she would never recover from this, never.

Footsteps behind her. Surely not Fernand? She dared not turn round to look; she quickened her already quick pace, though it surely wasn't necessary because, after that rebuttal, it couldn't be Fernand.

But she was wrong. "Odile!"

With a gasp of dismay and despite her high heels she broke into a sprint.

"Odile! Odile!"

She was now fleeing all out. She could hear him belting after her, calling urgently, "Odile!"

He caught up with her, grabbed her and swung her round.

"Odile, have you gone mad?"

"Have I gone mad!" she gasped indignantly. They were both panting so heavily with exertion and agitation that they could barely speak.

"You said . . ." she managed at last.

"Oh ignore what I said!"

"I was only doing what you. . . ."

"*Ciel!*" He made a wild grimace of frustration and despair to heaven, seized her and crushed her to him, bruising her mouth with the intensity of his kiss.

Fernand's lodgings were small and shabby, but this Odile never noticed when they tumbled in; the blackout curtains were undrawn across the window and the searchlights, crossing and recrossing and stabbing the sky in search of the raiders whose presence the sirens had just announced, sent a kaleidoscopic variation of light patterns flickering and fumbling across the floor, the bed, the walls, the ceiling, and in this bewildered and frenetic quaich of darkness and illumination they tore off their clothes, pressed themselves together, fell on the bed and completed a union of victory and despair as the ack-ack barrage crashed overhead and somewhere in the street outside a cascade of shattered glass showered over the pavement.

Afterwards they lay smoking cigarettes in the dark room, watching the window with its strips of sticky paper forming a lattice of false security between themselves and laceration. Above the dim façade of houses on the opposite side of the street was the moonless sky, at intervals brilliant with the searchlights and spangled with exploding shells, like fiery flowers in one swift instant bursting into bloom, and then expiring, petal by dropping petal.

At some moment in their timeless and tireless night a stick of bombs fell close, the first near enough to tell them the second would be nearer and the second so near that the third could only fall on them, or so it seemed as it came screaming down above them as they clasped each other in an urgency that could not be quickened even by the imminent proximity of violent death for, bomb or no bomb, they had already reached the climax of vehemency and the only step beyond was explosion: which came, while the whole house seemed to sway and take off into the air.

Presently Fernand made some Nescafé, boiling the water in a kettle on a gas ring that made a strange hissing sound. The night sky, red with distant fire, was closed from view by the now drawn blackout curtains; the dinginess of the cheap little room was harshly revealed by electric light, but to Odile it seemed a room with a special kind of beautiy endowed by circumstance. She absorbed every detail of it, trying to imprint it indelibly upon her mind's eye: the faded yellow wallpaper with green and brown flowers, the small cream painted fireplace with a little gas fire, gas ring and slot-meter box, the worn and faded green carpet, the miserable dressing table and narrow wardrobe, the washbasin in the corner with a tatty screen made of pleated mauve cotton fabric, the bedside table on which stood a small lamp with a dirty pink shade, another pink-shaded light dangling from the ceiling; the bed itself a single divan, placed against the wall; every object in the room cheek by jowl with the next and Fernand, in an incredible floral patterned silk dressing gown, gaudy as a bazaar, edging and sidling his way between this piece of furniture and that.

"Where on earth did you pick up that amazing garment?"

"In Casablanca."

"It makes you look like Max Miller."

"*Comment?*"

Fernand, a Frenchman in a terrible eye-searing dressing-gown, standing in the bedroom of a third-rate Pimlico boarding house, holding a tin of Nescafé in one hand and a kettle in the other, being told that he resembled an Englishman of whom he had never remotely heard, surveyed Odile with an expression so inimitably Gallic in its suspicion of and bafflement by all things Anglo-Saxon that Odile burst into hopeless laughter.

"I can't help it," she managed to say at last. "You're so . . ." And she became helpless with laughter again.

"Who did you say I looked like?"

"Max Miller. At least, your dressing-gown does."

"It's all I could find and I had to have one because I was staying in rather an expensive hotel at that point in time and ate breakfast on a balcony. I couldn't sit there naked."

"It would have been a less injurious sight. It's a wonder you didn't blind the waiter."

"A chambermaid."

"Bet she's still suffering from green splotches before the eyes!" And Odile started giggling again.

"Calm down, or you'll spill coffee all over the bed."

He got in beside her and they lay propped against the pillows sipping the coffee. Then suddenly Odile gave a sharp cry and jerked upright.

"Gosh! What's the time?"

"A quarter to eleven. Why? What's the matter?"

"Only a quarter to eleven? Are you sure? It must be much later than that!"

"We were in bed by seven o'clock, remember."

"I'm supposed to be spending the night at Maytrees. I forgot clean about it! They're going to be frightfully worried if I don't turn up, and don't telephone."

"Relax, Odile! You'll have to tell them tomorrow that you were caught in Town and couldn't phone because of the air raid. It's as good as truth. Relax." He pulled her back onto the pillows and put his arm round her; she rested her cheek against his shoulder. She murmured, "Do you remember *your* mother at Bolbec? Always following us around?"

262

"What hard things I said about her under my breath! And of course, you see, she was right. Here we are at last, just as she feared."

"Even Hitler hasn't been able to stop us." She added, "It was sheer luck, you know, that I was in Town this evening and walking along the Mall. Pure chance!" She paused, then asked, "Aren't you glad now, Fernand, that I chased you down the Mall, and caught you?"

"I'd lie if I said no, but at the same time I still say it would have been better for us both if you hadn't."

"But why? Imagine having missed this!"

"Because I have no room in my life, now, for you, Odile. I am entirely dedicated to France, the liberation of France. All my thoughts and powers of concentration are devoted to that, and that alone. It must be so."

He spoke with an air and expression of categorical virtue that was both impressive and maddening.

"I'm dedicated to beating Hitler, too," said Odile, "but that doesn't mean I can't be in love."

"I am not speaking of merely beating Hitler. I am speaking of liberating France; liberating her from her bonds, her torpor. Our Chief has told us. . . ."

"Your Chief?" intervened Odile.

"De Gaulle. He has told us that we, the FFL, must show the world, by our union, our renunciation, our spirit and our faith, that ours are the voices, political, social, moral, in which our country will rediscover her honour and grandeur. To that end we must sacrifice everything: our personal lives, in this struggle for France, stand as nothing. Our crusade is that of the Cross of Lorraine. To that crusade, for better or worse, I am committed, Odile. Not to you."

Odile, heaving a deep breath, got out of bed and stooped over the litter of clothes scattered about the floor. She found and picked up her bra and put it on. "What are you doing?" exclaimed Fernand.

"Getting dressed. I must go. I feel altogether too much like Queen Guinevere."

"What are you talking about?"

"I don't want to seduce you from your Holy Grail, Fernand."

He got out of bed himself, walked to her slowly, put his arms round her, picked her up, carried her back to the bed, dropped her on it and flung himself on top of her. "You can't walk out on me. One

263

day I shall be forced to walk out on you; that's the tragedy this war has inflicted on us, Odile. But you don't walk out on me." He unfastened her bra, pulled it off and began kissing her breasts. Odile kissed his dark, tousled hair and sighing, murmured, "Let's pray that it isn't a day that comes soon!"

XXXIV

At eight o'clock next morning they were walking across St James's Park. Fernand had to be in his office by eight-thirty, he had an appointment.

"Make a flying start, don't you?"

"*Voilà!*"

An iron rail, about a foot high from the ground, ran along the edge of the path separating it from the grass; Fernand leapt on to the rail and teetered along it rapidly, like a tightrope performer; after some ten yards, disguising the fact that he had lost his balance and was about to fall, he jumped off, waved his cap and shouted, "*Hop-là! Bravo!*"

Odile clapped enthusiastically. "*Encore!*"

"Thank you, but I daren't do it again; might break my ankle. Moreover, the Chief has a habit of taking a turn in this park in the morning before going to his office. I don't think he'd be too amused, between you and me, seeing one of his junior officers doing circus stunts."

"Oh!" She glanced across the park, grey and misty in the morning light. "One can't miss him, because of his height," said Fernand. "He's not here."

He put his arm through Odile's, drew her close to him and kissed her. They then walked on, beside the lake.

"Has General de Gaulle a sense of humour?"

Fernand broke into a laugh, as if at a comic idea. "Not precisely. He has a pungent wit, that isn't always appreciated."

"You haven't told me how you got here, yet. To England."

"I was taken prisoner of war. I escaped. I travelled to Morocco by boat; from Oran I went to Casablanca by train; I presently left Casablanca disguised as a Polish soldier, with a contingent of Polish troops bound for England. It all took much longer than that, but there you have the essence of it."

They reached the little bridge on the lake and paused on it. The morning smelled of autumn, with a touch of early winter; of mouldering fallen leaves; of last night's raid. The air was cold: the ducks quacked loudly, as if apprehensive of icy months ahead. Odile leant on the bridge rail, staring at the ducks and the island. Fernand stared at her. She felt his eyes upon her and said, with a slight smile, "If you stare at me as hard as that, you'll hurt your eyes."

"I want to remember you, and this bridge, and this morning after last night. A memory to carry about with me after we've said goodbye."

"But, Fernand, we're not saying goodbye now. I mean, we're saying goodbye now, but not for good! We'll see each other again, shan't we?"

"I've no idea."

"But you're not leaving England yet?"

"I've no idea," he repeated. "In any case, as things are at present there's no guarantee that we'll both still be alive this time tomorrow. You know that as well as I do."

She sighed. "I remember you saying that to me on the beach at Bolbec, that last morning. I said maybe there'd be no war, and you said, 'Yes, there'll be a war this time; you know it as well as I do.' Do you remember?"

"I remember. And I gave you a shell as a souvenir."

"I still have it."

"Never!"

"Of course!"

They burst out laughing. He put his arms around her; they leaned against the bridge parapet laughing and kissing.

"What a way to behave in a public park at eight o'clock in the morning!"

"All the same, I very much fear, my darling and beautiful Odile, that all you will be left with in the end will be a scallop shell and a broken heart."

"And you?"

"I shall be dead."

"Oh, don't be so Gallic and gloomy! Maybe our luck will hold; for just look how miraculously lucky we've been, meeting again like this." She kissed his hand and caressed it. "Suppose I'd let you escape from me last night; think what we should have missed!"

"That's perfectly true!" He allowed his tone and manner to lift. "But all the same, with the best will in the world I don't see how we can be too optimistic about future meetings when you spend every night in a cellar and I spend all my days in an office."

"That's true." It was now Odile's turn to look dejected. "What's more I don't see much chance of getting regular nights off. Mine's not like an ordinary job, or even being in one of the Services."

"Surely you could ask for one night off a week?"

"Ask who?"

"Your chief. Whoever your chief is."

"I have no chief. I'm my own chief. I'm the shelter marshal, full stop. That's the trouble; if there was someone else I could ask for permission they'd probably say yes and it would be easy, but when it's oneself. . . ."

"I understand perfectly. Like an officer always sees that his men are in comfortable quarters before he forages for himself. Which means he, poor fellow, spends a damn awful night."

"Precisely." She stared up the lake towards Whitehall, the strengthening morning light catching the trunks of trees and the paler stone of buildings behind them. "However, I honestly don't see why I shouldn't treat myself to a night off once a fortnight. Could you manage that?"

"Oh I daresay my powers of performance would stretch to once a fortnight, yes!"

"If the Blitz eases off I might wangle once a week."

"Exhausting!"

"And, of course, if only they'd stop entirely. . . ."

"I'd be prostrate!"

"No, be serious. If I can get a few nights off. . . ."

"Get what you can. Only not in office hours. The Chief, I fear, would not be sympathetic. He's not the Don Giovanni type."

She caught sight of his watch. "It's twenty past eight."

"*Mon Dieu*, so it is! Listen, where and when can I telephone you?"

"Oh lor, I don't see how you can! I'm not on the phone. Can I ring you anywhere?"

"Here's the Pimlico number." He took a pencil and a scrap of paper from his pocket and scribbled the number on it.

"Telephone me there between half past six and seven; I'll be waiting by the phone; it's in a call box in the hall."

"But that's when the raids start, half past six to seven!"

"To hell with the raids. I'll be waiting by the phone."

XXXV

"Look here Pete, I told you before and I ain't bleedin' well telling you again, if you ain't a good boy you won't be getting no present when Father Christmas comes round, see?"

And Marie gave Pete a brisk shake to impress this horrid fact upon him.

"When's he coming, Mum?" asked Rhona.

"Blimey Roan, if I told you once I told you fifty times; he's coming here tonight!"

Rhona had long since stopped believing in Father Christmas, but she was still deeply interested in receiving presents and was perfectly agreeable to the idea that someone pretending to be Father Christmas should be coming to Barrico Hold to hand them out.

"Is everyone going to get a present?" she asked, again for the umpteenth time.

"Cor strike a light Roan, give it a rest!" groaned her mother. "Start wishing Father Christmas had never bin invented, I shall, if you keep on like this! Oi, Pete, come back! Kergh, little bleeder's off again! Fetch him back, Roan; go on quick, fetch him back!"

Rhona darted off after Peter, who was apparently heading for the furthermost recesses of Barrico Hold. Marie said to Josie, who was sitting next to her with the twins, "You just wait till them two of yours are running about, both in different directions at once!"

"Enough trouble already, crawling," said Josie.

Old Mrs Tooley said, "Thought you weren't comin' to Barrico any more, Josie; thought you said you were going down the Tube."

"So she is," said Marie, "after Christmas. Just coming here over Christmas so's to get the presents for the kiddies."

"You going down the Tube, Marie?" enquired someone else, seated nearby.

"No. Suits me here in Barrico with my mates," said Marie.

"Tube's warmer in winter time," said Josie. "I get ever so cold here."

"It's better now we got all these partitions up," said Mrs Tooley. "Nice now we all got our own cubicles, like."

"I'd rather be down the Tube," said Josie. The London Underground had been invaded by shelter-seeking thousands early on in the Blitz; authority had had to concede to public demand for usage of the Tube passages and platforms as places of refuge. Josie had tried the Tube once or twice with friends and now thought it decidedly preferable to Barrico. "Safer too," she said.

"Barrico's safest shelter in London," said Mrs Tooley. "Proved it!"

"What, when they had that bomb back in September?" said Marie. "Yes, proved it then alright."

Josie shook her head. "You're wrong Mum. Tube is safest. Everyone says so."

At this point terrible yells and shrieks were heard; Rhona came, hauling a protesting Pete towards his mother. He was struggling and kicking so hard that his pants fell down, revealing white thready legs and buttocks bright scarlet with nappy rash. Marie gave a shriek. "Cor you wicked boy, now you lost your knickers! Come on, Roan; give me the kid. Can't you even keep the little bleeder decent?"

Everyone else was laughing. Marie grabbed hold of Pete and hauled his pants up. "You stop that hollering, Pete, will you? Give us all headaches with that bleeding awful noise! Father Christmas will hear you and then he *won't* bring you nothing, that's a dead cert!"

Pete roared, "I wanna . . . I wanna . . .!"

"What you want and what you get are two different things! You'll get your legs slapped if you go on like that!" Pete howled, his face scarlet, great fat drops of tears sploshing down his cheeks. Marie, her heart relenting, pulled him on to her lap, gave him a hug and said, "Here, tell you what! Go along with Roan and ask the young lady shelter marshal if she'll let you have a silver star to help with.

Roan, take him and ask the marshal if she'll let him help a minute with a silver star, just to keep him quiet."

"All right Mum," said the resigned Rhona. "Come on Pete, come and get a silver star! Here, come and see the Christmas tree!"

Odile patrolled cheerfully round the cellar, watching the scores of volunteers busy putting up the Christmas decorations. Over the past three to four months remarkable changes had taken place in Barrico Hold. Blast walls had been built, dividing the cellar for greater safety; these divisions had been sub-divided for social reasons, as well as for comfort. The "cubicles" as they were called, though "compartments" would perhaps have been a better word, each held some two to three hundred persons and each cubicle accommodated a different group: some of the groupings were determined by nationality (there were more than twenty-five different national groups down in Barrico Hold), some by age (the adolescent youngsters liked to gang up together), others by districts and streets. There was a contingent of bombed-out people from Silvertown, another from the Isle of Dogs, a third from Wapping Island, and so on. Street groupings, above all, were popular: this was scarcely surprising, for, in dockland, families had lived in the same streets for generations, forming what almost might be called street clans; neighbours who had known each other and lived next to or near one another from infancy and whose parents and grandparents before them had enjoyed the same neighbourly closeness.

Marie, who had been born and brought up in Stepney and had lived there all her life until her second marriage, had surely returned like a homing pigeon to her old street group, the group of her childhood, girlhood and early womanhood. Everyone knew her; she knew everyone. Deep inside herself, in a funny sort of way, she was happier now, down in Barrico, than she had been for years.

The extraordinary improvements that had taken place in Barrico Hold had been achieved through the efforts of the shelterers themselves. The most important step forward of all, the reduction of the shelter population by a good half, had occurred perfectly spontaneously; people, finding the overcrowding insupportable, had simply moved off to other shelters. Those who had remained behind had set about making Barrico "the best bleeding shelter in London, mate!"

There was now a Barrico Hold shelter committee, each cubicle choosing a representative to sit on it. Each cubicle, too, had its own warden, invariably a middle-aged matron. These were responsible for airing bedding, keeping the cubicle clean and tidy, preserving law and order therein, and so forth. Further general cleaning and maintenance teams were organized by the main shelter committee. There was a canteen and penny-a-cup soup service, initiated and run by volunteers drawn from the shelterers, and a laundry service. Everyone was keen to play some part.

Requests made by the committee for outside help had resulted in gifts of blankets, bedding, barley sugar for babies, books, clothing. Ante and post-natal clinics were organized; health visitors called. Evening classes in adult education were run. A piano arrived; there were sing-songs, religious services, parties. A chess club sprang up, a dominoes and darts club, knitting groups, sewing groups, a girls' skipping group, a boys' PT group. Barrico Hold also had its own Fire Guard, its own First Aid squad. For the past three weeks it had even had its own rudimentary news sheet and bulletin. The latest activity, stimulated by Christmas, was a choir which, like all the other developments, had come into being without any prompting from outside authority. The shelterers themselves had decided they wanted all these things and had then set about creating, or obtaining them.

Odile found it all fascinating and exciting. She was an essential part of this activity: a co-opted member of the shelter committee; chairman of a committee of cubicle wardens; she played the piano; organized a child-minding group in order to leave mothers free to enjoy shelter activities; helped organize talks and discussions. Indeed it was true to say of Odile, as it was of Marie, that she was happier now than she had ever been in her life before. To be sure, much of her happiness was due to Fernand's presence in London: though, so far, they hadn't managed to see one another more than once a fortnight, yet once a fortnight was bliss when compared with all those months when not only had she not seen him, but for much of the time had thought him to be dead. But Fernand's reappearance in her life was not the sole cause for her happiness; she was riding the high of the incredible mainspring of community endeavour and fellowship that was inspiring everyone down in Barrico.

Now, as Odile stood happily admiring the Christmas tree with all its handmade, which meant Barrico-made, decorations, a little girl came up to her dragging a grubby, smelly toddler. "Miss, can he have a silver star to hold?"

"He can hang a star on the tree if he wants," said Odile. "Is that what he'd like?"

"Wanna star, wanna star!" yelled the infant.

"You can't keep it, ducks, but you can hang it on the tree." And Odile gave the little boy a star and held him up so that he could hang it on a bough, the girl helping him. "There you are, isn't it pretty? Now everyone will enjoy it, won't they?" said Odile, beaming at him. He, wide-eyed in wonder, stared at the tall star-gleaming tree. "Bleeding luv'ly, ain't it all?" sighed the little girl. "Real Chrismassy Chrissmas this year, innit!"

Barely an hour later, Father Christmas arrived; the decorations had been completed just in time. The children had all been placed seated on the ground in front of the crowding adults, thus ensuring that the "little 'uns" would get a good view. Father Christmas had no reindeer or sleigh, which was a slight disappointment, but he was attended by Barrico Hold's youngest fire-fighting group: Nelson Tooley, Lenny Schreiber and fifteen-year-old twins, Fred and Gus. They had with them the handcart on which they normally conveyed their stirrup-pump, sand buckets, water buckets, shovels and so forth. Tonight the cart was piled high with magnificently wrapped parcels, a glittering, shining, gorgeous load. Behind the cart tripped a fairy in white and tinsel, with little stiff white wings, long pale blond hair with a star fixed in it, and carrying a wand with a star at its tip. Father Christmas (Clem heavily disguised in whiskers and beard) was, of course, greeted with a rousing cheer; Nelson and his gang of three and the loaded handcart brought even louder cheers. The fairy was received with cheers mingled with loud and appreciative wolf whistles.

Father Christmas joked and laughed his way through the crowd, stopping frequently to speak to the children. He took the parcels, one by one, from the cart; each bore a label saying what it contained and he relied upon the fairy, Nelson, Lenny, Fred and Gus to hand the gifts to suitable-looking recipients. The presents themselves were magnificent: they came from across the Atlantic and nobody in Barrico Hold had seen Christmas gifts quite of that splendour before. Dolls, trains, paintboxes, pencil cases crammed with pencils, teddy bears, Donald Ducks, Goofies, Mickey and Minnie

271

Mice, Snow Whites, Seven Dwarves, Little Pigs, Noah's Arks, bangles, necklaces, slippers, woolly gloves, pixie hoods, banjos, musical boxes, humming tops: there was no end to the wonders. Rhona got a skipping-rope, a box of embroidered handkerchiefs and a propelling pencil with six different coloured leads in it. Peter got a Donald Duck and a big coloured rubber ball. Gerry got a teddy bear and a pair of vivid red socks; Gary got a Goofy and some yellow socks. All the children were beside themselves with glee.

The distribution of gifts was followed by carol singing. Morwenna, who, as the fairy, had warmed herself up well and truly dancing about handing round gifts, now wrapped herself in her thick coat and had a cup of coffee with Odile at the canteen. "What are you doing with yourself over the rest of Christmas?" enquired Odile.

"Well, I'm afraid I shan't get home for it. We've a few more shelters to visit with Father Christmas tomorrow afternoon; we couldn't get round them all in one evening. And Boxing Day there's a big children's party, and it'll be all hands on deck for that. What are you doing?"

"I'm on duty here tomorrow; we're having a special Christmas dinner laid on by the WVS and naturally I shall be down here for that, and then I've forty-eight hours' leave, isn't that luscious? And I'm spending it with a friend."

"Not allowed to know who, Odo?" murmured Morwenna with a teasing smile.

"Not allowed to know who," replied Odile, dimpling. Morwenna thought to herself, "Well, she was bound to get over Fernand, some time or other."

Clem, still dressed as Father Christmas, came to join them for a cup of coffee. Morwenna introduced him properly to Odile and the three stood chatting and laughing. Then Clem said, "I better discard these pagan trappings and return as a man of the cloth." He vanished behind some screens and reappeared in his cassock and dog-collar to conduct a Christmas service, a simple one, designed for the children. They sang "Away in a Manger" and "Good King Wenceslas" and Clem spoke to them about the Prince of Peace. Odile, who generally couldn't abide the clergymen who came down to Barrico, was rather disarmed by Clem's unaffected spontaneity.

They ended up with "Hark the Herald Angels", and then Clem, Morwenna and the junior fire-fighters with their now empty cart departed, among rousing cries of "Goodnight!" and "Merry

Christmas!", to restack their cart and repeat their ceremonies all over again at the next shelter.

Revelries now erupted in many of the cubicles. It had previously been decided by the committee that Christmas Eve parties should be held in certain cubicles, while others should be left in peace for those shelterers who wanted to sleep. Marie's cubicle was one designated for sleepers; the children were put down in their blankets, the cubicle warden remained to keep an eye on them while most of the other adults removed themselves to make merry in another cubicle.

"Nice quiet night we're being given by 'Itler for Christmas, innit?" said Mrs Tooley appreciatively. "Wonder how long it will last?"

"Well, one thing I do know," rejoined Marie, with her broadest grin, "The buggers will have to wait with their next lot till I've had a good booze up!"

Some of the parties lasted much longer than others. Marie's capacity for revelry was immense once she got going; she was dancing long after the much younger Josie had retired, worn out. Finally there was a tremendous "Knees Up", with much shouting and shrieking laughter and then even Marie decided to call it a day and made her way, unsteadily, back to her cubicle, to find the rest of its occupants either snoring, or disposed to complain at all the noise Marie and her friends had been making.

"Never mind," said Marie, with cheerful philosophy, "Christmas only comes once a year!"

"Good job it does, if you're going to kick up a row like that every time it comes round," said a querulous old man who had not joined in any of the night's festivities.

"I enjoy a bit of Christmas every now and again," retorted Marie, with a slightly belligerent edge to her tone.

"Yes, we noticed that."

"No harm in enjoying yourself! No help to nobody having long faces around!"

"No help to nobody keeping everyone awake when they want to sleep, neither! 'Itler gives us a peaceful night for once, and you take over!"

"Cor!" shrilled Marie to the cubicle in general, "listen to him! Anyone'd think I'd been blasting off like a bleeding land-mine!"

"Nice Christmas Eve though, Marie," said Mrs Tooley soothingly. "Nice service. Nice that bit about the Prince of Peace."

"Yes, that made you think, didn't it?" said Josie. "Made you really stop and think about war and that, didn't it?"

Marie sat down on her blanket and, with difficulty, began taking off her boots. "Always be wars," she said.

"Why, Mum? Why must there always be wars?" asked Josie. "Don't see why."

"Maybe it's different for clergymen, maybe they do meet with a bit of peace and quiet along the way, but for ordinary people life's just one long battle and it's no use talking to me about any bleeding Prince of Peace! No more's it any good to talk to me about the Ligger Nations! One time, we had a clergyman up our way, up Bow Creek, who was always on about the Ligger Nations. Kept coming round with a collecting box, he did: for the Ligger Nations. Came to me with a bleeding collecting box!" Marie wrenched off her left boot and waved it at the company, warming to her theme. "Me, what couldn't even collect enough for the bleeding rent let alone the Ligger Nations! I said to him, 'Look!' I said, 'Look, no use talking to me about the Ligger Nations because if ordinary working people have to fight all the way along the line, wot hope is there of peace for the Ligger Nations?'" She paused and eyed her audience gloomily for a few seconds. Then, "Who are the sodding Ligger Nations anyway?" she asked, her manner deeply suspicious, her dark glance roving over the company.

There was no reply. Everyone looked uncomfortable. At last the old man said, feebly, "Dunno, mate."

"Are we a Ligger Nation?"

"Dunno."

"Don't do us no fucking good if we are, does it?" said Marie. "Don't stop 'Itler dropping this lot down on our heads!"

There was another pause; Marie, pulling off her second boot glared indignantly at them all; they shifted uneasily. Marie was known to sling boots with deadly accuracy when roused. Receiving no answers to her questions she at last drew a long breath, heavy with port and lemon, and said, "If you ask my opinion, you can stuff the Ligger Nations where the monkey stuffed his nuts, and the Prince of Peace too I reckon!"

"Cor Mum!" said Josie, shocked. "That's blasphemy!"

"Why?" Marie sounded surprised.

"Prince of Peace, that's Jesus! That's why!"

"Jesus!" Marie sounded genuinely amazed. "I thought it was one

274

of the Royal Family. That's the point I was making see?" She thrust her face fiercely at Josie. "I was thinking to myself while that young clergyman was keeping on at us; bleeding King can't stop the war, so what chance has the Prince of Peace got?"

Josie closed her eyes in mortification at having such a parent. "Cor Mum!" But the old man, for the first time that Christmas Eve, began to cackle with laughter until he was shedding tears.

"Oh, give it a rest, mate!" suddenly bawled little Mrs Green, the cubicle warden, who had been lying curled up under her blanket, but who now sat bolt upright, her patience exhausted. "Worse noise than all the rest of 'em put together, you're making! Wake the whole place up! Come on, give it a rest!" Then, as the old man still wheezed and coughed and cackled and gasped, Mrs Green grabbed hold of one of Marie's boots, pounded the floor with it like a chairman calling for order and screeched, in the piercing voice of the street vendor she had once been, "GOOD NIGHT ALL AND NOW BLEEDING GO TO SLEEP AND MERRY CHRISTMAS!"

From all over the cellar this display of high authority was good-humouredly greeted with laughter, cheers, friendly catcalls and answering shouts of, "MERRY CHRISTMAS!" Finally a voice sang out, "Sweet dreams old gal! Mind a reindeer don't get you!"

And the calm of Christmas night enfolded Barrico Hold.

XXXVI

Christmas Day dinner for over eighty people, at Tulip House, was an experience not to be forgotten in a hurry. The Mission was an old-established one with many friends, some in the unlikeliest of places; turkeys had arrived from a well-wisher who asked to remain anonymous. Tulip House must have been one of the few places in Britain where turkey was eaten that Christmas Day.

Just before the meal was served Father Christmas appeared with his attendant fairy, and gifts were given to the children. Father Christmas then presided at the dinner and carved the turkeys. The repast ended with toasts and speeches, the toasts being drunk in cider. Miss Widgeon and Miss Whitebeam, being teetotal, were innocently convinced that cider was a harmless beverage and produced it every Christmas; the flushed faces and lively noisy talk that ensued they always attributed to seasonal high spirits.

Morwenna was enjoying Christmas rather more than she had anticipated. Her rupture with Frank had at first left her desolate, if desolation meant a ceaseless gnawing sensation of empty despair. Fortunately there was so much to keep her busy at Tulip House that she was deprived of much opportunity to brood upon her loss; she suspected that Miss Widgeon thought up ways of occupying Morwenna's every moment as a form of therapy for a mourning heart: "Bad news about a friend." Above all, concluded Morwenna, devoting oneself to the problems and sorrows of others went a long way to ease the aching of one's own heart. So many of the people of the refuge had lost loved ones, lost everything; Morwenna felt almost ashamed to find herself moping over Frank.

So, to please Clem (who was tireless in his efforts to serve others) and to entertain the hundreds of homeless children in the shelters and refuges that Christmas, Morwenna had flung herself into the role of a fairy and had discovered herself getting a remarkable amount of fun out of the enterprise. Not only fun: there were moments when she was almost touched to tears as she handed a shiningly wrapped gift to some gaping, grubby toddler and saw the look of wonderment in the child's eyes.

Nelson and his crew had been invited to the Tulip House dinner; they became markedly merry on the cider and when Father Christmas and his party rose to depart on their next round of shelter visits their condition was, as Morwenna thought to herself (with a sudden sharp pang at the memory), distinctly akin to *Bublie crient e weissel E laticome e drinckeheil.* . . .

Everyone accompanied them upstairs to see them off; as they passed through the kitchen Clem suddenly grabbed hold of Lily who, in all innocence, was standing under the mistletoe and gave her a robust hug and kiss that brought the house down. She herself thought it the most tremendous joke, once she had got her breath back, and was still clinging to the dresser rocking with laughter as Father Christmas and his companions emerged into Sparrowgrass Row.

The afternoon was an uproarious success; from one Christmas Party to another they progressed, with the cheers and shouts of "Merry Christmas!" of their last port of call still ringing in their ears as they marched triumphantly into the next. Father Christmas was pouring with sweat inside his warm costume; Nelson and his stalwarts couldn't stop laughing; Morwenna's cheeks were an unwonted bright pink and her eyes shone as brightly as the stars in her hair and at the tip of her wand.

It was late afternoon and dark when they came away from the final shelter on their list. The fire-fighters had to get back to Barrico and duty, Clem had an evening service to conduct, Morwenna had to prepare suppers. At the corner of Burdett Road and St Paul's Way the little company, that had been so successful in distributing good cheer, broke up with handshakes and congratulations. Nelson, Lenny, Gus and Fred went one way with their handcart; Clem and Morwenna began walking off in the other. They could hear the wheels of the cart scraping along over the road surface, the sound, that had accompanied them on their Christmas touring over the past two days, suddenly held a moving nostalgia. Morwenna said, "Good old cart! I wonder if we'll be going round with it next Christmas."

"Please God there won't be any shelters to go round to, next Christmas."

"It's been fun though, Clem."

"Yes. It's been a wonderful Christmas. Everyone, everywhere you go, agrees that it's been one of the best Christmasses ever! And not only the merrymaking and the parties — the churches have been crowded and the services quite inspiring."

"That midnight service was marvellous."

"It was, wasn't it? I thought so; absolutely."

They trudged along the dark, empty street that was melancholy with the drained mood that always engulfs a Christmas Day afternoon. Morwenna realized, for the first time, that her blue satin fairy slippers pinched her feet.

Tulip House was deserted, everyone was over at a tea party in the main Mission building; even Miss Whitebeam had been wheeled across to it. Morwenna and Clem went into the kitchen. Morwenna said, "Like a cup of tea, Clem? I'm gasping for one."

"Wonderful suggestion!"

"D'you mind if I take off my shoes?"

"I'd object most strenuously."

Morwenna, laughing, removed them and, in stockinged feet, filled the kettle and put it on to boil. Clem removed his hood, beard and whiskers and said, "Whew!"

"We shan't forget this Christmas in a hurry, Clem."

"I suspect not."

"Gosh, you weren't half a success, though, as Father Christmas."

"You mean some of the munificence of our American friends rubbed off on me?"

"Yes. But you were pretty good too, yourself, you know."

"You were not that dusty as a fairy!"

Morwenna, taking the tea caddy from its shelf, burst out laughing. Clem, who was in his favourite position, propped against the dresser, suddenly swooped on her, said, "You're asking for it!" and enveloped her in an embrace that turned into a very long one. Morwenna realized that she had been standing under the mistletoe and, when at last their protracted kissing was over, that she had tilted most of the contents of the tea caddy on to the floor.

"Oh glory be, Clem, that's a month's tea ration for this household gone for a burton."

Clem, his voice sounding slightly shaky, said, "Get the dustpan and brush. We'll sweep it up. Nobody will ever know."

Morwenna got the dustpan and brush and together they knelt on the kitchen floor, Morwenna giggling wildly and Clem starting to giggle too.

"There's grit and dust and everything in it! They can't be given that to drink!" said Morwenna.

"Tea's made with boiling water. That'll sterilize it. We can't lose an entire month's tea ration because we kissed under the mistletoe. Imagine trying to explain that. . . ."

"To Miss Widgeon!" Morwenna chorused with him.

They roared with laughter at the impossible notion and, finding themselves under the mistletoe once more, began kissing again.

"It's true, perhaps I didn't know my own mind!" Morwenna thought, and then forgot about thinking.

Presently, as they sat drinking their tea, Morwenna said, "You know, Clem, I think perhaps I should tell you that I have been in love before."

"I realize that. In fact, I learned about it early on, while you were still in hospital. Something that Posy let drop. She made it fairly clear to me that you were, as she put it, 'sweet on a young officer'. I had a feeling she was trying to warn me off, giving me notice that I'd better not try to cut him out. Truth is, most unchristian of me and I should be ashamed, but even at that early stage I'd made up my

mind to jolly well cut him, or any other contender, out. I was going
to get you or bust, and that's the truth."

"And there was he referring to you as a doddery old clergyman!"

"Really?" Clem was highly amused. "Didn't you enlighten him?"

"I didn't have an opportunity. He, one might say, cut himself out,
or off, almost immediately after that."

"All for the best. It would have been a shocking thing had we
come to blows. But it's unseemly of me to gloat. Poor chap."

"He said I didn't know my own mind. I was too young," said
Morwenna after a pause.

"Youth and age survived the day; you too young, and me too
doddery. And here we are!" He took her hand.

"Yes. Here we are," said Morwenna.

XXXVII

Fernand loved dancing at the Lyceum: it was crowded, smoky,
dimly lit; he said it reminded him of the dance halls in Paris that he
had frequented as a student. "It isn't smart, but who wants to be
smart? I'm sure you have plenty of other admirers, Odile, to take
you to the Savoy."

"Oh stacks! And you know what a lot of time I have to kill!"

They shared this little joke ritual each time they went to the
Lyceum. They went through the ritual this evening and followed it
with a conversation that, though it never ran word for word the
same each time, was close enough the same nonetheless. After the
first few dances they always went to the bar and there Odile had a
ginger beer and Fernand a lemonade. And as he poured the
lemonade, his dark eyes slightly closed against the smoke of the
cigarette that he held between his lips while he used both hands to
wield bottle and glass, Fernand would explain why he had given up
alcohol, except a glass of wine when they dined. "You can't drink
and concentrate: truly concentrate. And I have to concentrate hard,
nowadays. On my job; on you. When there isn't much time left, one
has to learn to condense a whole life in a matter of mere months,

perhaps weeks! Every night we're together has to be a *tour de force*, for it's all we've got and are ever going to get, *hein?*" And he commenced laughing, catching the cigarette from between his lips just in time, as it was about to fall; wartime laughter; reckless, and at a notion that, without a war, would have seemed just the reverse of comic.

"So you keep telling me and so, I suppose I must believe you," replied Odile at the close of the conversation this evening; as usual half tempted to laugh with him and half in despair.

But at least she had the satisfaction of knowing that he now felt she mattered to him in equal proportion to the Cross of Lorraine: he had to concentrate on her, as well as on the liberation and renewed grandeur of France! Two months ago he had been convinced that there was no room whatever for an Odile in his life.

"Fernand," she said, thinking of this.

"What, *ma chérie?*"

"Nothing. Just that I love you, that's all," sighed Odile.

He put his face close against hers, staring deep into her eyes; she could smell his warm breath and feel it on her cheek. Sighing, she took his hand; his fingers were deeply stained with nicotine.

"You smoke too much, Fernand my darling."

"Again, concentration. I have to smoke a lifetime's cigarettes in a mere matter of months, remember!"

"It's not good for you."

"That does matter, doesn't it?"

"I shall really be amused if you live to be seventy-five."

"And I shall be astounded. Where should we retire to? Some-where nice and balmy, on the Côte d'Azur: Menton?"

"Menton will do nicely."

"Or would you prefer Bolbec? All those dear, far away memories."

"It would be rather windy in winter, wouldn't it? Windy and wet."

"You're probably correct. Menton would be better. Not that we shall ever get there; but, that left aside, Menton would be better. Why have you become so distractingly beautiful, Odile?"

"You can't see straight, mate, that's the answer. All this cigarette smoke. And the wretched lighting!"

"Shall we dance again?"

"Yes."

The red signals, indicating that an air raid was in progress, had been on above the dance floor all evening; the raid had started early and ferociously. This opening bombardment had scarcely been noticed by Odile and Fernand; they had been in bed. And now, at the Lyceum, the raid continued to be ignored, the crowded dancers behaving as if there were no bombers over London at all.

The band was playing a tango; Odile loved tangos. And Fernand was a marvellous dancer; he was one of those broad, muscular people who look heavy but in reality are remarkably light on their feet and adroit in their movements.

"Have you noticed," said Odile, after they had been dancing for several moments, "that the worst raids come at the weekends, now. Specially if I've been able to take a Saturday night off to be with you. Like I have tonight."

"Some wretched spy has reported to Hitler that a certain terribly dangerous Free French officer is in the habit of relaxing his guard on Saturday nights, and, such being the case. . . ."

A loud crash, and the lights flickered, went out, everyone groaned, then they came on again and everyone cheered and carried on dancing. A second crash, a little further away. The band struck up a rumba and the dance floor vibrated with the animated tempo of the dancers.

It was a fortnight after Christmas, the happiest Christmas of their lives, they both agreed; forty-eight hours of leave together, spent almost entirely in the shabby little bedroom of a third-rate boarding-house in Pimlico. They had given one another chocolates as an exchange of Christmas gifts, to fortify each other's energy, and they had eaten them lying in bed, laughing. Once they had gone round to a wine bar to have a drink and turkey sandwiches. Fernand had bought a bottle of wine and some extra sandwiches and they had taken them back to the bedroom and consumed them when they had woken up at two in the morning. Nothing had mattered in the whole world except themselves and one another.

Forty-eight hours was the longest period that as yet they had had alone together. But on the occasions when Odile managed to get a Saturday night off this gave them twenty-four hours. They met in Piccadilly Underground ticket hall at three, raced to Pimlico and bed and remained there until six or seven, went to Soho and ate at the Universelle, then went dancing at the Lyceum, wandered home on foot through a romantic blacked-out central London, were back in bed by two, stayed there until two or thereabouts the next afternoon, had a late lunch at a wine bar and after that walked to Victoria, where they said *au revoir* until the next time.

This evening, at the Lyceum, during another interval in their dancing, while they were drinking coffee, Fernand produced a small package from his pocket. "A present for you *ma'm'selle*, a little souvenir of our happiness together. For you to open after I'm gone."

"Gone where?"

"Away, of course."

A cold finger touched Odile's heart. "But you aren't going yet, are you?"

"I've told you, often enough, I never know when, or where, I shall have to go. The Free French resemble any other army: nobody knows when, or where, they'll be posted. There's the whole of the Free French empire left for me to be sent to, and as everything's becoming very fluid now, with all kinds of developments in North Africa, for example, the chances of my remaining here in London for much longer are pretty slender."

"Oh Fernand! How shall I live without you? You'll come back won't you?"

"I doubt it."

Odile's eyes flooded with tears. Fernand, seeing them, was clearly appalled by the result of his words. He gabbled quickly, "No, no, my sweet Odile I don't mean that! I mean, it's most unlikely I shall return to London. When next we meet it's almost certain to be in Paris, not London."

"Like I never joined you at the Sorbonne," Odile managed to say, somehow controlling her tears and her voice.

"*Tiens*, who knows, we may find ourselves together at the Sorbonne yet!"

"Two middle-aged students," said Odile wryly.

"There'll be a lot of things to catch up. Everyone will be catching up on everything, after the war."

She knew he didn't believe a word of what he was saying. It was only said to comfort her.

She repeated, "But you aren't going yet, are you?"

"Of course not, my darling. Of course not."

At midnight the raid was raging worse than ever; the band played louder and louder so that the dancers couldn't hear the noise outside. Odile found herself feeling increasingly uneasy. She had heard innumerable stories, since the Blitz began, of persons who had been seized with a strange uneasiness and, taking it as a premonition of disaster, had left the house or shelter they had been in, or, in another version of the tale, had cancelled going to their next appointment, or wherever it was that they were supposed to be going; in each variation upon this theme the leaving of a place, or the refusal to go to another, had saved the person's life from the bomb that had fallen.

Odile was not superstitious, but she was now feeling peculiarly uneasy, and she had heard of this kind of thing so often, from people of perfect integrity whose word she had no reason to doubt, that presently, at the end of a slow foxtrot, she said to Fernand, "Would you mind very much if we left? I would so awfully much like to get away from here."

He looked at her with concern. "My poor love, you're rather pale. Are you feeling ill?"

"No. I just don't feel at ease here any longer. I'd like to leave."

"Return to Pimlico and a little *tour de force, hein*?"

Normally they would have strolled back to Pimlico, exchanging long embraces on the way, but this night was not an inviting one for strolling and when a taxi came along the Strand Fernand hailed it. They sat in the taxi, and Fernand began to kiss her. Unfortunately the taxi driver was in a talkative mood, possibly to cover raw nerves. "They was bringing 'em out in blankets when I drove past, always a bad sign. What can't come out on a stretcher must've copped it nasty. And when I went back . . . cor, feel that?" As the taxi seemed for a moment to rise in the air and settle again. They sped down Whitehall, the road to themselves; the taxi driver resumed his conversation. "Well, as I was saying, when I went back that way they'd got it all cordoned off, and to judge by the number of ambulances I'd say it was a real bad incident." He chatted on, Odile paying him but scant attention and Fernand even less. The taxi reached their destination. Odile jumped out and ran up the front steps and opened the door with the key that Fernand had handed her in order to save time while he paid the fare. Then he raced into the house after her, laughing, while the taxi driver shouted effusive thanks from his cab. "How ever much tip did you give him?" asked Odile. "No idea. I didn't wait to count it. Must've been something lavish. Get upstairs!" urged Fernand.

But their way was barred by Fernand's landlady, a gaunt elderly woman who emerged now from the basement where she had been taking refuge. She was wearing slacks over her pyjamas, a shawl

283

round her shoulders, and her hair was put up in curlers under a pink lace slumber-net fastened with a bow under her chin. She informed Fernand that there had been a telephone call for him and a number had been left for him to ring immediately he got in. "I told 'em that you were usually late on a Saturday night, Captain Legrand, but, whatever the hour, they want you to telephone."

"Oh hell! You go on up Odile. Be with you in a tick."

Odile went to his room and started to undress. Fernand's landlady, she reflected, not for the first time, was a most broadminded, sensible woman; not all landladies allowed young men, even in wartime, to fetch girls home with them in the middle of the night. But she said she was used to military men; her husband had been a military man. And she could see that Odile was respectable. "Which is more than some might." Odile said to herself with a grin, as she removed her bra and leapt happily naked into bed.

Fernand pounded up the stairs and burst into the room. "I have to go out for a while. If I'm not back, don't worry. I shan't have been bombed, or anything like that. Telephone me tomorrow evening, here, at the usual time."

"Have to go out? At this hour?"

"To a small conference."

"At *this* hour?"

"It isn't all that late, for people who wish to sit up talking. And now lie down and shut up and leave me to get on with it! D'you think I want to go?"

He was snarling with frustration. Odile fell back on the pillows and covered her despairing face with the sheet. Fernand flung from the room, she heard him running downstairs, the front door slammed behind him, the sound of his footsteps hurried away up the street.

She lay in bed in a ferment of anxiety for him, though she didn't quite know why. She was wholly unable to sleep. She ached with unsatisfied desire, worry, and, presently, weariness from worrying. He didn't return. At nine the landlady knocked on the door, saying, "Captain Legrand has just telephoned. He asks me to tell you that he doesn't know what time today he'll be back and he thinks you should return home. He'll be in touch with you. He apologizes for spoiling your weekend."

Odile, all the unease of midnight more strongly upon her than ever, rose, made herself some coffee, then dressed and left the house. It was a cold, raw, January morning. She walked to Victoria: the air smelt of burning, wet charred wood, fallen plaster, bricks and mortar; the wind was full of dust from bomb sites, old and new; the sound of glass being swept up lacerated her already quivering nerves.

The Underground was in turmoil and it took her a long time to complete her journey. A guard on the platform told her that the Bank Underground had had a direct hit. "A lot of fatal casualties." Odile knew, as all workers connected with Civil Defence knew, that the tremendous confidence the public felt in the security of the Tubes was entirely misplaced. There had been several serious incidents involving heavy casualties: the blast travelled down the shafts and along the tunnels. Six hundred people had been killed in this way at Balham in October, for instance, and that was only one of several disasters. But as, for security reasons, there was no reference by wireless or newspapers to these horrors, few knew about them and the trusting tens of thousands continued to go nightly "down the Tubes".

Odile didn't know what to do with herself the rest of that Sunday. She darned stockings, tried to write letters, but her sense of deep personal disquiet made her wholly incapable of concentration. She couldn't sit still for more than a few moments at a time. She was relieved when the hour came to leave for Barrico.

She found the place crowded; last night's raid had put the wind up everyone again. That's what happened, these days: the raids slackened off a little in their intensity and people who had a home to stay in thought they'd stay there rather than turn out in the cold and go down the shelter; then there was another fierce night and off they all trooped to the shelter once more.

Odile made her evening patrol to see that all was well. Nowadays her progress on these patrols was slow, everyone wanted to stop her for a chat. And everyone had a particular desire to talk this evening, telling her about the previous night's harrowing experiences. The raid had roused particularly strong feelings in the East End, where it was being described as a "civilian killing" raid. The bombers had come in low, their explosives catching the shift workers on the way home. The streets had been crowded, the casualties heavy. "Jerry was out to kill us off. Kill as many of us as he could. And don't tell me someone hadn't tipped him off the best time to do it! Been told all he needed to know, in detail, Jerry had! Couldn't've done it, other-wise."

There had been no sing-song in Barrico Hold that Saturday night, but prayers instead. "That young clergyman, who came here at Christmas, he came in and gave us a service; said, nearer to death means nearer to God: that's right, innit? Times like these makes you feel it, don't they? A real good young chap, that. Talks like he means it. Said he knew how we was feeling after that packet; said he felt the same. Said he felt it might help for us to have a service, and it did."

"Hear about the Bank?" Connie asked Odile.

"Yes."

"That Marie Tooley, you know her?"

Odile didn't know Marie properly; it was impossible to know all the shelterers properly, but she knew Marie by sight and, even more, by shrill distant sounds. Connie continued, "Her daughter's copped it. Stopped coming here, the poor gal did, and started going down the Tubes; said they were safer. So she's been going down the Bank with her two little kiddies, twinnies. And now they've all three been blown to kingdom come, mother and her two little kiddies. Makes you run cold! Marie's beside herself."

"Oh Connie! When will all these horrors come to an end?" Odile's face looked grim and drawn.

Connie dropped her voice. "They're saying that chap's been here again. Him that goes round whispering, you know. Upset Marie Tooley ever so; suddenly found him whispering in her ear to surrender and none of this would be happening any more. The very night she lost her Josie!"

"Nobody able to nab hold of him I suppose?"

"He always catches people in dark corners, when they're least expecting it. She'd just been to the lav and was in a dark place between the cubicles. One minute he was whispering in her ear, then he was gone."

"We'll have to keep a special watch out for him."

"He's too crafty by half. Only starts whispering after a bad blitz, then vanishes again. Like a ghost."

"Nobody takes any notice of him, Connie!"

"Nobody takes notice of him, that's true, but same time it's an insult. Have a blooming Nazi creeping about telling us to surrender. Besides, you don't know what else he's up to. Wish I could get my hands on him!"

The night passed. As Odile was going off duty in the morning she was told that a telephone message had been left for her at the nearby Wardens' Post: because she was not on the telephone at the flat at Victoria Park she had arranged with the Post that urgent calls for her might be received there. She hurried to the Post, the strange indefinite dread of the past thirty hours or so strengthening upon her, almost stifling her. Her friend the warden grinned when she came in. "Aha! young lady! Cryptic message for you in mysterious foreign accent. Said, 'Now you may open the present.'"

"Was there any number for me to ring?" asked Odile, her voice quivering slightly.

"No, no number for you to ring, duck. No name. Nothing. Just this young foreign chap said to tell you that now you may open the present. Going in for being Mata Hari or something?"

"Oh rather! Just like Greta Garbo!" Odile managed to crack back. "Well, thanks for taking the message. See you!"

"Glad to be of help any time, duck. Ta-ta for now!"

Odile, her feet like lead, walked slowly away. The message could mean only one thing. Fernand had gone.

She returned to the flat, found the little package that Fernand had given her at the Lyceum and with trembling hands and tears in her eyes opened it. A small box; inside it a slender gold chain with a tiny scallop shell, made of coral, suspended from it. Within the scallop shell a single seed pearl that would sow, thought Odile, a thousand tears.

There was no message attached. None was needed. Odile knew that Fernand would never return and that what he had said on the bridge in St James's Park was true; she was left with a broken heart and a scallop shell.

XXXVIII

Morwenna, heavily laden with bags after a session of shopping for household supplies in Burdett Road, trudged slowly homeward to Tulip House. The February afternoon was a damp and dreary one, and the few people who were about looked as dreary as the weather. Winter seemed to have become a permanent fixture; spring, though officially only just round the corner, gave no sign of any intention of putting in an appearance.

Morwenna heard footsteps hurrying after her and, without turning round to discover their owner, knew that they were Clem's. She stopped, turned slowly. He advanced rapidly upon her. "Hey, young lady! let me carry those bags." "I won't say no, but I warn you they're heavy." Clem took the bags from her. "Great Scott! Whatever is Miss Widgeon thinking of letting you stagger about with appalling loads like this?"

"There wasn't anyone else to carry them and Lily needs fresh supplies."

"I shall have to find you a camel."

"What a lovely idea! But I'm afraid until that happens I shall have to make do with the occasional curate." Morwenna gave his arm a squeeze. "Where have you been this afternoon?"

"I've just seen Posy Cowper on her right road to Mile End Station. I'd have seen her on to her train, only I have to get back to the Mission."

"Posy! What, Posy's been in Bow, and without seeing me?"

"Don't be affronted, darling. She badly needed a confidential chat with me. Has a troublesome matter on her mind. She asked me to give you her love and promises to be in touch very soon."

Morwenna cast a disconsolate glance at Clem. "I really think she might have confided in me, too. I'd come to feel I was part of that family and quite supposed that they'd fully accepted me as such. Apart from poor Henry, of course; he was one of those naturally stand-offish types. Still, mustn't speak unkindly of him."

"You knew Posy's brother Henry?"

"Of course. We lived under the same roof. He got blown up at the start of the Blitz." Morwenna returned to her earlier theme. "I do wish Posy had felt that she could confide in me. I know I'd always be ready to confide in her!"

"When did you last see him?"

"When he left home, at the start of the Blitz. He went off to deal with gas mains in the emergency. Last any of us saw of him." Morwenna, as she spoke, suddenly slowed down her voice and her steps simultaneously, as if abruptly struck by a memory. "But I had a funny thing happen, Clem. One night, or rather early one morning, after a raid, I came out of Tulip House into the street, when it was just growing light, and a man bumped into me, and I could have sworn he was Henry Cowper! I was so sure it was Henry, I even called out his name. But he took no notice: hurried on and disappeared, and then I remembered it couldn't be Henry because he was dead. And I put it out of my mind and forgot all about it; but now, mentioning him again. . . . All the same, it couldn't've been!"

"When was all this?"

"Soon after I first came to Tulip House. Weeks after Henry was said to be dead."

Clem handed Morwenna the bags. "There's a café round the corner, wait for me there." And with these words he turned and began racing back along the street the way they had come. Morwenna, wholly nonplussed by this development, hauled her bags into the café, a small, dilapidated place, empty apart from the proprietor and a seedy companion who were seated at a table studying the greyhound racing page of a newspaper. To justify her presence, Morwenna ordered a cup of tea. Shortly afterwards Clem arrived, leading an out-of-breath Posy who looked as bewildered as Morwenna felt.

Clem propelled Posy into a chair next to Morwenna and ordered two more teas. Then, seating himself at the table, he said, "Now Morwenna, gently repeat to Posy what you have just told me about bumping into her brother."

Morwenna, in a low voice, repeated to Posy the tale of the mysterious encounter. When Morwenna had finished speaking Posy glanced across at Clem. "Makes what I've been telling you sound even more likely, eh?"

Clem nodded.

Posy turned to Morwenna. "You see, duck, night before last we had a break-in at Forty-Seven Rushton. Mum was sleeping in the Anderson, and I was on duty, so the house was empty. Now, when I say break-in, what I really mean is that someone had been to the house during the night and let themselves in with a front-door key. Must've done, because all the doors and windows were locked, and Mum had her front-door key, and the back-door key — we only have the one for that door — in the Anderson with her. Now, none of the windows had been broken and nothing forced open; not a burglar's job at all. So it's obvious it must have been a front-door key used, and that could only be me, or Mum, or Henry. What's more, nothing in the house had been touched, except some of Henry's clothes gone from his bedroom clothes-closet. I know what was in that closet, because after he had failed to come home in the first place, I looked to see if he'd taken any clothes with him, and he hadn't, except for his raincoat, and of course the working clothes he was wearing. Just what you would have expected, seeing he was going to deal with emergency damage to gas mains and intending to come back home afterwards. However, yesterday morning when I looked in his room, like I look in all the rooms every morning to make sure there's no ceilings down or anything after a night's bombing, I noticed the door of his clothes-closet ajar, and then I saw that his overcoat, suit, extra trousers and new shoes were gone, though they'd been there the day before. Well, what are you to make of that? Only one conclusion, far as I can see. Henry's still in the land of the living, and been home to fetch his clothes. He never went to see Mum in the Anderson, to set her heart at rest and say he was safe and well, but stealing in and stealing out again like a thief, hoping we'd never notice he'd been, never know he's still alive. And now you say you saw him not so long since, here in Bow. . . ."

"I wouldn't take my oath on it, Posy. At the time I thought I saw him, but the light was pretty poor. I thought I must have imagined it, which was why I put it out of my mind and never told you, or anyone. I just didn't see how it could've been Henry. After all, he's officially dead, isn't he?"

Posy nodded grimly. "Yes. Officially he's dead orright."

"Have you told anyone yet that you think he isn't a fatal casualty after all?" pursued Morwenna. This time Posy shook her head. "No, I wanted to talk to Clem first. Get some advice on what he thinks I should do. Haven't breathed a word of it to anyone else, not even Mum."

"And personally, as I've already said to you, Posy, I suspect that the poor chap's ill and needs help," intervened Clem. "I can only repeat that your best course is to tell the police, so that they can look out for him and get him into care if he needs it."

"Get him into prison, more likely!" exclaimed Posy. "Imagine how Mum would take on if it came out he'd been up to no good and was put away on account of information given by me."

"But why should he be up to no good?" asked Morwenna. "Oh, Henry's done some funny things in his time," replied Posy brusquely, and left it at that. Morwenna, sensing that to ask further questions would be unwelcome, said no more.

A silence fell between the three of them, broken at last by Clem, who said, "Whether you decide in the end, Posy, to tell the police or not, I'd place a note for Henry on his bedroom table, asking him to show a bit of faith in his family and confide to you what his trouble is; so that if he does return home again he'll know you are lovingly concerned for him. Love works wonders, Posy!"

"Yes. Except Henry's never lacked for being loved: been doted on by Mum all his life, he has, and fat lot of good it seems to have done him!" retorted Posy. "Still, I shouldn't speak to you like that; sorry." She rose to her feet. "You've been very kind, putting up with all this rigmarole, Clem. I'm sorry I've worried you with it, and I'll do what you suggest about leaving a note for him, and have a fresh think about reporting the matter. Trouble is, Mum. I'd do it if it weren't for her. But as things stand. . . ."

"I know. I fully understand." Clem patted Posy on the shoulder. "And if there are any further developments, or you simply feel the urge for another talk, at any time, just let me know."

"Very kind of you. I really appreciate it." Posy shook hands with Clem and turned to embrace Morwenna. "You'll never breathe a word of any of this to Mum, will you, duck?"

"Of course not! Absolutely not!"

They went out into the street. It was growing dark; "Don't worry about me Clem; I'll find my way," said Posy. "You help Morwenna with those heavy bags."

Morwenna and Clem walked in silence in the direction of Sparrowgrass Row. At last Morwenna said, "What an extraordinary. . . ! You can understand poor Posy being so distracted, but what do you suppose she means by 'up to no good'? And having done some 'funny things' in his time? He always seemed such a quiet, essentially respectable type to me."

"Personally I can only repeat for the umpteenth time that it all sounds to me as if Henry has been pushed over the brink by the bombing and acute strain of it all; a sort of shell-shock. Two or three of our parishioners have gone that way, and no surprise either. What astounds me is how the vast majority of people have preserved their nervous systems and sanity intact!" exclaimed Clem, adding, "But if you ever run into him again, Morwenna, let me know immediately, because I'm serious when I say I think he needs help."

"Do you always want to help everyone, Clem?"

"Everyone? No, I do not! There are some people, in my view, who have done a deal with the Devil. Hitler is demonstrably one of them, to start with! Nothing could be more evil than a creed of world domination by a master race, or persecution of the Jews, not to mention bombing and blasting innocent civilian populations. He preaches and practises all three. The last thing I'd want to do would be to help him! Indeed I can't imagine even a Miss Widgeon hoping to bring Hitler back to the fold with loving kindness. Only thing is to destroy him, root and branch, and that goes for all his henchmen too!"

"Onward Christian soldier!"

"'Fraid so! A regrettable world we live in, but it's what we've inherited and it's up to us to do our utmost to hand down something better. And the first step is to remove Hitler and his sort from the map. But all this has nothing to do with a chap like Henry Cowper. Whatever he has done in the past to make his sister shake her head over him, and I can't imagine it can have been anything that dire, I still maintain he sounds like a sick man needing help. Here's a nice quiet alley-way; give me a kiss before we reach Tulip House and Miss Widgeon."

The kiss was of short duration. A sudden well-known scraping of wheels accompanied by cheerful young cockney voices prompted Clem and Morwenna to disengage themselves hastily from their embrace as Nelson Tooley with his fire-fighting outfit of cart and comrades Lenny, Gus and Fred, came bowling merrily along the alley-way. The party this evening enjoyed the addition of a small skinny girl. Nelson hailed Clem without ceremony. "Hello Rev. Nice night to be out with a bit of fluff if it don't turn nasty!"

"Hello Nelson. Hello everyone. What brings you here?"

"Oh, just been for a stroll," said Nelson airily. "And we fetched the outfit along 'cos I thought that if anything started dropping we'd be ready and handy, see?"

"You live in expectation, Nelson," said Morwenna, amused, as always, by the boy's unquenchable gusto.

Clem said courteously, "Who is the young lady you have with you tonight, Nelson? I don't think I've met her before."

"She's my sister Roan. Fed up with sitting down in Barrico with her mum, so she's joined our outfit as messenger and private spy and tracker. Feels she needs a bit of a lark, don't you, Roan?"

Rhona, for answer, rose on her toes, twirled round lightly, and gave a happy giggle; a small girl anticipating revelry.

"First rate spy and tracker, old Roan is," said Nelson, eyeing his sister proudly. "You'd be surprised if you knew what old Roan does. She's a good 'un."

"Rather young for such adventures," murmured Clem. But Nelson merely repeated, "Old Roan's a real good 'un. One of the best!"

The fire-fighting outfit trundled amiably along with Clem and Morwenna, providing them with company they privately wished to be without. In Canal Road, near the bridge, Nelson halted and said to Rhona, "Well me old china, this is where you stop and watch out for a bit."

Rhona, with a broad smile, nodded vigorously.

"Orright. You know where to find us when you want us?"

"Yes."

"See you later then. Good luck."

And the party moved on, leaving Rhona, looking diminutive, standing against a wall beside the bridge, staring eagerly into the gathering darkness.

"You aren't going to leave her there all alone like that, are you Nelson?" exclaimed Morwenna, reprovingly. Nelson replied breezily, "Waiting for someone to turn up. She'll be orright. Wasn't born yesterday, y'know."

"She couldn't've been born that long ago, Nelson," said Clem, glancing back at the small figure by the bridge. "Don't worry, Rev," said Nelson. "Having the time of her life, Roan is!"

As they reached Sparrowgrass Row the sirens began to wail. "Nice and on time, ain't they?" said Nelson cheerfully. "On the early side, if you ask me," responded Clem. "I must confess I'd hoped for a quiet night tonight, or at least one that didn't start off too soon."

"Getting old," quipped Nelson. "Well here you are safe home at your front door, miss. Wonder you walk around in the dark with a dangerous man like him!"

"On form tonight, Nelson!" said Clem rather wrily, as Morwenna took out her front-door key.

"Who, you or me, Rev?" Roars of laughter greeted this one, from the rest of the outfit. Clem and Morwenna, with cries of "Good night!" hurried indoors. "That put paid to kissing you on the doorstep," muttered Clem, with a sigh. "And here, of course, is Miss Widgeon!"

XXXIX

Sunflower Ward, at break of day. The patients had finished their breakfasts, given them by the night staff now thankfully leaving for supper. The day staff trooped on with cheerful cries of "Good morning!"

The four original patients, from that now distant first-ever day at Plashett Wold in July, were still there, but all greatly changed in appearance and their state of progress. Mr Beauchamp, in a gaudy striped dressing gown in shades of pink, maroon and blue, was ambling down the ward en route for the bathroom: he looked completely grotesque, apart from the dressing gown, for he was in the process of growing a facial skin graft taken by a flap from the inner surface of his arm, which, supported in position by plaster, was held perpetually up to his head; the skin flap from his arm growing on to his cheek, the tissue kept alive and nourished by the arm of which it was still part, yet also growing on to his face, to replace the skin and flesh that had been burned away. The process of thus building up his face would go on for months, necessitating constant trips to the operating theatre. But this didn't prevent Mr Beauchamp from a display of tearing high spirits when he spotted the oncoming day staff. He burst into hurrahs! and, grabbing the first nurse to hand, who happened to be Wendover, he clutched her round the waist with his free arm and waltzed her down the ward. Cheering also came from Mr Alcott, in a dizzy sky-blue kimono with peach blossom patterned across it. He was standing at the bedside of another patient who, with one arm similarly affixed to his face and the other fastened across his chest, was merrily waving his feet about as a form of greeting. A large koala bear with a bright red nose was seated on his locker. "Good morning, Mr Plumbton!" Meantime the fourth patient, Mr Judd, who had had a foot amputated, as well as having had new eyelids and surgery to his left ear, came whizzing up the ward in a self-propelled wheel chair, shouting "Tally ho!" at the top of his voice. His dressing gown was bright orange, with a black and red dragon squirming across the back.

The patients on Sunflower vied with each other in their choice of gaudy and exotic dressing gowns, the amount of noise they could make, and the degree to which they could banish boredom from their lives. It was a ward for eight beds; four other young men, in a comparative state of progress, had been moved here from Daisy. The four cubicles on Sunflower accommodated four fresh cases, all perilously burned and all requiring a quiet that they could not possibly have found on the open ward, which at times resembled bedlam, especially when Sister Sunflower appeared, briskly trotting in. The patients almost raised the roof with their cries of, "Good morning Sister! Tally ho Sister!" The Sunflower responded with smiles, twinkles, jokes and laughter; she paused at the foot of each bed to bid an individual "good morning" to its occupant; everyone was asked how they felt, with everyone a joke was exchanged.

The explanation for this astonishing state of affairs on her ward had been given by Sister to the young nurses in one of her teaching sessions. "Ye'll have noticed, nurrses, mebbe, that I'm rather lax, as ye might think it, about the noisy behaviour of the patients on this ward. But the noise and high spirits of these young men is important to their recovery. For one thing it indicates their morale is high, and that's a splendid thing, and for another it is a sign of returning vigour, and that's a splendid thing. They've passed through a long and terrible experience, and they've still got a long way to go on the road to recovery, for as you know the dangers of infection are by no means over for them. But they've come through this far, and naturally they're relieved and delighted by that, and with God's blessing and skilled nursing they'll come through the rest. High morale is essential to their good recovery; nothing must be done to dampen them and so, within the bounds of reason, they should be allowed to let off steam. Ye might call it part of their treatment! But ye must bear verra weel in mind that, because we're allowing the patients a degree of laxity, this doesna mean that you nurses may show the slightest degree of laxity in *your* behaviour. Just the reverse! Friendly, aye; cheerful aye; sympathetic and understanding of their need to be noisy and a wee bit rackety. But noisy or rackety yourselves, or forgetful of your own orderly behaviour and discipline as nurrses, never! Now in fact I'm sure there's no need for me to remind you of this. I would be amazed if any of you behaved in any way other than as ye should. And now let us awa' on to the ward."

Demurely and respectfully the nurses followed her on to the

ward, there to pass from patient to patient: the young men, now finding themselves being discussed by Sister with complete objectivity, as surgical cases, became quiet. Her remarks were all kept carefully optimistic, the girls noticed: she afterwards took them back to the office and there enlarged upon the subject of bacterial infection, the bogey of the burns unit: "The patients, of course, must be themselves kept alerted to this danger, but they must not be intimidated by it. Vigilance is the watchword, nurrses."

She then dismissed them and they returned to work. And work her nurses Sister Sunflower most certainly did. "Hers may be the best ward to be on, from the point of view of training," Wendover would growl from time to time, "but it does make you jolly sympathetic to the anti-slave movement!"

Now that the girls were no longer junior probationers, but had become second-year nurses, they were allowed to "special" and each was assigned a case. To Pam's enormous pleasure she was assigned Pongo Plumbton. The reason for her satisfaction was partly because she had developed a special sympathy for him in the past, but also because his burns were more extensive than those of any other patient on the ward and he required most attentive nursing: that Pam had been chosen to special him was a recognition of her growing professional skill.

Although Pongo couldn't smile his one eye could now be most expressive and as he could also speak, though not very distinctly, he was able to make it clear to Pam that he approved of having her to concentrate upon him.

The nurses soon discovered that the high feather of their patients could not be sustained for more than a few hours at a time. They became tired and when they tired they grew irritable, like children. Visitors always wore them out and the nurses came to dread the outbursts and difficulties that followed as an aftermath of visitors. "Oh naughty paddywhacks, Mr Beauchamp!" Wendover was heard saying, in her best nanny accents. "I shall confiscate that nice box of chocolates that Mrs Beauchamp brought you, if you behave like this!" Mr Beauchamp's reply was indistinct, but might be judged by Wendover's response: "Then I *am* confiscating them until you jolly well change your tune!"

Pongo was not troubled by "visitor fatigue" as the nurses called it for, apart from daily appearances of Lady Grace and Lady Daphne, he received no visitors; there was nobody to visit him now that his old squadron had been posted to the Middle East. There was, of course, no sign of Poppy.

Although he chatted with Pam without inhibition on a wide range of subjects, the name of Poppy was never mentioned between them. He knew that Jos had been killed, though he himself never referred to it. He no longer watched and waited for visitors. He clearly took it for granted that nobody would come.

The weeks passed; carpets of aconites and snowdrops appeared beneath the trees in the garden, to be followed by the first brave few of the crocuses. Almond blossom trembled, delicately pink. Then Lady Daphne was placing a bowl of camellias in the ward.

The patients progressed back and forth between the ward and the operating theatre, to have the flesh pedestals of their grafts unrolled, fraction by fraction, as the flaps took. Pam much enjoyed preparing Pongo for these excursions to the theatre: the facial area that was to receive the extended graft was kept nourished with saline until the last possible moment, the part of the arm from which the increased flap was to be taken was made sterile, and covered with a sterile pad while the patient was taken to the theatre. This prepping, as the nurses called it, was all done on the ward. Pam and Pongo joked together as it was being done; then the pre-medical that he'd been given would make him drowsy. Pam always accompanied him to the door of the theatre, but she doubted if he ever realized this. Sometimes the probationers were allowed in the theatre as spectators, and for this they had to gown up and don masks; it was an essential part of their training for it taught them to become used to operations and not to faint. Pam never fainted: she loved the theatre. Boggy, though she never actually fainted, on one or two occasions had come close to it. Wendover was a dreadful one for passing out in the theatre. "I don't think I'll ever be able to stand it, I really don't!" But in due course she learned how to keep control of herself.

The problem with skin grafting was that the grafts didn't always take and the process had to be repeated. On Sunflower, thanks to the high morale of the patients and the vigilance of the nursing staff, there were few graft failures, and the patients continued to make excellent progress. Both Mr Judd and Mr Beauchamp were each allowed home for a few weeks, before returning for further grafts. Pongo's facial graft had been successfully accomplished; his next stage now was to have a new nose built up. This was done by bringing a flap of scalp down to the top of the eyebrows and neatly rolling it into a so-called pedestal, which fed the new nose. All the skin graft patients looked grotesque: if you weren't accustomed to the sight of them the only possible adjective to use was Franken-steinish; but the patients receiving grafts to build up noses were the hardest sight to take of all, with their rolled down scalps and embryonic appearance; the ghoulishness further accentuated by the fact that the flesh of the pedestal coming from the scalp sprouted hair.

Pongo had ceased to resemble the accepted notion of a human being. Pam noted that visitors were careful to avert their eyes from his corner of the ward. Lady Grace and Lady Daphne, by contrast, devoted more time to him than they lavished upon any other patient; all Lady Daphne's choicest flowers found their way to that corner. Sister Sunflower's attentions to him were unstinting and none of the nurses could do enough for him, while Pam, specialling him, crooned over him like a mother over her first-born. As she explained to Boggy, as they chatted together in her cubicle before bedtime one evening, it was the marvellous personality behind Pongo's appalling mask that mattered: his courage, his patient resignation, his good humour. "He really is a wonderful example to us all, you know, Bogs!"

"Becoming quite your hero, little one!"

"Yes, I suppose in a way he is," confessed Pam. "We all have our heroes," she added, with a slight smile and a glance at the portrait of Giles Sowersby that now stood, silver-framed, on Boggy's bedside locker.

Boggy laughed. "Oh, Giles isn't a hero! I'm in love with Giles. Two slightly different things."

Boggy was really in luck: Giles was now stationed a mere twenty miles from Plashett Wold. He telephoned her regularly; dashed into Cirencester, the nearest place for a cinema or a meal, to see her whenever their off-duty spells made it possible; sent her flowers. Boggy was in a state of non-stop mooning and spooning, as the other girls put it. They all envied Boggy her beautiful shiny romance, but it was an amiable envy untinged with jealousy, for they were all young enough, and self-confident enough, to believe that a similar shiny romance was waiting just around the corner for each of them.

"Giles is awfully like Jos, in some ways, isn't he? At least, judging by that photograph," mused Pam. Boggy said, "Yes. Though actually, much as I used to dote on Jos (for I suppose he really was my hero, before the Poppy thing happened, anyway), much as I worshipped him, I realize now that Giles has looks, charm, courage, everything, streets ahead even of Jos!"

"Lucky Bogs, to have your Giles."

"You've got your Pongo! And as you said, it's personality that matters, not what a chap looks like. I mean if . . . if Giles ever wound up like Pongo, which heaven forbid! but if he did, the real Giles would still be there to love."

"Absolutely Bogs, absolutely!"

Boggy, an enigmatic smile playing round her mouth and in her eyes, contemplated Pam thoughtfully. "Ah, love is a mysterious thing, my child! No accounting for it!"

"Love!" retorted Pam. "Don't be ridiculous!" At the same time, in spite of herself, she blushed deeply. Feeling herself blushing, she repeated loudly and firmly, "Don't be ridiculous!" Then, after a pause, during which Boggy continued to smile, Pam added, "Besides, when all's said and done, officially Pongo's still a married man, and now that Jos . . ." Her voice trailed off. Boggy, her smiling eyes suddenly snapping with indignation, burst out, "Surely you aren't suggesting that Poppy will try to return to Pongo? Cast him adrift while she had an affair with his best friend and then, her lover lost, back to hubby as a poor second? Even she couldn't stoop to anything quite so despicable as that!"

"Well, whatever happens you needn't start weaving novelette romances about young nurse falling for mutilated war hero, so don't try," rejoined Pam, somehow recovering her best brisk nursy voice and manner. "Concentrate on dreaming about Giles," she concluded, with a wave of her hand in the direction of the portrait. And with this Pam made to leave the cubicle. Boggy, with one of her gurgling chuckles, replied, "I'll do that thing, little one! Good night, and sweet dreams for you too!"

A few evenings later Boggy, with a conspiring air, came to Pam's cubicle. "Pam, little one, lend me your ear. I am seeking a partner in crime for a somewhat dicey op."

Pam, rinsing out stockings at her hand-basin, raised her eyebrows apprehensively. "Oh lor, Bogs, what are you up to now?"

"My birthday's looming on the horizon: next week, to be exact.

A Saturday. And with some guile I've wangled it as my day off. I was more than half anticipating that Giles would invite me to supper at a country pub, or something like that. But now he wants to take me out on the Town! I can't turn down that invitation, honeychile!"

"Which town?"

"Which town, says she! There's only one Town. London of course!" Boggy added airily, "Naturally I've accepted. Giles will pick me up at the Berkeley bar at eight. That's a hard date."

"Hard date's the right name for it, Bogs! How the hell are you going to manage it?"

The problem was one that bedevilled all hopes of ever having an evening's fun in London while you were on day duty at Plashett Wold. There was an evening train you could just catch if you rushed straight to the station from coming off the wards at eight-thirty; this got you into London just after ten, far too late for a theatre or dinner. Nurses on day duty had one night off a month; if you had somewhere to stay the night in London, you could travel up by this eight-fifty-five train and then you had all the next day to spend in Town, taking in a matinée or even a tea dance, after which you caught a six p.m. train that had you back at Plashett Wold in time for supper. Daring schemes of catching a later train and making an illicit entry through a window, thereby giving yourself dinner or a show in London, were fraught with peril: the late train was popular with members of the medical staff. In addition, even if you managed to dodge being spotted on the train, you had a horrid long walk in the dark back to the Manor. It was asking to be caught if you hired a village taxi.

All in all returning late to Plashett Wold from London was such a hazardous enterprise that nobody was on record as having yet tried it. But Boggy was explaining now: "I'll go up to London on Friday evening and stay the night at Brown's, while away the next day shopping and having my hair done, paint the town red with Giles, and he'll drive me back here; so there won't be any bothering with that late train. All I ask of you, little one, is that you put a bolster in my bed on Saturday night, and make sure the back door's open in the small hours of Sunday morning. Any attempt to climb in a window would involve acrobatics and mountaineering I'm not prepared to try. But if you can creep down round about three ackemma and open that door for me, so that all I have to do is sail in, well, I'll name my first daughter after you!"

"What if the back door bolts creak?"

"They won't creak. I'll oil 'em in advance."

"Suppose you're caught sailing in? Or I'm found in my nightie opening the back door?"

"For crying out loud, who's going to be patrolling this place at three or four in the morning? And if you're caught on the stairs in your nightie, why, you obviously walk in your sleep. Oh come on Pam dear, it's a watertight scheme!"

"Then why, if it's so safe, did you call it a dicey op?"

"Well, returning in the small hours, there's always a chance you might run into some miserable senior nurse pattering to the loo or something; but honestly, Pam, I don't think there's much real danger of coming unstuck. And even if I had to run the gauntlet of Matron herself I'd risk it on this occasion, for between ourselves, honeychile, I do believe he is going to pop the question!"

"Under those circs, Bogs, I'll suppose I'll have to become a partner in crime. But remember, if we get turfed out of the hospital you'll have a husband to support you, while poor little me will be on my uppers in the cold cold snow."

"Never fear, m'dear, I'll see to it that you're ensured a billet in the deep South of the good old US of A. Now come along, let's carry out a recce and take a squint at those bolts."

The bolts were certainly on the stiff side, but Boggy contrived to oil them in readiness for her escapade. She and Pam kept their plans a secret between them: Boggy didn't tell anyone else that she was having a date with Giles; she merely said she was staying a night with an aunt in London and would spend Saturday, her birthday, shopping and having her hair done in Knightsbridge.

On Saturday evening, while Pam was eating her supper and thinking of Boggy at some swish nightspot, Staff Nurse said, "Telephone for you, Nurse Spurgeon. Your mother."

"My mother? Golly!" What could have happened? It must be some calamity, for Ma to phone!

Pam hurried to the telephone booth in the hall. "Hello Mater! How are you? Is everything okay?"

"Couldn't be better, little one, couldn't be better!" came back a well known, gurgling voice. Pam gasped, "Bogs! It's you!"

"Yes, me. Thought I'd better disguise my identity. I just wanted you to be the first to know, Pam darling, he's popped the question and I'm wearing a most fabulous diamond and sapphire ring!"

"Oh Bogs you're not!" breathed Pam, delightedly.

"Oh Pam, I am! I'm angels ten, right over the moon! Can't tell you my state of bliss!"

"Where are you speaking from?"

"Café de Paris. Giles has booked us a perfect table, right beside the dance floor, Snake Hips Johnson and all! Everything too wizard for words!"

"You lucky kid!"

"Yes, aren't I? Horseshoes all over me!"

"Dear darling Bogs, I'm so terribly happy for you! And congratulate Giles for me. Got horseshoes all over him, too, landing a wizard girl like you!"

"Thank you Pam love, I'll tell him that."

"Thanks for phoning, Bogs. Terribly sweet of you."

"Wanted you to be the absolute first to know, honeychile! And don't forget that back door!"

"Come hell and high water Bogs I'll see to it."

"Do the same for you some day, Pam; do the same for you! Byeee!"

"Byeee!"

Gosh! Pam gasped to herself as she hurried back to the dining hall. Gosh! Good old Boggy! Lucky old Bogs! But she deserved every little bit of it. Wizard girl, Bogs!

The Sister in charge of the nurses' home made her rounds at half past ten, checking that everyone was safe in bed with the lights out. Boggy had told Pam that, for the past few nights, she had been sleeping with her dressing-gown over her, pulled well up above her head, as if for extra warmth and Sister, peeking in, had grown accustomed to seeing this. So now Pam, just after ten, stole into Boggy's cubicle, arranged the bolster in the empty bed to simulate a slumbering Bogs and put the dressing-gown in place; she draped some clothes over a chair to make it look as though Boggy had undressed, plopped her slippers on the floor beside the bed, wound up the bedside clock, opened a paperback and placed it face down next to Giles's photograph on the bedside locker and, these things done, turned out the light and left the cubicle, saying in a loud, cheerful voice, "Good night Bogs, sleep well!" .

Then back to her own cubicle and to bed herself, lying in the dark praying that Sister wouldn't be in one of her poke-nose moods.

All went well. Sister made her rounds and departed. Pam, who had set her alarm for two-thirty, placed it under her pillow so that it should wake her without rousing anyone else and endeavoured to sleep, but found it difficult because she was on utter tenterhooks. At last she drowsed off, to wake up with a jerk in what seemed no time at all with the alarm clock ringing in a muffled, protesting kind of way beneath the pillow. She switched it off, flicked on her bedside lamp, got out of bed and put on her slippers and dressing-gown, opened her cubicle door with as little sound as possible and crept along the passage and across the landing to the stairs. Down to the first floor; this was the dangerous part for it was here the senior nursing staff slept. Pam stopped, listened, then, as all was silence, she stealthily descended the next flight to the ground floor.

Along the passage to the back door. In addition to the bolts the door had a lock and key; in a trice Pam had turned the key and reached swiftly to slide back the bolts. Her great fear was that Staff Nurse in the room above might hear this operation; Pam, her heart thudding, waited a moment or so to make certain that Staff wasn't going to appear, investigating. But nothing stirred and Pam crept back up the stairs, crossed the danger zone of the first-floor landing; up the second flight, along the passage, and then she was safely in her own cubicle. Mission accomplished! Vastly relieved, she quickly fell back into sleep.

Six o'clock: they were all roused as usual to start another day. Pam dressed, left her cubicle and, with a slight tap on Boggy's door, opened it and peeped in, expecting to find Boggy in the final stages of preparing to come down to breakfast. But Boggy had not returned; the bolster was still in the bed.

Pam's heart dropped like a stone into her shoes; something must have gone terribly wrong! And the ghastly thought struck her that Boggy had been caught. Hastily Pam removed the bolster and placed it under the pillow. Then she hurried downstairs.

Over breakfast the other girls began to comment, "Where's Boggy?" "Must've overslept," said Pam. In her own mind she went through a list of possible things that might have happened. The car might have broken down on the return journey. Or, horrid thought, they might had have an accident. There was the remote chance, Pam supposed, that Boggy and Giles had ended the night in one another's arms somewhere in London, but it wasn't likely: Boggy had clear cut ideas about what was in the code book and what was not and always declared, "It's a wedding ring or nothing as far as I'm concerned, little one!" Nonetheless, that said, you could never be certain what a girl might do if she really got carried away!

However, all possibilities explored, the most probable likelihood was that Boggy had been caught on her return to the nurses' home and was now under lock and key, like a criminal. For a criminal she would be in the eyes of the hierarchy. And if this was what had happened then Pam's role as an accomplice would undoubtedly be exposed and she, too, would be up before Matron and out on her ear.

Like Bogs herself, Pam had been basically confident that the escapade would pass off without discovery. But now that she knew something had gone seriously wrong, she realized just how much it would ruin her life to be expelled from St Jerome's, and she wished, with all her heart and mind, that she had had the sense to refuse to agree to Boggy's scheme.

Yet there was still the remotest chance that Boggy would appear, saying that she had overslept, or felt unwell. She would be reprimanded for being late, but she wouldn't be expelled. But if she didn't appear now, for roll call, that would be it!

Boggy didn't appear. And Pam began to understand what feeling desperate truly meant.

Staff went off to investigate Boggy's non-appearance. Pam, like the rest of the nurses, hurried to the wards. Here, on Sunflower, she was plunged into the usual scurry and flurry of morning routine. She performed her chores feeling sick with the expectancy of being summoned, at any moment, to Sister, and attended Pongo with only half her mind on the job; he asked her if anything were the matter. She managed to summon a smile and say, "No, of course not."

Then Staff tapped Pam on the shoulder and told her that Sister Sunflower wished to see her in her office immediately. This was it!

Sister was seated at her desk when Pam entered. Pam stood at the nursing equivalent of attention, beside the desk.

Sister said, "I understand, Nurse Spurgeon, that Nurse Hope-Warrington is missing, and as you and she are known to be close friends I am wondering if you might be able to throw some light on the matter?" And she cocked a bright little eye at Pam.

There was a long pause while Pam wondered precisely what to say. Should she lie, and say she had no idea? No, it could only make things worse. Boggy had had it, now; lies couldn't help the situation in any way. Pam took a deep breath. Sister fixed her with a penetrating look and said, "Well, Nurse?"

Pam decided to put things as circumspectly as possible. "Nurse Hope-Warrington spent her day-off in London, yesterday, Sister, and I think she was planning to return by road in a friend's car."

"I see. But she hasn't returned."

"No," murmured Pam in dismal agreement.

"Who was this friend who was driving her back?"

"A family connection of hers, Sister. His squadron is stationed not terribly far from here. He was bringing her back. They had been out together."

"In London?"

"In London."

"I think you had better tell me all you can, nurse. It will be the most helpful course to all parties concerned, in the end, you know."

"Yes Sister. Nurse Hope-Warrington had been dancing at the Café de Paris, Sister."

"She told you she was going there, did she?"

"She telephoned me to say she was there, Sister. She had just become engaged and she wanted me to be the first to know."

"I see."

Sister paused, looking very grave, indeed grim. Then she said, "That will be all for now, nurse. You may go."

Pam returned to the ward. She had fully expected to be questioned about the unbolted back door: this would have been discovered, for sure. But Sister had made no mention of it. Pam reminded herself that there was nothing to link her with the unfastened door, nor would anyone ever be able to prove that it was she who had opened it. If questioned point blank she would have to confess. Otherwise, she would keep quiet about it. Luck might yet still be on her side!

At midday Sister Sunflower asked to see Pam again. "This really *is* it," she told herself. "Sister will send you to Matron and she'll tell you that you're expelled."

"Sit down, nurse," said Sister Sunflower. Pam, surprised, sat down, while Sister seated herself behind her desk. "It grieves me verra much to have to break this to you, nurse. There was a heavy raid on central London last night, and the Café de Paris received a direct hit. Nurse Hope-Warrington and her escort, Flight Lieutenant Sowersby, were among the fatal casualties."

Pam, stunned, sat motionless, feeling suddenly as cold as if she had been turned into stone. Sister resumed, "It seems that someone in the nurses' home had left the back door open for Nurse Hope-Warrington, thereby becoming implicated in this tragic flouting of the hospital rules, but under the circumstances it has been decided not to pursue the matter. Whoever it was that conspired with Nurse Hope-Warrington in this way will, I think, suffer enough, as it is, from the verra sad outcome, without having to be further punished. That will be all nurse. Get back to your duty."

Pam, with an indistinct murmur, rose from the chair and walked from the office. It was time for her to go the nurses' dining hall for dinner; but instead she went to her room and wept her heart out.

XL

2A Cheyne Mews, SW3
March 26 1941

Dear Morwenna,

I should have replied long before this, I know, to your letter about Jos. It was nice of you to write: I never heard a word from anybody else remotely connected with Parrocks! I can't imagine how such a lovely chap as Jos came from such a ghastly family. At least, they seemed ghastly to me, judging by the specimens I met: that grumpy prig of a brother, and that prize bitch, Boggy.

I shouldn't say this to you, I know, seeing that Boggy is a friend of yours. But the truth is, though I know she'll never face it, she was largely instrumental in destroying Jos. I know he was a hero to her, he was to his whole damn family; but that didn't help him much when it came to a little understanding from them all. As for Boggy, boy! did she put herself out to pull that hero down!

He was mad keen for me to get a divorce and marry him, and I, of course, was crazy about him;, but, thanks to bloody Boggy, the situation was quite impossible for us both. We were both bugged with guilt about Pongo. And it was good little Nurse Boggy who first started me off feeling so hellishly guilty — meeting me specially to deliver a lecture on my duty, and Pongo's sufferings, and all. Well, it lacerated me alright, though I was damn well not going to let *her* know it! And because I was lacerated, Jos got lacerated too. He knew the whole thing was tearing me in two; the awful decision I was faced with. Sheer agony. And agony for him too, for the only decent thing for him to do was to let me go back to Pongo. But, by then, Jos and I had both realized that we simply couldn't live without each other.

I shall always be convinced that Jos got out. A very gallant gentleman, a Captain Oates; only going out in a storm of flak, not a snow blizzard. Removed himself from the scene, to make it possible for me to do the right thing by Pongo. Maybe he only did it subconsciously, but nonetheless when he said good-bye to me at the end of that last leave, I knew, whether he was aware of it or not, that he was going to get himself killed.

And the tragedy is that I realize, worse than ever now, that it was only Jos I loved, never poor Pongo. Jos truly *was* my man. There's not the remotest possibility of there ever being anyone else for me. Above all no Pongo! There's never any going back. I'll let him divorce me for desertion.

I can't write any of this to Boggy, naturally, much as I'd love to make her squirm! All other considerations apart, the last thing I wish to do is open up a correspondence with *her*. But if you ever have the chance, you might just let that smug little customer know that she successfully ruined both our lives — Jos's and mine. I hope it'll be her turn, then, to feel guilty. Just pass it on to her that she did a thorough hatchet job on Jos — and me.

At the moment I'm working with NAAFI, of all things! Keeps me occupied. First chance I get, I shall probably head back home to Australia. 'Fraid I can't stand you Pommie lot! There was only one who was good — and he's gone.

Poppy

Tulip House, E3
March 27 1941

Dearest Pam,

Have received your letter containing news about poor darling Boggy. As you say it was a sad, sad letter for you to write, and I can't honestly think what to say in reply, except, as you realize

307

without my telling you, I'm absolutely shattered! What appalling bad luck, and just when she was on the brink of such happiness with Giles! The only comfort is that they couldn't have known anything about it, and they went together when they were both blissfully happy. I'll cling to that thought.

It's cheering to read that Pongo is proving such a tower of strength to you, saying you've taught him that life has to go on, however tough the going, and, having taught him that lesson, you can't pretend, now, that you don't know it yourself! I'm sure he means it, Jampot love, when he says he would never have survived without you, and you're to keep smiling for his sake. Hope you're obeying his instructions.

I've had a pretty amazing letter from Poppy Plumbton, saying horrible things about Bogs—I won't repeat them—Poppy, to be sure, doesn't know about Boggy's death. I think she, Poppy, is still half-demented losing Jos. One thing she *is* emphatic about, she'll never go back to Pongo. Says she'll head for Australia, leaving him to divorce her for desertion. I can't help feeling he's the lucky one!

I'll pass the news about Boggy on to Odo. Poor kid! she's very down herself, just now. Seems she had an old French flame resurface, much to her joy, for a month or two in London, but now he's gone and she says she knows she'll never see him again. Won't say who he was — not the confiding type, Odo: but I have my guess! Poor Odo! she looked so blissfully happy when I last saw her, or at least as blissful as any one *can* look in the middle of a war! Now she sounds completely desolate.

What a world it is! Everything, in every direction, splintering into bits; and the future, even a few hours ahead, absolutely uncertain; dark, like being in a thick fog. Even if you've a chance to be happy, you're almost afraid to be, because it's impossible to believe it will last.

Clem (he's a young clergyman working with this Mission and the one who saved my life when I was bombed and buried) says when the world is dark we should make the most of every beam of light that comes along, and in that way we help illuminate the darkness and find that there's a lot more light than we thought — but I don't know, Pam; sometimes I can believe in this way of looking at things, and then other times I can't.

I might as well confess that Clem has fallen in love with me: and well and truly so! I'd never supposed that clergymen fell in love, at least, not with such heady ardour! Not that he has yet suggested a handfasting or fossil room (Frank's private jargon!) but I think he *will* propose to me, sooner or later. I suspect he would have done so before now if it weren't for the fact that he's absolutely penniless, like all young curates. I've thought a lot about being poor, and a clergyman's wife and that, and I think I could cope with it. My trouble is that though I feel *certain* that I'm now in love with him (he's awfully sweet, and so touchingly means everything he says and does — besides being jolly brave too; everybody in this part of the world adores him — he really is one of those special people! not to mention good-looking though that's merely by the way) — where was I? Oh yes; the problem. You see, I don't yet feel that I've well and truly got over Frank. If they both appeared, walking up the street, I honestly couldn't say to which of them I'd run first! A purely hypothetical problem because there's no earthly possibility of Frank walking up the street; he's been sent overseas, Middle East I suppose, and anyway before he left he made it quite clear he'd finished with me. Thought me too young to know my own mind etc. Only hope I know it better now. I feel that I do.

So if and when Clem proposes to me, I shall say yes. I have an extraordinary sense that Fate has been at work with this one. Living in the Blitz has made me fatalistic, but I feel particularly so over Clem: the way we met, him digging me out; the way I sort of fell into this job at Tulip House; the way Frank broke everything off, out of the blue, leaving the way open for Clem.

Sorry to write so much about ME, but you asked me for news of myself! I realize this isn't much of a letter at a time like this: but what *can* one say that could even be faintly adequate? Try to keep smiling, Jampot love, like Pongo says. It's the only way.

All my love,

Morwenna

Maytrees
Tuesday evening

Darling Thingy,

As maybe Odile told you I really must give my deprived eyes the treat of seeing you both, so have booked for the three of us to go to a concert afternoon of May 10, Elgar's "Dream of Gerontius" conducted by Malcolm Sargent at the Queen's Hall. I'm telling you well in advance, so that you can make arrangements to have the afternoon free. I've told Odile too. I can't say how much I look forward to an outing with my daughters. Just like old times!

I'm due to be picked up by Sybil any moment, so have no time for more. Lots of love my darling,

Mummy

PS.   Your grandmother sends love too. Will write soon she says. Absolutely tied up in the vegetable garden, with spring sowing. At her age! I really hand it to her! Your father is talking about being posted to the Middle East, where, the Battle of Britain now being virtually over, the next battles must rage. He thinks, unless the Americans come in, this war will last into the next decade. Thank heaven we can't see that far! A black outlook. However, we'll get there!

XLI

Steve Tooley turned up totally unexpectedly while Marie and Gert were having a cup of tea in the room behind the shop one afternoon. There was the sound of Pete shouting jubilantly and then Steve, in Home Guard uniform, came in grinning all over his face, carrying the exultant Pete in his arms.

"Steve!" shrieked Marie. She leapt up, flew at him, started hugging him in a frenzy of joy. Steve, laughing, exclaimed, "Cor, lemme go, Marie, lemme go! You'll have me strangled, gal!" Pete continued to whoop; Rhona squealed, "Steve! Steve!" Gert shed tears of delight. At last the welcome calmed a little. Gert put the kettle on for more tea, Steve was given a chair and Marie seated herself opposite him, saying reproachfully, "You never told us you was coming 'ome!"

"Didn't know meself till the last minute. Got forty-eight hours' leave, and thought I'd better come and see how you was all doing after what you've been through." Steve was now grave; he looked sadly at his mother, his aunt, then back to his mother. "Very cut up I was, to hear about Josie and the twins. Real bad job, that was, Marie mate."

Marie's eyes instantly brimmed with tears. "Don't talk about it! Can't bear to think of it. Wickedness of it all, bombing little kiddies and their mothers!" Steve, in a gesture of dumb sympathy, leaned towards his mother and patted her on the arm. At this point Rhona interrupted with, "There's a man in the shop wants serving, Aunt Gert. Shall I serve him?"

"No. I better. You'll get the change wrong," said Gert. She wheeled herself into the shop; a seedy looking man asked for a packet of twenty Capstan. Gert served him. Rhona, who never ceased to find the shop a place of endless fascination, stood beside Gert and watched the transaction, missing nothing, eyeing the customer intently with a small smug smile on her face.

The sale completed, Gert returned to the tea table. "Well Steve, you're looking very well," she said, handing him his cup of tea. "Quite your old self."

"You're looking same as ever, too, Aunt Gert. Bombs don't seem to have got you down."

"Where's Roan?" asked Marie, glancing round.

"Dunno. In the shop a minute ago. Gone to play skipping with her mates I daresay," said Gert, pleasantly busy with the teapot.

"You ought to get out of the Smoke, Marie, with Roan and Pete," said Steve. "Go somewhere safe in the country. Don't want us to lose no more of the family."

Marie shook her head. "I'm staying here. Staying here in Stepney, where I belong. And my kiddies with me. Said it from the first, and I mean it. Besides, I have to be here, don't I, for Mick and Vi to find me when they get back."

Steve asked, "Where d'you think Mick and Vi have gone, Marie? Josie said they'd been took away, in that card she sent me, ages back. But took away where?"

Marie replied, testily, "I dunno. If I knew where they'd been took I'd know where to find 'em, wouldn't I? Stands to reason, don't it? All I know is, when I got back to Lucknow it'd gone. And Mick and Vi had gone. And I was took to one of them Rest Centres and if I hadn't walked out they'd have carted me off into the country and gawd knows how I'd've got back myself. Well, that's what happened to Mick and Vi, see?"

"H'm," said Steve. He surveyed his mother thoughtfully. She more than ever resembled a twist of rusty wire; her sallow face was gaunt; her hair, which she now kept permanently clamped to her head in metal curlers, was so clogged with dust and grime that it was impossible to decide whether she had grown greyer or simply dirtier. Her clothes were dustier, rustier; her boots were cracked; her person carried the sharp and acrid scent of crowded shelters and damp plaster dust and burned charred London that impregnated all and everything and, if you smelled of it, was as good as carrying a certificate guaranteeing that you were a veteran of the Blitz.

In short, thought Steve, Marie now resembled those citizens of beleaguered Madrid alongside whom he had lived and fought and bled. Marie had become a veteran of siege and bombardment: dehydrated and worn like a leather accoutrement of some long campaign; to a superficial eye so thin and worn she looked as if she would blow away, but, to anyone who knew anything true of a battle line, here, in this little woman, you were seeing a seasoned, hundred per cent, durable front-liner.

Steve's expression, as he contemplated Marie, grew deeply affectionate, he grinned and gave a slight shake of his head and then looked thoughtful again as she, her dark, bloodshot eyes flashing from under her perpetually furrowed little forehead and the array of curlers, continued, attempting to convince him, "See, with Lucknow gone they've not been able to get hold of me to tell me. Wouldn't know I'd come to Gert — never dream old Gert would still be here, sitting it out. I can't get hold of them, they can't get hold of me. Easy happens in times like these. Easy happens!"

"Yes," agreed Steve. "War's a right mix up! Easy happens you can lose one another in a war. But," his tone was cautious, "it's a long time now, Marie mate!"

"Not really," retorted Marie. "Not considering." She paused, then concluded, "Know it in my bones they've been took a long way off. Take 'em a long time to get back."

Further conversation had to be left for later; the hour had arrived to start for Barrico. Pete, protesting vehemently, was tethered in his pushchair and was given his flag to pacify him. A bag was packed with sandwiches, a bottle of tea and a spare bottle of milk for Pete. Steve asked, "How does Aunt Gert get there?"

"Gert don't. She stays here in her rabbit hutch."

"What, you been sitting there in that wooden box all through the

Blitz?" the astounded Steve gasped to Gert. "Gor blimey! Rather you than me!"

"Nothing else I can do," replied Gert. "Got to sit it out."

So that was that.

"Not that there's much chance of bombing tonight," said Marie. "Us lot copped it proper again three nights ago; went for the docks good and proper again, 'Itler did! Has to get his breath back before the next lot's ready. See," she explained to Steve, "it's getting him under, all this bombing London. He don't come every night no more, like he use to. It's wearing him down."

Steve burst out laughing. "Supposed to be the other way round, Marie!"

"Wotcher mean?" Marie suspicious.

"Supposed to be wearing you lot down, not Hitler."

"He may see it that way, but we don't!" retorted Marie. The family then set out for Barrico. But they hadn't trudged more than two hundred yards when Marie stopped short. "Ain't got Roan!"

"Ought we?"

"'Course we ought!" Marie stared belligerently about her, muttering, "That Roan, getting far too independent she is! Keeps going off. Taking up with Nelson, him and his fire-fighting cart. Well, have to go without her, I suppose. Daresay she's headed for Barrico herself." And they resumed walking.

"We're going to cop it bad tonight," remarked the wheezy old man in Marie's cubicle, as she and Pete settled down beside Mrs Tooley, who was already installed in her usual place. Steve had gone to see if he could spot Nelson. "Cop it something chronic we are, tonight," repeated the old man. "It's 'Itler's birthday."

"How d'you know it's 'Itler's birthday?" asked Marie.

"Lord Haw-Haw told us. 'Itler's gonna celebrate and we're gonna cop it."

"Nice of him to remember us lot on his birthday," responded Marie cheerfully.

Some time later the sirens sounded. Barrico Hold started to cheer and sing, "Happy Birthday".

Then the bombers thudded in and the barrage crashed out and everyone was announcing to everyone else, "Here come the birthday presents!"

"Not close fisted with 'em, is he, neither?"

"Generous lot, them Nazis are!"

"Hope we're soon giving the buggers something by way of many happy returns!"

The tumult became the loudest they had known to date, even worse than those first fearful days in September. The night outside rocked and was torn apart; they could feel London shuddering. The shelter hadn't been over-full at the start, but now more and more people arrived, white-faced, tumbling out of the roaring dark, breathless with terror and with hurrying to the shelter through the bombardment.

The electricity failed, Odile turned on the emergency lights. She resumed her patrolling, going from cubicle to cubicle talking to people. She had lost weight recently and looked drawn; the shelterers, remarking on this, said, "Well no wonder, poor young woman. She don't spare herself!"

Marie, as the night wore on, became increasingly anxious. Rhona had still not put in an appearance, and Steve, too, had vanished. Marie decided that he must have gone off with Nelson to fight fires. But whatever could have become of Rhona?

"I wonder if that whisperer will be down here tonight?" murmured Mrs Tooley to Marie. "Sort of night he chooses."

"He's a crafty one." The two women kept their voices low: the man was a taboo subject, people never spoke about him openly; he had a spectre-like quality that made you feel he wasn't altogether real and this in turn made him something, rather than someone, to fear. It was remarkable, too, the way in which he was never properly seen, and still remained at large after all these months. "You'd've thought the coppers would've nabbed him by now, but he always gives 'em the slip."

Presently Rhona crept in and dropped down beside her mother on the blanket. "You bad naughty gal, where've you been? You'll get blown to smithereens, and you'll have asked for it! Turn me white overnight, you will. Gone grey I have already!"

"Not been nowhere, Mum. Been talking with my mates other end of the shelter. Straight I have, really Mum!"

"Straight as a bleeding corkscrew," returned Marie, with disbelief. Rhona made no further contribution to the conversation and it lapsed.

At last the All-clear sounded and soon afterwards people began packing their things and leaving, anxious to return home to find out whether or not their houses had survived the night. The already bombed-out gave themselves up to resignation and sleep.

Marie and her mother-in-law prepared to leave for St Jerome's and their scrubbing. Rhona was to remain at Barrico until it got light, then she would wheel Pete home. The possibility that Gert might have been bombed during the night, any night, never crossed Marie's mind. Gert's place was inviolable.

At St Jerome's a bomb had fallen on the main medical block but there had been no more than a few casualties and things were already well under control when the scrubbing ladies arrived. Marie and Mrs Tooley did their work, had their cups of tea. Mrs Tooley went on to further jobs, Marie started off for home.

It didn't take her long to realize that the damage done during the night was, as she put it to herself, something out of the ordinary. The morning, in the early light, looked, sounded and smelled like a crisis. Marie began to get one of her funny feelings that there was real trouble in her camp. At the corner of Jamaica Street and Stepney Way she found Rhona and Pete in his pushchair. Pete was in one of his tantrums, fed up. Rhona just stood, peaky and pale, waiting for her mother. Immediately she spotted them Marie knew what must have happened. Her heart gave a great lurch and she broke into as brisk a trot as her boots would allow. Directly she was within shouting distance of Rhona she screeched, "What's happened to Gert?"

"Orright!" shrilled back Rhona. And repeating it reassuringly as her mother drew close, "Auntie Gert's orright. She got rescued."

"Shop's gone though?" Marie knew the answer to that one, without being told, and Rhona merely confirmed it with, "Disappeared."

Together they hurried to the scene of disaster. Gert's place was nothing more than a heap of rubble. The house next door was gone and the house next to that; three houses opposite were blasted through and through. The street was strewn in debris. Rescue and ambulance men were everywhere.

"Kergh!" said Marie. "It's a marvel your Auntie Gert came out of that other than in bits in a blanket."

Gert had been taken in by friends, the Trotters. Jack Trotter, the ARP warden who had built the famous hutch, had formerly lived just round the corner from Gert, but he had been bombed out earlier on and now he and his wife were living about a mile away, nearer the

315

Burdett Road. Here Marie hastened, to find Gert, seated in her battered-looking wheelchair and smothered white with plaster, holding court like an albino queen. Nelson and Steve stood either side of her, grinning. Nelson greeted Marie with, "Aunt Gert won't go to 'orspittal!"

"Don't need no 'orspittal," said Gert contemptuously.

"How ever you manage to come out of that alive, Gert?" asked Marie, agog.

Gert, with an air of total victory, replied, "Bleeding miracle Marie, that's what! In my chair, I was, in the rabbit hutch, with all the bleeding house on top of me! There I sat, and I said to myself, 'Well, this is all very nice so long as there ain't no fire!' So, I just sat and waited to be rescued. Had no choice, did I? And then I heard 'em getting at me. And after a bit I saw daylight. And then Jack got me out, chair and all, and wheeled me here. And here I am!"

"Blimey, Gert!" said Marie. All other words failed her.

"She takes the biscuit, don't she?" exclaimed Nelson proudly.

A family council of war was now held. Steve was anxious that Gert should be evacuated to somewhere safe in the country, but Gert refused to consider such a thing. The Trotters had assured her that, for the time being, she might stay with them and stay with them she would, said Gert, until the Council found her somewhere else to live. "Find me another shop," said Gert optimistically.

Having failed to persuade Gert to see reason Steve now tried, for one last time, with his mother. "Have to move away from Stepney now, Marie. You got nowhere to live; can't expect neighbours to take you in with two kiddies."

"Go with old Mrs Tooley up Brick Lane," said Marie. "She'll have us."

"She won't have room for you lot," said Gert.

"Orright, when her place gets too overcrowded me and the kiddies can go down Barrico. Perfectly nice place to be, any time of the day or night, Barrico is now. Don't mind living there all the time for a bit, if we have to. They done it up nice now, Barrico."

"Okay Marie, you win." Steve had said it often enough before; he had no doubt he would hear himself saying it often enough in the future.

So Steve, Nelson, Marie, Rhona and Pete set off for Brick Lane to acquaint old Mrs Tooley with the latest developments.

But as they walked amiably along the street Marie suddenly

stopped, her cheerful expression changing to a thunderous scowl as she stared Steve accusingly in the face. "You been fighting!"

"That's right, Marie. Fighting fires all night, with Nelson."

"Oh more than that, you 'ave! You been duffing someone up! I can tell!"

And she peered closely at the tell-tale puffiness across his slightly reddened cheek bones, a swollen lip, inflamed and swollen knuckles. Steve, remaining admirably deadpan under this gimlet-eyed scrutiny, said, "We all been in a fight, ain't we? Fighting old 'Itler."

"Fighting him all night," said Nelson. "Good night's work, wasn't it Steve?"

"You too, Nelson. You been at it too," said Marie, switching her gaze to Nelson. "Cor luv-a-duck, two of 'em in the bleeding family!"

"Oh come off it Marie," said Steve. "We've done nothing, except what you'd be proud of. Going up the boozer after this, Nelson and me are, to celebrate. Park Roan and the nipper in Brick Lane and come and join us."

"Celebrate what?"

"Never mind what. Just take it that your sons have done you and old England proud."

Marie, sensing she'd get nowhere with further questioning, gave up and accepted the invitation.

They were now approaching the mound of rubble that had been Gert's shop. They walked slowly towards it and halted beside it. At last Marie said, "Good old shop! Good old Gert's! Stood up to them bleeding bombs for six months on end and then only went down to a direct hit." She turned to Pete in his pushchair. "Come on Pete, give me that flag, there's a good boy! I'll get you another one, much bigger, but let your Mummy 'ave this one for now, darling." Pete didn't want to part from the flag, but his mother firmly took it from him and he forgot to start a tantrum in his surprise at seeing her now scramble up the mound of rubble, making her way up it on all fours.

Marie reached the top of the mound, balanced herself carefully and then planted the Union Jack firmly in the rubble. It was the ultimate in a gesture of defiance. Nelson and Steve helped her down. Marie stepped back several steps and stared, for a moment, up at the flag. "There y'are, Pete," she said. "There's your flag. You can be proud of it."

XLII

Ann, ringing and knocking at Sybil's front door, began to think that her friend must be out. "Blast! She said she'd be in all day, taking it easy and relaxing now we're having a spell of off-duty!" Ann stepped back from the brick and timber tudor porch and scanned the latticed windows of the ornately gabled and wisteria-draped house frontage. The wisteria, its new young leaves glistening, was not yet in flower, "Everything's late this year!" thought Ann, and at the same moment caught sight of a dressing-gowned figure, with deathly white face, peering at her from a downstairs window. "Good heavens, Sybil's been taken ill! All this strain of the past few months!" And, after a series of violently excited and indecipherable gestures intended to convey to Sybil that if she could only totter to open the door immediate help would be at hand, Ann leapt back upon the doorstep and, pushing open the letter-box, began calling, "Sybil! Sybil!"

After a few moments of intense suspense the door was opened, revealing Sybil in a floral dressing-gown, her feet bare, her hair tied up in a blue turban and her face thickly coated with a kind of cement which, in combination with her spectacles, gave her an appearance both ridiculous and unearthly. Between lips tightly congealed together she managed to mutter, "Face-pack!" "Oh my dear, so sorry to have disturbed . . .!" Sybil waved her hands imperiously to indicate that Ann should enter the room which Sybil called her "den" and, then hissed into Ann's ear, "Gimlet?" "Please!" Ann flopped on to a couch opposite the chair on which Sybil, obviously, had been sitting with her feet in a basin of water on the surface of which floated languid globules of oil. The room smelled deliciously of Floris "Roman Hyacinth". Beside the chair was a small table on which reposed a manicure-set in leather case, bottles of cuticle remover and Ardena Pink nail varnish, the Floris perfumed bath-oil and a tumbler of palest green liquid that could only be the drink optimistically described by Sybil as a "gimlet". Sybil was availing herself of the lull on the battlefront to spruce herself up and be in good trim for whatever came next.

While Ann contemplated these sybaritic accoutrements, Sybil

busied herself at the drinks-tray placed on her desk in the bay window. In due course she handed Ann a concoction of gin, lime cordial, ice and tap water (tonic water and soda now being pleasures of the past, and real limes or lemons never so much as even dreamed of). Sybil then seated herself in her chair, placed her feet in the basin of water and began to apply a second coat of varnish to her fingernails.

Ann, raising her glass to Sybil in a gesture of gratitude and appreciation, took a long mouthful of drink and let it glide slowly over her tongue and down her throat. "Glory be! I needed that!" As Sybil was unable to converse, there ensued a short silence, during which Ann relished her gin and Sybil finished her nails. Then, flickering her finger tips to help dry the varnish, she managed to enunciate, "What went wrong?"

"Everything! Quite the most frightful afternoon I've had for years! Can you imagine, the first day I try to manage an outing since the war began, and it has to be the day of the Cup Final — Arsenal playing Preston at Wembley; the Tube crowded with supporters, mostly drunk and all madly noisy; sheer chaos! Getting there was bad enough, but coming home!" Ann rolled her eyes and drained her glass with an air of desperation. Sybil rose and refilled it for her as Ann continued, "Of course, I hadn't planned to return home so early. I thought, things being so quiet at the moment, and you and I enjoying a break from the canteen, that I'd take the girls out for a bite somewhere after the concert, like we used to in the old days — a Corner House brasserie or something; the girls used to love that! School holidays, it was one of their favourite treats. Nothing in the least posh, but great fun! However, that idea fell flat on its face. Odile, who's looking absolutely washed out and at least forty — I was quite horrified when I saw her! plastered with make-up, of course, like she always is these days, but even that couldn't hide her drawn appearance — she had to get back to Whitechapel where, it seems, she lives next door to your Hugo and he had a friend coming out of hospital so Odile was due to cook a celebration dinner for them, while Morwenna . . . Thanks, m'dear: what a godsend you are!" as the second drink was handed to her.

Sybil reseated herself, feet in basin. Ann, after another gulp of revitalizer, continued, "Morwenna . . . you'll never believe this, Sybil. It's why I had to come and talk to you, rather than have to unburden myself to mother. She'd have a stroke! Believe it or not,

Sybil, Morwenna — knowing I'd planned a beautiful family outing, just myself and my daughters together — I mean I *am* their mother and even though there *is* a war on, one does want to see a little of one's own children!" Ann paused dramatically. Sybil, eyes wide behind her gleaming specs, nodded vigorously in sympathetic understanding. Ann recommenced, "Mor—wenna, my dear, arrives at the Queen's Hall with a young clergyman in tow! She kindly informs me that he isn't sitting with us, having a seat of his own, but we can all have a meal together afterwards! When I say, having tactfully waited until he has gone off to his own seat, 'Really darling, you know that this was going to be a nice outing of just you and me and Odile alone together, like old times,' this child announces that she's engaged to him and under the circumstances she had supposed I should only be too delighted to make his acquaintance. Engaged! To a curate from the East End! And she's not yet eighteen!"

Sybil, literally speechless and her facial expression of necessity wooden, managed to respond with a muffled gasp and a lifting of her hands.

"It turns out that he is the young man who saved her life when she was bombed, and works at that Mission thing to which she has gone. Which rather explains her sudden mania for doing good works, I feel. I must admit he's a perfectly presentable young chap; charming, in fact, and obviously from a good background: but his prospects! I mean, the Church!" Sybil's eyes glinted. Ann hurried on, "Yes, I know your grandfather was a bishop, Sybil, but how many clergymen become bishops? Most clergy exist in penury! Besides, her age!

"I managed to say, 'Don't be ridiculous, Thingy, you *can't* put the cart before the horse like this, you haven't even completed your education!' But all that produced was a withering look and, 'Mummy *do* grow up!' Then the concert started. Ruined for me, of course! In the interval we were joined by the curate: it seems that Odile already knows him. They talked about that air-raid shelter she works in, and somebody called Marie who has been bombed out of her own home and is now living round-the-clock in this air-raid shelter with her children. It seems that Odile, having lost an assistant named Connie, who has married and moved to Barking, has appointed Marie as assistant in her stead which may or may not work out and so they all chatted amongst themselves about all this and I felt completely left out and on the shelf! I grant that the curate made polite attempts to draw me into the conversation but I mean what was the point I. . . ."

"Time's up!" interjected Sybil. Ann, for a moment not understanding, stopped her recitation abruptly and stared rather bleakly at Sybil who, rising from her chair, hurried out of the room. Ann then realized that Sybil was referring to her face-pack and not to Ann's admittedly frenetic monologue.

Left on her own Ann leaned back, sipped her drink, lit a cigarette and felt immensely sorry for herself. The afternoon had badly disillusioned her. For weeks past she had created for herself the fantasy of recapturing those happy pre-war outings she had so loved sharing with the girls during their school holidays; eager, rosy little faces, carefree conversation, schoolgirl jokes and laughter: such fun, such enormous fun! And instead! An Odile looking older and more worn by sorrow and experience than Ann was sure she herself had ever, would ever, look; gallingly anxious to return as fast as she could to sordid lodgings in Whitechapel; while little Thingy coolly produced a fiancé and after the concert vanished with him to stroll across the Park and later have supper — Ann excusing herself from their company as she could see only too plainly that they wished to be alone.

The truth stared her in the face that she had lost her little daughters. Those happy outings with them would never take place again. The war had swept away her children and instead she was now mother of two young women, one of whom looked too adult for her years, while the other. . . .

"See what you think when you hear this!" Sybil had returned, her face cleansed of face-pack and unnaturally smooth and pink. She was waving a letter.

"Oh Sybil! You're not in trouble too?"

"Pam."

"Oh my dear! Not . . .?"

"No, not that kind of trouble. But grim enough." Sybil poured them each another drink. Ann lit another cigarette.

"Engaged to some young chap she's nursing, called Pongo. Says not to worry, they won't be marrying for ages yet; he'll be months longer in the burns unit having his face rebuilt, quite apart from the fact that he has to get his divorce."

"Sybil!" Ann gazed in horror at her friend. "That's even worse than a curate!"

"Infinitely!"

"When did this happen?"

"The letter arrived this morning. She'd love me to meet him, she says — no intention of doing so, of course! — but warns me to prepare for a shock because he's having facial skin-grafting and looks sub-human but is such a marvellous chap underneath." Sybil reseated herself. "I don't mind what he looks like; all honour to these young chaps, she can marry someone with no face at all if she chooses! But a married man, there I draw the line, and so should she."

A long and pensive silence fell between the pair. In the garden dusk was rapidly falling. At last Ann said, wearily, "They were bound to change, you know, in a war like this."

"I agree. Bound to change. And our trouble is, of course, having seen so little of them over the past months we haven't realized the extent to which they have changed. But this ridiculous business of becoming engaged, without giving any apparent thought, or bringing any sense, let alone morals, to bear. . . ."

"I must confess that Paul and I got engaged and married in the middle of the last war."

"Come to that, so did Arthur and I . . . Did your parents approve, Ann?"

"Mother, of course, was already a widow. And no, of course she didn't approve. Me, her only daughter, marrying a Frog . . . as she put it. You know mother!"

"The salt of the earth!"

"Maybe." Ann sighed and smiled simultaneously. "What did your parents think of Arthur?"

"Not much. They thought he was . . . rather common."

More drinks. More pensive contemplation of the darkening garden. They sat without lights, in order not to have to disturb themselves with the blackout precautions. They chatted in little spurts, about this, about that. The full moon rose. They watched it climb up a clear, cloudless, cold sky. "Fantastic sight!"

"Remember what happened the last time we had a full moon, Ann?"

"I do indeed! One of the worst raids we've had in the entire Blitz."

"We haven't had any bombers over for three weeks. I can't believe it, can you? Think he's had enough?"

"I'd like to think so, but. . . ."

322

"We mustn't drink any more," said Sybil, rising to her feet with a slight lurch and moving slowly to the window. "We may find ourselves having to take out the canteen."

XLIII

Morwenna and Clem lingered long over their meal together. He was not on Civil Defence duty that night and so there was no rush to get home.

Clem said, "I'm sorry that your mother didn't like me better."

"Oh it wasn't so much that she didn't like you, as that she didn't like you being there. But she'll come round to seeing our engagement in a better light in the end, or at least putting up with it. She's quite intelligent really! I only hope your parents approve of me."

"Can't fail to!"

"I wouldn't be so sure of that. I mean, my mother's a case in point of how strangely parents behave. Any normal woman would have immediately danced for joy at hearing that you were her prospective son-in-law."

It was dark when they came out of the restaurant. In the Underground they walked between rows of improvised beds laid out on the floor on either side of the corridors, with people sitting or lying on the folded blankets and old eiderdowns. On the platform where they waited for their train the bunks now installed against the wall at the back of the platform were occupied by regulars, many of whom had fixed up curtains to give greater privacy. The bunks, however, only accommodated a certain number of people and many more were bedded-down on the platform itself. A white line, painted the length of the platform, about a yard from its edge, separated the sleeping space from the part reserved for waiting passengers.

"There aren't so many people sheltering here tonight as you usually see," commented Morwenna, after a moment or two of contemplating the scene.

"People aren't using the shelters like they were. Let's hope it's not misplaced confidence."

At their feet, only just on her sleeper's side of the white line, a small girl lay in deep slumber on a dirty old blanket. She had no coverlet of any kind over her; she wore shabby street clothes and had an old knitted bonnet on her head. Her skirts had caught up to expose her little dirty thighs and knickers; one of the other shelterers, a derelict-looking woman, leaned forward and carefully readjusted the child's skirts, protecting her decency. There was something extraordinarily touching about the gesture. Clem said enigmatically, "That is civilization."

"You know, Clem, you wonder why I sometimes seem so dejected, but I still do find it so impossibly difficult to understand why all this suffering should be allowed. Don't you find this a most depressing time to live in?"

"I thought so earlier on, but now I've come to see it differently. People, ordinary, poor people, are proving themselves to be so wonderful that it fills me with hope. And with such an example of courage on their part, one can't help but grow courageous too. No," said Clem, looking up and down the platform at the grubby, shabby people in the dreary reduced light, "I think it's a time of hope and courage."

"Certainly, when it's all over, things will have to be very different," said Morwenna. "All these people will expect and deserve a very different way of life, Clem."

"They will indeed. And it's up to us to see that they get it." He squeezed Morwenna's hand hard. "We'll work for it together, my darling."

It was full moonlight when they found themselves back in the Mile End Road. The new double summer time had just been introduced, the clocks had been put forward by two hours, which meant that air-raids would now start later, if and when they occurred. The fact that they no longer took place nightly had removed much of the tension from daily life, a relaxation of mood which was reflected in the way in which Morwenna and Clem, arm in arm, now sauntered, almost in holiday style, through streets bathed in silvery light.

"How incredibly beautiful!" exclaimed Clem. "I'm positive it's been laid on specially for us. This really is our night! You wouldn't believe, unless you saw it for yourself, that a bombed East End landscape could look so magically lovely. Morwenna, sweetheart, I've never been so happy in my life as I am tonight!" And he took her in his arms and wrapped her into a kiss that only stopped when the nearby church clock struck, startling them both.

"Half past ten! We must step out. Miss Widgeon will be horrified at me keeping you up so late."

"Half past ten is scarcely late, Clem darling."

"It is to Miss Widgeon."

Miss Widgeon, hearing Morwenna's key turning in the lock, emerged from her office, wearing the expression of mingled relief and reproach common to all those who have waited up late for a returning prodigal. "Dear me!" she said. "I was becoming rather anxious. I expected you back hours ago."

"I'm afraid I led Morwenna astray," said Clem. "Persuaded her to have dinner with me in Town."

"We should have telephoned you, Miss Widgeon, to say we'd be back later than we'd originally planned," said Morwenna. Miss Widgeon replied, "That would have been thoughtful, dear. Never mind," she added, with a Christian determination to forgive, "I don't suppose it will happen again. And now up you go to bed, you must be tired out, I know I am; and as for you Clem, naughty boy, off you go and don't repeat keeping her out at this hour! It's eleven o'clock!" she concluded dramatically.

"Sleep well, Morwenna," said Clem. He and she exchanged a long look. "Sleep well Clem, and thank you for an unforgettable evening," said Morwenna.

And then the sirens began to wail.

For a brief instant Miss Widgeon, Morwenna and Clem stood motionless, while the air filled with the wailing as siren after siren picked up the chorus. Then Morwenna said, "We must get people into the cellar," and Miss Widgeon said, "I'll put the lights on down there." She made a hasty exit towards the kitchen. Morwenna and Clem, with a spontaneous movement of tacit understanding, fell into each other's arms. "At least let me kiss you good night even if it's now going to be anything but!"

The wail of the sirens faded, the drone of what sounded like hundreds of planes took over, and then a violent knocking on the door accompanied by Nelson's shouting forced Clem and Morwenna apart. He opened the door and at once Nelson was yelling from where he stood on the doorstep. "Quick, Rev, insanitaries! Thousands of 'em!"

Clem vanished down the steps into the street. Morwenna

snatched her tin hat from the hall stand, slammed it on her head, raced for the kitchen and started filling a bucket at the sink. The stirrup pump was kept ready in a corner; Morwenna seized it in one hand and took up the full bucket in the other and shrieked at Lily, who had now appeared bundled in a dressing-gown with her hair in small plaits, "Fill another bucket and fetch it out quick, Lily!" Morwenna then made for the street with Miss Widgeon panting at her heels.

The night throbbed with bombers, the incendiaries were falling like hail, the moonlight was made pallid by the brilliance of the German flares and people were racing about in all directions putting out fires. Nelson's squad was working away extinguishing flames behind the fish and chip shop. Miss Widgeon and Morwenna stared round bewildered, wondering where to start. Incendiaries were exploding everywhere at once. Then Lily emerged from Tulip House screeching, "Miss Widgeon! Miss Widgeon! The coal shed's alight!" "Open the side door for us, Lily!" They ran to the side door; Lily drew back the bolts and opened the door and they ran into the yard of Tulip House; a small space, as all yards were in that part of the world, with the coal shed hard against the house. Flames were already sprouting and licking in all directions and the house itself was in obvious danger. Morwenna began pumping while Miss Widgeon manfully directed the spray, but it was obvious that the fire was rapidly getting out of control. Lily had already brought a second bucket of water and now came gasping and panting with a third. Morwenna, seeing that the fire was going to defeat them and that Tulip House would burn, shouted in Lily's ear, "Run down the street and fetch Nelson Tooley!" Lily, grotesque in dressing-gown and plaits, teetered into the street. At the same time a window opened above them and Miss Whitebeam's foghorn voice came: "Isabella, Isabella, aim rather more to the left!" But Miss Widgeon was unable to reach from the ground and could not climb up. Someone came running with a ladder, Miss Widgeon took over with the pump and Morwenna climbed the ladder and directed water on the flames; at the same moment Miss Whitebeam emptied a large water jug from above. There was a hiss and then the flames sprang up as fiercely as ever. Another shower of water from Miss Whitebeam, this time from a basin, but as ineffectual as the first. Morwenna was now so hot from the flames and exertion that she was soaked in perspiration. She was too desperate to be scared.

Voices were shouting below, then Clem grabbed hold of her and lifted her down from the ladder and climbed it himself, and Nelson and his squad were in action like demons and Morwenna was running back and forth from the kitchen with buckets of water, and it seemed that everyone in the neighbourhood was there trying to save Tulip House and at last, after a nightmare struggle that might have lasted hours or merely ten minutes, the fire was out, the air reeked of charred wet wood and Rhona was squealing, "Come on Nelson, quick! It's all on fire round the gasworks!"

Away towards the gasworks tore the squad, Nelson yelling at Morwenna, "Fetch those buckets, miss, as many as you can!" He must mean empty buckets, thought Morwenna; she couldn't run two or three hundred yards with buckets filled with water. The empty buckets clanking and clanging, Morwenna pounded after Nelson's squad. On the way they passed a house with flames coming from the ground floor window. An old woman was screaming; Lenny rushed in the house and hauled out the old woman with her hair on fire, Fred tore off his coat and wrapped it round the old woman's head rubbing and pressing out the flames. Gus and Nelson ran into the house with buckets and stirrup pumps, Morwenna and Rhona ran to the house across the street and a woman was already running up the passage from the kitchen at the back, fetching a bucket of water; Morwenna and Rhona now ferried more and more buckets of water across the road to Gus and Nelson; Fred helped the old woman into the neighbour's house and ran to call an ambulance for her. The fire in the house was put out, the squad clatteringly assembled in the street and then went off at the double towards the incandescent gasworks.

But not only their local gasworks were turning the sky copper red. To the east a vast glare showed where Beckton gasworks were alight; dockland burned all the way from North Woolwich to the Pool, with Surrey Docks, on the southern shore, once more a furnace. Fires were raging in every quarter: Westminster and Marylebone, Waterloo and the Elephant, Hackney and Islington and St Pancras; the City. Within the space of half an hour London had been set ablaze by cataracts of incendiaries spilling from the bombers that never stopped coming over.

There seemed to be more of them overhead now than ever before; Morwenna's head drummed with their thunder. People were running, screaming and shouting, fire and ambulance bells clanged.

In the distance they could hear the thud of exploding bombs. Nelson halted to attack a fire in another little house; a man, his wife and two small children were carrying things out of the front door as the back of the premises burned. After a few minutes Nelson decided that the fire was too much for him; it was a matter for the fire brigade. Rhona was despatched to inform the firemen fighting a blaze in the next street, while Gus came hollering that round the corner an old girl's sofa was about to set the rest of her house afire.

Round the corner and into the house raced Morwenna and Fred: an incendiary had come through the roof, through the floor below and had landed in the front ground-floor room on the sofa. The tiny room was full of dense black smoke; it was impossible to fight the fire from inside so Fred dashed outside again and smashed the window. While Morwenna pumped on the pavement immediately under the window, Fred squatted on the sill and sprayed the sofa and managed to extinguish the fire. Then, to make quite certain the sofa wouldn't ignite again, they soused it with buckets of water.

Suddenly there came a thin whistling sound curving out of the sky. Fred shouted "Duck!" Morwenna flung herself face down on the pavement and the bomb exploded with a crash at the end of the street. Another whistle, another crash in the next street, a third crash and the final bomb of the stick of three dropped beyond the second. Morwenna, shaking, got to her feet; already the squad was pounding up the street towards the spot where the bomb had fallen. The air was full of dust and whirling fragments; a woman came from nowhere, shrieking with blood all over her face. Stretcher-men came running, rescue workers; Morwenna glimpsed Hugo, his face black with soot and glistening with sweat. Then Nelson had Morwenna by the arm and was pulling her away, shouting, "Come on, us lot aren't needed here. There's plenty for us to do over by the gasworks!"

Once more they headed for the gasworks. The bombs were now falling simultaneously with the incendiaries; the bombers came in wave after wave, flying so low they seemed to be thudding over at little more than roof-top level. Lenny bawled, "There won't be no London left after this!" and Nelson yelled back, "He ain't half mad ternight! Going for us all hammer and tongs!" "It's a reprisal raid!" shouted Morwenna. And she thought to herself, "It'll go on like this, reprisals, one against the other, for ever. No end to it!"

Around the gasworks all was one inferno: the streets and little squares, the moonlit landscape that Clem and Morwenna had strolled through a bare two hours previously, now illuminated more brightly than by any moonshine; not silvered, but luridly ruddied. Rhona, whose job was to find spot-fires of the kind the squad could cope with, came running to say that a newsagent's shop was burning. Away went the squad, to be greeted by the newsagent's hopeless cry of, "Can't do nothing! No water. They've smashed the mains."

A provident soul up the street had an old bath she kept filled with water for emergencies and Morwenna, Fred and Rhona filled buckets from this while Gus, Lenny and Nelson set about beating out the fire with shovels. After a struggle they managed to get the fire under control and then to extinguish it.

With no more water in the neighbourhood the streets around the gasworks were becoming a sea of flames. Families simply abandoned their homes and fled. There were many at home that night because the three-week lull in the Blitz had greatly reduced the numbers of those going to the shelters. Nelson and his crew abandoned fire-fighting and instead helped people move away to the safer streets.

Morwenna carried a wireless set from a house for one woman, two tabby kittens were thrust at her and she carried them, she gave an old man her arm and helped him away; everywhere were people helping one another and calling out the names of relations and cursing and crying and shouting. Fire hoses squirmed over the ground; the firepumps were drawn up all round the area of conflagration, but were useless because there wasn't any water. And presently the engines were summoned away to other fires where there was still water to fight them.

Fire had ceased to be fire in the sense that Morwenna hitherto had always understood fire: something cosy, domestic, confined to the grate. This was fire elemental, fire on the rampage, swelling and towering, consuming everything in its path in all directions at once; it beat up its own winds with which it fanned itself into even greater fury, and as it burned it breathed loudly and rhythmically like a living monster. It was more terrifying than Morwenna had ever imagined anything could be; she was sweating with the reflected heat of the blaze and yet at the same time icy cold with terror. She turned to Nelson, saying, "Let's get away from here, we can't do an atom of good. Let's find some more people to help somewhere else."

But Nelson had vanished. Every member of the squad had gone. Morwenna was gripped with panic: had they been swallowed by flames and she had never noticed? And she was on the point of breaking into screams at the mere horror of the thing when she spotted Rhona pelting along a pavement in the direction of a row of houses the nearer end of which was already engulfed by the fire. Morwenna began tearing after her.

The narrow street into which Rhona had turned was full of thick smoke. The burning houses were the opposite side to the pavement along which Morwenna raced after Rhona but even so the air was oven-hot and the flames seemed to be roaring into Morwenna's ears. She couldn't imagine why Rhona was speeding, it seemed, into the fire itself, but Morwenna dared not lose sight of her. It was like a nightmare in which she found herself doing things as if she were some person outside herself. Rhona raced on, Morwenna raced behind, steadily catching her up. Rhona now dashed across the street to the houses that had not yet been reached by the flames but soon would be. Outside one of them stood the squad's cart, the doorway of the house was open and Rhona darted into it. Morwenna darted after her. The house was in darkness; she could hear voices further along the narrow little passage that led from the front door to the kitchen at the back. Nelson's voice, Lenny's voice, Fred and Gus joining in and a woman's voice arguing, saying, "Leave me. Just leave me. You get out while you can and leave me. You got all your young lives ahead of you. I've had most of mine; don't matter if I lose the rest."

The passage was beginning to fill with smoke and Rhona could be heard squealing, "Hurry up, oh hurry up! The house will be on fire next!" Gus said, "We'll never move this chair, now. Get her out of the chair, Nelson, get her out of the chair!" A flicker of red light appeared at the kitchen end of the passage and bigger puffs of smoke: the woman's voice came again, "Leave me! Go on leave me!" Nelson shouted, "Don't be so bleeding silly! What d'you think Marie would say?" Morwenna had her electric torch in her pocket, she took it out and shone it to reveal an old wheelchair jammed across the passage, its occupant seated in it facing the kitchen; obviously the boys had been trying to pull the chair out and it had stuck. Nelson shouted, "Keep that torch on us!" Morwenna shone the torch while the boys struggled to lift the woman from her chair. The smoke was getting in everyone's eyes and they were all coughing; the woman continued to moan, "Leave me! leave me!" but they still struggled to get her out of her chair which was so awkwardly jammed and the passageway so narrow that it was almost impossible to get hold of her and lift her up and out. And then Nelson gave a shout and the others shouted and the chair-back collapsed and everyone was falling head over heels on top of one another and the smoke and fire came in a great surge forward up the passage as the boys half-carried half-dragged the woman out of the house to the pavement. "Quick. Get to the other side of the road!" bawled Nelson, and they dragged the woman across the road and sat her on the doorstep of the opposite house, propped against the door.

"You're orright now, Auntie Gert, you're orright now!" Rhona repeated over and over again in her high-pitched little voice. The woman sat gasping for breath and coughing the smoke out of her lungs. At last she managed to wheeze, "Yes, duck, I'm orright now, by the mercy of God."

"She can't stay here," said Lenny. "It's too dangerous." The fire was rearing up all round them and the smoke blew over them in gusts. "Get her on the cart," said Nelson. "Blimey, where *is* the cart!" The cart still stood outside the now well and truly burning house. Nelson darted forward, grabbed the cart and swung it sharply across the road. They picked Aunt Gert up and dumped her in along with the buckets and shovels and then they all started racing up the street away from the fire with the cart lurching and rocking. "Take her back to Tulip House," instructed Morwenna. Nelson headed the cart for Sparrowgrass Row. Aunt Gert said, "Twice in three weeks! Blooming twice in three weeks! Never've believed it if it hadn't happened to myself!" Nelson said, "You watch out, old gal; don't want you making a habit of it!"

Aunt Gert, as they neared Sparrowgrass Row, exclaimed, "Lor, I hope I look respectable, lying on my back in a cart with my knees up like this!" The boys broke into guffaws. Then Nelson burst out singing, "Knees up Mother Brown". The others joined in, Morwenna included, and finally Aunt Gert, who not surprisingly seemed a little hysterical, started singing too.

Then Nelson said, "Here comes the Rev on his bike. Wondering what we're up to, wheeling an old gal in our cart. He'll think we've took up kidnapping as a sideline!"

331

Clem, spinning along on a bike at the further end of the street, waved to them and came pedalling towards them. "Found you at last, thank God!'" he said.

"We rescued Aunt Gert!" shrilled Rhona. "Just in the nick of time! Fire came in at the back as we went out of the front!"

"Saved my life," said Aunt Gert. "Been left alone in the house I had, 'cos things had turned so nice and quiet with nothing doing for weeks, and now we've copped this packet! I'd've been burned to a cinder for sure if Nelson and these mates of his hadn't come and got me out." She added by way of apology for her extraordinary position and appearance, "I'm in this cart because I've lost my chair."

"We're taking her to Tulip House," explained Morwenna.

"A cuppa tea and I'll be right as rain," said Aunt Gert.

Clem said nothing; he merely looked at them as if he could find no suitable words to speak. He himself was black with soot, with his hair and eyebrows singed. At last, breaking into a smile, he said, "Yes, take her into Tulip House and give her a good strong cup of tea and keep me one too. Be with you all in a tick. I'm just dodging round the corner to check that the Mission House itself is okay."

The squad turned up Sparrowgrass Row, all bellowing "Knees up Mother Brown" again, a kind of chant of victory. Clem cycled off in the opposite direction. Morwenna glanced over her shoulder at him as he pedalled away. She had almost forgotten him during the frantic happenings of the past three hours, just occasionally wondering at the back of her mind what he was doing and if he were safe. Clem, in these raids, took incredible risks.

Now Morwenna watched him cycling along, as unconcernedly as an undergraduate riding up Oxford High. He skimmed round the corner into the next street, out of view. They stopped the cart and lifted Aunt Gert out and into the back yard of Tulip House. "Let me go first. I'll open the kitchen door," said Morwenna.

They heard the whistling overhead and Nelson shouted "Down!" and they all flung themselves on their faces, Nelson and Lenny covering Aunt Gert with their bodies. There was the usual fearful crash, the air sucked in and then shuddered out; another whistle and a crash, then a third; each, it seemed, almost on top of the other. Then they got up and ran to look along the street and all the houses at the corner were down, and Morwenna screamed "Clem!" and started running towards the corner, and Nelson pounded after her and caught hold of her and held her, shouting, "Stay here duck! Stay here with me!" And he held her, keeping her with him, while she struggled to join Gus and Fred and Lenny racing towards the gaping crater in the road where Clem had been. And then they stopped, and just stood still among the rubble, and Nelson led Morwenna back to Tulip House.

XLIV

Realization of the true immensity of the damage done came slowly, percolating through the blanket of official silence and censorship thrown over the raid: the outside world heard little or nothing of it; only the Londoners themselves knew what had really happened. "It's wrong to hate, I know," said Gert, "but I hate that wicked lot for what they done!"

"It was a spite raid," said Lily. "Wicked spite from start to finish. But never mind, they'll get paid back. Them that lives by the sword dies by the sword. Their turn'll come to cop it, you'll see, just as bad as we've copped it and worse. They won't know Berlin, they won't, when we've finished with it!"

Aunt Gert lamented, "All gone, the river and the docks we knew; all gone! I'll never forgive 'em for that."

"The river's still there," said Morwenna. Gert responded, "Yes mate, actual river's still there, but the river was more'n just water. The docks made the river, and the people made the docks, and all that's gone. Never be the same. Can't be!"

"The Lord teaches us to forgive and to turn the other cheek," responded Miss Widgeon, "but I must confess, after this, I find it very difficult."

"Blimey, Miss Widgeon, after that last lot we ain't got no other cheek left to turn," rejoined Lily.

"Everywhere you look everything's down." Gert continued her lament. "Nothing but holes and empty spaces."

The worst hole and empty space lay at the corner of their street; not only for Morwenna, but for all in the neighbourhood, for Clem had been loved by everyone. Yet after the service that had been held, not just in his memory but in the memory of all the parishioners who had died that same night, his name was not mentioned at Tulip House; not because they were not mourning him, but because Miss Widgeon and Miss Whitebeam, true to the tenets of their class and kind, considered open grief a form of self-indulgence; they were the old stiff-upper-lip school, the "bury your troubles in hard work and service" brigade and they kept everyone at Tulip House, and especially themselves and Morwenna, busily occupied from half past six in the morning until ten o'clock at night, hard at it, holding the tears at bay. And certainly with the house so full once more and the surrounding district still reeling from the raid, it was not difficult to find a thousand and one tasks.

A letter arrived for Morwenna from her grandmother.

Dearest child,

Your mother and I and Elizabeth are all very very sorry to learn, through Odile, that the poor young man you were hoping to marry was killed the other night in that terrible raid. Our thoughts and prayers are with you. Your mother will write as soon as she is able. She and Sybil are in the local cottage hospital at present, though not seriously hurt thank heaven, but cut and badly bruised and your mother with a broken leg and Sybil with broken ribs. Their canteen was called out that same night as you suffered your loss, and it was overturned by blast: they were very lucky to have survived if you ask me. What a war! the only consolation is the knowledge that we are winning, and will continue to win, though we still, I fear, have a long hard haul ahead of us. I always remember my grandfather, a seasoned old soldier if ever there was one, saying, "Only one thing to tell oneself, in the middle of a stiff battle, and that is, No way but forward!"

I always remind myself of that, dear, when I feel I need pepping up!

Love from us all,

Grandma

Odile's condolences had been brief, but poignant:

Your Clem and my Fernand, both gone for ever!

Those golden days before the war, when we genuinely believed

334

(at least I know I did) that the future was a kind of palace of delights, waiting to be explored, step by delicious step. And we would be happy all the way, because it is everyone's right to be happy. What a delusion!

It isn't any use trying to put sympathy or feeling into words, Thingy darling, because we're all too engulfed for words to mean anything any more.

Let's try to meet again soon, if we can. Until then, think of me, and I'll think of you. Odile.

A letter from Posy also brought sympathy — and some disturbing thoughts of a kind Morwenna tried to put at the back of her mind:

Dear Morwenna,

Feel I must drop you a line to say how absolutely shattered I am by the news about Clem, along with everyone else here in Cuddwell who knew him. He was one of the very best. We can't afford to lose people like him.

He risked his life, trying to save others, time and time again; you know all about that yourself! As for all the everyday kindnesses, well, I don't suppose any of us will ever know the half of them. A case in point was the way he troubled to listen to me on the Henry business. How many would have done that?

I'm afraid I wasn't as honest with Clem as I should have been though, about Henry. Truth is I had, still have, a very nasty hunch that Henry may drag our family's good name right through the mud, and this I couldn't bear to talk about, not even to Clem. Henry's always been a funny one; very quiet, very clean and tidy and polite, never given any real trouble to anyone in his life. But at the same time, never a character you could properly make out, not even properly get to know — and I'm his sister saying that! He never seemed to have any close friends, either. Or, let's put it this way, if he did have them, he never fetched them home. That, to my mind, always makes you think!

Before the war he took up learning German and went camping in Germany. Beautiful part of the world, he said. Came back full of Hitler, too — how Hitler was the one who did everything right, cured his country's unemployment and gave youth something to believe in. Things our system in this country couldn't do.

Well, we know there were plenty of people around before the war who sang the praises of Hitler and then came to realize how well and truly he'd led them up the garden path, and I must say that once the war broke out we heard no more talk like that from Henry. But with him, there had been more to it — he really did believe that the only hope for the future was if this country followed Hitler. Us and Hitler together would be the answer to everything. Really *believed* it. Said he'd do anything to make it come true. And what worries me is that he may now be doing something to help Hitler and against his own country. Which is why he went so mum, and now has disappeared. He wants us to take it that he's lost and gone, so that he can get on with his dirty work with nobody any the wiser.

I can see, of course, that I may be letting my imagination get the better of me. But there it is, sometimes you do smell a rat, and afterwards you think, "If only I'd taken steps!" So, after that long talk with Clem, and you telling me you thought you'd bumped into Henry, I went to the police. I told them about Henry being officially dead, and the break-in and stolen clothes making me think he must still be alive. But I didn't mention his interest in Hitler: if the police do find Henry then they'll discover what he's up to (if he *is* up to anything!) and if he isn't — well, then he's just gone loopy, pushed over the brink by the bombing, like Clem said.

Still, when all is said and done, Henry's my brother, my own flesh and blood, and you can guess how awful I feel, for whichever way it's looked at, it's bad — bad that I've shopped my own brother to the police, terrible that I felt the necessity to do it in the first place! If it hadn't been for Clem I wouldn't have done it, and he only saw the need for it because he thought Henry might be ill and needing help. I reckon if I had told Clem about my real suspicions of Henry, Clem would have said I must tell the police about that too! Well, I haven't. And I'm afraid I've let Clem down. I hope, if he knows about it, he'll understand.

I know that you and Clem had come to mean a lot to each other. I needn't say more about that. This is an awful war. I never thought it would turn out to be much of a picnic, but even I didn't realize how hard it would *hit*. Still, no good growing faint-hearted! Plug on — that's all we can do, Morwenna my duck, plug on.

Your affectionate friend,

Posy

PS. Still not said a word of any of this to Mum and don't intend to as long as it can be avoided.

PPS. If she knew I was writing she'd send her love.

Morwenna couldn't decide what to think of this letter. Poor Posy's distress was clear enough; but what to say to her? The likelihood of Henry Cowper being involved in treachery of any kind struck Morwenna as highly unlikely. He just didn't fit the bill! She much preferred to believe in him as a quiet, unsung war hero, an ordinary, unobtrusive chap who, when the need arose, had, like so very many others, done what he had to do. She had never much taken to Henry herself; there was nothing in his personality to take to. But that said and done, be fair to the chap: there was nothing in him to seriously take against, either! Clem, bless him, had got it right; Posy was letting her imagination run away with her.

Still, there wouldn't be much comfort for Posy in a letter telling her all this. She'd just feel more rotten than ever, at having shopped Henry, as she put it. So Morwenna delayed replying to Posy for the time being.

Morwenna now had three planks to cling to for comfort when she found herself with time to brood upon her loss. The first, and best, was that Clem had died happy: "I have never been so happy in my life as I am tonight!" He had died without suffering, instantaneously, skimming round the corner of the street on his bike in the expectation of being, within a jiffy, back in Tulip House kitchen drinking tea with Morwenna. If you had to die it was a good way to die. And as for the if and the why of the dying, "If your number's on it you'll get it; if it ain't you won't." Aunt Gert, sensing the girl's attachment to Clem, observed sadly, "That's what it is, you see duck. If it's written, it's written. Twice in three weeks I was saved by a miracle; first my hutch held, and next time the back of my chair gave way. But him, poor young man, he sailed right into that bomb as if his name was on it in plain black and white! Why the Lord

337

should spare me and take him, I can't think. He'd be a lot more use than me to be left down here, a lot more use!"

"God moves in a mysterious way," sighed Lily.

"Anyhow, there's no way but forward," said Morwenna, resorting to her second plank, provided by her grandmother. And she repeated it to herself, "There's no way but forward." There was no longer anything promising or bright about the way ahead; it was simply all that was left. "Plug on," Morwenna told herself, "plug on." Plank number three.

The days passed, the weather gradually grew warmer; Miss Widgeon planted mustard and cress in flower pots; dusty-looking wallflowers and lilac blooms appeared in the rectory garden.

Another letter arrived for Morwenna, this time from Parrocks. Morwenna had heard from Vicky, following Boggy's death, and had exchanged correspondence on that sad subject, but had heard nothing since. She opened this letter now with a strong sense of foreboding.

It was from Lady Sowersby, breaking the news that Frank, in Greece, was reported missing following heavy fighting. Though there was a possibility that he might have been taken prisoner, his family were not allowing themselves to be optimistic.

It would be wrong to hold out hope, Morwenna dear, when there are such very slender grounds for it (the letter had continued). The blows we in this family have sustained over the past few months have at least attuned us to disaster and we have learned to look it steadily in the eye, though God knows it has been a hard and heavy lesson! First we lost Jos, then darling Boggy and dear Giles, and now it seems that we have lost Frank. I had a suspicion that this might prove a sad war for this family, but I had no inkling, thank heaven, of what was really in store for us! If one could see into the future it would be difficult indeed to carry on.

The letter concluded with an invitation to Parrocks.

Why don't you come up at Whitsun for a few days? Do try! Frank, when he was last home on leave, was bitterly disappointed not to have you up here; he explained to us how hard and devotedly you were working in the East End blitz, but, judging by the news, things have quietened down now and however dedicated you are

338

to the work I am sure that a short rest could do you no harm: you have been in the London raids without a break since September! So do try to take a few days over the Whitsun holiday. We should all be so happy to see your bright young face; alas, most of the bright young faces are gone!

Morwenna, on reading this letter, had realized that Frank hadn't told his parents about their rupture. No doubt he had been too upset and angry to feel like discussing the matter with anyone. Lady Sowersby obviously had no idea that the affair had been broken off. In any case it didn't matter now. Frank was gone.

Because there was now no likelihood of a visit to Parrocks reinvolving her in any way with Frank, Morwenna, after some cogitation, decided to accept the invitation, providing of course that Miss Widgeon would allow her time off over Whitsun. Truth to tell, everything was so busy at Tulip House that she felt distinctly guilty in asking for a holiday. But Miss Widgeon proved sympathetic. "An excellent notion, my dear. In fact I was on the point of suggesting, myself, that you should take a little rest." So Morwenna wrote a letter of acceptance to Lady Sowersby.

She posted it during the course of one of her daily constitutionals with a band of Tulip House infants: no longer the same ones, the originals had all been found country billets, but a fresh intake who to all intents and purposes might have been the same little lot. They played on the recreation ground swings, all shouting at once for her to push them higher. At last, worn out by this exertion, she sat on a seat while they gambolled on the grass.

"Hello miss!" It was Nelson, carrying a large bunch of lilac and looking unusually shy.

"Hello Nelson. Nice to see you. What brings you to our lovely recreation ground?"

Nelson, with a bashful grin, replied, "I been tracking you down, that's what. Mind if I sit next to you?"

"Not in the least! Plenty of room."

He sat down beside her. "Aunt Gert tells me you're off on holiday tomorrow."

"Only for a short while."

"Do you good." He handed her the lilac. "Brought you that, as a going on holiday present," he said, his ears turning very red as he spoke.

"Oh, how beautiful Nelson. That is kind of you! How lovely it smells!" Morwenna buried her nose in the lilac, thinking to herself that without doubt it must have been nicked from the rectory garden.

"You deserve it, duck," said Nelson gallantly.

There was then a pause, during which Morwenna sniffed the lilac and kept an eye on the children and waited for Nelson to give tongue to whatever it was that he was obviously trying to get himself to say.

At last he mustered the courage, and began, "There's something I ought to tell you, miss. Only, if I tell you, it's dead secret, see? You'll have to give me your solemn oath not to split."

"Yes, Nelson. Of course I'll keep it secret."

Nelson drew a deep breath, "I thought a real lot of the Rev." He stopped. Morwenna said "He thought a real lot of you too, Nelson."

"I know he did," said Nelson. "That's why I've got to tell you what I'm telling you, see?"

He glanced round to make sure there was no one within earshot. They were alone in the rec, with the exception of the children. "I know the Rev thought a lot of me," said Nelson. "And when a bloke like that, a real good 'un, thinks a lot of you, it's not right not to come clean with him about what you've been up to; mustn't keep him in the dark."

Morwenna nodded. "You don't want to feel you've done anything behind his back."

"That's exactly it, miss!" Nelson looked relieved and glad that she understood. "And you see, there's something I did that the Rev might see as orright, and there again he might not. I was going to tell him about it, make a clean breast like, but he got blown up before I had the chance."

Morwenna waited for Nelson to continue.

"Well, the Rev's not here any more for me to tell, but I know you and him was, well . . . he was gone on you good and proper, wasn't he. Thought the whole world of you. And so, you being the next best thing to him, as you might say. . . ."

"Yes Nelson." Morwenna, close to tears, hid her face in the lilac.

"What I'm telling you is, there's some real wicked ones around, miss. You wouldn't know 'em, but there is, here in this very borough. In fact, one in pretty well the next street, there was! Just round the corner from Tulip House. The sort that wants the Nazis to beat us, wants us all to give in, surrender and that." Nelson paused again. Then he resumed, choosing his words with great care. "Well, if one of these Hitler lot got spied out and tracked down, and followed up, and put paid to on a dark night when there was too much other things going on for nobody to notice, what d'you think the Rev would say? Say it was downright wicked and sinful of them what done it, or say it was all for King and country and destroying the enemy?"

Morwenna sat still and thoughtful for several minutes, staring at the lilac, and then across the green grass of the recreation ground. At last she said, "I can't answer for someone else, Nelson, however close we were. All I can say is that Clem would probably have thought and said, as I'm feeling and saying now, that it was an awful thing to have to do, and of course you ought not to have done it, or," she corrected herself, "whoever did it ought not to have done it; but in a war such as this one, anybody who is on the side of the Nazis is the enemy, Nelson, and the enemy must be destroyed because in this war the enemy stands for truly evil things."

"You think the Rev would've said that?"

"I think so, Nelson."

Nelson drew a long breath of relief. "Well, that's what I think he would've said, myself. And, tell the truth, I think he might've done it himself and all." Nelson sighed and stretched out his legs, relaxing after a difficult session. "You'll be coming back here after you've had your holiday?"

"Yes, there's a lot, always, to do at Tulip House." She stood up. "I think I'll have to take this little band back now for their elevenses."

"I'll walk back with you," said Nelson. They rounded up the infants and shepherded them out of the rec.

"And you needn't worry, Nelson, I'll never breathe a word of this to anyone."

"I trust you, duck. You're as good as old Roan at keeping a secret. Know I can trust you by the look in your eye."

Morwenna said hesitantly, "They'll never find him, Nelson?"

"No," said Nelson. "Tipped him over the embankment wall into the river at Shadwell, we did, and even if they do fetch him out of the mud next time the river's low, who's to recognize him? And who's to say he didn't cop it from a bomb?" He gave Morwenna a grin and a wink. "Even the old Blitz can 'ave a good word said for it sometimes!"

"So that's who Rhona was watching out for, and tracking down!" thought Morwenna to herself, when Nelson had left her and she was back in Tulip House. "Well, I should never have thought it myself, but Posy, who knew Henry better, was right all along! One thing, she can never be told the true end of his story. The official line is that Henry went missing at the start of the Blitz — copped it from a bomb. More than that she'll never know."

And Morwenna hurried to the kitchen to get on with elevenses.

The midday post brought her more mail, including a letter that had been forwarded to her from Maytrees. It had an Egyptian stamp, and for a moment Morwenna merely looked at it in objective surprise; she could think of nobody she knew in Egypt. The address was typed, impersonal. Only one way to find out who had sent it and that was to open it. She turned it over to slit the flap. The name of the sender was typed on the back: "Captain Francis Sowersby". Morwenna startled Lily with her shriek.

"What is it?"

"Nothing," Morwenna managed to reply. "Burnt myself on the kettle. Not to worry."

At last she was able to take the letter upstairs to her room, to read it undisturbed. Dated the twenty-second of May, it commenced without preamble of any kind, as was usual with Frank's letters.

Resuming our conversation, so rudely interrupted by our having temporarily lost one another for the umpteenth time, due solely to my impulsive nature and explosive temper, let me first of all say that I can't pretend to be delighted at the thought of you in dockland, in what might be termed the eye of the Blitz, but I can understand your reason for feeling that you should do this thing; that your experiences of recent weeks, in the bombing, have left you with a passionate desire to help others in whatever way you can and, a specific appeal for help having been made, you feel impelled to take it on. It's only what I would expect of you; you may be Piglet sized, but you have the heart of a Heffalump!

As for you not knowing your own mind, I apologize and take it all back; I only said it, I fear, because I was so piqued and put out to discover that you knew your own mind in no mean fashion and, having determined to stick to your post under bombard-ment, stick to your post you would, despite all my appeals and blandishments. A most conclusive demonstration that you know your own mind, my love! We remain handfasted.

I have recently passed through a series of amazing adventures that will furnish me with anecdotes galore if I feel inclined to bore you, in between fossilizing, upon my return. Not that I anticipate many breaks for this kind of refreshment. The fascination of fossils for experts in the subject (and we shall become experts) will leave little time for recalling how I was left for dead in Thessaloniki etcetera. And by the way, I do hope this premature news of my decease hasn't reached the ears of my poor mother, or she will start doing something foolish and tiresome, like praying for me, which should be prevented at all costs. They whom the gods destroy, first get prayed for.

I don't suppose I shall be seeing you for quite a while, my little love, for this war, clearly, is now going to drag on. But however many good battles may lie ahead, the best of this war is over. Indeed, the best of all war is over. Our finest hour, the defiance of the enemy from the acropolis, is done. It was a marvellous hour to have lived through: the acropolis; the high citadel, the topmost place; and we defended it alone! Oh happy breed! For it'll never happen like that again. We're the last generation who'll know what it feels like; to stand in cold blood and high spirits on the ramparts waiting for the enemy. Future conflicts will be waged by heartless and mindless little robots pulling switches. And, let me add, these orgies of extermination won't be about freedom, either; they'll all have forgotten what freedom truly means, by that time. There are certain crimes that free men say "No" to. If and when those crimes take place it will be because the free are free no longer.

But cheer up! That's still a longish way off. So is the end of *this* war. We shan't need to follow the plan of our personal campaign, I surmise, because by the time I'm back with you your twenty-first birthday will most certainly have come and gone. But never fear, back I shall be, to spend what is left of eternity with you. And now, for the time being, I must sign off, leaving you, as always, with our watchword and battle cry, "Parrocks and the fossil room!" F.

Morwenna, suddenly weak at the knees, sank down to sit on the side of the bed. She reread the letter, "Resuming our conversation, so

rudely interrupted by our having temporarily lost one another . . ."
He was right, of course, they could never lose one another for good
and all. They were handfasted. It was Clem who had been, not a
dream, but an ephemeral love, skimming through her life on his
bicycle. Dear, darling Clem! And Morwenna's eyes filled with tears
at the thought of Clem as she sat holding Frank's letter in her hand.
"What a strange thing the heart is," she thought to herself. "And
how full of twists and turns life is, to be sure! And wartime life
particularly so. Twists and turns, and holes and empty spaces.
Hopes and. . . ."

Lily was calling to her: it was time to lay the table for the midday
meal. Morwenna slowly folded the letter and put it in her handbag.
She went on to the landing and paused there for a moment, before
going downstairs. From every room in the overcrowded house rose a
babble of voices: babies cried; a wireless played; Miss Widgeon's
authoritative boom could be heard coming from her office. This
time tomorrow Morwenna would be travelling up to Parrocks.
Suddenly she knew how thankful she would be to get away from
Tulip House and London, if only for a temporary break. She was
battle weary. It was time she had a rest from the ramparts.

Vicky met Morwenna at Stellafield Halt, greeting her with a warm
embrace. "Seems an eternity since I last met you here."

"Yes, the evacuee child who was going to learn to milk a cow."

They laughed; then, as they walked towards the car parked in the
tiny station yard, Vicky said, "I presume you've heard that Frank
has resurfaced, alive and well in Cairo?"

"I've had a letter from him."

"So have we. All about Thucydides and the lessons of war. He
said he had written to you, recommending the study of fossils. A
most peculiar chap, my brother!"

They got in the car and drove off, through a countryside vivid
with fresh young leaves. Cuckoos called in the woods. Morwenna,
stunned by the beauty of it all after months in East London, sat in
silence. Vicky, too, remained without speaking. But at last she said,
"I know I shouldn't say this, Morwenna, but I'm thankful, at heart,
that Frank is the brother who's survived; well, survived so far, that
is. Someone has to inherit Parrocks: it was either he, or Jos, and
though Jos was an adorable chap, as dear darling Boggy would have
said, he . . . well, he lived for the hour. If he had married Poppy he

would have been quite capable of selling Parrocks and going off to Australia. Whereas Frank and Parrocks are essentially part of each other. Even as a very little boy Frank carried, what can I call it, a sort of backlog of the past around with him. When he was quite a small child he shook me by saying to me, 'When your great-great aunt sat on that sofa I bet she didn't show her knickers!' The thought of our great-great aunt on that sofa had never so much as crossed *my* mind, but that child was obviously aware of her. So you see. . . ."

"Don't talk like that, Vicky! The war is nowhere over yet; none of us may be alive at the end of it. The Blitz has taught me one moment we may be here, the next gone for ever."

"I fully realize that. I was just speaking my thoughts; allowing myself, for a moment, to hope for the future."

"Keep our fingers crossed!"

"All the time!"

They reached the house. There were the steps on which Frank had sat waiting for Morwenna. She could almost imagine she saw him there now. Slowly she followed Vicky up the steps; Eliot opened the door. "Well, Miss Morwenna," he said, smiling broadly, "here's one returned from the wars. Let's hope soon to have the next!"

Morwenna, her fingers tightly crossed, stepped into the house, unable to see clearly for tears.

XLV

Marie was now settling down into her routine as assistant shelter marshal at Barrico Hold. At five-thirty each morning she left Barrico with Mrs Tooley Senior to scrub at St Jerome's Hospital. At seven o'clock they were given tea and biscuits and at seven-thirty Marie returned to Barrico, there to superintend the airing of bedding, the cleaning of bays, the disposal of waste, the purchase of supplies for the canteen, and any other chores and duties with which Odile required assistance. In the afternoons Marie had her time to herself; at six-thirty she resumed her marshalling. She proved a lively addition to the staff and, though Odile never could be quite certain of what might happen next when Marie was around, at the same time there was no denying that she was turning out to be a hard and conscientious worker.

One early morning at St Jerome's, while the usual chit-chat was going on over the cups of tea in the room reserved for the scrubbers and their cleaning equipment, a hospital porter appeared, to say that Mrs Marie Tooley was wanted by a police constable waiting in the front lodge. This information was received in tactful silence by everyone except Mrs Tooley Senior, who exclaimed, "My stars, whatever they want with you, Marie?"

"Search me," replied Marie, adding gloomily, "Expect it's Steve and Nelson with their bleeding duffing up. Someone's reported 'em, I bet! All that celebrating — tempting Providence!"

The porter conducted her to the front lodge where the constable was waiting. "Mrs Tooley? You're wanted at the station to help with a matter of identification."

Marie became the epitome of suspicion. "Identifying who?"

"They'll tell you all about it when you get there," he said. "Silvertown police station, it is. Not Leman Street." Leman Street was the local station.

Marie couldn't think why Silvertown police should want her. And then, suddenly, she had a brainwave: she remembered that she, several months back, had given descriptions of Violet and Mick to the police sergeant there. They'd been found♦

Joy lent her chronically tired feet wings. In no time she was back in the scrubbers' room announcing, "They've found my Mick and Vi!"

The news had a stunning effect for a few moments. Then everyone burst out, "Where?" Marie replied, "Dunno. That's what I'm going to find out, see?" And off she went, with everyone shouting, "Good luck, Marie!"

"Fetch 'em back with me!" were her final parting words as she hurried out of view, laughing with excitement.

Silvertown police station, boarded and bricked up like a fortress against blast and bomb-splinters, was almost the only building left standing in this blighted battle area, where squads of demolition men were now clearing the enormous mounds of rubble. The wind stirred great clouds of dust and grit, whirling them into the air. "London's grown such a gritty place. Never all this grit blowing around before the war!" grumbled Marie to herself, as she picked her way across the

346

desolate acres that had once, no so long ago, been crammed with streets and houses, pubs and shops. Now she couldn't have told you where she was, apart from having the police station as a landmark to head for.

At last she reached it and hurried up the steps and presented herself to her old acquaintance, the sergeant. She looked round eagerly, more than half hoping, indeed expecting, to see her Vi. The sergeant said, "You left us a description, about six months ago, of your missing husband and daughter."

Marie, nodding vigorously, said, "Yes, sergeant. I did."

"The demolition boys have come across this, mother, and we're wondering if you recognize it." He took a brown paper carrier-bag from under the desk and from this bag brought out an old navy blue shoe with a matching buckle on the front. It was so dusty and plaster-engrained that Marie stared at it in bewilderment: was it one of her old shoes turned up in the rubble of Lucknow Passage?

"Might be one of mine," she said doubtfully. "Don't remember it, though. Usually wear boots."

"It answers the description of the shoes you thought your daughter would be wearing at the time of her disappearance." The sergeant opened a large and heavy book apparently full of descriptions of missing people and read, in a toneless voice, "Navy blue Dolcis shoes, self-matching buckles, court style, medium height heels. Almost new."

"Yes, but," said Marie, holding the shoe in her suddenly trembling hands and slowly turning it over, "this isn't an almost new shoe. In a shocking state!"

"It's been lying buried in rubble for the best part of nine months, mother. If you look at it a bit more, you'll notice the heel is hardly worn down and hasn't been reheeled by a cobbler, hasn't been reheeled since being bought, that means; and you can still see the name, 'Dolcis' on the inside sole, and that's another indication it's a newish shoe and not been worn much. See?"

Marie said, "Where was it dug up? Lucknow?"

"No. Came out of the crater near where the pub was. The local warden saw your husband and daughter running along the street, past the pub, presumably making for the nearest shelter. No one ever saw them in the shelter; we can't trace them among the people evacuated from the area during the raid; there's nothing recorded of them at all, apart from having been seen running up the street past the pub seconds before the bomb fell that made that crater."

In silence Marie stood turning the shoe over and over. Then she asked, "Can I keep it?"

"If you want. Put it back in the bag for you, shall I?"

He took the shoe from her and dropped it carefully back in the bag.

"How's the rest of the family?" he asked her. "Doing okay?"

"Yes. Doing fine," she managed to say.

"Lucky to have a large brood of youngsters you're happy with," he said. "There's many been left with nobody at all." He handed the bag to Marie. "Goodbye mother. Mind how you go. Keep your pecker up."

"Thanks," said Marie. And made her way into the rubble-piled spaces once more.

Odile, at Barrico, was writing up accounts when Marie walked in. "Hello Marie. I was beginning to wonder what was keeping you."

"Been up Silvertown. To the police station."

"Oh? Nothing wrong, I hope," responded Odile, looking up from the accounts.

Marie drew a long breath, opened the carrier bag, took out something and held it out for Odile to see. A battered blue shoe. "There!" said Marie. "That's what they gave me, up the police station. Came out of a bomb crater it did, near our old home, or where our old home was before Hitler started on it."

She continued to hold out the shoe. Odile stared at it in silence.

"My chap and my Vi, running for the shelter when the bomb dropped. They must've gone sky-high together! My chap, they ain't turned up nothing whatever of him. And my Vi: just one bleeding shoe. All that's left of that lovely gal, mate! The rest is London grit."